For my mother.

About the Author

Catriona King trained as a Doctor, police Forensic Medical examiner and health service manager in London, where she worked for many years. In recent years, she has returned to live in Belfast.

She has written since childhood; fiction, fact and reporting. 'The Carbon Trail' is a standalone thriller set in New York City, USA. Catriona has visited the USA many times and has family there.

Catriona is also the author of the popular Craig Modern Thriller Series, which follows Marc Craig and his team through and beyond the streets of Belfast in their hunt for serial killers.

Acknowledgements

Thanks to Crooked Cat publishing for being so unfailingly supportive and cheerful.

Huge thanks to my family for giving me an interest in, and enthusiasm for, science.

Catriona King
Belfast, April 2014

Also by Catriona King

The Craig Modern Thriller Series

A Limited Justice
The Grass Tattoo
The Visitor
The Waiting Room
The Broken Shore
The Slowest Cut
The Coercion Key

Discover more at: **www.catrionakingbooks.com**

The Carbon Trail

Chapter One

New York City. Wednesday, September 3rd 2014. 10.45 p.m.

Greg Chapman stared at the tall man, shocked by how calm he felt. Thoughts crowded into his mind; the clearest one was that he'd failed. Someone else would take over now. He gazed at the smooth, black floor longing for sleep but fought the urge hard, knowing that it would be his final nap. There were so many things that he'd left undone. Marriage, kids, another trip home to see his folks.

The man watched Chapman in silence, holding something just beyond his reach, its outline blurred by the brightness of the room. Chapman needed all his strength to breathe, each gasp increasingly laboured as he approached his last. He'd always known that the job would kill him. It killed them all in the end.

***

Lloyd Harbor, Long Island. Thursday. 6.30 a.m.

The sound of rushing water knocked the man off-balance and he fell against the glass wall, scrambling frantically to steady himself with a hand. His grip failed and he hurtled towards the white-tiled floor, catching a glimpse of the water as it flowed towards the drain. Instead of the clear liquid that he expected to see, the outlet was filled with a dark-red pool that circled the rim twice before disappearing. The colour diluted slowly, melting to a faint trail of pink as the man watched in fascination. His fascination changed to fear when he realised that he was looking at blood.

The man searched his body for injury and pain. First his trunk and then each muscled limb, until, in a last effort to find the blood's source, he searched his face. As his fingers rushed across its contours he froze, stunned by its unfamiliarity. It was his jaw and his nose, yet he didn't recognise either. Logic cut through his shock. He had no wounds and no pain except a piercing headache, nothing to explain the water's colour. It wasn't his blood. And if it wasn't his, then who did it belong to?

The tint faded as the man gazed at it, until the water ran glassy clear. As he lay there, rained on by the warm shower, questions formed and broke in his mind before he could grasp them. Two solidified. Where was he? And what the hell was he doing there?

Suddenly the cubicle wall shook, jerking him from his thoughts and a hand loomed towards him through the mist. The man recoiled, until he saw that its open palm held no threat. Two long fingers tapped lightly on the glass, telling him that the hand was female. Blonde curls appeared, followed by a blurred face showing a look of concern. He smiled reflexly at the face's prettiness and then smiled again, touched by the stranger's caring look. The words that came next said that the woman was no stranger.

"Jeff. Are you OK? You've been in there for almost an hour."

The man recoiled again, shocked by her knowledge of him. Jeff. Was that his name? And if it was, then why didn't it sound familiar? He squinted to see her face and another question came. Who was she?

The woman's face pressed closer to the glass until he could see her large, dark eyes. They looked gentle. A second later the glass wall swung back and she came fully into view. She was small and slim, and her face and clothes said that she was somewhere in her thirties. She gazed up at him; her face wearing a look of concern, then leaned slowly behind him, turning off the shower with one hand. A large towel hung from the other, its weight implying comfort.

The woman reached up and draped it around him, rubbing gently at his back, then she moved slowly down his body, patting him dry as she went. She cared for him without embarrassment, implying an intimacy and knowledge long before that day.

As she drew him carefully from his glass cocoon and knelt on the floor at his feet, drying each toe as if he was a child, the man gazed down at the light tan of her hands. He already knew that her eyes were blue but when she glanced up he saw them clearly. What a blue. They were a dark French-navy and the fine lines at their edges creased-up in a smile, with an ease that showed she did it often.

The man gazed around the room as she worked. It was a large bathroom with white-tiled walls and a floor of honey-coloured wood, whispering taste and money. A feeling of peace enveloped him and he knew that he was safe there, wherever it was. From the blood to the woman and his name, he'd assimilated each shock as quickly as it had come. He stood unperturbed now, waiting for the next. It came in a glance. A wedding ring on his hand and then on hers. Married. And then another shock. His reflection in the mirrored wall.

He stared at himself as if he was a stranger. There was no flicker of recognition, no sense of familiarity as he stared at the toned forty-something across the room. It was an image of someone else. He touched his arm to test its reality and watched as the reflection touched his too. He smiled and he smiled back, handsome and tanned, without any sense of who he was.

When the next surprise came the man only glimpsed it. A small toothbrush beside the sink. She had a child. They had a child? He had no memory of any of it. He let out an anguished moan and the woman gazed up at him anxiously. He smiled, not wanting to make her afraid. If he was her husband he wanted to protect her. The thought told him something else. He cared.

His wife returned to her task; ministering to him with a tenderness that felt completely new. If someone had been this kind to him before then he'd forgotten. She wrapped a fresh towel around him and took his hand, leading him to a bedroom where he dressed in perfectly fitting clothes. Then breakfast in a kitchen whose sunny warmth echoed hers. She smiled at him over coffee, with a look that the man recognised as love. Wherever he was, he was home.

Chapter Two

7.00 a.m.

"Do you really have to go to work, Jeff? Can't Devon gather the data for once?"

Jeff stared at his wife blankly, with no idea what she was talking about. An honest answer would have said too much, so instead he just smiled and gave a reply so neutral that no-one could have questioned it.

"Sorry, honey. But yes."

She sighed and then nodded once, resigned. "OK, but don't forget we have an appointment to view a kindergarten for Emmie, at five. We can't miss it."

Just then a small figure appeared at the kitchen door and the woman turned and smiled broadly, holding out her arms towards a little girl. Jeff gauged her age as somewhere less than three and smiled as well, mimicking his wife. It was the right thing to do, but no paternal feeling followed. The girl climbed onto her mother's lap and the woman kissed her silky curls, talking to him over her head.

"Silly Daddy has to go to work. Let's drive him there after breakfast. We'll have him all to ourselves tonight."

Jeff nodded, recognising that it was his cue, but his mind was on other things. Where did he work? And what would he do when she left him there and drove away? When they'd finished their meal the woman handed him his jacket. A badge hung from the lapel. 'Dr Jeff Mitchell: Scrabo Research Enterprises'.

Jeff Mitchell, and he was a doctor, but what sort? He worked at some place called Scrabo; it didn't sound like any hospital he'd ever known. He dreaded to think what job he'd soon be showing his ignorance of and prayed that it didn't involve patients' health.

Thirty minutes later they pulled the front door closed and stood like a family in the leafy street. Jeff Mitchell gazed around him, searching for some landmark that he knew, but there was nothing. Just a quiet suburban road, full of trees and prosperous lives. The new model Lexus in the driveway showed that they had one as well.

He stared at the sky and then scanned the horizon. They were somewhere elevated, somewhere near New York. That much he recognised from the skyscrapers in the distance and the new One World Trade Center. He knew it was morning because they'd just had breakfast and the watch on his wrist said so. That was everything he knew about his life. His name was Jeff Mitchell, he was a New Yorker, married, a father and he was on his way to work. It was enough for now.

The woman started the car and they drove smoothly down the wide street. The trees at each side gave it a cosy feel and their leaves formed a rainbow of earthy hues. He could see the first fall shedding on the lawns below; autumn but not cold yet; September. As Jeff Mitchell gazed around and made small talk, his wife seemed unfazed by his vague replies. He wondered why and then decided to be grateful instead. Until he had some clarity, endless questions were the last thing that he needed.

Mitchell sat back, relaxing as much as he could on his way to a job that he had no idea how to do. As they reached the road's end and turned left at the junction, neither of them noticed the dark sedan pulling out behind. It followed at a distance as they drove through the suburban roads of Lloyd's Harbor, then left Long Island by the Midtown Tunnel. It was still with them fifty minutes later when they reached Manhattan's urban sprawl.

The traffic slowed to a crawl as they neared their goal and

cold drops of sweat trickled down Mitchell's back. He pictured the nightmarish day of meetings that lay ahead, with people that he couldn't recall. Pulling down the passenger visor, he stared at his face in the mirror inside; a complete stranger stared back, his blue eyes and strong bones still unknown.

The Lexus pulled up on West Street and a moment later Jeff Mitchell was standing outside a multi-storey tower signed 'Scrabo Research Enterprises', focusing so hard that he completely missed the sedan parking across the street.

***

Worth Street, Lower Manhattan.

Magee dialled the cell-phone number for the third time then sighed in exasperation as it rang out and cut to answerphone. Where the hell was Greg Chapman? He'd been tasked with a simple surveillance and he couldn't even manage that. He corrected himself immediately, knowing that his anger was masking concern. Chapman was a good agent, really good. It wasn't like him to go off piste. Some of the others, yes, but never him. Something was wrong.

Magee glanced at his watch. There'd been no contact from Chapman for ten hours; three check-ins missed. He started to wheeze and reached for his inhaler, sucking hard on it as he thought. Greg Chapman was dead, he was sure of it. Magee shook his head determinedly. No. Until he saw a body he wasn't giving up. He re-checked the time then lifted the phone and called Greg Chapman for the fourth time that day.

***

West Street, Manhattan.

The glass door rotated and Jeff Mitchell stepped hesitantly

into Scrabo Research Enterprise's bright entrance-hall. It had a high transparent ceiling and metal elevators racing for the sky. He watched as a throng of people rushed past him towards their work, all certain of their destination. He envied them.

Mitchell's shoulders were jostled occasionally with a "Hey buddy, move out of the way" but he held his ground, staring curiously after them. They were mostly young, male and female, in a uniform of t-shirts and jeans, bearing jokey slogans of 'scientists do it atomically' and 'I'm the biggest bang in town'. Some were older like him, dressed in suits and carrying cases. Mitchell watched as the throng narrowed to an orderly crocodile and wondered where it stopped. He stepped sideways and got his answer. A security guard stood fifty feet ahead, running a metal wand across each member of the queue. He took their bags and laid them on a conveyor that ran through an X-ray machine. They were being searched! For what?

Mitchell's thoughts were interrupted by a firm slap on his back. He jerked around, his fists drawn, ready to strike. Their progress was halted by the shocked smile of a dark-haired young man, his hurriedly upheld palms indicating peace.

"Wow! That was fast! Where the hell did you learn that?"

The young man's tone showed annoyance, despite the softness of his southern drawl. Mitchell held his fists in position, scrutinising the man, until instinct said that he was no threat and Mitchell dropped his arms down by his side. More questions raced through Mitchell's mind. Where had he learned to fight? And why were his reflexes so damn fast? The man stared at him, puzzled.

"Jeff?"

Mitchell glanced at the man's badge. 'Dr Devon Cantrell'. Devon. Karen had mentioned his name at breakfast. They worked together every day yet Mitchell felt like he'd never seen him before. The only thing to do was bluff.

"Sorry, Devon. You startled me."

Cantrell nodded forgivingly. "No problem. I know you're

stressed about the work. What time did you get home last night? You were still here when I left."

Mitchell shook his head. "No idea." It wasn't a lie.

Cantrell gestured him forward and they joined the queue.

"I bet Karen was pissed about that."

So that was his wife's name. Karen Mitchell. It had a nice ring to it. Cantrell was still talking. "Did you make any progress after I left?"

Progress on what? Mitchell shook his head slowly, knowing that the gesture would cover everything. They reached the guard and he greeted both men cheerfully by name. Cantrell dropped his briefcase on the belt, holding his arms high to be scanned. Mitchell mimicked his actions then followed him through, looking for answers.

"Do they really need to do that when they know us?"

The younger man glanced up at him curiously and then shrugged. "Even we could be psychopaths, and if someone brought a weapon in here they could wreak havoc. Besides, you know there are people who'd pay a lot for Scrabo's research, especially ours."

They entered an elevator and a slim brunette slipped in just as the doors started to close, smiling up at Mitchell knowingly. He had no idea who the girl was but he recognised her message right away. He was a player! Mitchell shook his head once and her face fell. He couldn't believe he'd done that to his wife, but then he'd no idea what he was capable of. Mitchell's thoughts flew back to that morning's bloody shower and he shuddered.

The doors opened on the fifteenth floor and Devon Cantrell exited, staring at Mitchell curiously as he lagged behind. The door went to close and he blocked it with his foot.

"Wake up, Jeff. It's our floor."

Mitchell followed him hastily to some glass double-doors where Cantrell inputted a code. Mitchell quickly memorised the numbers, certain that he'd be expected to know them next time. The doors slid open and the noise level rose as they entered a bright room lined with machines and people in white-coats.

People nodded deferentially as they walked past and Mitchell immediately knew that they were in charge. In charge of what? And which one of them was the boss? The answers came a moment later when Cantrell entered an office marked 'Deputy Director of Research'. Mitchell turned and saw his name on the door opposite, with 'Director' written underneath.

He pushed the door open and entered a small room, gazing around it. He obviously spent his days there but it was another place that he'd no memory of. Mitchell placed his briefcase on the desk and took in his surroundings. The office was warm and bright, courtesy of a wall-sized window onto New York. Its walls and carpet were pale and its shelves were stacked with books. Mitchell lifted one and opened it; a book on the fall of the Berlin wall. A history book. But he hated history. Mitchell was surprised by the knowledge when he knew nothing else about his life. And if he hated history so much then why have the book in his office at all? He lifted a second book, 'Graphene; Carbon Rediscovered' and began to read its dust jacket.

Suddenly a pain skewered through Mitchell's head. He gasped at its intensity and fell back against the wall, sliding to the floor and struggling not to throw up. The feeling passed as quickly as it came and shock took its place. What the hell had that been? And what had caused it? His last thought before the pain had been the book on carbon. Had that triggered it? Mitchell glanced cautiously towards the bookcase, feeling nothing new. He knew nothing about carbon, except that it was an element. Was it something to do with his work?

Mitchell scrambled to his feet and scanned the room, bracing himself for more shocks. There were none, only files and a computer. The only personal items were pictures of Karen and Emmie. He was in some of them, smiling proudly, hugging them for the snap. He had a happy marriage, or as happy as the woman in the elevator implied. He sat down and rubbed his temple, trying to remember more, but nothing came.

A manual lay open on the desk and Mitchell flicked quickly through its pages. They were covered in equations that he didn't understand and he broke out in a cold sweat. But they told him something; he wasn't a medical doctor, he was a scientist. Mitchell knew right then that he was screwed; he would never be able to understand all this. He could bluff the social side of life, but work was another matter, especially work this complex.

Just then Devon entered the room, carrying two coffee mugs. He put one in front of Mitchell then sat down, starting to talk. Mitchell sipped his drink and listened, watching the young man's enthusiasm as he talked about their work. If Devon asked him any questions he was in trouble. He needn't have worried. Devon talked in jargon for ten full minutes without drawing breath. Mitchell nodded as if he was listening, grateful for the chance to gather his thoughts.

He was a scientist; his subject was some sort of biophysics, judging by the equations. And he was successful at it - the boss of this floor. They were researching something important; now he just had to find out what. Devon's soft tones broke through Mitchell's reverie.

"It's all very well duplicating results once we've achieved a breakthrough, Jeff, but so far we haven't. What do you think?"

Mitchell startled, realising that he was expected to speak. He sat forward authoritatively, instinct telling him that half the bluff was in the delivery.

"OK. Let's go back to basics. What is it that's stopping us achieving it?" Whatever *it* was.

Mitchell fixed Devon with a challenging look that he knew no deputy could resist. He wasn't disappointed. Devon re-started, while Mitchell wondered where he'd learned how to bluff so well.

"OK. We know Graphene is just another form of carbon, with the atoms bonded together a different way. Just another allotrope, like diamonds or graphite. Yes?"

Mitchell nodded as if he understood. Graphene; the title of the book. So that was what they were researching. The name rang a distant bell, as if he'd heard it on the news, but that was as far as his knowledge went. Devon was still talking.

"OK, so what do we already know? We know that in diamonds the carbon atoms are arranged in a tetrahedral lattice, whereas in graphite, they're arranged hexagonally and in sheets. Graphene's just a sheet of graphite one atom thick, but that gives it special properties; it's light and conducts electricity very well." Devon shook his head, dejected. "But hell, the whole world has known that since 2004 and everyone everywhere is working to make money from it, including us."

Mitchell snorted derisively, deliberately goading Devon for more information.

"So you're saying that for ten years, no-one's come up with anything new on carbon?"

Devon shook his head impatiently. "No. No, that's not what I meant. We both know there are people out there doing brilliant work, like the research on T and D-Carbon. But that just means *we* need to go even further to make our mark."

Mitchell pushed his luck hard. "OK. So, two things. One, why do we want to go further, apart from our giant egos? And two, what specifically are we aiming for?"

Devon leaned forward, enjoying the debate. "You already know why we want to go further! There's huge money to be made. If we could find something completely new that no-one else has thought of, we'd make fortunes for Scrabo, the U.S. and ourselves."

"So what's stopping us?"

Devon didn't notice that his boss had only offered questions, not ideas. He answered cheerfully, pleased at the chance to show off.

"It's like you said last week. Instead of just working on existing carbon allotropes, what if we applied what we'd learned to carbon-based life? Carbon is a key component for all life on Earth, including making up nearly twenty percent of the human body. Just think about it, Jeff. If we could create a new form of carbon in living organisms, the sky would be the limit!"

Mitchell struggled hard not to show his surprise. Messing about with living things! This was heavy stuff. And yet… it rang a bell somewhere in his head.

Devon stared into space for a moment and then shook his head. "It's a dream. Sci-fi. No-one will never crack it. But just imagine the medical applications if we did."

Mitchell startled at the word 'medical'. Could it help explain his memory loss? He leaned forward eagerly. "Let's focus on the medical side for a minute. Any further thoughts on that?"

Before Devon could answer the desk-phone rang. Mitchell motioned him to answer it.

"Yes?... What, now? …Oh, OK then."

Devon dropped the receiver and sprang to his feet. "That was the Boardroom, they want us upstairs. I'll grab my laptop; it's got all the latest stuff."

Mitchell's cold sweat from earlier returned ten-fold. It wouldn't take a company Board long to realise that he knew nothing. Bluff only worked so far. He scanned the office urgently for something that might help him, already knowing that he wouldn't understand anything he found.

Devon re-appeared and one minute later they were heading for the twentieth floor. What happened there would stun them both.

Chapter Three

Karen read and re-read the hospital appointment letter, wondering how she would ever get Jeff to go, and whether she even wanted him to. If they didn't attend then they would never know the truth, and maybe ignorance was bliss. If the truth was bad news then what good would it do to know about it?

She'd been noticing changes in him for months. At first it was just the odd word that made no sense, then whole sentences that didn't fit. Jeff wouldn't discuss it and she couldn't make him, but she knew that there was something very wrong. Karen had told him that she was making the appointment, but she knew the man she married well enough to know how stubborn he was. Jeff wouldn't take anyone's opinion on anything, and even if he did he would never agree to what might come next.

Karen sighed heavily and placed the letter face-down on the desk, then lifted their ginger cat onto her knee, stroking its fur for comfort. She turned to look at her toddler daughter. She was playing happily on the floor, her blonde curls bobbing in the light. Emmie sensed her mother's gaze and smiled up impishly, showing her small white teeth. Karen envied her childish innocence. It kept her safe from the hard choices in life.

She knelt down beside her small daughter and lifted a wooden block, adding it to an already high tower. The little girl clapped her hands, easily pleased, and her eyes sparkled just like her father's did when he laughed. Karen's eyes filled with tears and she turned away quickly, before she spoiled her daughter's happy game. After a moment she pushed her sad thoughts firmly to one side and turned back to enter her three-year-old's world. She would be an adult later; when she had to.

***

Mitchell led the way from the elevator and their feet sank into the thick carpet of the twentieth floor. The reception's walls were covered in soft grey tweed, and marble tables and exotic plants were scattered all around; the place reeked of power and money. They walked towards the visitors' desk under the gaze of a bored looking blonde. The woman looked them up and down disdainfully, her baleful stare a security scan. Finally she pressed a button and waved them towards a set of smoked-glass doors.

The doors slid back to reveal a short corridor and within seconds they'd reached the maple door at its end. Devon stopped, hesitating. Mitchell leaned past him and knocked the door hard, opening it on 'enter'. Both men were stunned by the sight that greeted them.

Three sides of the large Boardroom were made of ceiling-to-floor glass, yielding a view over Manhattan like nothing Mitchell had ever seen. The Goldman Sachs Tower stood straight ahead of them, glinting in the morning sun. It seemed so close that they could have leaned down and patted its roof like a child's head. Further left the West Street Building appeared, a testament to Gothic style, showing that New York had room for both the old and new. Mitchell stood in the doorway drinking it all in. He was dragged from his sight-seeing by Devon's cough, reminding him of where they were.

They turned to see an oblong conference table fringed with chairs. Three men of varying ages and uniform prosperity were seated on them. The tallest one stood and gestured them to sit, then he wandered to a coffee halt, indicating two cups. Mitchell shook his head but Devon took a cup for comfort, nursing it gratefully between his hands.

Mitchell scanned the men carefully, assessing them just as

they assessed him. One was slim and saturnine, dark–haired and olive skinned. He looked Spanish. No, Brazilian. Mitchell wondered how he could be so sure. The second man was short and round, with thinning hair and a hooked nose. He could have been from anywhere, but his prominent jaw and perfect teeth made him American through and through.

The tall man took his seat again and clasped his tanned hands together, resting them on the table. White metal squares glinted at his cuffs, bearing the logo N.S. Mitchell wondered if the S stood for Scrabo. The guy certainly acted as if he owned the place.

Neil Scrabo was slim and muscled, his grey hair slicked back from his forehead in a style favoured by men of wealth. His eyes were small and looked perennially unsmiling. The whole impression was of pure steel.

Scrabo stared at Mitchell coolly, as if summing him up. They held each other's gaze until Devon finally spoke, uncomfortable with the vacuum. He talked quickly and opened a folder that Mitchell hadn't noticed before, distributing A4 sheets covered with equations and graphs. Devon's tone was more hushed than earlier, as if he was in church, or the headmaster's office. His face said it was the latter.

The young scientist spoke for a full five minutes without drawing breath, outlining the point that their research on carbon had reached. Then he paused, waiting for questions. There were none, only the same cool silence that had greeted their arrival. Finally Neil Scrabo unclasped his hands, ignoring Devon completely and fixing Mitchell with a challenging look.

"Everyone has this! The whole world has been researching Graphene for a decade." The grey-haired man lurched forward. "We need something new, ahead of the curve. Not just the same bloody stuff!"

He slammed his palm hard against the table and Devon jerked back, caught unawares. Mitchell didn't flinch, just tensed imperceptibly. The man was a bully and Mitchell knew with sudden certainty that it wouldn't work on him.

"We pay you both handsomely, the government gives you subsidies and you've had every research facility that a scientist could ever want. Yet after five years this is all you have?" He looked pointedly at Mitchell. "You came from Harvard with the best references I've ever seen, Mitchell. Live up to them!"

Devon babbled in self-defence, protesting that a breakthrough was closer than they thought, then Mitchell's baritone broke suddenly through his noise. Mitchell's next words shocked everyone, including him. Instead of displaying the ignorance that he was certain he would, he started talking knowledgeably about carbon atoms and bio-variability, words that an hour earlier he was sure he didn't know.

Mitchell nodded Devon to pull up a diagram of carbon, watching as the structure rotated on the laptop's screen. He pointed to its small atomic size and spoke at length about its abundance on earth. After a ten minute lecture on carbon's potential Mitchell had managed to quieten them all. He paused and poured himself some water, taking a slow sip and making them wait, then he turned to his host and half-smiled.

"You know that there are several forms or allotropes, of carbon? Graphene is one of the newest, with different properties."

Scrabo nodded, curious as to what Jeff Mitchell would say next. Mitchell was proving a worthy adversary. It surprised him; scientists weren't normally known for their balls. Mitchell kept talking.

"I'm convinced that we can make even newer forms."

The short man sat forward, his face reddening. "What use is all this? Financially, what use is it?"

Mitchell glared at him. The man was so blinded by dollars that he couldn't recognise the breakthroughs that the research might bring. Before Mitchell could respond the saturnine man did it for him.

"Don't be a dickhead, Murray! If they make a new form of

carbon, think of the possible applications. It could make us a fortune."

Murray's eyes opened wide in realisation and Mitchell could see him doing the sums. Whoever discovered the next allotrope of carbon held a fortune in their hands. Devon stared at his boss incredulously. They'd been talking about new allotropes downstairs, but making them was still fantasy! Mitchell ignored Devon's stare and carried on.

"Carbon is the fourth-most-abundant element in the universe and all known life on earth is carbon-based. Including human life. Our bodies are almost one fifth carbon. I've been developing a new form of carbon in living organisms, based on known research but much more advanced. It's early days but…"

He paused and looked pointedly at the water carafe. The olive-skinned man jumped up and refreshed his glass and Mitchell took a sip before continuing, watching his audience as he talked. Scrabo was leaning forward now, his hands clasped so tightly that his tanned fingers were white. Gone were the hostile words of earlier, replaced instead by urgency and greed. They had an audience now, instead of an inquisition.

Mitchell looked at the three men in turn, not knowing what would emerge from his mouth next. He was as curious to hear it as they were. The words didn't disappoint him.

"It has the potential to alter the physical properties of living organisms in ways that….well; let's just say that they look very promising."

Mitchell stopped abruptly and watched their reactions. They ranged from awestruck to base. Devon was leaning forward, gawping, completely unaware that Mitchell had actually managed to develop such radical work. They'd just been theorising when they'd talked about it downstairs! The short man started running algorithms, all of them financially based. Mitchell watched as his thoughts externalised, covering his round face with greed. The Brazilian looked astonished.

Only the grey-haired leader didn't blink. Instead, Neil Scrabo relaxed until the colour returned to his hands. A smile twitched at his lips and he sat completely silent as noisy questions filled the room. Scrabo let the babble run on for a moment and then raised a hand, stilling the noise. Then he asked the only question worth asking.

"What do you need?"

Four words that deserved a hundred answers; money, staff, equipment, the list went on. Scrabo was surprised by Mitchell's reply.

"Nothing. Just time. Ask me again in three months."

Scrabo nodded and Jeff Mitchell stood, signalling Devon to follow and bracing himself for a flood of questions during their five floor descent. Questions that he knew he could answer now, without any idea where the words were coming from.

Chapter Four

By the time they'd reached his office Mitchell had had enough of Devon's inquiring mind. He grabbed his jacket from the cupboard and descended the fifteen floors to the street, inhaling the autumn air gratefully. Mitchell stood watching Manhattan's traffic, its speed a blur of yellow cabs and lost tourists then he looked through it, to the still centre of the busy street.

On a small island between the carriageways sat an oasis of flowers and trees. The trees were straight and tall, stretching skyward as if they were reaching for the sun. The flowers at their feet danced like pretty children, turning their faces towards the crowds for anyone who chose to see. Mitchell gazed at them for a moment and then turned sharp right, following the sidewalk instinctively towards his goal. He had no idea where he was going but his morning had been so full of shocks that he'd stopped being surprised by anything that he did.

Mitchell walked for a full five minutes, guided by some internal GPS. First straight, then right down Laight Street and right again, until he entered a small square whose sign said Regan Plaza. He walked on, finally stopping when he reached a small café. Its window was bowed, with lead-glass tiles lined-up along the base. Small tables decked with red gingham sat inside and a matching awning extended over the square. It looked like something from a Dickens' novel. Mitchell stood admiring the coffee-shop's quaintness for a moment then he pushed open its low front door, smiling as he was announced by a tinkling bell. A beaded curtain hung to one side of the dim room, its colour matching the gingham. The whole place felt welcoming, but despite that the café was empty, with no patrons or staff to direct him to a seat.

Mitchell took a seat by the door with his back to the wall, eyes watchful. He was surprised when an old woman emerged from the kitchen, rustling the curtain's beads as she passed.

She was small, as women of her age often were, with a softness that passed beyond her plump face. It was smooth and unlined, yet her age was stamped like a hallmark on her brow, years of life seared into its pale skin. The woman smiled at him in greeting and Mitchell recognised her, but with no idea from where. She peered closely at him through the gloom and her smile widened, her heavily accented greeting saying that they were friends.

"Jeff! It is so good to see you. We had thought that you were lost."

Mitchell smiled and stood, pulling out a chair for her to sit. The old woman spread her long skirt wide, smoothing down her apron before she sat, then she gazed curiously at him.

"Where have you been, Jeff?"

Her accent was Eastern European; Russia or the Baltic States. Mitchell resisted the stereotypes that it provoked and stared at the woman calmly. She took his silence as a prompt.

"Last night. Where were you? We waited until two. We were sure that some harm had touched you."

Her smile changed to an anxious look and she lifted a worn, brown hand, resting it gently against Mitchell's cheek. He felt no urge to recoil, letting her hand rest there for a moment and covering it warmly with his own. Mitchell compared his reaction to the old woman to his response to Devon's backslap that morning and smiled. He loved this woman and she him, he could feel it. But who was she? Mitchell searched for the words to frame an open question, one that would glean information while giving none. He needn't have worried; the woman's next words told him everything that he needed to know.

"Ilya said that I was being foolish. Daria he said, the boy will be having love. He can't always be working for our future."

It told Mitchell a lot. She was called Daria. From that and the man's name he knew his guess at Russia had been right. She obviously played some mothering role in his life. And Ilya? What role did he play? And what was the future they were all working towards? Mitchell knew that he couldn't ask questions without giving away the fact he remembered nothing, so instead he merely nodded. Daria smiled again, a wide, crooked smile that radiated love, then she stood up slowly, age making her frail.

"Now you will have Pelmeni; I made some fresh this morning. Then you will tell me of your wife and child and make me young again." She waved dismissively at a door that Mitchell hadn't noticed before. "Your work can wait for today."

***

After a lunch of bread and dumplings Mitchell stood to leave, no better informed about his work there than when he'd arrived, but learning more about himself by the minute. After he'd eaten he'd walked towards the door the woman had waved at, only to be stopped by her chiding him to take a day's rest. He would have to wait to find out what lay behind it. Promising to return the next day Mitchell pulled the front door behind him and walked briskly from the square towards the main street.

He was involved with Russians in some way; but how? Who was Ilya? Daria's son perhaps? She couldn't be running the café alone; her struggle as she'd carried in the food had shown Mitchell that she needed help in every way. What was his role in this mysterious future? Had he helped them with money, or were they related in some way?

Mitchell stopped and gazed at his reflection in a shop window. His dark-blonde hair, six-feet-plus height and blue eyes were all American; there was no doubt of that. Except...

perhaps his eyes were set at a slight angle, his cheekbones a little too high? He shook his head and laughed at his imagination. He was about as Russian as Oreos. As Jeff Mitchell stood laughing he completely missed the sedan behind him, following him back to work.

***

The rest of Mitchell's day was spent batting off Devon's endless questions, and his own. The time passed in a flurry of meetings with juniors, and interrupted attempts to switch on his PC. At four o'clock he gave up and grabbed at the rescue afforded by the ring of his desk-phone.

"Hello. Jeff Mitchell." The more times he said his name the less familiar it felt.

"Hi, honey."

The soft, east-coast lilt that came down the line made Mitchell glance quickly at the photo on his desk. The smile that had greeted him that morning beamed back and he said his wife's name softly.

"Karen."

She laughed and her high cadences wrapped themselves around him, pulling him back to that morning when she'd towelled him dry.

"Don't sound so surprised! Are you ready to go, babe? I'm parked out front."

"Go?"

Karen sighed in mild frustration and then stopped herself, keeping her tone light.

"Don't you remember? We're going to see a kindergarten for Emmie, unless you don't want me ever to practice law again?"

She laughed again, to soften the effect of her words. Mitchell smiled at the normality of her chatter, after the day of puzzles that he'd just had.

"I'll be down in five."

He dropped the phone; feeling strangely excited by the family evening that lay ahead, as if it didn't happen to him every day. It was closer to the truth than Mitchell knew.

Chapter Five

"What do you have to report, Brunet?"

Claude Brunet glanced at the car-speaker as he swerved the sedan around a corner, struggling to keep up with Karen Mitchell's Lexus. Mothers shouldn't be allowed to drive that fast - it went against nature somehow.

"Well?"

Magee's voice was impatient and Brunet could read his thoughts. He wasn't Magee's best agent by a long chalk, a fact that he was reminded of every day.

"The wife collected Mitchell from work an hour ago. They're heading down the Jericho Turnpike now. The kid's in the car."

"Where are they going?"

Brunet squinted at the speaker, tempted to bite back sarcastically with. "What am I? A fucking psychic?"

There was no point. He was too far down the agency's pecking order for a free shot at Magee, so he hazarded a guess instead.

"Long Island somewhere. Home, or somewhere for the kid. Probably the last one – home's further north."

Domesticity while Rome was burning. Magee snorted. It was a deep dark sound, with a slight wheeze signalling ill-health. None of them had seen Magee for years, but Brunet pictured him sitting in an armchair now, like Blofeld in a Bond movie. All that was missing was the cat.

"Try Chapman's cell-phone again."

There was no point in Brunet saying he'd already tried it six times that day, so he grunted "OK" and signed off, knowing that he'd be checked-on again in another hour. Roll on retirement.

He followed the Lexus at three cars length just like he'd been trained, and glanced through the windshield at the wet streets. Leaves of differing size and type were strewn across the road, their colours still green. The first fall. Soon to be joined by amber and red of every shade. Some of them floated across Brunet's view, caught in a breeze that made them soar then fall finally to ground, to be broken beneath the car's wheels.

Brunet's reverie was interrupted by the Lexus signalling left, into a cul-de-sac with a single-storey building at its end. Its colourful windows and rainbow sign said that it was a junior school. Brunet parked three cars beyond the junction. A sleek sedan would be too easily spotted in the dead end, amongst the family vans and SUVs. Jeff Mitchell seemed to have missed their surveillance over the previous nine months, but even he couldn't miss that.

Claude Brunet watched as Mitchell lifted his daughter from the car and followed his wife towards the school, then he unclasped his seatbelt and sat back, resigning himself to a long wait. He clicked on the radio absentmindedly. Sheryl Crow was singing 'All I wanna do'. He liked the song; it reminded him of feeling young. Brunet listened through one chorus then dialled it down low and pulled a scrap of paper from his pocket. Punching the numbers on it into the car-phone he listened for the seventh time that day while Greg Chapman's cell-phone rang out.

***

The kindergarten corridor was long and warm, with bright collages of string and paint displayed along one wall. Names were scrawled beneath each one in crayon. Children's handwriting; the letters square and jumbled, shifting randomly from large to small. First attempts at writing that most exciting thing of all; their name.

The wall was a rainbow of Kylees and Selenas, Justins, Ryans and Todds. Little people with adult names that they would soon grow into. As Mitchell gazed at the tableau a warm feeling engulfed him and he smiled down at his little girl. Emmie's eyes ran enthralled across the pictures and she pulled at his hand, straining to be set free. Mitchell unlocked her fingers and she flew down the corridor touching the wall, as each new thing became a joy.

He smiled at his daughter and then his wife and his hand reached instinctively for Karen's, entwining her fingers. All the excitement of a date swept through him, followed by a faint blush as if it was the first. Why did he feel like this? Their child said that they'd been a couple for years, even if he couldn't remember a single day of it. Karen gazed at him lovingly and for a moment Mitchell stopped wondering who he was, seeing himself the way she saw him and taking comfort from it. His thoughts were interrupted by the sound of a door opening and a high, light voice echoing down the hall.

"Mr and Mrs Mitchell?"

Mitchell turned to see a short woman walking towards them. Karen answered yes and freed her hand, extending it to shake.

"Mrs Baxter?"

The woman smiled. She was dark-skinned, with soft black eyes and a smooth, round face. She could have been any age from thirty to sixty, only her choice of clothes pointing towards the higher end.

"It's lovely to meet you both. This must be Emily?"

Her accent was as soft as her face, with a music that hinted at a different land. Mitchell wondered where. South America perhaps, or the Caribbean.

"Such a pretty girl. And what a nice dance."

Mitchell turned to see his daughter pirouetting down the hallway with a confidence that said she took ballet; another thing that he didn't know. Emmie travelled the full length of the corridor, turning slowly, her gold curls catching the light. Mitchell smiled at how much she looked like Karen. The teacher's next words said that he was wrong.

"Goodness, but she looks like her Dad!"

Karen laughed. "That's what everyone says"

Mitchell peered at his small daughter and saw that they were right, feeling a bond that hadn't been there before; it was as if he'd been looking at her through glass. He'd had few feelings for anyone he'd met that day. Was he in shock from seeing the blood that morning, or was it something else?

Emmie spun to a stop and smiled up at him with the bluest eyes Mitchell had ever seen. They were his eyes, and the simple genetic fact made him want to hold her. He scooped her into his arms and she snuggled in, totally safe, then they walked into the kindergarten to view her new world.

***

Claude Brunet yawned loudly and glanced at the time. Five-thirty. He yawned again then gazed through the sedan's tinted windows at the narrow suburban street. It was filling with cars of every sort and children of differing ages were spilling out of a door beyond the kindergarten. They clambered into the cars and Brunet watched as they chattered about their days to a varying level of parental interest. He smiled nostalgically. His own kids were grown now but he could remember them at every age, even though Magee hadn't allowed agents time off for the school run.

A cool breeze made Brunet shiver and he watched as it ruffled the branches of a tree overhead. The light was fading quickly, heralding evening. He cranked up the heating and dialled Greg Chapman's cell-phone again; call number eight. This time it cut straight to answerphone; switched off or a dead battery? Where the hell was Greg? This wasn't like him. He never missed a check-in; he was almost anal about them. Now he'd missed twenty hours' worth.

The flash of a car indicator made Brunet jerk upright and he readied to pull out. The Lexus emerged quickly from the cul-de-sac and drove past with the woman driving. Mitchell was reading something on his lap, completely oblivious to their tail. Brunet knew he was good but he wasn't that good, Mitchell should have spotted the sedan that time. Something was distracting him.

Brunet waited until the Lexus reached the junction then he followed at a distance, relaxed. He knew where the Mitchells were heading. The kid was in the car, and it was getting late. They were going home. He followed slowly, resigning himself to hours more in the car. With Greg gone he'd have to wait for Richie Cartagena to relieve him at nine o'clock. As the Lexus pulled into the driveway in Glove Lane, Lloyd Harbor, Claude Brunet settled back and turned the heater high, resigned to a long evening watch.

Chapter Six

"Jeff, can you get some tomatoes from the fridge? I thought we'd have pasta."

Mitchell set his daughter down on the kitchen floor and watched as she danced into the family-room. She'd be lying in front of the box watching cartoons until dinner. He wondered how he knew that and then shrugged. Pretty much every kid did it, and besides, information had been popping randomly into his head all day. He'd given up looking for 'the why'.

Mitchell scanned the bright kitchen and finally found the fridge, yanking its steel door back. It was packed with food. Meat and vegetables crammed in beside children's yoghurts and chocolate treats. He smiled at the good motherhood that it implied.

"What do you think?" Karen's voice rang out across the large room.

"About what?" Mitchell wondered whether it might be a trick question.

"What do you think of the kindergarten?" She carried on, not waiting for a reply. "I liked Mrs Baxter, didn't you? She was cosy."

Mitchell gave a loud laugh and its suddenness caught Karen unawares. Cosy. The word was perfect for everything about the 'Rainbow Kindergarten' and he said so.

Karen talked on brightly as she chopped the tomatoes and Mitchell reached automatically for the pasta jar, set high up on the wall. She smiled as he poured a glass of wine and then sat on a stool chatting to her as she cooked. Jeff looked better than he'd done for weeks. Perhaps she'd been worrying about nothing.

After dinner they told Emmie she was starting school and she ran around the kitchen gabbling happily that she was a 'big girl now'. After her bath and story she fell quickly asleep and Karen snuggled up beside Mitchell on the settee and dozed. He smiled to himself. Married life felt good. It would feel even better if he could work out why it all seemed completely new.

***

11 p.m.

"You're late. You were meant to be here two hours ago."

Richie Cartagena paused halfway into the car and squinted sceptically at Brunet. The words that followed were said in a deep New York accent.

"You want me to take over or not? I can go away again you know."

Brunet waved him in, irritated. "Stop messing about and get in. You're letting the heat out."

The young man glared at him, unimpressed by his colleague's mood.

"Listen. It isn't my fault that Greg's gone AWOL and we have to cover for him. I've done nine shifts already this week. How do they expect us to stay alert if we're wrecked? Magee needs to find us some help."

The grey-haired Brunet shrugged, disinterested. He wanted to get home, not have a debate.

"Take it up with him. Mitchell's in bed and everything's quiet. I've tried Greg's cell eight times now. The first seven it rang, now it's just cutting to answerphone. He's forgotten to charge it."

Richie snorted. "Or switched it off. He's probably shacked-up with some woman and doesn't want disturbed." He couldn't hide the envy in his voice.

Brunet shook his head. "Not his style. Greg might be single but the job comes first. Besides, he'd have phoned in sick. Something's happened to him, I'd lay my life on it."

"Like what?"

"No idea. He reported last night at twenty-two hundred then nothing since. He was outside Scrabo Tower and Mitchell was working late." Brunet hesitated then said the words no-one wanted to hear. "I think he's dead."

Richie's hand flew instinctively to his gun. "You think Mitchell did it? That means Greg must still be at Scrabo."

"Probably. But Magee won't let anyone search; just said Mitchell's to be watched around the clock."

"How could Mitchell get the better of an old hand like Greg? He's just a scientist."

"We both know that he's more than that." Brunet indicated the notebook sitting on the dashboard. "He went to the café again today."

Richie raked his black hair slowly, then he reached into his jacket for a packet of cigarettes, tapping one out. "OK. Go home. I'll take it from here."

Brunet stared pointedly at the no-smoking sign then opened the driver's door. Richie waited until he'd disappeared into the waiting van then he lit up, thinking about Greg Chapman and preparing for a long night.

***

Mitchell woke at a sound in the back yard, instantly alert. He slipped out of bed and went to the window, searching for the source, but there was nothing to see. Moving quickly through the house, he turned each corner sharply, prepared to do whatever came next. A minute later he found the cause; a bin had blown over outside. He smiled and relaxed his fists, wondering which instinct had taught him such stealth, then he went back to bed and slipped between the covers, gazing at his wife's outline in the dim light.

Karen turned towards him in her sleep and Mitchell could just make out the curve of her cheek. He peered hard through the darkness until all her features appeared. Tendrils of blonde hair strayed across her face and he stroked them back gently and gazed at her. Her nose was small and fine, turned up slightly at the end. Her mouth was full and soft and he wondered what it would feel like to kiss it, suddenly shy at the idea. As if Karen read his mind her eyes opened, surprising him. She gazed at her husband for a moment, gauging his thoughts as he tried to gauge hers, then she moved closer, until she lay so close that they almost touched.

Her dark eyes urged Mitchell on and he reached out tentatively towards her in the dark then stopped, still too shy to touch. Karen stared into his eyes, puzzled, then she leaned forward, closing the gap between them. After a moment she kissed Mitchell softly, until instinct overcame his shyness and he took her in his arms, kissing her deeply. Mitchell drew her against him until she could feel his desire, then he slipped her t-shirt quickly over her head, gazing at her full breasts in the moonlight.

He found them with his lips and tongue, circling them gently and sucking just hard enough until Karen moaned. He didn't question how he knew what she wanted, he just did. Mitchell slid his tongue between her thighs until Karen was wet and begged him to take her, but instead he returned to her breasts, slowly running his tongue across her nipples until she could bear it no more and begged him for release. Finally he entered her in one hard, smooth movement, thrusting in a way so rhythmic and familiar that Mitchell knew they'd been lovers for years. Building together in a steady, forceful dance they both came, their sighs filling the night air, then they fell back into a dreamless sleep, oblivious to their watcher in the street below.

Chapter Seven

Friday. 5 a.m.

The morning light hit Richie's eyes like a blow and he jerked awake, hacking hard and convinced that he'd never been asleep. Grabbing urgently for a cigarette to calm the first cough of the day he peered through the window's condensation, rubbing it away with his hand. It was early. A glance at the clock confirmed it; five a.m. The Lexus sat untroubled in the driveway and the Mitchells were still in bed; he'd got away with dozing this time.

Richie yawned widely, not bothering to cover his mouth. There was no-one around to tell him off and boys would be boys, after all. He opened the car door and stepped out onto the sidewalk, stretching hard, confident that he wouldn't be seen; only the cats and birds were dumb enough to be awake this early. A sudden buzz of static told Richie that he was wrong. Magee's wheeze reverberated around the car like a health warning and Richie climbed in again urgently, pulling the door shut behind him in case the neighbours heard.

"Richie. Where are you?"

Even Magee called him Richie. Not out of fondness, out of laziness; his surname took longer to say. Richie pressed the speaker's button and answered.

"Richie here. What can I do for you this fine, bright day?"

The voice wheezed again then grew stronger. Richie was sure that its strength increased when Magee was bollocking them.

"Don't get smart with me, son. Where's Mitchell?"

"In bed if he's any sense, like I should be. When are you finding us some cover, boss?"

"When I see fit. How do you know that he's in bed?"

"The car's in the drive, the bedroom curtains are closed and I didn't see anyone leave the house all night."

The last bit was a lie but a pretty safe bet. There was no way Magee could know he'd been asleep unless he had someone watching him as well, and they were too short-staffed for that. Magee's next words made him wonder.

"Hmmm… I believe you, despite the fact that you've been asleep all night."

What the hell? There was no way he could have known! Magee was already on to other things.

"Did you try Chapman again?"

"Brunet tried him eight times. The first seven rang out and the last cut to answerphone. I've tried twice; answerphone both times. My guess is his battery's dead."

And him too probably. The words went unsaid but they sat heavily in the air between them. Richie decided to be hung for the whole sheep.

"Greg was at Scrabo Tower on Wednesday night. If he's hurt he must still be in there, boss. We should go in and look."

"No. I'll say when that happens. If Chapman followed Mitchell into the building then he knew the risks. We have cover coming from Boston later, so you and Brunet will get some rest soon."

"Who?"

"Pereira."

Richie swallowed hard. He'd dated Rosie Pereira two years before and it hadn't ended well. Magee knew all about them.

"Follow Mitchell until Pereira relieves you at two. And Richie…"

"Yes, sir?"

"Stay awake until then."

***

Daria Kaverin pulled back the curtains and gazed through the café's windows, tutting at the grime that had built up in a week. They needed washed but physical tasks were beyond her now. She sighed heavily; old age was a terrible thing. Then she gave a small smile - at least it hadn't affected her brain.

Soon Jeff Mitchell would visit again and they would be ready. The work he was doing would change all their fortunes, and help take back their country from the maniac who ran it like the west; allowing corruption and lechery at every turn. They might only be a small group but with what Mitchell would soon give them no-one would defeat them. She could finally leave this godforsaken country and go home to Russia, to spend her last few years in the place where she'd spent her first.

***

Karen glanced shyly at her husband as she slipped Emmie's dress down over her head, smiling at the memory of last night. Jeff had made love to her differently than usual, gentler somehow. She'd really liked it. He's still been full of energy and strength, like the man she'd married, but his passion had been unselfish, far more than it had ever been. He'd taken his time, making certain that she was satisfied before he pleased himself; he'd never been so generous before.

Karen admitted it to herself reluctantly. She'd always loved her husband, but no-one could ever have called him an altruist. But now...Jeff felt different somehow; she struggled to define it and then gave up. Just different.

Mitchell smiled at his wife with the confidence of being on more solid ground. He'd felt as if he'd been getting to know Karen last night, although his body had said that he already did. The look on her face said something had changed between them too, in a good way. Something was better, but what? The moment was broken by Emmie jumping onto Mitchell's lap, and giving his stubble a tug.

"Ow! What did you do that for?"

"Because you're funny, Daddy. Funny, furry face".

Mitchell rose to his feet, lifting his daughter high in the air and smiling up at her. "Funny, furry face, have I?" Then he set her on the ground with a playful growl. "Well, then, you'd better run, because old furry face is coming to get you."

Karen laughed as Emmie ran around the room squealing. Richie pulled his earpiece out quickly as a high-pitched sound pierced his ear. He cursed the sensitivity of the bugs they'd put in the house then he realised what the noise had been. Mitchell was playing with his kid! He'd never done that before. Jeff Mitchell was being less of a bastard than usual for some reason, but it wouldn't last, no-one ever changed that much.

Chapter Eight

Friday. 2 p.m.

The sedan's passenger door opened sharply and Richie turned to see a pair of slim thighs wrapped in tight, black trousers standing outside. He would have known those thighs anywhere. He threw out a curt "get in" and gazed straight ahead through the windshield, craning his neck to see the top of Scrabo's impressive tower. The company certainly knew how to spend money. Still, in Manhattan a business' image was everything; that and the research that made them billions.

Richie didn't turn as Rosie Pereira slipped into the car; instead he lit a cigarette slowly, cracking the window open just an inch.

"Is this it then?"

Pereira's voice was husky, as if she smoked twenty-a-day, except that it came naturally to her, like the musical lilt from her first tongue. It was a lethal combination.

"Is what it?"

Richie tried not to glimpse Pereira's dark curls out of the side of his eye. Two years apart wasn't long enough for their effect to have waned. She pointed at the skyscraper overhead and snorted derisively.

"This. The great case that's going to make your career. Watching some scientist stare down a microscope?"

Richie hit back fast.

"Mitchell's not that sort of scientist. More the atom-bashing type. And yes, this is it."

Richie stubbed his cigarette on the dash and threw it out the window, then he turned his brown eyes slowly towards her, braced for the effect that she always had. His thoughts were cooler than he felt; all the bracing in the world wouldn't work against Rosie.

Richie gasped inwardly at her face, just as he'd done so many times before. Untamed blue-black curls spiralled to her shoulders, framing slim cheekbones that provided the scaffold for a pair of sloping black eyes. Below an aquiline nose Pereira's full lips half-curled into a sceptical smile. If she'd been a man that smile would have made Richie want to smack her one, but on her it looked inviting, begging to be kissed off her mouth. He steeled himself against her effect and turned to face front again.

"It's surveillance; what did you expect? You got somewhere better to be today?"

Richie paused, willing himself not to ask the question that would expose his hurt, but the words marched out unstoppably. "New husband?"

As soon as he'd said them Richie wanted to bite them back, but Pereira had already heard. Her smile widened, not sceptical now but sarcastic. Her tone matched his for acidity. "Same one that I left you for."

Richie recoiled as if she'd punched him and she instantly regretted her cruel words, but it was too late. His door flew open and he was out in the street, her only handover a sharp. "Check the log."

Then he was into the waiting van and Rosie Pereira was alone, running through the exchange in her head. Why the hell did they bring always out the worst in each other? She already knew the answer. Pereira shook her head sadly then sat back for a day spent watching the all-American scientist whose research could bring the country down.

***

Devon Cantrell glanced up from his computer as Mitchell entered, carrying sandwiches from the canteen. The younger man flicked on the percolator then he raked his hands through his long dark hair and tapped twice on his keyboard with a puzzled look.

"Did you log-in on Wednesday evening and forget to log-off, Jeff? You're showing as logged-in just before 18.30, but you never logged-off again. It was slowing down my intranet so I had to get security to check it yesterday evening after you left."

Mitchell shook his head, genuinely confused. "Why would I do that?"

He hesitated, struggling to recall his movements on Wednesday evening, the night before his blood-stained shower. After a minute he gave up and grabbed a seat. Mitchell gazed at his deputy's open face and decided to take a chance.

"To be honest Devon, Wednesday's a blur. I can't remember anything before yesterday morning at home."

"Nothing? What about the firm's annual barbeque last weekend? Do you remember that?"

Mitchell screwed up his face in concentration then nodded hesitantly. A meshwork of images formed slowly in his mind; picnic rugs on the grass and a small baseball diamond with people all around. Karen and Emmie were there and he was on the rug beside them drinking beer.

"Vaguely. But Wednesday's hazy. Tell me what we did."

Devon poured the coffees then unwrapped his sandwich, staring curiously at his boss.

"It was pretty much like any other day. In early and work all day, except for breaks. When I left at six o'clock you were still here. You said you had some stuff to finish up. You don't remember any of it?"

Mitchell shook his head. "Nothing."

Devon scanned Mitchell's face then gave a wry smile. "Maybe you were working on that new stuff you told the Board about."

There was a huff in his voice but Mitchell let it pass. He turned Devon's PC screen towards him and typed in some words. A table flashed up and he scrolled back through the logs till Wednesday night. Devon was right. He'd logged-on to his computer at 18:26, but there was no activity after that. Mitchell had a bad feeling about it.

"What did security say?"

Devon shrugged. "That you must just have forgotten to log-off. There was nothing new on your screen and your files were untouched, but they changed your password just in case. You know what they're like."

"Why didn't you mention this to me before?"

"I was busy this morning, supervising the new intern, and you had to leave early yesterday so I didn't want to call you at home. What was that about anyway?"

"Emmie's new kindergarten. Karen wanted me to take a look."

As Mitchell said the words he felt more ownership of his family than he could ever recall. He was proud of them. The realisation pleased him, but the thought that he hadn't felt it before nagged at something in the back of his mind. Devon's next words pulled him from his reverie.

"Great...Look, Jeff, I don't want to make a big deal of this, but shouldn't we check the tapes in reception and the lab just in case? If your computer was wide open someone could have accessed our results." He paused and then continued. "And you still haven't told me about your new carbon allotrope."

Mitchell stared at him, not reacting.

"What you told the Board about yesterday. It was as much news to me as them. I really want to hear about your work on carbon-based organisms."

A surge of anger flooded through Mitchell and he fixed his deputy with a cold look. He felt furious but he didn't know why. All he knew was that he wanted to reach across and choke the life out of his friend. Mitchell raced through the possible reasons for his anger. He didn't mind Devon questioning him about his poor memory, or even theorising about new allotropes as they done before they'd gone to see the Board- that wasn't it. And checking the security tapes was just routine.

Mitchell found the reason for his ire quickly. Discussing carbon theory the day before had been fine, but he didn't want Devon asking anything about the actual research on carbon-based organisms that he'd told the Board about. Mitchell knew instantly that he would kill his deputy if he did.

With a huge effort Jeff Mitchell re-arranged his face into a smile and patted the young man reassuringly on the arm.

"I just exaggerated to the Board yesterday to get them off our backs. It's only theory, Devon, just like we discussed. It hasn't got off the page, but if it ever does then you'll be the first to know."

"But if it's something for the company surely they should have been told before?"

Mitchell's forced smile widened. "To be honest the concept is so far 'out there' that I didn't want to tell anyone and look stupid. I only mentioned it yesterday because the Board backed me into a corner. And you heard them, they're happy to give me time to firm it up. "

He stood up briskly, making it clear that the discussion was at an end. "Now, let's go and view the tapes for Wednesday evening. That way we'll find out if I'm losing it completely."

***

Karen wandered aimlessly around the law library, lifting books and flicking idly through them, then replacing them without reading a single word. Finally she gave up, too preoccupied with her feelings to concentrate on Tort, and decamped to the coffee-shop on the corner to make sense of her week.

Jeff had seemed so much happier in the past two days,

different somehow. Karen searched for the words to describe it and stumbled onto one; kinder. He was kinder. Jeff had never been cruel to her exactly, well not physically, but his sharp words had made her cry plenty of times. Not enough to make her leave him, or even to stop loving him, but enough to make her wish that he would change.

Karen loved her husband but even she knew that he was a rigid man, cool and organised to the point of being obsessive, but that was to be expected from his job and his time in Iraq. He'd gone over as a surgeon on a short commission but left in 2003 to go back and study biophysics, finishing his PhD at Harvard and starting a career in research. Scrabo Research Enterprises had head-hunted him in 2008 and then their life together had changed. Jeff had become secretive, disappearing without a word, sometimes for days. He always returned, but without a word of explanation, refusing to answer her questions, even about the smallest things. Eventually she'd stopped asking, learning to be grateful for whatever she got.

In the past few months there'd been something more; Jeff had been vague and forgetful, always complaining of a headache that tablets wouldn't shift. She'd watched him, worrying silently but knowing that there was no point asking him how he felt. His answer would always be the same; silence.

She'd loved him anyway, even as he was, but in the past two days she'd seen a different Jeff, a softer man, and she liked the change. Karen closed her mind to the bloodied shirt she'd found in the laundry basket the day before, and prayed to whatever God was listening that the change was here to stay.

***

The video footage in the Tower's main reception was unambiguous. Mitchell peered at the images again but there was no doubt; it was definitely him. He'd walked through reception's metal detector at 4:35 on Thursday morning and exited the building through the West Street door.

After he'd logged-on to his office computer around six p.m. he hadn't hit a key, yet he'd been in the building for another ten hours. What had he been doing for all that time? Had he worked on someone else's PC instead of his own? And if so, why? Mitchell banged his hand against his head in frustration. Why couldn't he remember?

Devon watched his boss' confusion helplessly. Something was wrong with Mitchell but Devon was certain that even he didn't know what. They entered the elevator and descended to the basement laboratory on the lower-fifth floor, exiting into the cold air. As Devon walked towards the lab's door, he missed Jeff Mitchell's expression change from confusion to blind rage.

Devon punched in a code and scanned his retina and the steel door slid back quietly, revealing the high ceilings and low lights of the best equipped lab in New York. As he punched in a second set of numbers the lights brightened automatically and a soft whirring started, signalling the machines awakening from their sleep. There were millions of pounds of equipment and even more valuable knowledge locked inside this room.

Devon gestured towards the cameras overhead. "Let's take a look at the tapes. Maybe you came down here to work on Wednesday after I left?"

Mitchell felt himself coil like a spring. Something had happened here on Wednesday night, he was sure of it. His instinct said that it hadn't been good, and that it had to stay a secret. Mitchell watched as Devon turned away to start his search and visualised how easy it would be to snap his neck. He reached out his hands towards his deputy and then gasped, shocked by his own actions. What the hell was wrong with him? Was he prepared to kill for some secret that he couldn't even recall?

Devon heard Mitchell's gasp and turned, seeing the pallor on his face. He stared at him anxiously.

"Are you OK, Jeff? You're as white as a ghost."

Mitchell's heartbeat slowed ominously and a terrible dread overwhelmed him. There was something in this lab that he needed to hide, but he didn't know what it was. He nodded Devon on, following slowly as they entered a small security room and Devon clicked on a screen. Images of them both appeared and Devon waved, watching as he waved back. The timer showed 15:10 on Friday September 5th. So far so accurate. Devon tapped a key and a wall of files appeared; archived tapes for each day of the month. He clicked on Wednesday's tape and fast forwarded it to 18.26; the time that Mitchell had logged-on upstairs.

Mitchell's fists clenched and he got ready to strike. He didn't know what the tape would show, but he knew that Devon might have to die as a result. He was shocked by the thought, but part of him felt that it was inevitable.

The timer on the screen reached 19.00 and the basement lab's doors slid open. Mitchell appeared, dressed in a suit like every day. He walked slowly towards a steel door at the far end of the lab and opened it using a code. Devon clicked again and the interior hallway behind the door appeared, leading to a refrigeration room and a small office on either side. Half of the office was laid out as a lab, with a desk, computer and work-bench; the other half lay behind ceiling-to-floor glass, creating a small, glass room secured with a door.

Devon turned to Mitchell with a wry smile. "Your inner sanctum."

"You've never been in there."

It was half-statement, half-question and Devon frowned as he replied.

"In your research suite? No way. I know where I'm not welcome. You were very clear on that."

Mitchell eased more information from Devon like an expert, enough to find out that he'd had the inner research suite built to specification fifteen months before, without ever telling Devon why. They watched the tape as Mitchell entered the suite's office at 19:05, then as he moved to the desk and started typing. Ten minutes later he walked to the work-bench and read some papers. He looked just like a scientist carrying out research. Devon looked up from the screen and smiled.

"You must have been doing your new carbon allotrope work. Maybe that's why you didn't log-off upstairs? You just forgot."

Mitchell nodded but his thoughts said no. If Scrabo's computers were all on one system then his work in the suite should have shown-up on the intranet, and Devon would have seen a log-off time on his PC upstairs. It could only mean one thing; the computer in the research suite was a stand-alone, disconnected from the Net. But why would Scrabo allow that? Surely they would want a back-up of everyone's work? Mitchell answered himself immediately. Scrabo hadn't allowed it. Whatever research he was doing in the suite he was doing it alone.

Devon fast-forwarded the tape to four-thirty a.m. on Thursday, just when Mitchell should have been leaving the lab. Static filled the screen. Devon rewound to find out when it started. At 22:30, Jeff Mitchell was seated at his desk in the research suite's office, and then suddenly nothing; the screen turned to static. Devon pressed fast-forward and they watched six hours of a flickering screen. Finally, at 4:30 on Thursday Mitchell reappeared, sitting behind his desk in the same position he'd been in when the screen had gone down. Two minutes later they watched as Mitchell tidied the office and turned off the computer, then the lights dimmed and he locked-up the suite for the night.

Devon clicked on the main lab screen. It showed Mitchell leaving the basement laboratory at 4:32. He'd exited the building three minutes later. Devon clicked repeatedly, searching for other views, but for six hours Jeff Mitchell was nowhere to be seen. Finally Devon scanned back to the research suite. Mitchell watched as Devon went back and forth, frustrated, comparing the views of the suite's small office six hours apart.

Devon upped the magnification and Mitchell stared at himself on the screen, shuddering. His shirt was covered in dark patches and Mitchell knew instantly that they were blood. He'd gone from looking pristine at 22:30 to dishevelled at 4:30. What the hell had happened in between? Devon asked the same thing.

"What happened to your shirt?"

Mitchell shook his head, his mind a complete blank. He had no memory of anything on Wednesday, much less the time that he'd spent in the lab. But he was relieved; Devon had seen nothing so that meant he wouldn't have to kill him. Devon Cantrell would never know that a faulty camera had just saved his life.

"I've no idea, Devon. The first thing I remember is being in the shower on Thursday morning."

Devon leaned in, peering at the screen and Mitchell thanked God that the tape was in black and white. He decided to try a bluff.

"The stains look like coffee."

"You'd never bring coffee into the lab, Jeff! Could it be blood? Were you injured?"

Mitchell feigned confusion.

"On Thursday morning. Did you have any injuries?"

"No, nothing." It wasn't a lie. He hadn't been hurt. Whoever'd owned the blood in his shower it hadn't been him.

Devon persisted. "Maybe you fell."

He paused the tape and enlarged the frame still further. Mitchell's dishevelled look certainly fitted with a fall. Devon scrolled through the other files then he stopped abruptly, throwing Mitchell an accusing look. He clicked on a frame from the research suite office, enhancing it. There it was, small but undeniable; a coffee cup was sitting beside Mitchell's computer as he worked. His bluff had paid off!

"Shit, Jeff, you know that you can't bring coffee into the lab!"

Mitchell nodded apologetically, grateful for the get out.

"I must have been tired and needed a pick-me-up." He embellished on his mistake. "I obviously fell and knocked it over my shirt."

They watched the tape in silence until the end then Devon clicked off the screen. He wandered around the main lab for five minutes and returned with a puzzled look.

"There's no cup anywhere. You must have cleaned it up. Can you let me into the suite to check?"

Mitchell looked at him and shook his head. "I can't remember the code." It was true, but even if he had done he would have lied. Whatever he did in that suite Mitchell knew that he didn't want Devon to see; he was certain the security camera inside spent a lot of time turned off.

Devon shook his head. "How long have you been forgetful like this?"

"I don't know. I think Karen's noticed it. She hasn't said anything, but she looks at me sometimes like...well, you know."

"I won't say anything about this, Jeff, but you need to see a doctor. OK?"

Mitchell nodded then smiled, pleased. Not because he'd kept his secret, whatever it was, but because he didn't have to kill the man in front of him. Because if Jeff Mitchell was confused about a lot of things in his life, he was absolutely clear that he would have done that.

Chapter Nine

Rosie Pereira stretched her arms wide and scratched herself, then she shook her head and tutted. Working with men was turning her into one, next thing she knew she'd be watching baseball and swearing at the screen. Her mind drifted back to Richie and she felt a small pang of regret at their conversation. She hadn't meant to hurt him but he always riled her. Had done ever since they'd met in training. She knew exactly why. He made her feel vulnerable, and that was something she couldn't afford.

She closed her eyes for a moment and pictured the first day that they'd met; Richie standing in his crisp white shirt and pressed trousers, with her dressed exactly the same, wishing she was in a pretty dress the moment he'd glanced her way. Each time she'd turned round Richie had been smiling at her, and she'd involuntarily smiled back. After that they always seemed to end up near each other; in lectures and the canteen, training and in the car-park. Meaning to go straight home to their other halves, but never quite making it beyond the gate, without 'just a quick drink at Mac's?' emerging from one of their mouths.

Pereira shook her head hard, trying to wipe out the images and with them the feelings that she still had. It didn't work. She could still remember the fullness of Richie's lips on hers and his strong hands stroking her, unexpectedly gentle. Richie had held her as if she was delicate and could break. He'd been right. She could break and she had, into a million tiny shards of love and loss.

A single tear escaped from her eyes and slid in slow motion

down her cheek, its heat burning a path. Pereira let it fall, watching it slowly in her mind and feeling it cool as it reached her neck. It fell alone. She'd already cried millions of others since the day she'd made her choice. A choice she'd known every day for the past two years that she shouldn't have made.

Richie had been so much braver than her, so much truer. He'd always known what they had together and that even if she wouldn't leave Joey he had to leave his wife. To stay with Dina any longer would have betrayed all three of them.

Richie was brave in every way. But she wasn't and she'd betrayed them both. Staying in the half-life of fondness and safety her marriage offered, instead of seizing the real love that she felt for him. She'd regretted it every day, as life heaped on yet more things to tighten her chains. Each time she saw Richie she lied to him, and to herself. Full of banter and sarcasm, pushing him away with her words. Pretending that she'd chosen well, and yet every minute praying that he'd see the truth and pull her into his arms. Pull her out of her cowardice into the life that she was supposed to have with him.

Pereira dreamed for a moment longer and then dashed away the tear, half-dried now against her skin. Then she sat forward, the professional again, and scanned the street ahead. There was still nothing happening, so she sat back again to wait.

***

4.30 p.m.

Mitchell pressed randomly on the keys of his laptop and glanced at the clock. Four-thirty. Soon he'd have the weekend to cope with. He braced himself for the conversations ahead, where he'd hold back, delaying one beat to search for clues in Karen's words. At least he could relax with Emmie. She knew even less about their life together than he did.

He turned his chair towards the window and scanned the

street. The Goldman Sachs Tower stood opposite, casting its wealthy shadow on everything around. Thousands of glass towers shone across New York, their mesh of windows forming a rainbow. It joined a real one, caught by the falling afternoon sun. Mitchell squinted up at the clouds, searching for faces in them like a child. Images half-formed and faded as he watched. Whose face was he searching for? He barely knew his own, so how could he find someone's that he didn't know?

Frustration overwhelmed him suddenly and Mitchell slammed his fist down on the desk. Why couldn't he remember things and why did he have this constant bloody headache? Why didn't he know the people in his life, when they so obviously all knew him? And what internal homing device had led him to that café the day before, where the old woman had greeted him so warmly? A warmth that he'd felt too, even before she'd told him her name.

A brisk rap on the door jerked Mitchell back to earth and he fixed on a smile and turned. Instead of the Devon he expected to see, the brunette from the elevator was standing by the door. Mitchell caught his breath. The elevator's lighting hadn't done her justice. She was beautiful. Her hair flowed across her shoulders in skeins of smooth black silk, making a dark contrast to her alabaster skin. Her lips were curved and red, parted in a smile that promised everything, without a word. But it was her eyes that really told her story. They were a pure moss-green, rimmed with lashes so long that they touched their white surround. Mitchell couldn't breathe, afraid to break the spell.

The young woman stared back at him, slipping languidly into the office and locking the door. She crossed the room without a word, until she stood so close that Mitchell could feel her warmth. He did nothing, just sat very still, paralyzed by her closeness. The woman gazed down at him, her pupils widening with each slow blink. She reached forward and stroked Mitchell's face, then she slid onto his knee and firmly kissed his mouth.

Mitchell's body hardened in response and he took her in his arms, returning her kiss with a passion that he'd never felt before. The feeling shocked him, not because of his lust but because he felt detached from it, as though the feeling belonged to someone else. His body reacted instinctively but his mind raced, confused. Was he really this man? Having sex in the office, while his wife and child waited for him at home?

The woman ran her tongue across Mitchell's lips and desire overwhelmed him. He slid his hands up her soft, pale thighs, stopping six inches from the top, then his touch changed instinctively to feather-light strokes, beating a rhythm on each inner thigh until she moaned. Mitchell slipped his fingers gently beneath the girl's thong and traced lazy circles, until her moaning grew louder and she whispered his name. As her orgasm built Mitchell stood, and in one swift movement he'd laid her on his desk, all caution gone.

Mitchell gazed down at the woman's firm, slim body, every inch of it smooth and un-obscured and felt his pulse start to race. He stroked her, slowly at first and then faster, until her sighs grew in volume and she called his name aloud. A moment's caution rose and Mitchell pressed a finger to her lips, but it passed as soon as it appeared. As the girl's body pulsed beneath him Mitchell entered her with one hard thrust and drew her higher. He moved back and forth to some silent, primal beat, until his hardness was like stone and finally he came inside her, moaning, his moment of release echoed in her green eyes.

Mitchell fell across her, spent, and after a minute they drew apart in silence, the only word said since the woman had entered the room her uttering of his name. Mitchell stared at the lithe brunette and at what they'd done and confusion overtook him. Who was she and why did this all feel so familiar? And who the hell was *he*? What sort of man fucked a woman half-an-hour before his wife collected him for home? Mitchell's guilt threatened to overwhelm him but his satisfied lust pushed it quickly away. He felt like an observer in his own life. Part of him knowing that what he'd done was wrong, the other part smirking inwardly at his afternoon delight.

The woman dressed herself sensuously, fixing Mitchell's eyes as she rearranged her clothes. When she finally spoke, her voice was dark and cool, with a European edge.

"Thank goodness for that. I thought you were ignoring me yesterday."

"Who are you?"

Mitchell uttered the words before he could censor himself and immediately wished he could bite the question back. The woman's eyes widened suspiciously and she scrutinised his face. She looked like a cat, and not a domestic one.

"Are you being funny? You know exactly who I am!"

Mitchell gathered himself and smiled, covering the fact that he didn't know her name.

"Humour me." He gave her a knowing smile and the brunette nodded slowly.

"Ah, OK. We're playing a little game." She gazed up at him. "I'm Elza Silin, Dr Mitchell. Your friendly office spy."

She stood so close to him that their knees touched and she slid her dress provocatively up her thighs, toying with him again. Mitchell caught another glimpse of lace and felt himself throb. He reached across and stilled her hand, smoothing the dress back down and searching desperately for some memory of her from the past.

"What is your mission, little Elza?"

The woman smiled and shrugged, playing along. "Why, to keep you happy of course, Dr Mitchell. And under surveillance." From the look in her eyes Mitchell knew that she wasn't joking. "We can't have our most valuable asset unhappy in his work."

He stroked her arm, playing the game. "And what value could I possibly have to you? Such a beautiful woman must have hundreds of wealthy boyfriends." He paused and then added pointedly. "Who aren't married."

Mitchell looked in her eyes for some sign of pain but there was nothing. It was sex; impure and simple. Or she was hiding her feelings well.

"But I'm here to look after you, Jeff, and to make sure you don't change your mind about the deal."

"And that is?"

As soon as he'd said it Mitchell knew that he'd gone too far. The question had displayed his ignorance. Elza stepped back quickly and scrutinised his face, confusion and suspicion blending to make Mitchell wary of her next words.

"You're not playing a game! What's going on?" She stared hard at him and her next words were a threat. "You're backing out, you spineless bastard! If Ilya hears of this he will kill you."

Ilya. She was working with the woman in the café! They were using this Elza to keep an eye on him. Mitchell knew that he had to act quickly and his brain ran the permutations so fast that he was shocked. Kill the girl; but that would mean disposing of her body, and security in the building was too tight. Push past her and escape; but by the sounds of it, this Ilya would soon follow. Pretend to be ill so that she forgave his lapse; no, too contrived, she'd see through it in a heartbeat. Charm her into believing that he'd been joking? The look in her eyes said that she was beyond that. No, the first line of defence was attack. It was only afterwards Mitchell realised that he'd considered murdering a woman as lightly as having a beer.

Mitchell stepped forward so quickly that Elza fell backwards. He caught her with his left hand, his reflexes lightning fast, then his voice dropped to a growl.

"Who the fuck do you think you're talking to? You're so far down the pecking order I could scrape you off my shoe and not notice. Don't you know that I'm testing you, bitch?"

Elza Silin's eyes widened, first in scepticism and then, as Mitchell's grip tightened, in fear. She knew he could kill; he'd done it before.

Mitchell hissed in her ear, pressing his advantage. "This mission is too important to take anyone on trust. Now, answer the question I asked you about the deal!"

Elza winced as Mitchell tightened his grip and her eyes begged him for mercy. He released her abruptly and she fell to the floor. Mitchell could tell that she was frightened and the knowledge made him hard again. He was shocked. Now he enjoyed hurting women! What sort of a bastard was he?

"The p…process. The new work on carbon that you've been doing. You promised it to us. That is the deal."

Mitchell gazed down at the young woman for a moment then he leaned forward menacingly until he was close to her face. Elza scuttled backwards towards the door, trying to widen the gap. Mitchell forced his next words out aggressively through his teeth, bluffing to cover his ignorance.

"Tell Ilya that you've done your part; fucked me and kept me happy. You can also tell him that when I make a deal I stick to it. Just make sure he sticks to his part."

Mitchell turned and stared out the window, making his voice cold. "I'm tired of being spied on. I don't want to see your whoring face again."

Elza glared at his back and then gathered herself, exiting the office in a rush. She left Jeff Mitchell wondering what kind of animal he was, and exactly what sort of mess he was in.

Chapter Ten

Friday. 5 p.m.

Pereira dragged herself from her day-dream and focused on the tall figure of Jeff Mitchell leaving Scrabo Tower. She watched as he squinted down the street, shielding his eyes from the late afternoon sun then checked his watch as a stream of cars pulled up to the kerb and slipped away again, full of suited husbands and wives. The Lexus that Mitchell had been waiting for finally arrived and Pereira reached forward, tapping the car speaker until it crackled into life. "Car two, come in." The crackles said that someone was at the other end.

"Target approaching the car. Any instructions?"

There was a moment's silence when Pereira thought they hadn't heard then it was broken by a clear male voice. She smiled to herself; Richie. His accent was unmistakable, as was the way he twisted the letter 'Y', making it a word all on its own.

"Yo. Stand down. I have eyes on. I'll take it from here." Then another moment's silence, broken by a grudging "Have a good weekend."

Pereira went to return the wish then stopped herself. Richie would be spending his weekend alone and that was her fault, no matter how she tried to dress it up. She swallowed hard, hard enough for him to hear it on the other end and read her thoughts. Neither of them spoke for a moment, then the receiver crackled again and he signed off, putting a full stop to their unspoken words.

***

Saturday. 9 a.m.

Mitchell had managed to get through Friday night without revealing the extent of his memory loss. It was helped by his genuine end-of-the-week fatigue and Karen's allowances for it. He'd wanted to do nothing more exciting than slump on the couch and watch the game, so she'd sat in the chair beside him surfing the net while Emmie played at their feet, until her bedtime had taken her and Karen away.

Mitchell had watched the screen without seeing it, trying to make sense of the previous two days. Finally he'd given up and devised a strategy to cope with the weekend. It comprised five words; keep busy and don't talk. Now it was Saturday morning and he was planning to do just that.

Karen handed him a fresh cup of coffee. "Honey, I'll do the grocery shopping after breakfast."

Mitchell smiled at his wife and shook his head. "Not today you won't. We'll do it together tomorrow."

Karen shot him a questioning look as she poured-out Emmie's milk and Mitchell elaborated.

"Today we're taking Emmie to Boomers Amusement Park and then to the County Fair."

Karen's mouth fell open and Emmie jumped up and down in excitement, knocking over her milk. Karen watched as Mitchell mopped it up quickly then lifted Emmie from her seat and threw her giggling into the air, as she squealed "Boomers, Boomers" again and again.

Karen couldn't believe her ears. Jeff had a routine at the weekends and nothing and no-one could change it. Friday nights were spent winding down and watching the game, just like the night before, but where he normally insisted that Emmie was in bed by seven, last night she'd played at his feet and climbed all over him until nearly ten o'clock. Saturdays and

Sundays saw her doing the shopping alone while Jeff read a book in his study, or caught up on the scientific journals that he'd missed reading during the week. Sometimes, if he was in a good mood, they'd go out somewhere for Sunday lunch. If he was in a good mood.

Jeff's plans for today were unprecedented! Emmie was three-years-old and in all that time her father had never offered to spend a Saturday somewhere just for her. Quick tears pricked at Karen's eyes and she turned away before the others could see them fall. She wasn't sure why she was crying at first, and then she realised; she was happy. She brushed the tears away and turned back to the family scene, then listened as Emmie gabbled excitedly about all the amazing things she would do that day.

***

Richie spent the day following the Mitchells from the fun-park to the County Fair and growing more incredulous by the hour. He'd been tailing Jeff Mitchell for nine months and in all that time he'd never seen him give a damn about his wife and kid, never mind spend time somewhere that they might enjoy.

Richie parked the sedan and followed the small group at a distance, sure that at any moment Mitchell would meet someone to pass on information to. But there was no-one, not unless a giant clown was a spy.

By six o'clock Richie's suspicions had almost gone. Mitchell was just being a Dad, and a good one at that, judging by the happy little girl asleep in his arms and the smiling wife by his side. The change made Richie uneasy in the way change always did. He walked back to the car and radioed Magee with a request that took his boss aback.

"There's something going on here, sir. I want to stay on Mitchell all weekend."

Magee was firm. "Impossible. You need some sleep."

Richie nodded to himself then varied his request. "OK. Then how about if I do nine to twenty-one hundred and someone else does the rest? Just today and tomorrow?"

"Why?"

"There's something up. Mitchell's behaving totally out of character. In a good way, but still, something feels off."

Magee thought for a moment and then nodded to himself. Richie was a good agent. If he felt there was something up then there probably was.

"OK. Nine to nine today and tomorrow and keep the recordings from the house. Let's see what Dr Mitchell's playing at now."

***

By Sunday afternoon Richie was even more confused. Mitchell was cutting the grass like a regular family guy. He was pushing a mower around while Emmie sat making flower chains at his feet. The picture was so idyllic that Richie almost wanted to take a photo. Judging by the way his wife was hugging Mitchell, things were good in the bedroom as well.

Karen pushed her hair back behind her ear and knelt down at the edge of the grass, tidying the flower bed with a trowel. She smiled, remembering the day before. It had been wonderful from the moment they'd woken-up to the hours they'd made love for that night. She'd never seen Emmie so happy. Jeff had taken her on every fun-park ride, long after she had said stop, and Emmie had gone to bed tired and covered in candy floss, refusing her bath because she wanted to smell it in her sleep.

They'd walked back downstairs together after tucking her in and Jeff had poured them both a drink. He'd put on one of the romantic CDs she'd bought hopefully over the years, but never played, then he'd taken her hand and held her close as they danced slowly to the sound of Adele. He'd undressed her there in the living room and made love to her. Tenderly and intensely, as if he was willing her to look deep into his soul and see what was there. Karen had, and they'd connected like never before, until they'd fallen asleep on the rug to be woken by the morning light.

Karen smiled at the memory and glanced shyly towards her husband as he cut the grass. He smiled back as Richie watched them, recognising the look. Yes, it said sex, but it said far more than that. Mitchell's smile promised to love his wife and take care of her until he died. Richie felt a sharp pang of jealously. He pushed it away quickly. Karen Mitchell deserved some happiness; his instinct told him she'd had little enough of it in the past few years.

By Sunday night Emmie was exhausted, the grass was cut and they had a weekend of happy memories that would take a long time to fade. Karen cuddled up to her husband on the couch, trying to push away her growing concerns about his vagueness. Jeff couldn't seem to remember even the big events that they experienced together. She hadn't been testing him, but when Emmie had asked that morning about where and when she was born he couldn't recall the hospital or even the date. Karen had been gripped by fear as she watched her husband struggle to remember, then laugh and say "you've always been here, honey."

It had satisfied Emmie but sent a shiver of fear down her spine and she'd made up her mind to remake the clinic appointment soon. There would turn out to be nothing wrong, she was sure of it, but she needed to hear a medical expert confirm her view.

Karen Mitchell hugged her husband hard then leaned up and kissed his cheek as he smiled at her, amused. She turned back to the movie to enjoy what she had, while she still had the time.

Chapter Eleven

Monday morning came much too fast and with it the early morning routine of families all across the state. The weekend's slow touches were lost in a clamour of showers and oatmeal, lost sneakers and hair ribbons. Until finally at seven-thirty the front door slammed behind them and Emmie was strapped in her car-seat. The click of seat-belts and the bright flash of the indicator woke Claude Brunet from his daydream. He yawned as he watched the Lexus pull out, counting to five before following it down the suburban street.

Karen indicated left and smiled brightly at her husband as she turned. Her outward grin was matched by a bubble of joy in her heart. She knew it was love. No. It was 'in love'. She was in love with Jeff again, after ten years of marriage and six of limbo. She didn't know why he'd changed when he'd joined Scrabo in 2008, but he had. It had been subtle at first, and in small ways. He stopped smiling at waiters, after usually exchanging a friendly word. He'd become sullen and secretive, sneaking off to take calls late at night. She'd been afraid to ask who he was speaking to, in case he had a lover and left her alone. Then his sullenness had changed to open aggression, snarling when a meal was five minutes late or one minute overcooked. He'd stopped holding her hand and listening to her day, always somewhere else in the distance. She didn't mind for herself, but Emmie's hurt eyes when her father pushed her away had been hard to bear.

When the forgetfulness had started the year before she'd grasped at it as a reason for the man that Jeff had become. A guide to all his meanness. This wasn't the Jeff she'd married. He'd been fit and lean, just out of the military, back from Iraq. Never soft or indulgent, but brilliant and funny. Exciting, and always hers. This Jeff was angry and cruel.

And now? Something was different again. He looked the same; still handsome, still tanned, still fit and tall, but he'd changed in the past few days. Still forgetful, even lost sometimes, but loving, oh so loving. The weekend had been like a second honeymoon, except that this time his love had extended to Emmie, even to the waiters again. Karen didn't know what had happened or why, but it felt like the man she'd married had returned, except much much nicer than he'd ever been.

***

Brunet watched as Mitchell disembarked and headed into Scrabo Tower then he radioed in his location and settled down for another boring watch. He clicked on the radio but a Springsteen CD started to play instead, against regulations. Richie. Brunet shrugged. Whoever had written the regs had never spent twelve hours cooped-up in a car.

After three tracks Brunet unclipped his seatbelt and pushed open the car door, stepping onto West Street to stretch his legs. A sea of people in suits washed past him and his eyes locked on the women. Manhattan certainly had some beauties. Sex and the City hadn't done them justice. Women of all colours and ages strode past, all of them rushing somewhere else. Pink suits with sneakers, a pair of heels in their bag for when they reached work. A blue suit with dark pumps; blond hair flowing straight and gleaming down a slim back. Brunet was so distracted that he almost missed Jeff Mitchell re-emerging from Scrabo Tower fifteen minutes after his wife had dropped him there. Brunet jumped hurriedly into the car and grabbed at the speaker mike.

"Mitchell's on the move. I'm in pursuit."

He pulled the sedan into the morning traffic, keeping his quarry in sight. Claude Brunet completely missed the fact that he was being watched as well.

***

Mitchell had no idea why he'd suddenly decided to get some air. Or why his feet were carrying him down Laight Street and through the alleys again, deep into Manhattan's heart. It was as if he was following some instinct that the scientist in him didn't understand. After five minutes he entered Regan Plaza and found himself standing once more outside the small café. A sharp tapping noise made him turn quickly, poised to fight or flee. Mitchell held his breath, scanning the deserted square, until a sparrow pecking water from a trash-can explained the clicks he'd heard. He exhaled noisily and smiled at his own reflexes. He had no idea where they'd come from. He'd been in the military, sure, but he somehow doubted that the medical corps had majored in martial arts. A final sweep of the square revealed nothing but the bird, so Mitchell pushed open the café's door and went inside.

Daria Kaverin was standing by the old-fashioned till, counting her meagre takings. She smiled brightly as Mitchell entered, offering him some tea. He declined, saying he would take some later then he walked unhesitatingly towards the door that she'd waved at the week before, growing more certain by the moment about what he would find lying behind.

Brunet slipped into an alley across from the café, grateful for the bird's thirst covering his steps. He tapped once on his lapel mike, signalling that he'd reached his location and the message from Magee came back loud and clear. Watch and wait; nothing else. Mitchell was more useful to them free right now. Magee wasn't certain what he was up to yet and action couldn't be based on vague suspicion. They would only get one shot at Mitchell leading them to his bosses, and finding out what *they* were planning was the Holy Grail.

Brunet's eyes locked on the café's small door and he prepared to wait for as long as it took. He didn't see the sudden movement behind him, but he felt the blade slicing through his skin. It slipped between his vertebrae and severed the spinal cord without a sound. A moment's searing pain was followed quickly by a gasping death, his last breath freezing in early morning air.

Claude Brunet's last fall was slowed by a woman's bloodied hand, as she lowered him silently onto the urban ground. Elza stripped off her latex gloves and walked away without a backward glance and as Brunet breathed his last, Jeff Mitchell slipped deeper into a world of betrayal and lies.

Chapter Twelve

Monday. 12 p.m.

"What are you working on?"

Mitchell looked up, pulling on his screensaver with a tap. Devon was standing in his office doorway with a look of curiosity on his face. As Devon talked on in his Texan accent Mitchell smiled at how much it reminded him of Dallas, a show on CBS when he was a kid.

"Is that the stuff you talked to the Board about? The new allotrope?"

Devon glanced at Mitchell's screen then continued without waiting for a reply.

"Hell, it would be great if it were really possible, Jeff, but I just don't see how our research could be extended to manipulate carbon-based life. Still, the applications would be awesome."

Devon stopped suddenly, staring into space as if he could visualise them, then pulled himself up short and grinned at his boss.

"You really were just bull-shitting the Board to keep the money coming, weren't you?"

Mitchell's smile grew wider and he nodded. The truth was that his words to the Board had shocked him just as much as Devon, although he felt certain that there were facts behind his claims. He'd thought about it and the logic was impeccable. But until he knew why he felt so disconnected from everything, and why he'd been covered in blood five days before, it was better if Devon believed that he was scamming funds to keep their research alive.

Devon's amused expression changed to one of concern. "Did you tell Karen?"

Mitchell gazed at him, puzzled.

"About last week's memory lapse in the lab?"

Mitchell thought for a second then nodded. Let Devon think that he'd confided in Karen, it would keep him quiet. But there was a lot more he needed to know before he was ready to talk to anyone, even her. If Karen thought he was losing it he'd end up in the nut-house before he'd bottomed everything out.

Devon stared at his boss for a moment, unsure if he was being bull-shitted or not, then he shrugged and jerked his head towards the door.

"Lunch?"

"I want to tidy some stuff first. I'll meet you in the canteen in ten."

As the door closed Mitchell tapped his screen back to life and watched as pages of equations scrolled down. He knew he should understand them but he didn't. He only knew that he'd found them an hour before, in a folder hidden deep in his hard-drive. Daria had said that they'd be there, in a file marked 'Café', but that she had no idea what the contents meant. That made two of them. She'd talked him out of opening the door in the café again, telling him to read the file instead.

Mitchell pulled open the top drawer of his desk to grab some paper and was surprised by the sight of a cell-phone sitting amongst his pens. It hadn't been there on Friday and it definitely wasn't his. Who could have left it there? No-one had access to his office except Devon and the cleaners.

Mitchell turned the phone over tentatively then pressed the 'on' switch, waiting for the screen to light up. Nothing. It was dead. He gazed at it for a moment then called reception.

"George? Hi, it's Jeff Mitchell up on fifteen. Could you tell me who cleaned our section this week?"

"Hold on, Dr Mitchell. I'll check the rota."

The security guard came back after a moment. "It was two guys called Abassi and Joe this weekend. Is there some problem?"

"No, no problem. Do you have a number for them?"

"Sure. They work at Ubrite Cleansing in Brooklyn. The number's 347-378-02869."

Mitchell thanked him and ended the call, preparing to re-dial. His finger halted in mid-air. It might be better to find out more about the phone before telling anyone that he had it. It might be nothing, or it could help him to make some sense of things.

***

The phone store on Hubert was noisy. Offers for free gifts, from laptops to televisions, covered the windows on lime-green stickers. Insistent girls wearing matching sashes handed Mitchell leaflets as he browsed. He quickly found the two things that he was looking for and ten minutes later he was back in his office. As the charging symbol appeared Mitchell pressed the cell-phone on, inpatient to find out who owned it. The handset was black and anonymous and looked like it belonged to a man. When the screen lit up with the image of a baseball Mitchell was sure of it.

The cell-phone rang immediately with a message saying that its voicemail was full. A series of texts followed, leaving Mitchell wondering what to do first. Read them and feel like a voyeur, or listen to the answerphone and invade the man's privacy completely. He opted for the latter, hitting the answerphone symbol and placing the phone on speaker on his desk, five seconds later the recorded message told him to press 'One' for voicemail.

Mitchell knocked the phone off abruptly and moved swiftly to the door, checking the corridor outside; it was empty. He re-entered the office and locked himself in then hit the symbol again. A minute later, he'd listened to over twenty messages in four different voices looking for someone called Greg Chapman. The name sounded strangely familiar, but Mitchell couldn't remember from where. The voices ranged from official to anxious, female to male; all of them asking one thing. Where was he? The last message had been left a day before, as if they'd located Chapman or given up.

Mitchell scribbled down the detail from each call. Whoever Greg Chapman was, he was making a man called Magee pretty mad. He sounded like the boss. The other messages were less authoritative; colleagues or friends? The woman didn't sound loving exactly, but she was warmer, younger, warning Chapman that her boss would be pissed if he didn't return their calls soon. A secretary? Working for whom? Magee?

Greg Chapman had obviously lost his phone, but how had he lost it at Scrabo? It was a secure facility. Maybe someone Chapman knew had lifted his phone by mistake and brought it into Scrabo with them? Perhaps Chapman had given up looking and bought a new handset by now. The idea was squashed when Mitchell dialled the cell's number from his desk-phone. It rang loudly, confirming that the line was still live. The phone provider would have killed it dead if the owner had reported it lost.

Mitchell flicked the answerphone to greetings and listened to Greg Chapman's voice. It was deep and soft and Mitchell was certain that he'd heard it somewhere before, but where? Maybe the guy worked at Scrabo. Mitchell lifted his desk-phone quickly and dialled through to personnel. A girl answered brightly.

"Human Resources. Jenny speaking."

"Hi, Jenny. It's Dr Mitchell in R&D here."

"Hello Dr Mitchell, how may I help you?"

"I'm trying to find if we have a Greg Chapman working here. He's left something on our floor."

"Just hold on, I'll check."

"Could you check the names of the cleaning detail for this floor as well, please? He might be one of their crew."

"No problem. I'll call you back."

She called five minutes later with no news, but a suspicious tone in her voice.

"There's no-one of that name at Scrabo, or in any of the cleaning teams. What did you find? It could be a security breach."

Mitchell whipped out his ready prepared excuse.

"Sorry for bothering you Jenny, I've just found out that my wife lifted a work colleague's phone by mistake and put it in my briefcase. It must have fallen out when I opened it earlier."

"Oh...well maybe security should have a look, just in case."

"Don't trouble them, please. I've just spoken to the owner, Mr Chapman, and he won't be happy if someone looks through his personal stuff. I'll give it back to him tonight." Mitchell cut the call with a hurried. "Sorry to bother you. Thanks."

If no-one linked to the firm had dropped the phone, then who had? And why did the name Greg Chapman sound so familiar? Mitchell pressed the text symbol; there were fifteen unread. He opened them one by one. The messages got more irate as they progressed, ending with someone called Richie Cartagena texting. 'For fuck's sake Greg, call Magee, or your ass is on the line.'

Mitchell scrolled to the outgoing calls. The last one had been made at ten o'clock on Wednesday night. Thirty minutes before the tape had gone dark in his lab. Were they linked? What the hell was going on here?

Just then his office door rattled and he looked up to see Devon pressing his face against the glass.

"Hey, Jeff. Put those girly mags away and open the door. We've work to do."

Mitchell wrenched the charger from the wall and pushed it into his case with the cell-phone. Then he opened the door with a forced grin, joining in Devon's joke.

"You got it in one, buddy. But hey, you've got to do something to liven up a boring day!"

Chapter Thirteen

3 p.m.

Rosie Pereira stood at the corner of West and Vesey scanning the street for Brunet's car. It was nowhere to be seen. He'd missed five hourly-check-ins and Magee had messaged her to get downtown stat to see what was going on.

There was nothing to see. No Brunet and no car. It wasn't like him. If it had been Richie, ten minutes disappearing for a cigarette would have been par for the course, but not Claude Brunet. He wasn't the sharpest knife in the box but he *was* the most conscientious. Something was wrong.

Pereira pushed her dark glasses higher up her nose and stared at the glass tower across the street. God only knew how long it had been left without surveillance. Brunet had radioed in at eight-forty to say that he was following Mitchell. Brunet had been OK then and still OK ten minutes later when he'd watched Mitchell enter the café, from the alley across the square. Then nothing. For all they knew Jeff Mitchell could be out of the country by now.

Pereira tapped her earpiece and waited for an open line. Thank God for Bluetooth. Now that every asshole in New York walked around talking to themselves, government agents didn't stand out at all. Her earpiece whined and she started to report to Magee.

"There's no sign of Brunet at the Tower. Or his car. Do you want me to head to the café or wait here?"

She listened in silence as a curious teenager looked on and

then jumped as she stuck out her tongue. After a minute Pereira nodded her head.

"OK, send Richie with a car. I'll wait here until then."

Stepping back into the shadows, Pereira watched workers enter and leave Scrabo LLC, unable to shake the feeling that Claude Brunet was dead. No-one had been allowed to go more than an hour without checking-in since Greg Chapman had disappeared, and now Brunet had missed a handover. That would make two men they'd lost in the past week.

They'd all known that Chapman was a goner the minute he'd missed his second call, although no-one had wanted to admit it. He was ex-special forces and tipped for the top, and if one of the agency's best could disappear, then their enemy was way more skilled than they wanted to believe. So they'd kept calling his phone, just like she was doing now with Brunet's.

Five minutes later a dark sedan pulled up to the kerb and the driver's side window wound down. Pereira nodded at Richie and climbed in, signalling him to park across the street. She smiled at him despite the gravity of the situation. His jet-black hair was standing on end and she knew that he'd just woken up; it had stood up like that every morning they'd slept together. The memory seared through her and she turned on him angrily to cover the pain.

"Where have you been?"

Richie sat as far back as he could in a car and raised a questioning eyebrow.

"What do you mean, where have I been? Having a fricking life, that's where. Some of us do, you know. What's eating you anyway?"

"Brunet has disappeared."

"What?"

Pereira nodded gravely, pushing a strand of hair behind one ear. It was a familiar gesture and it made Richie want to touch her.

"He was following Mitchell. His last contact was from

outside the café just before nine o'clock and now he's missed our handover."

"You think Mitchell got him?"

Pereira shook her head. "It's not his style. But someone did. Magee wants me to stay here – another car's coming. You're to check out the café."

A worried look flashed across her face and Richie wanted to stroke it away, but he knew that any move to do so would earn him a slap. When Pereira spoke again it was almost a whisper.

"He's dead, Richie, I know it."

He went to contradict her and then swallowed his words. She was right; it was the only thing that made sense. They wouldn't have wasted time lifting Brunet, he was disposable. They all were. That made two agents down. Whoever Mitchell's bosses were, they weren't playing for laughs.

Richie glanced at Pereira's slim hand resting on the passenger seat. Her wedding ring was nowhere to be seen. She caught his look and jerked her hand away, sliding it quickly beneath her. Just then the speaker crackled with word of the second car. It was rounding the corner as they spoke. Pereira opened the passenger door then turned back to face Richie, her eyes bright with tears.

"Be careful, Richie. These bastards aren't playing."

She was out of the car and across the street before he could reply.

***

5 p.m.

"I'm off home, Jeff. You staying late?"

Mitchell glanced up from his computer and nodded at his deputy.

"Emmie's got some dance class so Karen's not collecting me for an hour. Might as well work."

Devon smiled. "Kids, eh? I've all that to look forward to."

He nodded goodbye and left though the outer office, flicking off the workstation lights as he passed. As soon as the glass doors slid closed Mitchell shut down his screen and pulled the cell-phone and charger from his case. He flicked to outgoing calls and scribbled down the numbers. One toll-free number had been dialled six times on Wednesday and then nothing after that.

Mitchell turned to the incoming calls and made a second list. The toll-free number appeared twenty times, some matching the voicemail times. Whoever Greg Chapman was, he worked for these guys.

Mitchell reached into his pocket and pulled out the brand-new SIM he'd purchased for the phone, then he slipped it into the cell-phone and hit dial, listening as the toll-free number rang. After three rings it cut to an automated line, instructing him to enter his code. Mitchell hung up and tried again, repeating the action five times, knowing that even the least sensitive security system would be alerted after that.

He was right. The cell-phone rang sixty seconds later. Mitchell stared at it, knowing that if he answered he would open a big fat can of worms. He'd already opened it; they would trace his location any minute and then God only knew who could come steaming through his door. Mitchell set the cell-phone on the desk, put it on speaker and pressed answer. The male voice that spoke wasn't one that had left a message, but then why did he expect it to be?

"Who are you?"

Mitchell sat in silence staring at the phone.

"Why are you calling us?"

More silence.

"We can trace your location."

This time, he heard a rustle and a second man's voice came on the line.

"We know you're in Scrabo Tower. We can be there in five

minutes."

The way the man said it made Mitchell sure that he wouldn't come. Mitchell swallowed, knowing he was out of his depth, but strangely curious. He recognised the second man's voice without any idea from where. Finally Mitchell spoke.

"But you won't come, will you?"

There was no answer, just a soft wheeze at the other end of the line. Mitchell decided to push it.

"Why not? No, let me guess. If you came you think that you would blow something, don't you? What? What would you blow?"

The voice came back loud and clear. "I don't know what you're talking about. This is a classified number. Don't call it again."

The phone clicked off and Mitchell stared at it for a moment then he pressed redial, listening as it cut to a local burger bar. He sat for a full five minutes, gathering what little information he had. He'd found the cell-phone of a man called Greg Chapman; Chapman didn't work at Scrabo, yet his cell was there. When he'd called the toll-free number on the cell they'd traced his location at Scrabo in seconds, yet for some reason they didn't want to take it further. Classified number? What exactly did that mean? Government? Probably. But the U.S. Government, or someone else's? The voices had sounded American but that meant nothing nowadays. Every country had their spies living there; it was practically compulsory.

Mitchell turned his thoughts back to the phone's owner. Greg Chapman didn't have a woman who loved him, not unless he had another cell-phone just for her. In five days of calls there'd been no frantic female voice, begging Chapman to phone and say that he was OK, just workmates warning him that the boss would be pissed. Mitchell thought of Karen and smiled, thanking his lucky stars for her. At least someone would notice if he disappeared.

He swopped the SIM back and scrolled though the

documents on the phone. There was nothing personal, only a picture of the New York Yankees. At least the guy had good taste. So who was Greg Chapman? And what was his phone doing in his drawer? Suddenly Mitchell's desk-phone rang angrily, jerking him from his thoughts.

"Mitchell."

"Hello, Dr Mitchell. It's reception here. Your wife's arrived to collect you."

Mitchell glanced at the clock, shocked that his detective work had swallowed up a whole hour.

"Thanks. Tell her I'll be down in five."

He pushed the phone, charger and SIM into his desk and made for the elevator, trying to work out what to do next.

***

Pereira's car speaker buzzed and she glanced at the clock. It was too early for check-in. It had to be Richie.

"Where are you, Rich?"

"How'd you know it was me?" Richie didn't wait for an answer, the woman was a witch. "I'm in Regan Plaza. I can see the café's door from here." He paused long enough for Pereira to know it was bad news. "I've found Brunet."

"Where?"

"In an alleyway opposite the café. He's dead. It looks like a mugging."

Pereira snorted. "Mugging, my ass."

Richie cut across her. "I said it looks like, as in mock-up. It's a hit, no question. And a clean one. They severed his spinal cord."

A moment's silence marked Claude Brunet's death and their thanks that it wasn't one of them, then it was back to business.

"Any activity in the café?"

"No. It's closed-up for the night. I've got the cleaners on the way for Brunet. I'll wait until they arrive."

The cleaners; an innocent euphemism for a nasty job that someone had to do. Richie paused for a second, knowing that his next words would rile Pereira even more.

"Magee called through. There's something up. The agency had a phone-call from Scrabo Tower."

"Greg?"

"No. Someone else. No name and the number was clean."

"Are we going in?"

Richie snorted and Pereira arched an eyebrow, annoyed.

"You really think Magee's going to blow nine months surveillance for a wrong number, even if it's not?"

Her voice was cool. "You mean they've too much invested to blow it now. Even for their dead employees."

"Something like that." There was silence for a moment until Richie broke it. "What time are you off duty?"

"Not until midnight....You?"

"The same" He paused for a moment and then continued. "That's two of us gone."

"We don't know that Greg is dead."

"Yes we do."

She fought the urge to say the words that both of them knew were coming next. Richie said them for her.

"Life's short, Rosie. Too short."

Pereira nodded to herself. He was right. They'd waited for too long. "Where?"

"Bar Seven Five on Wall Street, at the end of the shift. We can have a few drinks."

The bar in the Andaz Hotel. Pereira knew exactly what would happen if she went there and she was ready. It didn't need to be remembered anymore, it needed to be done.

***

7 p.m.

Karen Mitchell handed her husband a cup of coffee and smiled. "How was your day, honey?"

Mitchell glanced at her and Karen knew instantly that something was wrong. "What's the matter?"

"I'm not certain anything is. It's just…"

"What?"

"I found a cell-phone in my desk at work and it didn't belong to me."

He pulled out his own phone and flicked it open to the number reception had given him a few hours before.

"Who are you calling?"

"The cleaning crew for the Tower. They must have found the cell and thought it belonged to me."

Mitchell dialled the number and it rang several times. Just as he thought that everyone had gone home a woman answered, in a soft Hispanic accent.

"Hello"

"Hi. I wonder if you can help me? I need to speak to whoever cleans at Scrabo Tower."

Her voice became anxious, as if she was used to being told off. "There is a problem? You are not pleased with the work?"

"No, no, it's nothing like that, don't worry. It's just that someone left a cell-phone in my desk and I'm trying to locate where they found it."

Her relief was audible and Mitchell wondered what sort of ogre she had as a boss. "Scrabo Tower. Let me look. When did you find it?"

The phone must have been left in his desk at the weekend; he would have noticed it the week before.

"I found it today. It must have been left Friday to Monday sometime."

"Yes, here it is. A black phone, yes?"

"Yes."

"OK, they found it in the lab on the lower-fifth floor. We checked and the lab boss is a Dr Mitchell so they left it in his desk."

"That's me."

"It is not your phone? It is damaged?"

"No…I mean yes, yes it's fine." Mitchell's mind flashed back to the blank video-tape. "When did they find it, and where exactly in the lab?"

He could hear the woman flick some pages before answering. "Near the steel door at the back of the main laboratory. On Thursday morning."

Near the research suite, the morning after the blank stretch on the tape. The woman's voice cut through Mitchell's thoughts

"You're sure that this is OK?"

"Yes, it's fine. Could you tell me when the operative who found it is in work again?" Mitchell scrabbled around for an excuse to talk to him. "I'd like to give him a reward. It's a valuable phone."

The woman's voice filled with relief. "OK, yes. Tomorrow at twelve. His name is Abassi Idowu. Thank-you, Senor."

"No. Thank-you."

Mitchell cut the call and turned to see Karen watching him. The look in her eyes said she wanted to know what it was all about. Mitchell had no answers, so instead he did that most husbandly of things. He kissed her then turned on the TV to watch the news.

***

Bar Seven Five

The elegant bar was nearly full when Pereira entered and she cast a look around, praying that Richie was already there. He was nowhere to be seen and she felt suddenly self-conscious, moving into the shadows to avoid the barman's eye. His wasn't the only gaze Pereira needed to escape. A crowd of suits had spotted her, and one, the bravest of the pack, was sent to fetch.

He was almost forty, tall and slim with longish hair and a modern suit that said marketing or the arts. At another time he might have been her choice, but not tonight. The man smiled as he approached, glancing at Pereira's left hand and seeing that it was bare. He stopped six feet away, far enough away to be no threat but close enough for his intentions to be clear. Leaning forward decisively he closed her off from the rest of the bar, making them a couple for all to see.

Pereira stepped back and looked the man straight in the eye. Her message was unambiguous. 'I may be here alone but you aren't my prince'. Her suitor was undeterred. He went to speak just as a deep New York voice cut cleanly through the bar's perfumed air and Richie stepped forward to kiss Pereira on the cheek.

"Sorry I'm late, honey. The traffic on the FDR was rough."

Richie stared at the man unflinchingly and for a moment they locked eyes, until Richie's rival conceded defeat and melted into the crowd to find another prey. Richie gazed down at Pereira and she turned her body towards him, leaning forward for a kiss. It was soft and long and they were completely oblivious to the stares of the other people in the bar.

Pereira's lips lingered long enough to tell Richie what they both already knew. Two years had been too long; they couldn't wait a second more. He smiled and beckoned the barman for a bottle and two glasses. Then they walked into the lobby and booked a room where they could finally be alone.

Chapter Fourteen

Tuesday. 11a.m.

Neil Scrabo lifted his whisky glass and walked to the wall of windows that extended his luxurious office across New York. He gazed blindly at the vista, thinking and calculating, as he drank too early in the day. He'd suspected that Jeff Mitchell had been on to something for a while, but Thursday's admission had been the first time he'd had an inkling of what it was. Now he couldn't shake it from his mind.

There'd been something strange about Mitchell at the meeting. Distant somehow. As if he was an amused spectator, instead of an employee being held to account. Devon Cantrell had been his usual pathetic self; panicking at the sight of a well-cut shirt and an expensive manicure. Always much happier in his grubby scientist's world. Still, people like that were useful. They didn't get above themselves. And they certainly never challenged their betters in the way that he suspected Jeff Mitchell would.

Scrabo gazed up at the new One Trade Centre, or Freedom Tower as it was called in NYC. Admiring its sharp, clean lines, he tutted irritably as a helicopter swooped across his view, loaded with badly dressed tourists gawping at his world. He turned abruptly and pressed the intercom.

"Sylvie, ask Dr Cantrell to come up and see me."

Scrabo turned back to the window and smiled. If Mitchell had discovered what he thought he had then his world would soon extend much further than New York.

***

Elza sat back from the café's small table and crossed her long legs, lighting her fifth cigarette of the day. There were no-smoking signs everywhere in New York, but they didn't apply to her. She threw a benign smile at the old woman opposite and after a few long drags she slowly stubbed out her smoke and stared at her.

"Well?"

Daria Kaverin smiled at the arrogance of youth and thought wistfully of when it had belonged to her. She topped-up her tea from the Samovar then wagged a finger in remonstration.

"You were careless."

Her voice sounded tired, even to her; broken by the unfamiliarity of English and the wavering timbre of age. She spoke again, this time more firmly.

"I said to watch Mitchell and keep him happy. That was all."

Elza went to object but a wrinkled hand gripped hers. It squeezed hard until the girl's green eyes teared-up. There was no mistaking the old woman's message; do your job. Daria released her grip abruptly and turned back to her tea, staring into its steam as if her rheumy eyes could read the future there. When she spoke again her contempt was almost palpable and the younger woman leaned back to escape its force.

"We knew they were watching him and we had it all under control. Our research facility had already been moved. But you…you had to go and kill one of them outside my café, you stupid bitch!"

Daria's thin hand shot out again, this time grabbing Elza's neck. She squeezed so hard that the young woman gasped for breath and her hands flew to her throat, struggling wildly to break the grip. Daria stood abruptly, not loosening her hold, and pushed the girl backwards in her seat.

Her eyes weren't rheumy now; their brightness held a coldness that Elza had never seen before. A small smile twisted

Daria's thin mouth as the girl's lips blued from lack of air and she scrambled frantically to escape. Then, just as swiftly as it was formed the grip was loosened, and Daria returned calmly to her seat.

She sipped at her tea and watched, uncaring, as Elza gasped for breath. Both of them knew she would have finished the job if it had been required. After a moment's pause Daria spoke in a menacing hiss.

"You stupid Shl'uha. Your job was surveillance and sex. To keep Mitchell happy until we were ready to move." Her voice rose. "But instead you kill a man! And not just any man, but one of *them.*"

"But, he was…"

Daria quietened the girl with a wave of her hand.

"He was what? Following Mitchell? So what? They've had him under surveillance for months. But they knew nothing for sure. Now they will try harder. We will have them crawling over us, searching for connections."

She stopped and shot Elza a venomous look.

"Do you know why you're still alive?"

Elza's hand flew to her throat protectively and she shook her head.

"Instead of Mitchell coming here now to work he must be brought to a new research facility. You will bring him there."

"But he hates me. He told me never to speak to him again."

Daria raised an eyebrow questioningly.

"When was this?"

Elza smiled slyly, remembering, and Daria wanted to slap her pretty face.

"We had sex in his office and then he got angry with me. Like he'd suddenly developed a conscience about his wife." She snorted. "That was a first. We've been fucking for two years and he's never even mentioned her, except to say how boring she was. Now he suddenly turns moral!"

"Did he say anything more?"

"Just that when he made a deal he stuck to it. And he didn't want to see my whoring face again. But..."

"What?"

"I don't know exactly. There was something in his attitude. Different, somehow. When I mentioned the deal he asked what it was, then tried to cover it up by saying he was testing me."

Daria's eyes widened, then she shook her head. Mitchell had been to the café the day before and he'd been fine. She would have spotted anything amiss. She smiled frostily. The girl was imagining things; getting emotionally involved.

"Do you love him?"

"What?"

"Do you love Mitchell? Do you have visions of him leaving his wife and sailing into the sunset with you?"

Elza flushed and turned away from Daria's cool gaze, trying to mask her feelings before she answered the question; too loudly.

"NO!"

It was too vehement a protest and Elza knew it. Her mind raced, the thoughts tripping over themselves. *Did* she love Mitchell? She'd been watching him for two years and their longest conversation had been coital. But... Something tugged at her heart and she knew that the old woman was right. She hated Daria for her scrutiny; and for her insight.

Elza turned back to her interrogator. Instead of the slap across the face she expected she was greeted by an amused smile and a look of...what? Understanding? No, definitely not that. Pity, it was pity. Daria felt sorry for her! In that instant Elza saw past Daria Kaverin's grey hair and dry skin to the beauty she must once have been. A beauty who had known love and lost it. The two women sat in silence for a moment, each locked in their own thoughts, until Daria pulled herself upright and smiled.

"I know now why you killed for Mitchell. Do not worry; we covered it as a mugging. It is good to know you will kill to protect the mission." Daria's voice became solemn. "You may soon have to do so again."

***

Mitchell ended his call to Abassi Idowu and leaned back in his chair, feeling even more confused. The cleaner said he'd found Chapman's phone on Thursday morning, near the research suite door. But according to the computer no-one but Devon and he had entered the lab since last week. How had Greg Chapman left his phone there? And when? The logical answer was sometime on Wednesday evening. That was when the missed calls had started piling up on Chapman's phone.

But Chapman couldn't have been in the lab on Wednesday night or he would have remembered seeing him there. Unless Chapman had been part of the cleaning crew? Except that he wasn't. They'd had the same staff for two years and none of them was called Greg.

Mitchell sat for a moment, going round in circles and trying to think of other trails to pursue. All of them led back to Jenny in personnel and she'd been too curious the day before on the phone. It would be tempting fate to call her a second time.

His thoughts were interrupted by a sharp rap on the door. It opened before he had time to say yes. Devon was standing there, his face flushed. Mitchell gazed at him quizzically.

"What's wrong with you?"

Devon sat down without preamble and started talking at breakneck speed.

"Twentieth floor... The boss... What'll I do?"

He wasn't making sense and Mitchell said so, making him start again.

"I've had a call from the twentieth floor. Some girl called Sylvie."

"She's the P.A. to the Board. You remember? The blonde at the front desk."

Devon nodded and kept going. "The boss, Neil Scrabo, wants to see me."

Mitchell leaned forward, more interested now. "What about?"

A look of panic raced across Devon's face. "How do I know? If it was anything about research he'd have called you." His panicked look spread. "I'm getting the sack, that's it. I'm getting the sack! What'll I tell Amy? We're still paying off our college loans."

Mitchell shook his head emphatically. "If you were getting the sack I would know. Hell, they'd expect me to tell you. You're not getting the sack." He rubbed his face tiredly. "It must be something to do with the work."

Then Mitchell had a sudden thought. If the Board had noticed his forgetfulness, maybe they wanted Devon to keep an eye on him. He could do without it, but it wasn't Devon's fault. Mitchell looked at the younger man and smiled encouragingly.

"There's one way to find out. Go and see him. If he asks you about the allotrope or me, say I'm working on it and I'll report to the Board as soon as I've got something for them to hear."

He smiled again and waved Devon from the room. "Now, go. The sooner you see Scrabo, the sooner we'll both know why."

***

Karen wandered around the store with a faint blush on her face. It wasn't the sort of place she usually shopped, but then she didn't have a second honeymoon every week. She fingered a black lace camisole and rubbed its soft silk between her fingers, imagining her husband's strong hands stroking her breasts. A small shiver of pleasure ran down her spine and she giggled, feeling more like a high-school sophomore than a thirty-five-year-old wife.

Her thoughts were broken by the knowing look of the store

assistant. Karen dropped the lace and glanced away but the assistant had seen it all before. She stood up from her chair, smiling and wandered over to help her shy customer find the right size.

***

Devon's summons to the twentieth floor was interesting. Mitchell had no doubt that he'd leave with Neil Scrabo's instructions to keep an eye on him ringing in his ear. It didn't bother him unduly, he could handle Devon. It might even throw some light on things. All he had so far was scientific knowledge that he couldn't remember acquiring, an urge to drink Russian tea that kept taking him to a café where he had obscure conversations with an old woman, and a beautiful girl who knew him a lot better than he recalled.

Elza was already watching him; Devon would only be more of the same. There could only be for one reason for all the scrutiny; he had something that other people wanted. Mitchell thought of the door in the café and the file on his computer that he didn't understand. Yes. He had something that was worth a lot of money to someone.

He wandered into the bathroom beside his office and washed his face, staring at himself in the mirror. The face that gazed back felt less familiar by the day, instead of more. Reading between the lines at home, he was different with Karen too. Nicer somehow. She seemed happy about it. Elza had seen the difference as well, but she'd been less impressed.

Drying his face, Mitchell leaned back against the sink, thinking. Elza was the key. If she was watching him it was for a reason. Someone was telling her to do it and they were the people with the answers. Perhaps he'd been hasty kicking her out, she could be useful. He made a mental note to find her later then returned to his office and the search for Greg Chapman.

Chapter Fifteen

Pereira gazed at herself in the wing mirror and blushed, half-embarrassed by the memory of the night before. She stared hard for some sign of guilt, but all that stared back at her was pleasure. She tutted angrily at herself. She'd been unfaithful to her husband; at least she should have the good grace to look ashamed. The way she'd been raised a lightning bolt should be striking her dead by now!

A vision of Richie stretched across the hotel bed flashed into her mind and she felt the warmth of arousal spread between her thighs. She was about to chastise herself again when static from the dashboard told her to expect a call. Two seconds later her daydream was shattered by the sound of Magee gasping angrily down the line.

"Two agents dead. Two of my most reliable men!"

The night before's pleasure made Pereira bold and she answered her boss back too quickly with anger in her voice.

"We don't know that Chapman is dead yet, but we should pick up Mitchell and sweat it out of him."

It was a mistake. Disagreeing with Magee was never a good idea, but disagreeing and having ideas of your own was grounds for being sacked.

"Don't argue with me, Pereira, and leave Mitchell alone. It was incompetent surveillance that led to all of this."

She opened her mouth to object but her words never reached the air.

"I want this operation rolled up as soon as possible. I'm sending two more agents to back you up. You'll work with them to find out what Mitchell's up to; and quickly or heads will roll. Do you understand me?"

The only answer Magee wanted was yes, so Pereira obliged.

"Where's Mitchell now?"

"Still in the building, sir."

"No more trips to the café?"

"No." She hesitated for a moment then decided to push her luck.

"If Mitchell knows about Brunet's death, won't the café be off limits now?"

Her question was greeted by a wheeze then a long silence. Finally Magee spoke.

"Much as it grieves me to say it, you're right, Agent Pereira. They won't risk using the café again. That means they'll have to contact Mitchell in some other way."

He thought for a moment then spoke decisively.

"Mitchell should be home for the night by seven. I'm calling you all in for a meeting at nine o'clock."

The line went dead and Pereira made a face at the receiver. Few of them had ever met Magee, and she wasn't eager for the introduction. Then she smiled. A meeting meant she'd get to see Richie again, even sooner than they'd planned.

***

Devon coughed nervously and stared at Neil Scrabo's back as he stood by the window, perusing the city. A phrase popped into Devon's mind. 'Master of all he surveys.' He searched his memory for its origins but his reverie was broken by Scrabo turning to face him. Devon dropped his eyes to avoid Scrabo's gaze; he remembered it from Thursday's meeting and it wasn't a kind one.

Neil Scrabo scanned the man in front of him, placing him firmly in a box marked 'followers'. In his experience men fell into one of two groups. Leaders and followers. He preferred the second. Followers were easy and largely predictable. With the right motivation they did whatever they were told, and he had a bank account full of motivation.

He walked towards Devon with one hand extended and a whisky in the other. Devon was taken aback by Scrabo's bonhomie and stared at his hand like it was a snake. He grasped it awkwardly at the last moment then sat hastily in the indicated chair.

"Tea or coffee, Dr Cantrell?" Scrabo's mellifluous voice became almost confiding and he indicated his glass. "Something stronger perhaps? Feel free."

Devon shook his head nervously, certain that it was some kind of sobriety test, and instead croaked "Coffee, white please." He took the proffered cup with a shaky hand, his mind racing through the reasons that he might have been summoned. Scrabo took his seat at the head of the table and sipped his drink, then he asked the question that Devon had been dreading.

"Do you know why you're here, Dr Cantrell?"

Devon shook his head once and then realised that he should speak.

"No, sir."

The words squeaked out obsequiously and Devon could have kicked himself. They'd sounded much more assertive in his head.

"I'll tell you then. It's about Dr Mitchell."

It was what Jeff had thought. Devon's sense of loyalty was offended, just as his heart sank.

"Dr Mitchell is…"

A raised hand halted him and Devon fell silent, inwardly annoyed at being dismissed. Scrabo's next words mollified him slightly.

"I have the greatest respect for Dr Mitchell, and his work. As I have for yours."

Devon eyed his boss with suspicion but it waned slightly at

the sincerity in Scrabo's eyes. Scrabo continued.

"But I'm worried that we're stressing him too much. Dr Mitchell is doing ground-breaking work and I want to make sure that we don't push him too hard. Do you understand?"

Devon searched the older man's face for signs of deceit but found none. He nodded, relieved. He'd had his own worries about Jeff recently and it would be good to confide in someone. So why did it feel like snitching? Scrabo saw his hesitation and jumped in.

"I can see that you're concerned about being disloyal." Devon nodded. "That's commendable, but please don't be. Our concern for Dr Mitchell's health is genuine. He has a brilliant mind and sometimes brilliant people drive themselves too hard."

Scrabo reached over to a small laptop, pulling up the screen with a tap.

"I know that you and your wife both have college loans. The repayments can't leave much spare cash from your salaries each month?"

Devon froze, guessing what Scrabo's next words would be, and just how tempted he would be by them.

"In anticipation and gratitude for you taking care of Dr Mitchell, one of our most valuable assets, the company repaid your loans this morning with no obligation. If you feel that you can't do what I request, I'll totally understand. Your loans will still be repaid, with no hard feelings."

Devon's mouth fell open in astonishment at Scrabo's generosity. He was genuinely concerned about Jeff's health! Scrabo watched in amusement as Devon's naiveté made him take the bait. Devon started to talk. Over the next five minutes he outlined his concerns about Jeff Mitchell's forgetfulness, the late night lapse in the laboratory and his unexplained absences from the office.

"Jeff thinks that I don't notice he's gone, but …"

Scrabo listened attentively with a paternal look on his face.

He poured more coffee and asked the young man to keep a close eye on his Director, promising his continuing support and reward.

***

The chat with the cleaning firm had only told Mitchell what he already knew and the database searches had yielded nothing. He'd tried everything from the Yellow Book to 192, all without finding a Greg Chapman in New York. No-one could just disappear, not unless the government didn't want them found; very possible in Chapman's case. Mitchell took a swig of cold coffee and made a face; time for a trip to the canteen. He was halfway there when inspiration struck. Real Estate records. Everyone would cover their tracks in the obvious ways but maybe house purchases had slipped through the net.

Mitchell headed back to his office and started the search. An hour later he smiled in satisfaction. There he was; Greg Rudy Chapman, Washington Avenue, Prospect Heights. They'd even thrown in his date of birth. Chapman was forty-two, a year older than him. It opened the door to more searches and half-an-hour later Mitchell had Chapman's college and Marine records, even his parents' middle names. He was an only child with a good degree and ten years' service in the military under his belt. The last two spent in Delta Force.

It was when Mitchell looked at Chapman's employment record that things got really interesting. Greg Rudy Chapman hadn't worked since he'd left Delta Force, except that Mitchell knew that wasn't true. He'd spoken to his shadowy employers the day before. It all added up to one thing. Chapman had joined a government agency, and that government was looking more American by the minute.

Mitchell glanced at his watch. Five p.m. There was no sign of Devon and the outer office was clear of people, already half-way home. He thought for a minute then pulled out his cell-phone, dialling home. Karen answered his call in two rings.

"Hi honey. What's up?"

"Karen, don't worry about collecting me tonight. I'm working late, so I'm not sure what time I'll be home."

Karen smiled to herself. This was the dynamic man she'd married. She loved the new softer Jeff, but the more he focused on his work the less time he would spend worrying about his poor memory.

"Sure. Don't worry about us - I'll take Emmie over to Mom and Dad's and see you later."

Mitchell smiled to himself. Other men in the office talked about their difficult wives but he couldn't imagine Karen ever being anything but sweet.

"Thanks, babe. I'll see you then. Bye."

He clicked-off the phone and turned back quickly to the computer, with one eye on the door, half-expecting Devon to walk in. Five minutes later Mitchell was in a cab heading for Greg Chapman's apartment, to find out how Chapman's cell-phone had ended up in his lab. He didn't notice Elza watching him as he exited the tower, or the dark sedan following him down the street.

Chapter Sixteen

Devon wandered back to the office slowly, composing himself in case Jeff was still there and saw the deceit written on his face. He corrected himself. It wasn't deceit, it was concern. They were all concerned about Jeff; he was just the one who could observe him at close quarters. A quick thought came that Scrabo might ask Karen to watch him too, but Devon shook it away instantly. There was no way Karen would tell them anything about her husband. He'd seen the way she'd looked at Jeff that morning when she'd dropped him off. She was in love with her husband, the sort of love that meant she would hide anything that might hurt him.

Not that he was trying to hurt Jeff, God no. He liked him. He'd always been a good boss, willing to share his knowledge, not sparing in his praise. And lately…well lately he'd been nicer, easier somehow. No, he wasn't trying to hurt Jeff Mitchell; he was just keeping an eye out for him. For the work.

Devon nodded in self-justification and lifted his jacket, then he pulled his door behind him, casting a quick look at Mitchell's darkened office across the hall. He stood for a moment, considering, then he opened Mitchell's door, scanning the room quickly. It looked the same as always. Devon walked to the desk and tugged at the top drawer. It was unlocked; the sign of a man with nothing to hide. He tried the others one by one; they were filled with nothing but the detritus of office life. Devon turned towards the computer then he shook his head; that was a step too far. He left the room as swiftly as he'd entered; the snooping would have to wait for another day.

***

Washington Avenue. Prospect Heights.

The yellow cab halted abruptly, throwing Mitchell forward in his seat. He shrugged to himself. New York cabbies weren't renowned for their charm. That cost extra. He paid quickly and stepped out onto the broad suburban street. It was lined on one side with tall brownstones, on the other sat diners and shops. Inner city it might be but the neighbourhood was still OK. It was when the girly bars moved in that you knew you were in trouble.

Mitchell glanced quickly at the address he'd scribbled down then he marched towards a house with a flight of high steps leading up to a green front door. It was a deep moss colour, like the Massachusetts countryside. He wondered when he'd been to New England then remembered Scrabo mentioning Harvard and chalked it up as another memory lapse.

As Mitchell climbed the steep flight he felt his sense of familiarity grow. He'd been there before, he was sure of it. He reached the top and scrutinised a row of buzzers with names beside each one. Chapman was written just where the address had said it would be, beside number thirty-two. He buzzed once, half-expecting an answer, but there was none. He rang again just as the green door opened and a young woman emerged. She looked at Mitchell warily and then smiled, seeing his finger poised on thirty-two.

"You looking for Greg?"

Mitchell smiled involuntarily. He recognised her and he knew her name!

"Yes, Annie. Is he in?"

The woman stared at him curiously, but without any fear, Mitchell's middle-class preppiness giving her comfort.

"I'm sorry, but how do you know me?"

Mitchell didn't know, but he knew the wrong answer would earn him a slammed front door and a call to the cops.

"Greg told me all about you."

Annie blushed, giving him more information. She found Greg Chapman attractive, maybe they'd even dated. No. He was certain that they hadn't. Now, how the hell did he know that?

"I don't think Greg's in. I haven't seen him since last week, but you can try knocking his door."

In the time it took the thoughts to flash through Mitchell's head, Annie had let him in and waved a cheerful goodbye. The door swung closed behind him and Mitchell found himself standing in a high-ceilinged lobby typical of the building's type. Yards of brown-beige wall were broken only by a cycle rack and a row of mail-boxes. The tiled floor's once bright glaze was worn dull by years of hard shoes.

Mitchell squinted at the boxes, running his gaze along them until he reached number thirty-two. If Chapman wasn't upstairs he'd break the box open before he left and see what he could find. Mitchell's curiosity was growing by the minute. He knew the street and this building; he'd definitely been there before. His heart raced as he climbed the three flights to number thirty-two, more certain with each step that the apartment's interior would be familiar as well.

Mitchell's hands grew clammy with sweat and he felt something that he knew he hadn't felt for years. Fear. He was afraid. Afraid of what? There was no threat here, he was certain of that. Then it came to him. He was afraid precisely *because* he knew that; because he knew so much and couldn't remember how. He'd been here before but he couldn't remember when. The knowledge that he'd forgotten so much scared Mitchell stupid. *Was* he losing his mind? Was Karen right? Did he need medical help?

As Mitchell reached the landing he turned instinctively to his left, walking until he was outside number thirty-two. He knocked the door once, not expecting an answer, then he reached above his head without thinking. There, on a narrow ledge above the door lay a key, just where he knew it would be.

Mitchell reeled back in shock then gathered himself quickly. If anyone saw him entering a stranger's place he'd be in trouble, far better to feel shocked inside.

Ten seconds later Mitchell was standing in Greg Chapman's apartment. He stood in the hall for a moment, scanning the abstract prints and the pale-pine floor. He liked it, it was tasteful. He walked from room to room opening each door, already knowing what lay behind them. Each room disconcerted Mitchell more. He knew Greg Chapman, he was certain of it, and he'd been here before. Maybe that was why he had his phone. But if he knew Chapman so well then why couldn't he remember a single thing about him?

At the final door Mitchell paused. It had to be the living room; it was all that was left. If there were clues to Chapman's life they would be in there. He paused for a moment then grasped the handle and pushed the door open wide.

The room was wide and bright, with sunlight streaming in through windows along two walls. The pale wood of the hall gave way to a deep wool carpet that said louder than any words this was the place Greg Chapman relaxed. Mitchell gazed around him feeling strangely at home. The furnishings were clean and pale, no children's sticky fingers or pets' hairs to make a mess. A kitchen area in one corner held a dining table, its glass top covered by a thin patina of dust. Magazines lay on a worktop; car and boat monthlies, too impersonal to give anything away.

Mitchell stood in the silence searching for clues to who Greg Chapman was. He knew instantly where he would find them. Turning towards the corner where a high-end sound system stood gleaming in the still air, he lifted the open CDs. They were jazz and blues, but not the mainstream stuff that everyone knew. This was real fan stuff. Cannonball Adderley and Ike Quebec, Jimmy Smith and Dexter Gordon. Mitchell chose one by Gordon and slipped it on, turning the volume down low, then he reached across and poured himself a bourbon, certain that it would have a taste he enjoyed.

As Mitchell listened to the music he lifted the only photograph in the room. An elderly couple smiling at the camera, with their arms around a brown-haired younger man. Parents smiling the way they always did, proud of their son. It was the only personal thing in the room. There were no cards from friends, no picture of a woman, no signs of entertaining or love. Greg Chapman lived for his work. He was a loner. No. He was lonely. Mitchell was certain of it.

Mitchell sat down on the settee and stared at the photo. Greg Chapman. So that was what he looked like. His face felt too familiar for them not to know each other. If only he could remember how.

As Mitchell made himself at home in Chapman's apartment Rosie Pereira stood in the street below, staring up at the third floor. A chill ran down her spine. Mitchell knew where Greg Chapman lived. That could only mean one thing; he knew where Chapman was. If Mitchell had harmed him then she'd kill him herself.

***

Worth Street. 9 p.m.

Richie pressed the street level buzzer and the agency's side door swung open noisily, accompanied by a hoarse. "You're late."

He took the stairs two at a time until he reached the appointed office, then slowed and tugged his suit jacket into neatness, pushing cheerfully at the door.

"I'm sorry. The traffic was crap."

Five faces turned towards him in unison, Eric Dane's and Pereira's stifling a laugh. An older man at the table waved Richie irritably to a seat. Richie didn't know him, but then this was the first time that any of them had been called to Magee's office.

Memos were the usual mode of contact, but he supposed that having two agents down called for extreme measures. Richie guessed that the man was one of Magee's minions, wondering when they'd meet the great man himself.

"Can I get a coffee first?"

Richie's tone bordered on insubordinate and the blush that had covered Pereira's face since he'd entered took on a deeper hue. The others watched him with a mixture of awe and amusement; everyone except the older man. He tapped at his watch pointedly and then turned back to a pile of papers, nodding Pereira to pass them around. There was a moment's silence while they read and then Richie spoke again.

"Has anyone heard from Greg?"

The man sighed in exasperation and put down his file. The sigh became a wheeze and Richie's mouth fell open in realisation. It was Magee! Richie kicked himself for not knowing and then again for the casual way he'd behaved since he'd entered the room.

Magee stared at him balefully and Richie stared back, unable to conceal his surprise. Magee was an odd looking man, with a round, fleshy face and dark circles under his wet blue eyes. He reminded Richie of an actor from Hollywood's film noirs; Peter Laurie. He'd been Humphrey Bogart's nemesis many times. Magee's odd appearance was enhanced by his habit of sniffing and then gasping for air. The man couldn't help his asthma but Richie did wonder if he used it for effect.

In the few seconds it took Richie to have his thoughts, Magee was having his own. It wasn't that he didn't like the younger man, actually he did, what he knew of him from their remote conversations in the car. Richie record proved he was a good agent and he had a certain boyish charm. Someone else in the room obviously appreciated it even more than he did and they'd be having words about that soon. But Richie's need to make a joke of everything alternately amused and irritated him. It reminded Magee of someone else he'd once known. There was silence while the others watched the silent interaction, then Magee finally answered Richie's question in a tone of frayed tolerance.

"We'll get to Greg later. First, I'd like to introduce our two new agents."

He turned towards a slight blonde woman, whose regulation suit fitted her like a glove. Pereira sniffed. They never fitted like that without tailoring.

"This is Agent Howard. Amelia. She's joining us from the Maine office."

The woman nodded graciously, her fresh preppiness giving her a regal air. Richie smiled to himself. Rosie wasn't going to like her. A quick glance told him that she already didn't. Magee talked on, gesturing towards a well-toned man younger than the rest. He had a blond buzz-cut and the edge of a small tattoo peeped out from underneath his cuff. Ex-military, there was no doubt. Richie bet he'd be called Brad or Todd. He was right.

"This is Brad Whitman. He's been an agent in Virginia."

Headquarters. Richie sighed inwardly. A desk jockey with an ego the size of the Pentagon.

"They'll be taking over Brunet and Chapman's duties until further notice. Now, I want to discuss what occurred this week."

Richie and Pereira took it in turns to update the newbies on the operation then Magee chipped in with background. He ended by playing the call from Chapman's cell-phone the day before, shocking them all.

"We don't know who the caller was, but it came from Scrabo Tower."

When Magee had finished he nodded at Pereira and she turned to the back page of the papers he'd handed out.

"The map in front of you shows the route from Scrabo Tower to Prospect Heights. Greg Chapman's home address."

Richie raised a questioning eyebrow and she nodded.

"Jeff Mitchell caught a cab to Chapman's apartment block at seventeen-ten today. He entered the building at seventeen-fifty, after talking to a girl who was exiting the block. He spent seventy minutes inside the building, leaving at nineteen hundred, so it's safe to assume that he entered an apartment inside the building, in all likelihood Greg Chapman's apartment. When he left I radioed for cover." Buzz-cut nodded graciously. "Then I entered the building and checked Chapman's apartment for forced entry. There was none. That means Mitchell had a key."

Richie leaned forward, interrupting. "If it was Greg's apartment he entered and he had Greg's key then he must have taken it from him. That settles it, Mitchell did something to Greg. He knows where he is. We have to lift him."

Magee raised a hand to still him and nodded Pereira on.

"Nothing was disturbed in the apartment but there was a newly washed tumbler on the sink. As if Mitchell had a drink while he was here."

A shocked look crossed all their faces. Drinking from the glass of a man you'd killed. That was cold.

"I went downstairs and checked the post-boxes. Number thirty-two, Greg's post-box, had been broken open. I don't know if it was today or not, but there was no mail inside, not even junk. I sealed the box and reported in. Brad can tell you the rest."

Whitman unfolded his broad arms and spoke. His voice was surprisingly soft, with an accent from somewhere on the west coast. Richie could picture him hazing new kids in a frat-house named something Greek.

"Mitchell called a hire cab at nineteen-hundred and I tailed it from Chapman's apartment to his home in Lloyd Harbor. He arrived home at twenty-ten and the local cops are keeping a watchful eye on him until I get back. My understanding is that he doesn't tend to go out in the evening on weekdays. His wife's Lexus was in the drive."

Richie nodded. "They have a young kid. A little girl. Keeps them in a lot." He turned to Magee abruptly. "How much more proof do we need to move on this guy? Brunet got killed tailing him and now Mitchell's at Chapman's flat, acting as if he owns the place!"

Pereira nodded in agreement, throwing in her fifty cents. "And how does a scientist afford a house in Lloyd Harbor anyway, without getting money from somewhere else? Mitchell's as dirty as hell."

Magee thought for a moment before speaking.

"I understand the urge to avenge your dead colleagues."

"We don't know that Greg is dead."

Magee ignored the comment and continued calmly. "Or search for your colleagues. But we all know that there's more at stake here than agents' lives. If Dr Mitchell has made the breakthrough that we think he has, then we have to follow this right through to the end and catch whomever he's dealing with. This is too big an operation to blow for revenge."

Richie came back at him instantly.

"How about for honour and loyalty then? Greg could still be alive and where I come from we don't leave our men to die if we can still save them!"

Magee's eyes narrowed and he stared coldly at him. "Be careful, Agent Cartagena. Once you cross that line there's no way back. You're not the only one who gives a shit here!"

Pereira was shocked by Magee's unexpected swearing. She'd heard it plenty of times from others, but with him it just didn't seem to fit. Magee stood up abruptly, pushing back his chair.

"This isn't a debate. They know we're watching now so we need to wrap this up quickly. You have your orders; follow them. Find out who Jeff Mitchell's about to sell his research to."

Chapter Seventeen

Wednesday. 2 p.m.

The morning flew by in a haze of trivia but by two o'clock in the afternoon Mitchell was finally alone. He stood by the window of his small office, opening it the limited distance allowed by building regulations. If people wanted to commit hari-kari they'd have to do it on somebody else's watch; Scrabo's architects were determined to stop their staff messing up the sidewalk.

Mitchell sucked in a draft of cool air. The first hints of winter were appearing and then withdrawing, so that people could fool themselves that autumn would last forever and New York's snow and ice would pass them by this year. He smiled to himself, remembering Septembers in Florida, no hint of frost ever dimming the heat there.

The question came one second later. Florida? When had he been there? It was something else to ask Karen, in a way that wouldn't make her think he was going mad. It wasn't the only new question he'd had since yesterday. How come he'd known where Greg Chapman's key was kept? The mail that he'd stolen as he left Chapman's building hadn't thrown any light on their acquaintance. It was just a collection of circulars and bills that told him what he already knew; Chapman hadn't used his phone since Wednesday last. That and the fact he was forty dollars overdrawn at the bank. Mitchell rubbed his eyes tiredly, searching for something that explained Chapman's cell-phone being found in his lab, but there was nothing.

He turned back to his desk and sat down heavily, thinking about the green-eyed girl who could be his best lead and wondering how to find her in a building with five hundred staff. He knew nothing about her, except her first name. Still, a woman called Elza wouldn't be commonplace anywhere in America. He lifted the phone and made the call.

"Jenny? It's Dr Mitchell in R&D. We talked a couple of days ago."

The girl's voice was cheerful, holding none of Monday's suspicion.

"Yes, Dr Mitchell. How may I help you?"

"I've found a bracelet in my office this morning. It seems to be my week for finding things."

He laughed and she joined in.

"The thing is, I had a meeting yesterday with a staff member called Elza and I think that it might be hers."

"What was the meeting about?"

It was on the tip of Mitchell's tongue to say "none of your damn business" when he saw her question's validity. The meeting's content might told HR which section Elza worked in, if they'd had any other business but sex. He swallowed and then told the lie that would cast the widest net.

"International research."

"Oh. I'm not sure what section that would be, it's probably better if I search for her by name."

There was a moment's silence while Mitchell willed the woman on, then a soft intake of breath that showed she'd had success.

"We're in luck! There's only one Elza in the company. Isn't that strange? She works in interpersonal relations."

Elza was very good at it.

"I'll transfer you now."

Mitchell was about to object when the ring tone was interrupted by a husky voice. There was no doubt who it belonged to.

"Can I help you?"

Mitchell hesitated for a moment, remembering Elza's slim thighs, and bit back the urge to suggest a re-match. It might have to come to that to get her information, but suggesting it would be a step too far for his married guilt. When he spoke his voice was authoritative, no hint of confusion to re-ignite her doubts.

"Come to my office at five."

Elza's only answer was a gasp, as if he'd caught her unawares. Good. He wanted her off-balance. She'd had the advantage the week before but now he knew more, and as a wise man once said, knowledge was power. Mitchell cut the call before Elza could say another word, then lifted it again to call the other woman in his life. He gave Karen the excuse about working late that he was sure he'd given her many times before. It wasn't a lie, just a different type of work tonight.

***

Pereira towelled herself off from her shower and dressed in a long t-shirt and sweats. She grabbed a white wine and flicked on some music, curling up on the settee to think, before her husband Joey came home. As she let the soft melody wash over her, tears sprang into her eyes. They teetered on her dark lashes then rolled slowly down her cheeks, followed by more; until there were so many that she swallowed hard, gasping for breath.

Why was life so crappy? She loved Joey, really loved him. They'd met at high-school and held each other's hands through everything since. Pereira thought of his soft face and blue eyes and smiled, until her smile dissolved quickly in her tears. She loved her husband; she should be happy. She was lucky; lots of her friends were still searching for Mr Right, long into their thirties. She knew she was lucky. So why was she crying?

It was stupid to ask why, when the answer had sat across Magee's office the evening before, chewing the end of his pen and scraping half-heartedly at a stain on his tie. Her heart warmed at the thought of him and she gave a wet smile. Richie.

As she thought of his wide grin and his long soft kisses when they were alone, the warmth in her chest became a wave of excitement, a bubble that rose up, enveloping her completely. Then the tears came again and this time she understood why. She was in love with Richie, totally, completely, head-over-heels in love. She wanted to see him every morning and sleep with him every night, and that was what he wanted too. If only it was that simple. If only it didn't mean ripping another life apart.

***

The limousine stopped outside the elegant apartment block on Madison Avenue just as Neil Scrabo emerged through its gilded-glass doors. Nodding to the concierge who held the car door open, Scrabo climbed in, settling on its long back seat. Five seconds later a cigarette was in his mouth. After a few slow drags he pressed a switch, lowering the glass partition and revealing a black-suited chauffeur whose fit alertness said that he was much more than that.

Scrabo inhaled again, slowly, letting the smoke fill his lungs and carry his drug of choice swiftly to his brain. He'd tried every illegal substance that there was, but none of them gave him the hit that nicotine did, so he'd returned to his boyhood vice. He'd go to hell his own way, no matter how politically incorrect it was. After savouring the burn for a moment Scrabo spoke.

"Take the Palisades Interstate, Tom. We're meeting some new friends. And remember to load your gun."

***

5 p.m.

The outer office on the fifteenth floor was empty, the only light visible coming from a desk-lamp halfway down the room. Mitchell walked towards it and then froze; every instinct telling him that someone else was there. He readied himself for a fight just as a velvet voice broke the silence.

"Hello, Jeff."

Mitchell relaxed immediately, watching admiringly as Elza's curves emerged from the gloom.

"You certainly like to make an entrance."

Elza Silin stood completely still, as if someone had pressed 'freeze'. Only her eyes moved, running slowly across Mitchell's face as if she was trying to read his mind. Finally she shrugged, as if what she'd read had been boring, and turned her attention to their surroundings, scanning each desk for information.

Mitchell watched her and a grudging smile tugged at his mouth. There was something magnificent about Elza. Sex oozed from her every pore, but she didn't hide it apologetically like American girls did, embarrassed and shy. She embraced it, breathed it, used it like a weapon; every inch of her lethal.

He felt himself moving towards her, sucked in by her unapologetic sensuality. Then he was at her side, inhaling her perfume, knowing that the scent was addictive but already powerless to resist. Mitchell reached forward and stroked Elza's face, tracing each curve and edge with his finger, then he pressed it hard against her full red lips, as if they were ripe fruit that would yield juice. With one step she was lying against him and Mitchell felt her high nipples harden against his chest. Elza thrust her hips into his until they melted into each other and his need to take her overwhelmed him, no matter how hard he tried to push it away.

Chapter Eighteen

6 p.m.

The limousine pulled up to a pair of high, iron gates and a voice whose first language was Asian barked a question through the intercom. Tom Evans threw the camera a bored look and grunted a reply. He didn't like foreigners; they'd caused him problems in the past. He'd conveniently forgotten that his father was from Africa.

The gate opened inwards and Evans drove smoothly up the curved drive towards the house. House was the wrong word for it. Mansion would have been nearer the mark. Scrabo was loaded so he was used to driving him to luxurious places, but even so, this was something else.

The white stone edifice loomed impressively against its backdrop of the Hudson Highlands, staring down at New York as if it was its front yard. It was five stories high, not including the turrets, and as wide as a baseball field. The place looked like a medieval castle; the only thing missing was a drawbridge.

Evans pulled the car to a halt and sat awaiting his boss' instructions. The glass partition slid down and Neil Scrabo leaned forward, offering him a cigarette. Evans took it gratefully and they sat in silence for a moment, savouring the smoke, Evans' alertness level rising with each puff.

After several minutes the mansion's front door opened and a guard in an olive-green uniform emerged He carried a PPS-43 submachine gun; standard military issue, but not in America. Evans reached for his Glock but Scrabo's hand on his shoulder told him to stand down. They watched as the guard waited by the door and a small, East Asian man marched past him towards the car.

Evans got out and held the door wide for Scrabo to emerge. Scrabo walked towards the man and Evans watched as they bowed then shook hands, barely surprised when Scrabo started to speak in a foreign tongue; the benefits of an expensive education. The words sounded Chinese, but what did he know? The only Chinese words he knew were on a menu.

The sign for Evans to follow came in a backward glance. He walked close behind his boss, studying the armed guard and ready to take a shot if he made one wrong move. It never came and two hours later they were heading back to Manhattan, in a partnership with North Korea. It was the step too far for Tom Evans that would finally bring Neil Scrabo's empire down.

***

Mitchell reached over and stroked Elza's thick black hair, gazing down at her satisfied face. He hadn't meant for this to happen again and he could feel his guilt about Karen starting to grow. He pushed it away firmly. This wasn't love and it wasn't a betrayal, it was necessary, he was sure of it. He didn't know how just yet, but the woman beside him was the key to information. Information that would tell him just what was going on.

Elza smiled up at him dreamily and Mitchell smiled back. There was no sign of suspicion in her eyes; he was safe for now. His next move was important. He had to find out what Elza knew, in a way that implied he already knew it.

Mitchell lay back on the office floor and made his voice as neutral as possible, then he played the bluff that he thought might draw her out.

"The café's getting hot."

Elza turned quickly to stare at him. Her eyes were quite uncanny, green and clear, so clear that Mitchell could almost see through them. He wished that he could, perhaps then he could read her mind. In the second that it took Mitchell's thoughts to form, Elza was forming her own. They ran across her face in a mix of questions and calculations, until they finally settled on scrutiny. Mitchell held the girl's gaze, counting the seconds until she called him out, until finally Elza sighed.

"You're right. The agency already knows about it. One of them followed you there on Monday."

The agency? Holy Shit! His bluff had hit the jackpot. The number he'd dialled was an agency of some sort. Was that what they'd meant by classified? Which one was it? CIA, FBI, NSA? It didn't matter; they were all the same. Dangerous. Mitchell's mind raced so fast with the possibilities that he almost missed Elza's next words.

"I had to dispose of him. I covered it up - made it look like a robbery. But the agency recovered the body, so Daria said it's just a matter of time before they send someone else."

Mitchell's mouth half-opened in shock. He closed it hurriedly before Elza noticed and stared at her, unblinking, trying hard to hide his disgust. She'd just described killing a man as casually as if she was ordering a drink. Elza kept talking, completely missing his look.

"The big meeting's organised for Thursday night, but we can't use the café anymore." She stood and dressed slowly as she talked. "I'll let you know where."

She made for the door then turned back to Mitchell with a coy smile.

"Don't worry lover, I can deal with the spooks. You just worry about your equations. Then we can all go home."

Somehow Mitchell didn't think 'home' meant where he'd slept last night.

***

"Honey, can you put Emmie to bed? I've got to tidy up."

Mitchell jerked himself from his thoughts and turned questioningly towards his wife. Karen sighed inwardly at his vagueness and repeated her request. Mitchell nodded and stood to lift Emmie. She was having a tea-party with her dolls at his feet and he watched as she kissed each one good night in turn then turned her sunny face towards him with a smile. The gap between her front teeth was beginning to close as more teeth grew, and her baby curls were long tendrils of gold that hung around her face. A tear sprang to Mitchell's eye, surprising him and then he realised why it had come. He didn't want to leave her, or Karen, but if Elza was right then whatever crap he'd got himself into would make it inevitable soon.

The questions had been coming thick and fast since he'd seen Elza that evening. What sort of people was he involved with? And what part did Daria play in all of this? Mitchell thought of the old woman's softly lined face, trying to imagine her as anything but someone's Mom. As someone involved in murder. He couldn't get his head round it, but she obviously was.

Which equations had Elza meant? His screen was covered with them every day; how the hell could he choose which ones they wanted? He understood some of the science he read at Scrabo now but it came in fits and starts, and it definitely wasn't clear enough to help him with this.

Mitchell's mind flew to his discussion with the Board the week before. When he'd mentioned the new carbon allotrope they'd got very excited; it had to be linked with that. He'd been trying to find out more about it since he'd said the words that day, but there was nothing that could possibly be relevant on his PC at Scrabo. Nothing except perhaps the 'Café' file that Daria had pointed him to and he didn't understand anything he'd read in that.

Just then Emmie's tiny hand took his, pulling Mitchell from his reverie and into a pink bedroom at the top of the stairs, where an hour of bedtime stories pushed all thoughts of equations from his mind. As Mitchell finally tucked his daughter in and turned to leave her room he realised that Karen had been watching them from the doorway. The grin on her face said that she'd seen him reading 'The Three Pigs' and mimicking every voice.

Mitchell ushered her down the hallway, tickling her playfully, and Karen turned, reaching up to kiss him. When she pulled away he saw real love in her eyes, not the lust that he'd seen in Elza's hours before. Jeff Mitchell knew then that no matter what plans anyone had for him leaving, he wasn't going anywhere at all.

Chapter Nineteen

Thursday. 1 a.m.

Neil Scrabo gazed around the Boardroom, ruminating. The North Koreans were a tricky bunch, but clever, he had to give them that. All the power held by one family that marketed itself so well their people treated them like Gods. He steepled his fingers thoughtfully; he'd never understood religion, except for the social kudos that it could bring. He didn't like religious people much; irrational mass hysterics, all of them. Whether it was incense or begetting, four arms or orange robes, they were all the same in his book. Idiots. Kneeling and praying had been the ruin of too many good suits. He believed in what he could touch.

Scrabo smiled to himself, acknowledging the irony. No-one could touch carbon atoms but they would make him a fortune soon. Scrabo amended his beliefs to include anything that made him money. That was his God. But if people wanted to act like deities then what did he care? He was a pragmatist. The North Koreans had money and he wanted it.

Scrabo turned his thoughts back to reality. Mitchell had said he'd found something that could make them all rich. All he'd asked for was time. Not more money, nothing for himself, only time. It made him suspicious. In his experience men who couldn't be bought were unpredictable. They had principles and principles always cost money.

If Mitchell really could produce a new form of the carbon in living things, then the sky was the limit medically. But medical advances weren't what the North Koreans had in mind, and they weren't what they would pay him for. Even he'd been taken aback at the figure they'd named that evening. It would make him richer than Bill Gates and there was no way Jeff Mitchell's principles were going to stop him achieving that.

Scrabo walked to the window and gazed down at the street below. The cabs blazed a trail of yellow as they rushed from here to there and the New Yorkers looked tiny, like insects. They were insects, and soon he'd be able to buy them all. He scanned the fading evening sky, wrapping the island in a red-grey gloom. He'd be able to buy Manhattan as well. If that meant Jeff Mitchell had to be persuaded to part company with his principles then that was exactly what would occur.

***

Mitchell's eyes sprang open and he gazed around him for a moment, confused. The room looked unfamiliar then he saw the blonde head beside him on the pillow and remembered where he was. He'd been dreaming of somewhere else and in an instant he worked out where. Greg Chapman's apartment! In his dream he'd been sleeping there, in Chapman's large pine bed.

The thought disturbed him and he slipped quietly out of bed and headed downstairs. He gazed out the kitchen window at the front lawn; neat and full of flowers. Karen had made him cut it at the weekend, bedding down for the autumn. Mitchell admired his domestic handiwork, sipping espresso while he thought.

First he'd known where Greg Chapman had kept his key and now he was dreaming that he'd slept in his bed. Had he been living a double life, with a bachelor pad hidden away? Mitchell shook his head. No, there was nothing to back that up. Every year of his life had been accounted for by Karen, through some judicious questioning. And there were photos of him at college, in the military and at his job. There was no way he'd have found the time for a parallel existence. Besides, the man in Greg Chapman's photo definitely wasn't him.

Maybe he was losing his mind. He knew that Karen worried that he was. He'd seen the way she looked at him. She said that he'd been vague for nearly a year, pressing him to see a doctor. Maybe he should if the past few days' events were anything to go by. Was Elza even real? And the café? What if it was all a hallucination? He had a genius level IQ and everyone knew that it was a fine line... Maybe he'd finally crossed it and the agency was a fantasy as well?

Shaking his head, Mitchell tried to clear his thoughts. As he gazed out again at the grass Karen watched him sadly from the doorway, sensing his confusion. Her heart tightened and she made up her mind. It was time for the hospital appointment that she'd been putting off for months.

***

7.30 a.m.

Devon closed Mitchell's office door quietly behind him and glanced at the wall clock. Half-past seven; Jeff wouldn't be in for an hour yet. Plenty of time. He sat down behind the desk and switched on Mitchell's computer, reaching into his top desk-drawer to see what he could find. The search yielded nothing but rubber bands and chewing gum, plus a year old copy of Playboy that hadn't been there two days before. It was folded at Miss September; she bore an un-nerving resemblance to a brunette Devon had seen in the staff canteen.

Devon searched the other drawers quickly as the PC's screen booted-up. At the back of one lay a cell-phone that he hadn't seen before. It wasn't Jeff's, unless it was an old one bought before his time. Devon turned it over in his hand, wondering if he should press it on, then his thoughts were interrupted as

Mitchell's computer sprang to life.

He turned to the keyboard and typed in 'Einstein', the password that Jeff always used. It didn't work! Devon flicked an anxious look towards the door and then back at the screen. When had Jeff changed his password? Then he remembered. Security had made Jeff change it after he'd failed to log-off the week before. But to what? They'd have given him a temporary password but Jeff was bound to have altered it to something easier to recall.

Devon racked his brain for a moment, and then jotted down a list. After two more attempts the computer would lock him out so he had to get it right. He typed in 'Karen' and pressed enter. Nothing. Cold sweat dripped down his back as he typed in another word for his final shot. The screen changed quickly to a row of folders. Success! Devon smiled to himself; Jeff had made 'Emmie' his new password. He was turning into a real dad.

Devon scanned the folder names quickly and clicked on the one marked 'latest'. It held nothing but the work they'd been doing together that week. He clicked on all the recent files, then on any others that he could find, but none of them yielded anything resembling the carbon-life work that Mitchell had described to the Board. Maybe Jeff *had* been bluffing last week, because Scrabo had put him on the spot? As soon as the thought occurred to him Devon rejected it. No. One thing Jeff Mitchell wasn't was stupid. A lie to the Board would be career suicide and he'd worked too hard to get where he was. Jeff was doing the carbon-life research for sure, but he was hiding the data very well.

Devon clicked to enter the document library. He'd just started scrolling through the files when a loud crash in the hall made him jump. He shut down the computer urgently and wiped the keyboard with his hanky, as if some passing C.S.I. would check it for prints, then he stepped to the door and opened it just a crack. What Devon saw made him heave a sigh of relief; a cleaner was in the hall outside, picking-up a broom from the floor. She leaned it against her trolley and entered the main office, turning her back just long enough for Devon to slip across the hall to the safety of his own desk. He had nothing concrete to show for his burglary, but perhaps that meant something as well.

***

As Mitchell hung up his coat behind the office door his thoughts were still on his interrupted night's sleep. Why had he dreamed about Greg Chapman's apartment, and why did he have such strong memories of Florida? He'd never been there, he was certain of that. He'd checked with Karen the evening before, covering his questions as vacation ideas. Yet he was still sure that he knew it and knew it very well. Mitchell made a note to look into it further and turned to switch on his PC. Suddenly he stopped and sat back in his chair, gazing warily around the room. Something was different. Someone had been in his office, and not just to clean. He scanned the office and then his desk. The bottom drawer was open half-an-inch. He yanked it out and searched hurriedly through the detritus for Chapman's phone. It was still there! He thanked God and then searched the other drawers but nothing was out of place.

Mitchell turned back to the computer. If his suspicions were right then it could yield useful information. He typed in his password and went straight to the controls. Someone had accessed his computer at 7:40, fifty minutes before he'd got in. They knew his habits and they knew him, well enough to guess that his password was his daughter's name.

Mitchell grabbed the phone to call security and then froze, as an instant message popped onto his computer screen. Ten numbers and a message. 'Go home tonight as normal, then come back to the office at eight and wait for our call.' There was no signature but Mitchell knew exactly who it was from; Elza.

He lowered the phone and watched as the message dissolved, then he logged-on to the internet, trying to find something that the numbers could fit. There was nothing that made any sense. They were too few for latitude and longitude and everything else was too obscure. Mitchell thought of the call that he'd been about to make and decided against it, narrowing his possible intruders down to two. The only two that it could be. Elza or someone working for the Board. That could be anyone, but Mitchell knew who was the most likely; Devon. Mitchell smiled coolly to himself. As long as he knew who they were then he was one step ahead.

***

The Andaz Hotel. New York City.

Pereira gazed at her lover and smiled, then her smile turned to tears and she dashed them away angrily. Richie murmured in his sleep and rolled towards her, his tanned arm falling across her naked lap. She stroked his jet-black hair, surprised every time by its softness despite the wax he put in it; his daily attempt at being cool. Richie was cool, he didn't need to try. It was part of him, like his full lips and dark brown eyes. They changed colour to hazel when he smiled, a legacy of his Irish Mom.

Pereira traced his jawline with her finger and then ran it down his spine. Richie shivered in his sleep and turned again, onto his back, his arms flung wide. She smiled at his unguarded posture, only ever in bed. He was too good an agent to have it otherwise.

The white sheet slipped down from Pereira's breast as she moved to sit astride her lover, moving sinuously until Richie's arousal matched her own. She slipped him inside her and rocked back and forth until Richie awoke, giving her a sleepy smile. Pereira placed his hands on her hips and moved faster, desperately seeking some refuge from her guilt, until finally a familiar warmth flooded through her and she finally fell across him, her sighs mixing with her guilty tears.

***

Mitchell knew why someone might think his work important enough to kill a man to protect it, and why the Board had tried to turn Devon into a spy. If he'd discovered a way to manipulate carbon atoms in living things then the applications were endless. The best were medical, helping mankind; he didn't want to think about the worst. He glanced at the photograph on his desk, smiling at Emmie's cherubic face. His research could make a difference to her future; good or bad, depending on whose hands it fell into. Whose hands were safe? Not Elza's that was for sure. What about Scrabo's company Board?

Mitchell remembered the look on Murray's face as he'd done the calculations the week before. It had been pure greed. The Brazilian had talked about medical advances, and maybe he really believed that's what the company would use it for, but Mitchell wasn't so sure. There'd been something in Neil Scrabo's eyes that'd said he had other ideas. Whoever held the key to manipulating carbon-based life held the human race's future in their hands as well. The research couldn't be allowed to reach the wrong people. Mitchell shuddered for a moment, visions of a 21st Century Dr Mengele filling his mind. Then he shook himself. It was all hypothetical. If he had managed to discover a new carbon allotrope then he'd no idea when or where he'd done it, or where the research was now.

Mitchell thought for a moment longer then clicked on the 'Café' file. It hadn't been opened since Monday by him. He gave a sigh of relief and pressed print, watching as pages of data spewed out. The equations in the file were the key to something, but he didn't know what yet. Putting the prints in his briefcase, Mitchell deleted the file then scanned his PC to remove any trace. They might still find the file's shadow, but not without knowing where to look. Daria knew of its existence and that meant that Elza would as well and he definitely didn't want anything falling into her hands.

Mitchell sat back heavily in his chair and rubbed his face. He liked Devon, but it had to be him that had accessed his computer; no-one else would have thought of his password being Emmie's name. He'd known that Neil Scrabo wanted Devon to watch him but not that he would try to access his work. His young deputy was playing a dangerous game, far more dangerous than he could possibly know. If Elza knew that Devon was spying she would kill him. Worse, she would kill his family too.

Scrabo must have told Devon some bullshit story to make him look for his research, probably that they were worried about him cracking up. That and the threat of losing his job if he didn't cooperate would incentivise pretty much everyone. He hoped that Devon had got a hefty payment from Scrabo as well. He didn't begrudge his young deputy whatever he could get from the bastards; he'd probably earned it in long hours over the years. But Devon was a dead man if he didn't stop looking.

Mitchell rubbed his temple, trying to get rid of the headache that had been nagging at him for hours. He had to find out who Daria and Elza worked for, and why Neil Scrabo suddenly wanted his research so fast, when he'd said last week that he would wait three months. Once he had all the facts he could make some decisions.

Mitchell shook his head tiredly. All this interest in something he didn't even understand yet, but until he did, he had to warn Devon off, or he would lose his life.

Chapter Twenty

11 a.m.

"Where are you from, Devon?"

Devon glanced up from his file, surprised to see his boss standing in front of his desk; he hadn't heard Mitchell enter. Devon closed the file he was working on hastily, knocking some papers onto the floor. He rushed to gather them, blushing as he tried to calm himself down. Guilt was making him nervous; Mitchell couldn't possibly know that he'd been searching his office.

"Austin, Texas. Didn't I tell you?"

The younger man sat back, attempting a relaxed pose. Mitchell lifted a chair and sat down opposite, smiling amiably.

"Ever been to Florida?"

Devon shook his head slowly, wondering if it was a trick question.

"Not since I was a kid. My Dad used to take us there once a year for the rodeo at Kissimmee. Never liked the place myself – too spread out." He smiled, remembering. "I'm a small town boy. White picket fences, swings in the yard; the works."

"You went to the University of Houston, didn't you?"

"For my first degree. It was U.C. Berkeley for my doctorate."

Devon gazed across the desk at Mitchell, feeling like he was being interviewed. Mitchell already knew all this stuff so why ask it again? Devon opened his mouth to speak, hoping that he sounded braver than he felt.

"Did you need me for something, Jeff?"

Mitchell stared hard into his deputy's eyes, deliberately holding the gaze for a second longer than he should. It had the desired effect. Devon's earlier blush deepened and he glanced away. Mitchell pressed his advantage.

"Were you in my office this morning, Devon? Before I came in?"

Devon stared at Mitchell, shocked. How the hell had he known? Then he realised. Mitchell couldn't know for sure; he was fishing. Mitchell watched the thoughts running through the young man's mind, each one of them reflected on his face. Devon was deciding whether to lie to him or not and searching for a good one. Mitchell decided to save him the trouble.

"If you were in my office searching for something, I wouldn't bother. I don't keep anything important on that computer."

It was true, except that anyone listening would have thought that Mitchell actually *did* know where he kept important information, instead of still searching for it himself. Devon's mouth opened to speak and Mitchell raised a hand, silencing him.

"I know what you were looking for, Devon. Don't. It's more trouble than you need. If it's Neil Scrabo that hired you, tell him that you tried and couldn't find it."

Mitchell fixed the younger man's eyes and made his voice as threatening as he could. "Stop spying for them, Devon, for your own safety. This is the only warning that you'll get."

Devon's mouth closed slowly as Mitchell rose and rested his hands on the desk, leaning towards him. He spoke with more intensity than Devon had ever heard.

"There are people much more dangerous than the Board or Neil Scrabo in this world, Devon. They've already killed for this research and if they find out that you've been looking for it they'll hurt you and Amy very badly."

Mitchell watched as his words slowly sank in. When he was satisfied that Devon had heard, he stood back and smiled kindly at him.

"I'd hate to see that happen, but these are very bad people. Tell the Board that you tried and failed, and then take a week's holiday from today. You're owed the time."

Mitchell turned and left the office so quickly that Devon thought he'd imagined the whole exchange. He knew that he hadn't imagined its message.

***

"The café's a bust, Richie. They won't use it after Brunet's death."

Richie Cartagena watched mournfully as his lover slipped out of bed and headed for the hotel-room's shower.

"They'll have to meet somewhere, Rosie, and soon, now that they know Mitchell's under surveillance. Things are getting too hot for it to go on much longer."

Pereira's voice echoed from the bathroom.

"Do you think Mitchell killed Brunet?"

Richie shook his head firmly then realised that she couldn't see him. He yelled across the room.

"Unlikely. Jeff Mitchell's a lot of things, but a hands-on assassin isn't one of them. He'd think that it was beneath him."

"He has military training."

Richie laughed sceptically. "That doesn't make him a trained killer, babe. He was an army surgeon; we're talking special-ops training for the way Brunet was killed. Mitchell must have a guard dog; they wouldn't trust him enough to leave him unwatched."

Pereira re-entered the room and Richie watched in silence as she dressed in her black suit. He preferred her naked. He reached out for her and Pereira playfully skipped away, restarting the conversation.

"Is Magee any closer to narrowing down who *they* are?"

"The money's on Russia, because of the café, but who knows? That could just be some old cold-war spook at headquarters getting paranoid. My money's on the Arabs. Saudi or Iran. Syria's too hot at the moment for them to go looking for new toys."

"And Jeff Mitchell's just a straight forward scumbag who's selling his wares for the highest price?"

"Looks that way." Richie squinted at her, puzzled. "Why? Have you got a different theory?"

Pereira bit her lip thoughtfully before answering. "It's just… something doesn't fit. Mitchell's the original all-American boy. He fought for his country in Iraq and he has the perfect family and a good lifestyle. Why would he be prepared to throw it all away for a life in exile, or in prison?"

"He wouldn't be the first."

"Yeah, I know. But it's not as if Mitchell can't know that he'll get caught eventually. And can you imagine the wife and daughter wearing Abayas in some country with Sharia law?"

Richie shrugged. "Maybe he plans on going without them. He might have another woman lined up."

Richie didn't move quickly enough to avoid the slap heading his way.

"Ow! What the hell was that for? I was only saying."

"You were only saying too much, Cartagena, that's what! You've no romance in your soul."

The look in Richie's eyes told Pereira not to say any more. He'd given up his marriage for her. Romance was all he had. She changed the subject hurriedly.

"Anyway, an all-American boy living in Iran? Why?" Pereira paused for a moment then grinned. "Twenty dollars."

"What?"

"I'll bet you twenty dollars that Jeff Mitchell doesn't run."

Richie rubbed his arm and considered. "With or without the wife?"

"Either way. Mitchell won't leave the USA."

Richie thought for a moment and then extended his hand. "Done. Easiest twenty I ever made."

***

By the end of the day Devon had left New York. Mitchell congratulated himself. He'd saved Devon's life and thwarted the Neil Scrabo's intentions in the process. But Mitchell knew that losing Devon wouldn't stop Scrabo for long. He would find another way to get hold of his work.

For all the Board's talk of giving him time to develop his research, Scrabo wanted it now. As soon as the thought entered Mitchell's head he knew that he was wrong. Not in his estimate of Neil Scrabo's greed but in own use of tense. It wasn't time 'to develop' his research that he needed; he'd already done it! Mitchell was suddenly certain that he'd already developed the carbon-life allotrope; he didn't waste time wondering how he knew, he just did. So where was it?

The scientist in Mitchell kicked in, running through the protocols that he'd learned throughout the years. If he'd developed a raw hypothesis then the next stage was to do trials. That meant he had to have somewhere to run them. But where? There was high security everywhere in Scrabo Tower. How could he have developed trials there without someone finding out? And there was no-where at his house that would even vaguely suit. That left somewhere else, somewhere that he'd had the equipment and space to carry out his tests.

Mitchell racked his brains, searching for answers, but there was nothing. Since last week his life had just been home and work. Then it came to him. The café. He must have carried out the trials there; it was the only other place that he'd had access to. Was that what the old woman had meant about his work? When he'd been there last he'd gone to open the door beside the kitchen, but it had been locked and she'd refused to give him the key, chiding him to take a rest. He'd known then that there was something behind there, now he had to find out what.

Mitchell grabbed his briefcase and exited the office quickly. He was just about to lock the door when some instinct made him look more closely at his keys. There were four of them. House, office, the key to the Lexus and one more. It was nondescript, like a million others. And small, so small that the lock it fitted had to be custom made. Why hadn't he noticed it before?

Mitchell stared at it for a moment knowing exactly which lock it would fit, then he raced to the elevator, desperate to prove his theory. Common sense had returned by the time he reached reception and he walked calmly past the guards and exited the building, calling Karen to delay her lift until six o'clock. That should give him time to check things out.

***

5 p.m.

Richie changed the radio station and settled back to listen to some blues while he waited for Karen Mitchell's Lexus to arrive. Instead he saw her husband walking swiftly along West Street, heading in the direction of the café. Richie radioed in that he was following and pulled out into the early evening traffic, slowing the sedan to a crawl. Magee wheezed down the line that he was to wait; Brad Whitman was on his way and they were to tail Mitchell together. After Brunet and Chapman, Magee didn't want any more heroes, no matter what they thought Jack Bauer might have done.

Richie ignored him and kept on driving. If Jeff Mitchell was heading where he thought he was, then no amount of Magee's shouting was going to stop him giving chase. Richie watched as the scientist turned into the narrow side-streets that only ever led to one place. Mitchell was definitely going to the café. Richie checked his gun and exited the sedan, keeping to what few shadows there were. He tailed Mitchell as tightly as he could without being seen, until the narrow Manhattan streets opened into the small, paved square with trees at its corners and the red-awninged café set to one side. The café lay in darkness, closed for the day and Jeff Mitchell was nowhere to be seen.

Richie glanced involuntarily at the dark alley where Claude Brunet had died. There was nothing to mark his last stand. It would be the same for all of them. The alley was full of large bins that no-one could have squeezed between, that only left one exit from the square and he was blocking that, so where the hell had Mitchell gone? Richie stared up at the rooftops then scanned the square again, scrutinising every inch of it with well-trained eyes. There was no sign of life anywhere. Not a light or a sound. Jeff Mitchell had simply disappeared.

Richie stepped back into a side-street and weighed his options. Common sense said Mitchell had entered the café, but if he followed him in there, the whole operation would be blown. If Mitchell spotted him, ditto. There was no way for anyone to leave Regan Plaza except via West Street so that was where he would wait.

Richie re-traced his steps until he was back on the main drag. Ten minutes later a dark car pulled up on West Street and Brad Whitman leapt out. He didn't see Richie until he stepped into his path and pulled him into the shadows, staring him into quiet. Forty minutes later Jeff Mitchell walked past them, his cell-phone clamped to his ear. They heard enough to know that he was calling his wife to be collected. Richie waited until Mitchell was ten feet in front of them then he radioed Magee.

"Mitchell was in the square for nearly an hour. His wife's collecting him now. Whitman will follow them while I re-check the café. I'm due to handover anyway."

The wheeze that followed drowned out Magee's words so Richie asked him to repeat.

"I said if the café is shut, what was Mitchell doing there?"

"No idea. But I'll tell you this much, his briefcase is a lot fatter now than it was when he went in."

***

As the Lexus pulled into the driveway Karen Mitchell turned off the engine, glancing at her husband. He looked stressed, more stressed than he'd looked for weeks. She'd got fed up waiting for him to agree so she'd gone ahead and made the doctor's appointment for the next day and Jeff was going to attend whether he liked it or not. As Karen went to get out of the car she was surprised by Mitchell's hand on her arm, asking her to stay. She turned towards him and saw sadness in his eyes that she hadn't noticed before. Karen opened her mouth to speak, but Mitchell got there first. He gazed intensely at her.

"Karen, do you love me?"

His tone said that this wasn't foreplay. Karen took her husband's hand, squeezing it in her own as she replied.

"With every part of me."

Mitchell gazed at her for a moment until she saw tears in his eyes, then he spoke again.

"If I ask you to take Emmie away somewhere with no warning, will you do it for me?"

Karen's heart tightened with anxiety.

"Why? What is this about, Jeff?"

Mitchell gripped her hand and repeated his words. "Will you do it, Karen?"

She shook her head. "No, not without you."

He grabbed her shoulders hard. "You must. Even without me. Promise me that you'll do it."

Mitchell's eyes were burning and Karen felt his grip tighten. He was scaring her and he knew it, but he had to make her hear. Karen scanned her husband's face, then fixed his blue eyes with her own and nodded, feeling relief relax his hands.

"Jeff..."

Mitchell looked at her, pleadingly. "Please don't ask, Karen. Just trust me, please."

She nodded and he leaned forward, kissing her lightly on the cheek.

"Now, I have to go somewhere. Kiss Emmie goodnight for

me. I'll be back in a few hours."

"I'll be here."

Karen walked into the house without a backwards glance and Mitchell leapt into the driver's seat and checked his watch. Seven p.m. If he drove like the devil he'd just make it back to the office in time for Elza's call. He felt like he was about to be put through some kind of test, but a test of what? As Mitchell reversed out of the driveway, he was suddenly filled with dread about what he would find at his journey's end.

Chapter Twenty-One

Mitchell sat in his office and waited impatiently for Elza's call. It finally came at half past nine.

"Are you alone?"

"Apart from the blonde cheerleaders."

Elza's mouth twisted in a sneer.

"Very witty; I hope you're still laughing in an hour's time. Now, follow my instructions. Put the numbers I gave you into your computer and another message will come up containing a code. Key it into your car's GPS and follow the directions as you go."

Mitchell gripped the phone in fury.

"If you'd just given me an address I could have gone there directly from home, instead of all this bloody subterfuge."

"You like subterfuge, remember? You were bred for it. Besides, we have our reasons."

The line clicked off and Mitchell shook his head, wondering what Elza had meant. She seemed to get some sort of kick from all this cloak and dagger stuff. Mitchell got the code then went to the Lexus and tapped it into the GPS, waiting for a map to pop up. Instead directions to Miele Park in the Bronx appeared. Mitchell was puzzled; it wouldn't take him an hour to get there. Then he understood. When he got to Miele Park he'd be given another direction. So that was the way it was going to be; drip-feeding him directions to test how much trust he deserved. And whether he was being tailed.

Thirty minutes later Mitchell was on the I-295 and he finally put his foot down and started to think. The fourth key on his fob had fitted the locked door in the café, just as he'd thought he would. He'd never been past the café's front area during previous visits, always only a customer. But when Daria diverted him away from the door it had made him curious, and as soon as he'd seen the key he'd known with certainty that it would fit. Mitchell thought about what he'd found there that evening and frowned. As he thought about the room's contents he pulled into the overtaking lane, accelerating past a school bus full of kids. They cheered at him through the windows, heading home after a good day; still innocent of the bad things in life. Mitchell wished that he was.

The door-lock in the café had been small and custom-made and it responded smoothly to the key. Mitchell hadn't known what he'd find behind it. On his first few visits to the coffee-shop he'd thought it was a store cupboard, with shelves and tins and maybe sacks of flour. Today he'd wondered if it could be a small lab where he carried out his secret research trials. No, he hadn't known exactly what to expect, but it certainly hadn't been what he'd seen inside.

Mitchell slowed the car to fifty, not noticing Brad Whitman sitting three cars behind him in the adjacent lane. Mitchell could picture the locked room in the café clearly, as if he was still there. Its high white walls and smooth dark floor had stretched back for hundreds of yards, making him walk outside the building to check how the large space could possibly fit. He'd found his answer quickly. Behind the coffee-shop's cosy front sat an old warehouse that he'd never noticed. It looked abandoned, barely warranting a second glance, but it was linked to the café via the locked door. The café was the perfect front for secrets and one look back inside the room had shown Mitchell just what those secrets were.

Instead of tins and sacks of food there were shelves and high work-benches. Cables on the wall hinted at rows of computers that were nowhere to be seen. Abandoned cages sat in one corner and he'd shuddered at what they might have contained.

The place had been cleared out but there was no mistaking what the warehouse had once been. A sophisticated research lab. His research lab. They'd emptied it as best they could, but Mitchell knew a lab's layout well.

He'd stood in the room searching for remnants of information to give him answers. Not whether he'd been there before; flashes of memory and a sense of familiarity had already told him that, but answers about what he'd been researching, and how far he'd managed to progress his work.

There hadn't been much left but he'd crammed whatever papers he had found into his briefcase and they were sitting in the Lexus' trunk now, waiting for him to make sense of them. What had he discovered that everyone wanted so much? Had he really cracked carbon bio-engineering? Was there even more?

A light flashing in Mitchell's rear-view mirror pulling him back to the present and he realised that he'd slowed the Lexus to a crawl. He raised a hand apologetically and pulled into a slower lane then cracked open a window to keep himself alert. It wouldn't do to get killed in a crash before he'd got answers. Mitchell checked the GPS quickly; his turn-off was next. Just as he indicated he noticed a sedan with tinted windows do the same. It looked familiar. Then he realised. Of course…They'd been watching him.

Images flew into Mitchell's mind, slotting into place all at once. He couldn't believe that he hadn't seen it before. The sedan that was parked across from Scrabo Tower, on his street at home and now here. Were they working with Elza? Or were they government men? Thirty seconds later Mitchell had his answer. A dark green van pulled in behind the sedan and even in his mirror Mitchell could tell that it was too close. The sedan's driver seemed not to notice the van for a moment and then without warning, the sedan accelerated past Mitchell, swerving in and out of the lanes with the van following close each time.

They were three car lengths in front of him when the van

finally made its move. It pulled alongside the sedan and Mitchell watched, shocked, as the passenger window slid open and the unmistakable shape of a gun barrel emerged. The faint pop and muzzle flare were over before anyone else had seen, but their result was very clear. The sedan swerved wildly to its left and then left again, scattering cars furiously around it, trying to clear a path. It ricocheted off a small Honda, rolling it over, throwing sparks up from its wheels. As Mitchell watched the Honda's driver struggle to free himself, the sparks became flames and the car turned into a supernova in his rear view.

Mitchell swore aloud, glancing back at the funeral pyre, but the fast flowing traffic was only heading one way. He grabbed at the car phone to dial 911 and then thought again. Someone else would do it and he couldn't risk the cops' lives by involving them in his mess, not until he knew exactly what it was. The road ahead equalled the road behind for carnage as the sedan mowed down everything in its path, the driver far beyond controlling it. Mitchell watched as it hit two other cars, scattering them like pool balls with the same effect as before.

The vehicles far ahead of him had managed to clear a path and Mitchell wondered how they knew to do it. The sound of rotor blades overhead gave him his answer. A police helicopter was hovering above the scene, alerted by a concerned citizen. They'd used a loudhailer to direct people out of the way just in time to avoid the sedan.

The runaway car hit the highway barrier, buckling the steel beneath its wheels and making a noise like a crushers' yard. As Mitchell held his breath the sedan cut through the metal obstacle like heat through snow, plummeting over the road's edge to wreak more havoc on the road underneath. A moment later Mitchell heard a loud splash and exhaled, relieved. They were on the Throgs Neck Bridge and there was only water beneath them. He thanked God for the small mercy. Enough people had died because of him today.

The traffic slowed down to gawp and Mitchell used the pause

to search for the van. He saw it abandoned a car length ahead, its work done. No-one would follow him to the meeting now; Elza and her allies made sure of that. It answered his questions; the sedan had been a government tail. The van had risked civilian lives to kill the sedan's driver and no government agency, no matter how maverick, would ever have done that. The knowledge that he was being watched by the good guys was strangely comforting, but whoever the green van's driver was, Mitchell had no doubt that they worked with Elza, and whoever Elza worked for didn't want an audience tonight.

Mitchell edged the Lexus into the left hand lane and indicated, slipping quickly off the main drag and onto the Cross Island Parkway until he picked up his route. He drove slowly, checking his mirror every few yards like a man on the run, but there was no-one there. The van had done its job. Ten miles later the GPS told him to turn again, onto a farm road that tested the Lexus' suspension to the hilt. It went on for miles, running between fields of high grass. Mitchell was surprised; he hadn't known that there were fields this close to the city. Then he glanced at the milometer; he was forty miles from the office!

The track narrowed until the walls of yellow-green foliage grew so close that Mitchell could have touched them and there was no way to go but ahead. He drove until the evening sky was dark and his car lights kicked on. The only sound to be heard was a hawk overhead, swooping towards the car. Wherever he was going it was certainly out of the way.

A half-hour later the track opened suddenly into a clearing, where a small one-storey farmhouse sat surrounded by cars. Not the pick-up trucks that the rural location hinted at, but high-end limos with foreign makes. Mitchell was puzzled but the GPS confirmed that he'd reached his destination. Any doubt was quashed by the sight of Elza slipping elegantly from a dark Mercedes outside the house's front door. She strolled towards him like a panther and Mitchell's body twitched from lust. It was just a reflex, like blinking, something over which he had no control. It was nothing to do with love; that belonged to Karen. Mitchell smiled confidently as Elza reached the car.

"Interesting journey?"

Mitchell stepped from the Lexus and stared at her, hiding his disgust with a wry smile.

"You could say that - the fireworks were unexpected. There were casualties."

Elza shrugged, dismissing the deaths. "We protect our assets." She entwined his fingers with hers and gazed at him pointedly. "What's ours is ours."

The meaning was clear and Mitchell knew that Elza was applying it to more than work. He realised something that he'd missed before. Elza had feelings for him; maybe even love. The knowledge gave Mitchell an edge and he stored it for future use. Elza held his gaze for a second longer then they moved towards the house, the moment gone. As they walked she whispered instructions to Mitchell under her breath.

"Ilya you will know. But there are others inside; men you know nothing about."

Ilya. Mitchell had heard the name from her and Daria. He'd be expected to know him. How could he cover the fact that he didn't?

Elza stopped walking and stared up at him gravely. "We're nearing the end now, and that means they will want results. You must finish your work quickly. These people don't play games. You understand?"

Mitchell understood completely. If he didn't finish his work soon, they would dispose of him and take it for some puppet scientist to complete. He nodded and Elza smiled, opening the front door wide. This time Mitchell half-expected what lay ahead. The farmhouse's plain exterior covered a wood-lined entrance hall, with doors leading off to a series of rooms. Mitchell knew that one of them would mimic the laboratory at the café. Large and clean, but this time with the shelves filled with books and laptops on every bench. His new lab. Mitchell smiled inwardly; very clever. He admired their resourcefulness if not their goals.

Elza walked ahead and opened the first door on her right, showing Mitchell into a small, pale-walled room. Four men of different hues sat at a table. Mitchell recognised one of them but he couldn't remember from where. He was a powerfully built man of around seventy and he shot Mitchell a smile that said he knew him well. Ilya?

Mitchell didn't know the others but he recognised their greed. They wanted power. Money would follow but it was almost incidental for men like this. They already had more than they could spend. Power was what drove them, the power to control other people's lives.

A small man at the table stood up to greet him, beaming with bonhomie. He was wearing a suit so white that Mitchell was reminded of an old movie about a fabric that was always clean. He smiled at the incongruity of his thoughts and the small man smiled again. He looked Arabic. It was confirmed when he spoke.

"Salam. Dr Mitchell. I am Behrouz Javadi."

Mitchell's hand automatically flew to his chest, lips and forehead in greeting. "Salam."

"Please sit. Coffee? Or something cool after your long drive?"

"Coffee's just fine."

Mitchell cradled his drink as he scanned the room. There were two other men at the table and two men by the door that he hadn't noticed before. They had bulges in their jackets that had nothing to do with style. The men at the table were a mix of Arab and Slav and Mitchell knew that he was looking at an alliance; between Russia and the middle-East. Middle-East where? The answer came soon.

"You know Ilya of course."

The old man that Mitchell had recognised smiled warmly and Mitchell nodded in return, struggling to recall anything about him.

"This other gentleman is a colleague from Tehran."

Iranians. Mitchell wasn't surprised. The Iranians had kept pretty quiet throughout the Arab Spring, watching carefully from the side-lines, determined not to let it happen to them. They'd always wanted nuclear power, but the West had been watching. If they obtained his carbon research they would have an asset worth far more than that.

He'd guessed at Russia from Daria and Elza, but an alliance with Iran was something new. It was like a scene from a cold-war movie except that the sweat trickling down Mitchell's back said that it was very real. Why the hell had he got involved in this? Was it for money? Could he really be that mundane?

Ilya waved Mitchell to a seat and Elza was dismissed; a woman unimportant in a world of men. Mitchell smiled inwardly, knowing she wouldn't like it. Javadi turned towards him oozing warmth.

"Ilya tells me that you have a family. A wife and a little girl?"

The words carried a clear threat. Mitchell nodded, not trusting himself to speak without using his fists. Javadi smiled at him again, like a snake-charmer playing a tune.

"Would you like to take them with you?"

To where? Where the hell was he going? Mitchell knew that he couldn't ask or it would give the game away so instead he just nodded again.

"That can be arranged. Of course it is dependent upon your work proving to be of use."

Javadi gestured towards Ilya. "I am told Ilya has known you for many years, Dr Mitchell. Since you arrived here as a child?"

What the hell was Javadi talking about? Arrived from where? He'd been born in the U.S. Mitchell searched his memories frantically for clues. Images appeared and then dissolved before he could grasp them, leaving panic in their wake. Suddenly the answers that he'd been avoiding were staring him in the face. As Mitchell turned towards Ilya a different image of the Russian appeared. A man thirty years younger, cheering him on while he played baseball at school. Was Ilya his father? No. Mitchell rejected the idea as soon as it appeared. Father implied something positive and Ilya definitely wasn't that. He was something much darker. He was his handler.

The word flashed into Mitchell's mind as if he'd known it all his life. Ilya was his handler and he was a sleeper! An agent brought to the U.S. so young that he'd been bred to integrate. Speak like an American, dress like one, be one. To sleep amongst them, until the moment that he was activated and his handler wanted payback.

He was Russian! Ilya had brought him here and brought him up. He'd taught him everything. Even given him a legend that said he'd had parents called Jane and Stephen Mitchell who'd died when he was ten. Ilya had paid his way through college, and watched as Jeff Mitchell developed into an asset that they could use.

The knowledge nauseated Mitchell. He wanted to retch but he knew he couldn't. It would tell them that he'd forgotten everything and was shocked by the truth. Mitchell locked down his emotions to stop his thoughts from showing on his face. He was a spy, a Russian spy and he'd soon have to leave everything that he knew. He was a traitor.

In that second Mitchell saw something else behind the images and he grabbed at it and held it tight, using all his strength to smile. No. He wasn't a traitor, not unless he chose to be, and he never would. Forcing himself to relax Mitchell turned towards Ilya and spoke warmly, using their past relationship to best effect.

"Ilya was like a father to me."

Javadi nodded. "I am also a father. I know that love."

Javadi paused for a moment and then reached out his hand for Mitchell to shake. It was a signal. They trusted him. Ilya snapped his fingers immediately and a man entered the room, carrying a case. He distributed the hand-outs inside it and left.

The Russian opened the document in front of him and motioned them all to do the same. It contained a short summary sheet, backed up by two pages of graphs. Mitchell knew exactly what it was; his research. And he knew what came next. He'd be expected to run through it. Mitchell closed his eyes for a second and prayed that he would perform like he had in Scrabo's Boardroom, then instinct kicked in and he did.

Mitchell ran through carbon engineering in ten minutes, the point that the world's research had reached and how he'd managed to take it further. He ended with a minute on new carbon allotropes then updated them on what Scrabo's Board had asked him to do. Mitchell had the sense that his research had gone even further than he was admitting, but he couldn't remember how.

Mitchell laughed. "Scrabo said they would give me the time to develop it."

Ilya interjected. He had a deep, rough voice with a Slavic accent but there was something warm about the man. Mitchell could imagine them being close once, even though he couldn't remember.

"Mitchell will work at Scrabo Tower and also here. Once he has taken things as far as he can, we will leave. He will give Scrabo only what the rest of the world already has. The Americans will never get their hands on his real work." He turned to Mitchell, smiling. "Is that not so, Durak?"

Durak. Mitchell recognised the pet name and felt unexpectedly sad, but he had more important things to worry about. He rubbed his temple hard; thinking about Neil Scrabo's spying attempts. He couldn't tell these men about them or Scrabo and Devon would be the next ones in their graves. Who did Neil Scrabo want his research for; his company, America or the highest bidder? Mitchell settled on the last, wondering who the highest bidder was these days. Clearly not the men in front of him; they wanted his research for free.

Mitchell asked the most innocent question that he could

think of, just to test his nerves. His voice surprised him with its calm.

"How can I work here without my absence being noticed? We're almost sixty miles from New York."

It was a logical question but it made them all smile. Ilya answered him.

"Haven't you noticed where you are, Durak?"

Mitchell looked at him blankly.

"You're eighteen miles from home. You drove out of the city and back to Long Island again."

Mitchell thought about the route he'd come and then realised that they were right. The directions had led him out to the Bronx and then back to Long Island. Drip-feeding him directions had ensured that he'd got confused. Clever.

"We wanted to smoke out your surveillance and stop them tailing you here."

"Who were they?"

Ilya shrugged and nodded to the men by the door. One of them spoke in an American accent. A mercenary working for the biggest pay-day.

"FBI, NSA, who knows? They've been watching you for months and they'll keep on doing it. We just didn't want them to tail you here."

Mitchell smiled to himself, feeling safer at the mention of the acronyms. Javadi stood-up abruptly and the others did the same. Only Mitchell remained in his seat.

"We are pleased, Dr Mitchell. Keep on with your work and Ilya will give you an extraction date. It will be soon. Until then, do everything as you normally do. Now, the woman will take you to your new laboratory and then show you the short way home." He glanced at the Rolex on his wrist and smiled coolly. "You should be there just in time for bed."

Javadi turned on his heel and exited the room, followed by the other men. Ilya waited behind. He rested his hand on Mitchell's arm and smiled.

"You're doing well, Durak. Very well. Soon this will be over and we will all go home."

The old man left the room quickly, nodding at Elza to lead Mitchell to his new lab. Mitchell buried the questions racing through his mind and followed her, looking around him as they walked and memorising each detail for future use.

Elza stopped and turned, scanning her lover's face as if she could read his thoughts. She noticed everything; he would need to be more careful. Mitchell smiled brightly and ushered her politely ahead. He would consider his next steps well away from Elza's prying eyes.

Chapter Twenty-Two

Richie yawned and slid down the car seat, trying to get comfortable. He was bored and tired and in need of a shower. He'd almost been home when Magee had radioed him to babysit the house, while Whitman swanned off, tailing Jeff Mitchell to God knows where. He glanced at the clock; it was almost midnight and they still weren't back. Mitchell's rendezvous must have been miles away. Just Whitman's good luck to catch the overtime.

Just then a pair of headlights flashed in Richie's rear-view mirror and he jerked upright, recognising the Mitchells' Lexus. Richie smiled, knowing that he would soon be off duty. Whitman wouldn't be far behind so he could cover the rest of the watch. Visions of a hot shower and bed with Rosie Pereira filled Richie's mind.

The Lexus pulled past him into the driveway and Jeff Mitchell climbed out, pulling his briefcase from the boot. He stood for a moment scanning the street, as if he knew someone was there. A quick salute in Richie's direction confirmed it. Mitchell had seen him! Richie slipped down towards the floor then thought better of it and sat up again, returning Mitchell's salute with one of his own. Mitchell must have known he was being tailed for a while. They obviously weren't as slick as they thought they were.

Richie wondered when Mitchell had noticed them first. Probably on a trip to the café. It didn't matter. It was unlikely to alter his behaviour and it definitely wouldn't change theirs. Richie made a note to get better at surveillance and then glanced back at the Mitchell's house, watching as the lights came on in the study downstairs. The Doc was burning the midnight oil. Richie speculated for a moment on what Mitchell might be doing, then gave up. Either he'd be staring at equations like the nerd he was or thinking about the meaning of life.

Craning his neck, Richie scanned the street for Whitman's car. Where the hell was Brad? He wanted to get some sleep before it was time to come back to work. A moment later Richie got his answer, when the radio crackled into life. Magee's gruff voice announced matter-of-factly that Brad Whitman had been killed and that Howard would be relieving Richie soon. He would give them the details at a meeting at nine a.m.; the local police could cover their surveillance for an hour. Richie knew just how much the NYPD would love that; he'd been a cop before he'd joined the agency.

Richie's thoughts moved to Brad Whitman. He hadn't known the guy but he was sorry that he was dead. Whitman had survived years of combat, yet died two weeks into working for Magee. If Iraq doesn't kill you, New York will. Jeff Mitchell was a bastard who'd caused the death of another good agent.

A sharp tap on the sedan's window told Richie that the cavalry had arrived. He nodded gratefully at Amelia Howard and handed over. He knew there was no point trying to sleep so he called Rosie Pereira and headed for the nearest bar.

***

Karen Mitchell stood by the study door watching her husband read. Jeff had frightened her earlier, but she knew that he'd meant to. It was his way of making her take him seriously. She had. She'd sent the babysitter home and locked herself and Emmie in upstairs until she'd heard the Lexus return. Emmie had been asleep for hours, oblivious to everything but her dreams. Ignorance was bliss.

Mitchell sensed that Karen was there and turned, momentarily taken aback by his wife's beauty. With her long white nightdress and blonde curls rambling across her shoulders she looked angelic; like everything good in the world. Karen walked towards Mitchell and he reached out a hand, pulling her onto his knee and holding her close. She smelled of vanilla and he buried his face in her hair, searching for comfort. His work had taken him into a dark world and she was the polar opposite. She and Emmie were pure and clean and he would do anything to protect them.

Mitchell broke their embrace slowly and gazed into Karen's navy-blue eyes, reading the fear there. Without her make-up on she looked like a girl, but Mitchell knew that she was wiser than him in many ways. He went to speak but Karen kissed him gently, stilling his words. Mitchell kissed her back passionately, until he felt tears on his face. He stared at his wife but her eyes were dry; the tears were his. He dashed them away and then spoke.

"Karen, I'm in serious trouble and I need you to trust me."

Karen's large eyes widened, then she nodded and Mitchell knew that no matter what he said next she would still love him.

"I've been carrying out some high-level research and there are some people who are prepared to go to any lengths to get it."

Karen cut in anxiously. "What is it? Give it to them, Jeff. Just give it to them!"

Mitchell pressed a finger to her lips and gave a weak smile, then he shook his head.

"I'm not sure how far the research has progressed."

"But it's your research, how can you not know?"

Mitchell rubbed his forehead. "The problem is that I can't remember. I can't remember a lot of things these days." He missed the frightened look in her eyes. "But I know where the work is heading and I can't let it fall into their hands."

"Why not?"

Mitchell stared at her gravely. "Because if they get it they can pervert it, and use it to harm millions of people."

"How?"

"I've been working on new forms of carbon."

He paused and Karen stared blankly at him.

"In living things, Karen."

Her blank look deepened then she spoke. "I know you work with Graphene. Electrical conduction. But where do the living things come in?"

"All life on earth is carbon-based, including us. I think…I think I've made a new form of carbon. I've learned how to alter the carbon atoms in living things..."

Karen understood immediately and her face fell. Whoever held the key to manipulating carbon-based life held the key to advances that could save millions of people, or weapons that could destroy them. The ramifications made her feel sick. She broke Mitchell's embrace and moved away.

"How could you Jeff? How in God's name could you?"

Mitchell slumped in his chair and held his head in his hands.

"I can't remember discovering it and I've no idea how far the research has gone, that's what I have to find out. It must have happened when we were researching the applications of Graphene." He shook his head quickly to clear his thoughts and then stood up. "What's done is done. The discovery's made. What I need to do now is find out how far it's developed and keep it away from these bastards."

"Who are they?"

"Some sort of Russian, Arabic partnership."

Her eyes widened. "Oh God!"

"Scrabo's after it too."

"But don't they own the work? You did it on their behalf."

"The company only has copyright for work that they've paid me to do, anything I developed on my own time belongs to me. Anyway, it's not Scrabo LLC that wants it, it's Neil Scrabo himself." He sighed heavily. "He has Devon spying on me."

Karen's mouth flew open. "Devon? No! He can't know what

Scrabo wants it for."

Mitchell shook his head. "No, I don't think that he does. I told him that I was on to him and sent him away for a few days. He'll be safe as long as Scrabo can't find him." Mitchell stared at her intently. "You have to trust me, Karen. I'm going to string them along until I work out what to do."

"But you can't even remember what you've been working on. They'll realise what you're doing, Jeff. It's not safe."

"I can bluff until I find out. The work's too complex for anyone but another scientist to question me on. I'm going to keep you and Emmie safe, and when I find out how far it's progressed, I promise that I'll destroy everything. I just want to do some more digging and then I'll contact the Feds. They'll protect you."

"And what about you, Jeff?" She hugged him tight. "I'd die if anything happened to you."

Mitchell smiled down at her. "Then I'd better make sure that it doesn't. For all our sakes."

Chapter Twenty-Three

Friday, 12th September. 9 a.m.

"Whitman was killed before he could find out who Mitchell was meeting."

"Bloody waste of life."

Magee rounded angrily on Richie, his face a deep red. It was a shade that Richie had never seen before.

"Whitman did his job and he did it without complaining, Cartagena, which is more than I can say for you."

Magee ran out of breath and sucked at his inhaler, then he tapped the screen in front of him and an aerial view of the farmhouse that Jeff Mitchell had visited appeared. The house was set in acres of high grass with only the space it stood in carved out. There was no-where to turn a car but in front of the house; Brad Whitman's sedan would have been spotted in seconds. If he'd parachuted in nearby, high visibility would have resulted in him being shot before he hit the ground.

Richie nodded, understanding.

"I'm sorry, boss. All I meant was that, thanks to the tracker we put on the Lexus we could have waited until Mitchell arrived then got satellite images of the people he was meeting. Whitman would still be alive."

Magee shook his head. "We have the images but they're no use. They concealed their faces and all the car number plates were false."

A soft voice interrupted him. "An agent was our best chance of getting close enough to capture their faces on film, Richie.

Brad knew the risks when he volunteered."

Richie turned towards the gently said words and instantly felt bad. Amelia Howard's face wore a sad expression. Whitman had been her friend and he'd gone to almost certain death without a complaint. He'd been a brave man. Richie nodded at her in respect as Pereira watched them both jealously. She joined the discussion with more than a hint of chagrin.

"It's still a waste. All we know now is that they've shifted operations to some farm in the backside of nowhere and we've still no clue what Mitchell's been working on."

Richie nodded in agreement. "Whatever it is it must be something serious, judging by the security. They weren't playing when they killed Brad."

Magee interrupted the exchange in a weak voice. His asthma was getting worse, and some people wondered why the agency didn't retire him. Richie knew exactly why. Magee had mentored the Director when he'd first joined and he said Magee was the brightest men he'd ever met. Magee's trade-craft might be rusty these days and he wouldn't fancy his chances in a chase, but he still had his brain.

"We have every branch gathering intelligence, but the only whisper we have is about the Russians. They're the prime movers in this, but they won't be the only ones interested, you can be sure of that. As for what Mitchell's working on, we have to assume that it's related to carbon. It's his field of research."

Richie cut in. The others admired his hutzpah; if any of them had done it Magee would have had their heads on a plate.

"What? Some new application of Graphene? No way. This can't just be about electronics. Half the world is already working on that. Mitchell must have found something totally new."

"Like what?"

The room fell silent as everyone struggled to answer Magee. Eventually he restarted.

"What Mitchell's working on isn't our problem. We have scientists working on it back at base. Our job is to find out who the buyers are."

"We could always try bringing Mitchell in and asking him."

Everyone turned to look at Amelia Howard. Richie thought she'd undone another button of her shirt and he craned his neck to check. Pereira spotted where he was looking and interjected, mocking Howard's idea in a caustic tone.

"Yeh, OK. Excuse me Dr Mitchell, would you mind telling me exactly what you've discovered and which of the USA's enemies you're selling it to?"

"We don't have enemies nowadays, do we? Aren't they all just competitors?"

"Whatever."

Everyone laughed except Magee. He was rubbing his chin deep in thought.

"That's not a bad idea, Howard."

"What? You've got to be kidding, boss!" Pereira's voice and expression stank of sour grapes.

"I'm not saying that it's a brilliant one, but it's something for me to think about."

"Lift Mitchell? He'll say nothing and lawyer up."

Richie leaned forward, shaking his head at his lover. "I'm not so sure he would." He told them about Mitchell's salute the night before. "He obviously knows that he's being watched and he wanted me to know he did. There was something about that salute…"

"What?"

"Give me a couple more days watching him, and I'll tell you."

Magee thought for a moment and then nodded. "OK. Business as usual for two more days, then we'll talk about bringing Dr Mitchell in."

He turned towards Richie and nodded, trusting the younger man's gut.

"Focus on the wife and daughter, Richie, the others can watch Mitchell. Then we'll see."

***

3 p.m.

Pereira was surprised to see Karen Mitchell's Lexus arrive outside Scrabo Tower at three p.m., two hours earlier than normal. She was even more surprised when the Mitchell's headed towards North Moore and turned into 14th Street instead of heading home. The car pulled to a halt outside a glossy building, whose red 'H' said medical centre loud and clear. Who was seeing a doctor? Not the daughter, she was still at kindergarten. It had to be Mitchell or his wife. The solemn looks on their faces said that it wasn't for something small.

Pereira followed on foot and watched the Mitchells take the elevator to the seventh floor then she checked the index board. There was only one specialty on the seventh; neurology. Professor Robert King. A quick search on the internet said that he was a specialist in memory loss. That could be caused by any one of a hundred conditions and she didn't know which Mitchell was seeing him yet. Pereira checked her watch then made a call, adopting a heavy Brooklyn accent.

"Hello. Is that Professor King's clinic?"

"Yes, may I help you?"

"I'm Sergeant Cartagena of the NYPD." She smiled to herself as she said Richie's name; it had a nice ring. "There's a silver Lexus blocking the road down here and I've got it registered to a Karen Mitchell. Someone saw the couple who parked it entering your building so I'm ringing around trying to see which clinic they're at. I need them to move it."

"I'm sorry. We don't give out patient information."

Pereira raised her voice authoritatively.

"Lady, they're blocking a street. I could have it towed but I'm trying to be nice here, on account of they might be sick. Just tell me if a Karen Mitchell has an appointment in your clinic this afternoon."

The receptionist sighed heavily and Pereira heard a keyboard being tapped. The woman spoke a few seconds later, her voice still reluctant.

"We don't have a Karen Mitchell, but a Jeff Mitchell is seeing the Professor at three-thirty. Shall I send him down?"

"Don't stress it, I'll check on the street and come up."

Pereira walked quickly to the sedan and radioed Magee with an update. It might be something or nothing, but it was interesting either way. If Jeff Mitchell was sick it might make him vulnerable. Or it might just make him run.

***

Jeff Mitchell left the clinic two hours later with his decision made. All he had to decide now was when. The diagnosis had been clear and the MRI scan confirmed it, he had a brain tumour and it was inoperable. He was going to die, and soon. The only thing he could hope for was that radiotherapy would slow its growth, but that would mean time in hospital and he couldn't afford to be away from work right now.

Mitchell gazed sadly at his petite wife, her delicate face swollen with tears. He wasn't sad for himself; he deserved everything he got as far as he was concerned. He'd been ready to sell deadly research to the Russians. He was a spy, for God's sake; a sleeper agent. Except now he'd woken up, and it wasn't in a way that either Ilya or Elza was going to like.

He needed time to think things through so he'd lied to the Professor, promising that he would start radiotherapy the following week. Karen had given him a sceptical look and made him swear. She knew him too well. Mitchell had sworn to keep her happy; one more lie wouldn't make any difference to his afterlife or the damnation that he was sure awaited him there.

One look at Karen Mitchell's face as they walked towards the Lexus gave Rosie Pereira her answer. Mitchell was sick, very sick judging by his wife's tears. Pereira didn't pity him; Mitchell was a traitor ready to sell his genius for the highest price, but her heart felt for the woman by his side.

There was silence in the Lexus as they drove home, Karen sobbing quietly and her husband deep in thought. The tumour explained his failing memory, but it didn't explain his intimate knowledge of Greg Chapman's life. Chapman held the key to something and he was determined to find out what. Mitchell made up his mind to go back to Greg Chapman's apartment and follow whatever trail he found there.

He squeezed his wife's hand and smiled sadly. They'd had years together but he could only remember the last week; it seemed so unfair. But his diagnosis had convinced Mitchell of one thing. He would die to protect Karen and Emmie, because he had nothing else worth living for.

***

After hours of crying and talking, Karen finally fell asleep. Mitchell carried her up to bed, smoothing down the covers and switching off the light. He stood in the darkness watching her breathe. Karen made him happy and he knew that she'd loved him for years. Mitchell thought of his tiny daughter, with her curls and dimples; Karen's mini-me. The thought of someone harming them made him understand the urge to kill, but he was smarter than that, even with only half his brain. He would find another way to keep them safe.

Mitchell walked downstairs to the study and flicked on a lamp, lifting the briefcase that he'd left there the night before. After he'd seen his farm laboratory ideas had flooded into his mind. He'd covered the papers from the café with them. Just random snippets, scribbled in the margins, but he had to make sense of them now. Pouring himself a whisky Jeff Mitchell sat in his well-worn chair and started searching for answers while he still could.

Chapter Twenty-Four

1 a.m.

Elza flicked through the channels, staring blindly at the TV screen. The Iranians had thought that a door would stop her hearing; don't let the feeble woman hear the big men's talk. But the bug she'd planted in the room after they'd swept it had fed every word into her ear. Most of it was boring; macho posturing and bullshit. Only one bit had made her listen hard. Mitchell was planning to take his wife and child with him when he left. If he took that anaemic bitch Karen anywhere it would be over her dead body. She hadn't been screwing him for two years just for fun.

Elza slammed down her wine glass and then gazed at her hand, watching as a shard of glass pierced the skin. Drops of blood ran along its edge then fell slowly to the floor, one by one. She stared at them for a moment then lifted the cut to her mouth and sucked it dry as she made her plan. Jeff Mitchell was her future and anyone who got in her way would have to go.

***

Mitchell stared at the pages until their edges blurred and the words became shadows merging into one. He knew exactly what he'd been researching now; altering carbon-based life. He'd told the Board the truth. Mitchell corrected himself quickly. No, he'd told them part of the truth, not the whole truth, so help me God.

He poured himself another whisky and organised his thoughts into two parts, his work and the mess that he'd made of his life. Had his life led him astray in his work, or vice versa? He settled on the latter. If he'd been in the States since childhood, then he'd been groomed for this work from the off. But how had the Russians known that he'd be bright enough even to go to college? Mitchell shrugged; the Russians. He still acted as if he wasn't one of them, except that he was.

Mitchell answered his own question. They'd known that he'd be bright enough to go to college because they'd IQ tested him as a child. They'd selected him for the task specially. He'd been talent-spotted for his brain, just like athletes who were hot-housed young.

Mitchell was shocked by the wave of grief that suddenly overwhelmed him. Warm tears streamed down his cheeks, freed by the bad news that he'd got that day. The tumour was the end of his future, except that it had never really been his, had it? He thought of his family asleep upstairs and then of the Russian family that he'd never known. Who were his real parents? Not the two people whose picture he'd been shown at ten, told that they'd died in a car crash, that was for sure.

Mitchell startled at the crystal-clear memory. It was the first clear one he'd had of anything before the morning of his blood-filled shower. He concentrated, pushing hard at the past, trying to retrieve something more. He searched for things that had happened before he was ten, struggling to see his mother's face. But there was nothing. She was gone. He prayed that she was dead, so she hadn't had to miss her child for all these years.

Sipping at his whisky Mitchell turned his thoughts back to work. If Ilya had bred him for logic then he would use it against him now. OK, what did he know? The whole world was working on Graphene, looking for new applications that would make them millions. Its conduction properties weren't new; everyone knew about them and about its high ratio of strength to weight. Devon had been set to work on that, while he'd obviously focused his research in a completely different direction. Totally new forms of carbon.

Graphene was only one form of carbon, like Diamond. But they were both inert substances and he'd been curious to see how making a newer form of carbon might affect living things. Mitchell read a scribble he'd written at the side of a page. 'Carbon applications– inert and dead.' There was a space and then one more word. "Living?"

He slumped back in his armchair, staring into space. Inert carbon could be anything from a diamond to a lump of coal. But dead? That implied something that had once been alive. What had he been referring to? Plant life? A dead leaf? His mind flew back to the farm lab that Elza had shown him to. He'd expected to see most of the equipment that was there. Glass, steel and technology, just like in Scrabo's basement lab. Theoretical work. Carbon manipulation at an atomic level.

What he hadn't expected were the small steel cages lined up against one wall. He'd noticed some in the café's lab but dismissed them. But now there were more. What species were going to be kept in them? The largest cage would have held something the size of a small dog. Was his work really being trialled on more than dead leaves? Dead animals? Live ones? If it was then that Mitchell understood the need for secrecy; the animal welfare people would never countenance this.

Mitchell shuddered and glanced at his Labrador, Buster. He was lying against the room's radiator even though it was turned off; ever optimistic. Mitchell beckoned him over and stroked his pet's coat thoughtfully while he read. The papers were clear. He'd made a breakthrough in his research at some point. He'd managed to alter an ivy plant, re-combining its carbon atoms into something entirely new. People had been genetically modifying food and plants for years but he'd created an entirely new genus just by re-arranging its carbon! Still, the discovery wasn't that exciting, there had to be more to his work than this.

He wondered idly why he hadn't published the research in

any journals and then he pictured the tabloid headlines. “Scientist plays God.” The controversy would have halted his work for years, not to mention the religious backlash. And that was only a plant. He could imagine what would have happened with animal trials. Mitchell rifled through the rest of the pages searching the scribble-filled margins for more clues, but there was nothing except one word; 'Archaeus'.

Mitchell thought for a moment, racking his brains for what he knew about the term. It came from an obscure medieval science called Alchemy, famous for believing that lead could be turned into gold. Archaeus described the 'Life Ether', a grey area where matter transmuted into living energy; the Vital Spark of living things. The philosophy had been debated for centuries but discredited long ago.

Mitchell shook his head, smiling. The reference was cryptic, even for him. How could an abstract concept like Archaeus possibly be relevant to his work? He was an evidence-based scientist, a biophysicist; he dealt in hard facts, not fantasy.

He turned his thoughts back to the cages in the lab and shuddered, ruffling Buster's coat apologetically. If he'd applied his carbon research to plants, it wasn't a huge leap to think that he'd managed it with animals as well. If he had then it would explain the need for secrecy and the work's monetary value. Whoever had that research would make billions. The applications were endless. Mitchell thought of the possibilities, imagining biological weapons too awful to name. He couldn't let the Alliance get their hands on it. Or anyone else.

Mitchell poured himself another drink, trying to drown a nagging thought at the back of his mind; the thought that he'd taken the work even further than this. 'Archaeus'. He'd no idea what it referred to but he didn't like the sound of it.

Somehow Greg Chapman held to key to everything. He was sure of it. His brain tumour might explain him forgetting if he'd met Chapman, but it wouldn't explain him knowing about his apartment key. And there were other things. Knowing the name of Annie, the girl at Chapman's building. His and Chapman's similar taste in music and booze, and his clear memories of Florida, somewhere that he'd never been.

Mitchell made a decision. He sat for a moment longer formulating his plan, then he rose to go to bed. Buster jumped to his feet hopefully, barking for a walk but he was disappointed when his master headed upstairs for the few hours left of the night. Tomorrow Jeff Mitchell was going to find some answers.

***

Saturday. 8 a.m.

Karen watched as her handsome husband straightened his tie and tears started to fill her eyes. Mitchell gave her a mock frown.

"If you're going to cry at me all the time, then I'm going to feel even worse." He smiled and pulled her close. "Cheer up, honey. I'm not dead yet and I'm a long way from giving into this thing."

Karen pressed her head against his muscled chest and whispered so that Emmie couldn't hear. She was playing happily in the corner and they wanted that to continue for as long as it could.

"Do you have to go into work today, Jeff? It's Saturday."

Mitchell smiled down at her, stroking her hair. "The sooner I get things sorted at work, the sooner I can start treatment."

She stared hard at him, as if doing so meant that she'd see the truth. "Will you go for radiotherapy, Jeff?"

Mitchell held her at arm's length and smiled again, nodding. "I promise that I'll start it one day next week."

Karen opened her mouth to object and Mitchell pressed a finger to her lips.

"Trust me, please, Karen. I have loose ends to tie up. I may need to take a trip away for a day or two, I'm not sure yet. But

I'll be at the clinic next week, I swear."

It was only half a lie. He'd be there if the Alliance didn't kill him first. Mitchell kissed his wife gently and then turned her towards the door, smiling.

"Now, go get the car ready, or I'll be late for school!"

Chapter Twenty-Five

Neil Scrabo fixed his cufflinks and stared at his reflection. He was aging well, even if he did say so himself. He'd age even better with fifty billion in the bank. He slipped on his jacket and tutted, thinking about Devon Cantrell. He'd made a pathetic spy; Mitchell had caught him within the week. He'd deal with Cantrell once he returned from leave. Scrabo shrugged pragmatically. It was his own fault - he should have used a professional. This time he would. He walked down the hall and pressed the intercom.

"Tom. Join me in the study."

A moment later the fit shape of Tom Evans filled the study's doorway. He stood legs apart, hands crossed in front of him, like the ex-army ranger that he was. Scrabo stared at Evans coolly, assessing him before he spoke.

"How are you on surveillance?"

Evans considered his boss carefully, wondering what he was up to. If it was linked with the North Koreans then he didn't want any part of it. Scrabo paid him well, but not that well, and he was more patriotic than Scrabo knew. If Neil Scrabo was selling the Koreans information, he'd take steps to stop it that he wouldn't like. Evans thought for a moment then decided that it was best to keep close to the action. It would make it easier to keep an eye on Scrabo's game.

"OK."

Scrabo nodded, satisfied by the monosyllabic answer. He didn't need Evans to think, just to do what he was told. Scrabo took a seat behind the desk and scribbled a note, then stared at his bodyguard.

"I want you to follow a Dr Jeff Mitchell. He's working on something and I want to know what it is, and who he speaks to."

"Where can I find him?"

Scrabo handed him the note. It held details of Mitchell's work and home. Evans read for a moment then slipped it into his pocket.

"Report back on everything he does. But if you see him making a move to leave the country, kill him."

Evans thought for a moment and then nodded, turning on his heel to leave. Scrabo's voice halted him.

"And Tom."

"Yes?"

"I don't want any loose ends, so make sure that you kill his family as well."

***

The Lexus deposited Mitchell outside Scrabo Tower and he waved at Emmie, watching as the car pulled off. He walked towards the building's rotating doors like he did every day, but instead of walking through them he waited and as soon as Karen's blonde hair was no longer visible in the traffic he hailed a cab to Prospect Heights. Forty minutes later he was standing at Greg Chapman's mail-box, rifling through the circulars and bills that were all Chapman ever seemed to receive. Then he took the three flights to the apartment and let himself in.

Mitchell stood in the wooden-floored hall searching for some sign that Chapman had been back between his visits. But there was nothing. The rooms held the same lonely pall that they'd held five days before. He entered the living room and looked around. The air was stale and still, as if no-one had been there for years.

Mitchell lifted the picture of Chapman's parents, wiping

some dust off the glass. Chapman looked happy in it. Normal somehow. Mitchell wondered why he thought that he might not be, but that was the power of the unknown. What we didn't know or understand, we had to find a story for. He corrected himself. He *did* know Greg Chapman. He knew his taste in music and his parents' smiles. They felt familiar, as if he actually knew the people too. More familiar than Ilya had felt.

Mitchell turned, searching for something but not knowing what, then his eyes lit on a bureau that he'd missed before. In an instant he knew exactly what it held. He pulled open the third drawer down with a certainty that came out of nowhere. A lock-box lay inside. It held a handgun and I.D., he was certain of it. They had to be spares; no agent would ever go unequipped.

Mitchell found a kitchen knife to pry it open and two minutes later the box's contents were spread out in front of him. A gun and I.D.: he'd been exactly right. Mitchell lifted the large revolver and examined it. It was huge, bigger than he'd noticed the NYPD carrying and theirs weren't petite. He checked the cylinder. It was full. Whatever Greg Chapman had done for the government he hadn't sat behind a desk. The I.D. card confirmed it. Greg Chapman stared unsmiling into the camera, the seal of the United States stamped across his face. Mitchell turned the card over in his hand, searching for clues, but there was nothing. No acronym to say which agency Chapman belonged to. That could only mean one thing. Whatever the unit was it was too secret to give its name. Covert ops.

Without warning a searing pain in Mitchell's head knocked him off his feet. It felt like a screw was being driven through his skull. He held his head for a minute, squeezing it hard in a vain attempt at relief and wondering if this was what the tumour would feel like until he died. As quickly as it came the pain subsided, leaving something else in its wake. With sudden clarity Mitchell knew Greg Chapman was an only child and that he'd grown up in Florida. In St Augustine, the oldest

European settlement in the States.

Mitchell felt a sudden pride in the fact and then he shook himself. How the hell did he know that? And why did Florida feel so familiar to *him*? He'd been feeling it for days. He must have noticed something about Florida on his last visit to the apartment.

Mitchell clambered slowly to his feet, testing the ground, then he searched every room for clues. There was nothing, only a framed map of the east coast hanging on the bedroom wall. St Augustine was on there alright, but it sat amongst hundreds of other names. It wasn't highlighted in any way that would have caught his eye.

There was only one explanation. He must have met Greg Chapman and they must have talked about Florida. He'd obviously forgotten the meeting; but that was a definite possibility with his brain tumour; after all, he'd forgotten his own wife! He knew that Chapman had visited Scrabo Tower; how else could his phone have got there? Mitchell wandered back to the living room and sat on the low leather couch, racking his brains for more clues, until the changing light said that it wasn't morning anymore and he needed to leave. He had his plan. He was going to pay St Augustine a visit and find out exactly why Greg Chapman was so important to him.

***

12 p.m.

First Greg, then Brunet and now Whitman, all missing or dead. Someone badly wanted Jeff Mitchell protected. Richie corrected himself. It wasn't Mitchell they were protecting so much as his research, and if his neurologist was right, he wouldn't be producing much more of that.

It hadn't taken them long to access the clinic's records and get a second and third opinion on Mitchell's MRI. There was no doubt about it, Jeff Mitchell was screwed. Not only did he have a Glioma, the most malignant brain tumour you could get, but he had it in his brainstem, where one cut would turn him into a courgette. The stats were stark, only thirty-seven percent made it beyond a year.

Richie rubbed his neck in empathy. He despised the man, but you wouldn't wish that fate on a dog. It made the choices tricky for them too. Lift Mitchell and get whatever information they could from him now, while he could still speak? Or follow Mitchell to the handover, and try to catch who he was selling it to? Mitchell might be desperate after his diagnosis. Unpredictable. Richie damn well knew that he would be.

He shrugged. Strategy was Magee's problem not his. Richie glanced at the sedan's dashboard, checking the time. Mitchell's wife would be back from the store soon. Richie smiled at the thought. He liked Karen Mitchell. He knew that he shouldn't, but he did.

Yes, she'd married a bastard, but then smart women sometimes made bad choices. Look at Pereira. Images of both women sprang into his mind. Karen Mitchell was doll-pretty, not an exotic beauty like Rosie that was true, but there was something sweet about her, in the blonde cheerleader mould. Richie had a fleeting image of her in a short skirt waving pom-poms and quickly pushed it away.

Just then the Lexus pulled up and Karen Mitchell stepped out. Richie watched her lift some groceries out of the trunk then stand there for a moment, staring into space. She looked sad, as if she was going to cry. He felt strangely protective towards her. She was innocent in all of this; they knew that from the bugs they'd put in the car. Karen had known nothing about her husband's research until Thursday night. She just knew that she loved him and was going to lose him soon. Richie frowned to himself as he watched her open the front-door. Depending on what Mitchell did next, she and her daughter might be lost too.

***

Elza gazed out a window on the tenth floor, aimlessly shifting files in an imitation of work. It was the weekend and she was stuck in the office, but when Mitchell was at Scrabo Tower she had to be too. Ilya had wanted to stop her watching him, arguing that Mitchell was one hundred percent loyal; he would never back out so near the end, despite the Arabs' concerns. Elza agreed about Mitchell's loyalty, but she needed her surveillance to continue; it would give her access to his wife. A word to one of the Arab's bodyguards, questioning Ilya's objectivity, had produced the desired result.

A memory of the way the guard's lip had curled when she spoke to him leapt into Elza's mind. He'd looked at her as if she was dirt; a woman. Worse, a Russian whore. She thought that she'd got past hurt feelings years ago, but it had stung. It hadn't deterred her though. She'd dropped the pebble of doubt in the pond and watched as its ripples reached the ear of Javadi. He instructed her to keep tailing Mitchell, despite Ilya's objections.

Elza scanned the open-plan office where she stood, and sighed. On week-days it was filled with women with bad hair and cheap clothes; she stuck out like a sore thumb. If she was here to observe Mitchell she could have done it a damned sight better from the office beside his on the fifteenth floor, but Ilya found it amusing to keep her in Scrabo's admin office five floors down. Mitchell knew that he was being watched, so there was no logical reason to maintain a façade now; it was just Ilya's revenge for her going behind his back.

Elza's thoughts were interrupted by a spider dropping onto the file in front of her and she watched idly as it meandered across the page. She lifted a stapler and held it above the small shape, watching as the sudden shadow made it stop, as if standing still would make it invisible somehow. She held the stapler there for a moment and then placed it to one side, almost hearing the arachnid's sigh of relief. Then, just as its walk restarted Elza slammed her hand down hard, ending its life. She gazed at the wet remains, admiring the way they smeared across the page then returned to her plans for Karen Mitchell and her brat.

***

Sunday. 8.30 a.m.

Tom Evans gave the large motorbike a baleful look. A car would have been more comfortable, but Scrabo had insisted on him using a bike, saying that he could tail Mitchell better in Manhattan on two wheels. He had a point. It was easy enough to follow someone through the main thoroughfares in a car, but when the streets got narrow or rough, four wheels didn't cut it. Evans scrutinised the glossy machine then sat astride it. It was more comfortable than he expected, but then it was high end. A Yamaha YZFR1. Nought to sixty in under three seconds. He'd like to see Jeff Mitchell try to lose him on this.

Evans stepped off again and looked down ruefully at his suit. It was creased already, he'd have to go home and change. He glanced at the time; eight-thirty. Mitchell's wife had dropped him at the office thirty minutes before and Scrabo had made sure the scientist would be busy until lunch. Jeff Mitchell was going nowhere until this afternoon; plenty of time to head home and swop his Armani for a pair of jeans. Evans jumped into his car and exited the basement garage, thinking as he drove.

He'd follow Jeff Mitchell and report back to Scrabo like a good little spy, just long enough to get his bonus; then he was out of there. But not before Neil Scrabo had been dealt with. He might not salute the flag anymore, but the North Koreans were a step too far, even for him. Once the money was in his account, Tom Evans planned to give Scrabo up to whoever would listen.

***

Pereira rolled over in bed, revelling in her Sunday morning lie-in. She wasn't on duty until four o'clock; well, not unless another one of them got killed. She shivered at the thought and pulled the covers tight over her head, fending off the morning's autumn chill. She wanted to sleep and forget all the crap of the past week, but her brain wouldn't let her rest, so she lay with her eyes closed, thinking instead.

Joey's warmth was still in the bed beside her and she rolled into it looking for...what? What *was* she looking for? Clarity? Absolution? A wave of guilt overcame her and she rolled away again. She had no right to take comfort from his imprint. She'd betrayed him with Richie again, after two years of promising herself that it was over. It didn't matter that her infidelity was with the same man. In some ways that was worse. It wasn't just sex; there were feelings involved. Yes, there were; a lot of feelings. It was emotional infidelity as well as physical this time.

Pereira hid her face in her hands, wanting to run away. Just take the car and hit the road like some Kerouac girl. Why couldn't she? Just leave Joey, leave Richie, leave the bloody job. New York was full of other jobs and she had savings, she could survive. As soon as the question formed Pereira had the answer. If she stayed in New York Richie would follow her. Joey wouldn't, the loss would debilitate him, but Richie would hunt for however long it took. He'd force her to look into his eyes and say that she didn't love him, and she could never say that.

An image of Joey's face filled her mind, his sad eyes mourning her loss. She wanted to hold him, hug him and tell him it would all be OK. Except that it wouldn't. Suddenly Rosie Pereira's mind was clear, clearer than it had been all week. She pulled the covers off and sat up, staring around the room. Her decision was made. She couldn't live like this any longer, torn between two men. She had to make a choice, any choice, and she had to make it today.

Chapter Twenty-Six

Sunday. 12.p.m.

Two research staff sat in Mitchell's outer office, diligently completing their paperwork for the quarterly research meeting the coming week. At twelve o'clock they filed off the floor for lunch and Mitchell was finally left alone. He slumped behind his desk, with his head in his hands. His hair was getting long; he'd need it cut next week. He smiled wryly; the radiotherapy might save him the cost.

Mitchell stood up and looked in the mirror behind the door, searching for some sign of cancer, whatever that looked like. There was none. He looked just the same, with only his forgetfulness and an opaque mass on some scan to say that he was going to die. They were all going to die; it was just the speed of it that distinguished him from the rest. Who knew, maybe he'd get hit by a truck before the cancer got him. It would be quick anyway.

As soon as the thought occurred to him, Mitchell knew that he wasn't speculating, he was making a choice. A choice to take his own life instead of rotting away slowly in some hospital bed. He felt better immediately. It wouldn't be a truck of course, but something more controllable; less mess. But the principle was still the same; death by his own hand, in his own time.

He'd plan it once everything was finished. First he had to stop the Alliance getting their hands on whatever research he'd developed and Karen and Emmie had to be protected. Then he could die in peace. Mitchell looked quickly at his watch.

welve-thirty. Time to find out more about Greg Chapman.

***

Pereira dressed in her duty suit and strapped-on her gun, then she lifted her bag and headed for the door. Magee had been surprised when she'd called him. He didn't give his agents much time off, so they usually stayed as far away as possible from him when he did. He'd been curious on the phone and asked what the meeting was about, but Pereira wanted to say things to him face to face. It would add to his stresses but she couldn't help that.

She dumped her car in the agency building's car-park and took the elevator to the third floor, walking confidently past the guard. Lily, Magee's secretary, glanced up at her and smiled. She liked Rosie Pereira. She talked to her as if she was a human being, which is more than she could say sometimes for her boss.

"He's expecting you, Agent Pereira." The girl inclined her head towards the door and waved Pereira in.

Rosie smiled in return and headed for the half-glass door. She stopped midway, taking a deep breath. If she did this there was no way back; Magee wasn't a forgiving man. She nodded to herself, feeling a freedom that she hadn't felt in years. Then she knocked the door firmly and walked towards the rest of her life.

***

Mitchell adjusted the rental car's mirror and then looked down at the map. If he took the 278 he'd be at LaGuardia in time for the 15:20 Delta flight and in Miami by 19:00. He'd told Karen he'd be home sometime on Tuesday and she wasn't to worry. Mitchell pictured the way she'd looked at him that morning, stroking his face in concern. Of course she was going to worry. She would worry about him now until the day he died. He shook the image from his mind and pulled out of

Scrabo Tower's car-park into the bright Manhattan afternoon, heading for Florida to find some answers.

Tom Evans followed through the traffic at a safe distance. Mitchell was heading for the airport, he was certain of that. Where was he flying to so urgently? And for how long? Evans' curiosity was piqued. He'd seen Jeff Mitchell's face when he'd left the garage; he was a man on a mission.

Evans patted his pocket. His passport and credit cards were always packed. Then he patted his underarm holster, feeling his Glock.. He would never get the gun through airport security, so it would have to stay locked in the bike. Evans shrugged. He wouldn't need it. Mitchell was no threat and by the preoccupied look on his face he would never even notice that he was being tailed.

Chapter Twenty-Seven

Lloyd Harbor. 5 p.m.

It was only five in the afternoon but the sky was already growing dark. Winter wasn't far off. Richie pulled his jacket around him and cranked up the heating, wondering where everyone was. He hadn't seen the Mitchells all day and Pereira had been due to relieve him an hour ago. He was just reaching for the radio when the Lexus approached, indicating to pull into the drive. Richie watched as Karen Mitchell climbed out. She looked especially pretty today. Her hair shone like strands of white-gold and she wore a cornflower blue jumper that made her eyes flash when she turned. But it was what she did next that made her beautiful.

As she lifted her daughter from the car-seat she gently stroked the hair from the girl's small face and kissed her forehead, hugging her tight until she giggled. Karen laughed with her and they entered the house giggling together. Richie wondered what they would do next and wished that he could see. He pictured them playing a game on the rug or watching cartoons. He'd done that with his Mom and the memories had never gone. Karen Mitchell was a good mother and he was going to protect her, or die trying.

A sudden burst of static assaulted Richie's ears. Just as he grabbed for the receiver to stop it Magee's voice rasped out. He sounded pissed about something.

"You're being relieved late today."

There was no preamble and no warm platitudes. Still, at least you always knew where you were with Magee; usually in the shit. Richie decided to risk getting in deeper.

"Where's Pereira?"

The only answer he got was "She's asked for a transfer. Howard's doing the next shift; she'll relieve you at midnight" then more static. Richie asked him to "say again" but only silence answered him and he knew that Magee had hung up. It was an abrupt exchange, even for him. Richie grabbed urgently for his phone and dialled Pereira. Her cell cut to answerphone. The message was new. "Agent Pereira is on holiday. From September 30th this agent will be working out of the San Francisco office."

What the fuck? Richie's mouth fell open. Rosie had asked for a transfer and hadn't even told him! He dialled her personal cell but it only reinforced his confusion. "Hi, it's Rosie. I've gone away for two weeks."

Anger overwhelmed him and in a moment of pure rage Richie dialled her landline at home. A man answered. Joey. He sounded bereft. Richie almost cut the call but he needed to know.

"Hello. Is that Rosie Pereira's residence?"

The man sighed and then answered in a soft voice.

"It was. She's not living here anymore."

"What?"

The word was out before Richie could stop it. The man spoke again, sounding curious.

"Who is this calling?"

Richie considered hanging up but that would only cause suspicion. Anonymous calls to an agent's home could bring the Special Forces out.

"It's Richie Cartagena, Mr Pereira. Rosie and I work together."

"Ah, yes, Agent Cartagena. She's mentioned you."

Richie wondered in what context but Joey was still speaking.

"I'm sure you'll find out soon enough, so there's no point in me denying it. Rosie's left me. She's requested a transfer to the west coast and taken two weeks leave, starting today. I came home to find a note and she's not answering either of her phones."

Richie's heart went out to the man then his own pain took over. At least Pereira had left her husband a note; he'd had to find out from Magee! A faint glimmer of hope rose in his chest. Perhaps that meant that she'd left her husband for him and was going to call him later? The hope died as soon as it was born. Her husband obviously knew nothing about him. Another hope rose. Maybe Pereira hadn't mentioned another man at all, so as not to hurt him. Richie needed to know, so he asked the question, phrasing it carefully.

"She didn't tell you why she was leaving?"

Joey Pereira's voice was dull now, almost wary. As if he was imagining the years of pain ahead and guarding himself against them already. He answered the question, telling a stranger his news as if there was no-one else that he could tell.

"She said that she wanted a divorce but that there was no-one else...We were married for eight years. She's just thrown it all away..."

He sounded completely lost and in that instance Richie knew exactly what Rosie had done, and why she'd done it. Her love for him wouldn't let her stay with her husband, and her love for her husband wouldn't let her be with him. She'd walked away from both of them and she was going to keep on walking, no matter what he did. Richie's next words were heartfelt.

"I'm very sorry, Mr Pereira. I really can't tell you how sorry I am."

Richie cut the call gently then sat back and closed his eyes, thinking about the woman he loved and starting to say goodbye.

***

Florida. 11.50 p.m.

Mitchell pulled the rental car into a layby and checked the map, yawning. It was nearly midnight and he needed some sleep. Tomorrow was going to be a long day. He'd formulated a back story that would let him ask questions about Greg Chapman that no-one would query. He was a colleague of his from work. Government work. Their security clearance had to be renewed every year, and he'd been tasked with doing Chapman's background checks. Just some routine questions, folks. Nothing to get worried about.

Mitchell smiled ruefully. People didn't question the government, not half as much as they should do anyway. The dark suit in his trunk and the fake I.D. he'd made would fool everyone. Except the cops, and he was staying well away from them.

He drove off the I-95 and followed the signs for Escobar's Motel. Ten minutes later he was pleasantly surprised to see a horseshoe of quaint wooden buildings. Mitchell checked in and had something to eat and by one a.m. he was asleep, completely oblivious to the man who'd parked outside and bedded down for the night.

***

"Where is he? You should have told me that he was going away!"

Ilya looked up from cutting his cigar and fixed Elza with a stare.

"Why should I tell you your job? You were the one who wanted to keep following him." He snorted. "You're so damned good at it that you missed him leaving the state."

Elza's fury boiled over and she slammed her palm down on his desk. Ilya sprang to his feet and thrust his head forward, stopping half-an-inch from her face. She pulled back in reflex but held her ground. Ilya's next words were soft but there was no mistaking their chill.

"Be very careful, woman. You are disposable. Be under no illusions about that."

He sat down again slowly and turned his attention back to his cigar, ignoring her venomous stare. Elza asked the question again, more slowly.

"Where has he gone? ....Please."

Ilya smiled to himself, knowing that the last word had almost choked her.

"That's better. You're learning your place." He smiled sarcastically. "I imagine if Mitchell had wanted you to know where he'd gone, then you would. But I'll put you out of your misery. He's gone to a meeting with a scientific peer of his. He'll be back on Tuesday."

"But you know I've been tasked to observe him! You should have told me so that I could follow."

Ilya waved a hand dismissively. "Mitchell told me where he would be and I trust him." He stared into her wide green eyes, watching the pupils shrink in anger. "Besides. You'd better get used to being alone. When he leaves America he's taking his wife and daughter with him and I don't think there'll be room for a whore as well. Now, get out."

Elza glared at Ilya for a moment longer before turning on her heel. He laughed coldly as she walked away and Elza made up her mind then that Ilya Tabakov would be joining Karen and Emmie Mitchell in the ground.

***

Lloyd Harbor.

Richie was staring into space when Amelia Howard arrived to relieve him. He jerked himself upright as she opened the car door. Howard smiled wryly. He'd been asleep. One look at his eyes told her that she was wrong. He'd been crying. Richie caught her look of concern and realised how he must have looked.

"Don't worry, I'm not losing it. Just a bit of personal business."

She smiled sympathetically and nodded. "I know. I heard about Pereira."

Richie looked at her, shocked and then shrugged. Everyone in the office must have known about their affair, so much for being discreet. It made Magee's way of telling him even crueller. Howard read Richie's mind and shook her head.

"Magee didn't know how to tell you, so he asked me what to do. I suppose he figured that a woman might know what to say. I told him to keep it short and factual."

Richie nodded slowly. There'd been nothing else that Magee could have done. Any attempt at sympathy would only have made him feel worse.

"Trust me. He made it both of those."

They sat for a moment in the dark then Richie started reporting, ending with. "There's no sign of Mitchell yet. Just the wife and daughter at home since four p.m."

Howard nodded. "Don't worry about Mitchell; he's not coming back tonight. Magee knows where he is, although he's not sure why."

Richie gave her a curious look. "OK. I'll bite. Where is he?"

"Florida. Well, to be more accurate, halfway off the 1-95 in a motel at the moment."

"What the hell is he doing there?"

"We're not sure yet. I tailed him to LaGuardia and he took a Delta flight to Miami. That's why I was late. Magee has the Miami office watching him."

"Is he running?"

"Without the wife? No. He only hired a car at the airport for two days. But he's looking for something that's for sure, and tomorrow we should find out what."

***

Florida. Monday. 7 a.m.

The early morning road stretched ahead of Mitchell, dusty and dry. Solitary houses were dotted here and there along the route, only their design and the power lines overhead saying that the century was the twenty-first instead of the nineteenth. Mitchell half-expected a lone horseman to appear and say 'Howdy'.

Every now and then a town appeared, its sidewalks and palm trees lit by the heightening sun. He liked the solitude of the place; it made a pleasant change from the congestion of New York. Mitchell bit off a chunk of pretzel and cranked up the CD, glad that he'd resisted the lure of the eggs and bacon the motel's menu had advertised. They would have been great and he could almost taste their salty favour now, but he'd needed to get on the road early. He could only stay away from work for so long before his presence was missed. If his watchers in the sedan hadn't raised the alarm by now, then Elza would have.

Mitchell shrugged, uncaring. Ilya knew he was on a trip, although he thought it was to do with his research. The old man could handle Elza for him. Besides, everything seemed much less important now that he knew he was going to die. Mitchell smiled, correcting himself sarcastically. Everyone knew that they were going to die, they just didn't know how soon. He was just lucky that way. Mitchell caught himself agreeing with the caustic thought. He *was* lucky; it would give him the focus to do what he needed and not many people had that.

He shook the serious thoughts from his head and day-dreamed unhindered for an hour. An image of Karen's face filled his mind, the way she'd looked when he'd first seen her on the morning of his blood-tainted shower. Except that couldn't have been his first sight of her, they'd been married for ten years by then, so why was it his first memory? Why so precise? The disease in his brain didn't explain that.

Mitchell racked his mind for some glimpse of their first date, their wedding, and Emmie's birth. But there was nothing, a complete void where the images should have been. Karen said that he'd sat with her all through labour. He'd laughed at her story of how he'd done the crossword and played with his phone but he couldn't argue with her; he had no clear memories of anything before that morning in the shower. He hadn't even remembered he was a sleeper! Mitchell corrected himself. He'd remembered some things, when Ilya had pointed out his past, but they'd been shadowy images with only vague feelings attached.

Suddenly a car accelerated past him, jerking him out of his dream. Mitchell glanced in his rear-view mirror. A blue Ford Taurus had been sitting behind him for miles. His paranoia rose briefly and then he shrugged again. It was a free country and he didn't own the roads. If they wanted to tail him they could, whichever group they were, but it would be a very dull job.

Mitchell thought about where he'd be going soon if Ilya had his way and shuddered. The negative things he'd heard about Russia couldn't all be true, especially not nowadays, but it definitely wasn't the West. He wanted Emmie to grow up as free as a bird, not get thrown in jail for singing punk-rock songs in a church. They weren't leaving the USA, he'd made up his mind on that, what he wasn't sure about was how he could prevent it. But he had the seed of a plan and he intended to action it soon.

After an hour more driving a signpost for St Augustine appeared and Mitchell pulled the car off the highway gratefully, tired of driving in a straight line. The turn led to a back road with sparse housing on either side. Occasional school children wandered past on their way to class, some of them eager and others bored; the usual range of schoolmates. If there was a school then there would soon be a town. It wouldn't be St Augustine yet, that was at least ten miles further on, but there would be a rest-stop and a diner and he needed to freshen up.

Mitchell glanced at himself in the mirror. His clean-cut look was getting grubby, time for a shave and fresh shirt to change him into a government man. He spotted a diner five minutes later and pulled in, watching in his rear-view mirror as the blue Taurus whizzed on past. It hadn't been following him after all. Mitchell laughed at his paranoia and grabbed his bag, heading to clean-up. Just as he entered the diner's wash-room the Taurus returned and parked unseen in the shade.

***

"Jake. Have you got a copy of that order?"

Jake Anderson looked up from his screen and nodded. Then, like the high-school basketball player that he'd been, he rolled-up the piece of paper and lobbed it expertly into Ruth Lemanski's tray. She smiled and shook her head. The place got more like college every day. Lemanski unfolded the paper and spread it flat on her desk, reading the instructions, then she picked up the phone to the sender.

"Agent Magee?"

Magee wheezed in the affirmative.

"It's the Miami office here. Agent Lemanski. I was just reading your memo on a Dr Jeff Mitchell and I have a couple of questions."

"Wasn't it clear?"

Lemanski stared at the phone, surprised by Magee's rudeness. Then she shrugged. Perhaps it passed for humour in New York.

"Clear enough and we've got satellite covering him right now. I just wanted to check some contingencies."

Magee sighed noisily and Lemanski glared at the phone, screwing up her face. Jake caught her look and laughed. She put the call on speaker and he wandered over to listen as she carried on.

"You really just want us to observe? Even if Mitchell breaks the law?"

"Yes."

"How far does that go? Is breaking and entering OK, but murder isn't?"

Magee raised his eyes to the ceiling. This was what came of working with other teams. You had to break them in like a pony.

"Dr Mitchell won't murder anyone. He's looking for something down there, that's all. We just need to find out what. Let him break and enter and ask questions all he wants. If he kills someone then let us know, but don't lift him. He'll be back here on Tuesday and we can deal with it then. But be very clear; he's not to be hurt or halted. This operation has taken months to build and it's vitally important to national security."

Lemanski raked her hair, irritated. This was way above her pay-grade and she knew that one more smart word could have her on surveillance for a month. But… Jake caught the glint in her eyes and shook his head. Too late.

"Great. So we'll just eat popcorn and watch the bodies pile up and I'll tell my boss to send you the bill, will I?"

Jake winced and waited for the backlash. It didn't come. Instead, Magee laughed. It was a half-wheezing, tired laugh but it was definitely a laugh. Lemanski was off the hook. More than that.

"You do that, Agent Lemanski. And if you're ever looking for a transfer, give me a call. That's a New York mouth you have there."

A second later the line went dead and the agents stared at each other and laughed. If Lemanski had tried that line with Brookman he'd have had her on a charge. Maybe working in New York wouldn't be so bad after all.

Chapter Twenty-Eight

Lloyd Harbor. Monday. 8.30 a.m.
The Lexus reversed slowly out of the driveway. Slowly enough that Richie could sense Emmie's quietness, and see the signs of a night spent crying written on Karen Mitchell's face. He knew how she felt. He'd spent the night before tossing and turning, running his last conversation with Rosie through his head a million times.

He'd made Rosie happy, he knew that he had. She loved him and he loved her. X plus Y equals Z; it was the simplest equation in the world. Except that they'd had another variable; her husband. Richie rubbed his forehead hard, trying to erase his memories, but even if managed to forget her face, how could he forget the way he felt? It was no comfort at all that Joey Pereira was suffering too, if anything it made it worse. Rosie Pereira had made two men miserable and herself, just because she wasn't brave enough to choose. The thought caught Richie unawares and he repeated it aloud.

"She's a coward."

It felt like sacrilege. To think it was bad enough, but to actually say the words. And yet it felt right, Pereira *was* a coward. Yes, she'd take a bullet for him in a heartbeat, but face her own emotions? My God, no. That was far too frightening. A step too far, even for a woman with bravery awards.

Richie said it again, louder, testing the words. It didn't feel like sacrilege this time, it felt right. Accurate. Rather than face a tough decision Pereira had hurt three people, herself included. Hurting three people instead of one, how was that brave in anyone's book?

If anyone had called her a coward yesterday he would have leapt to her defence, but not now. The knowledge made him feel better and Richie could feel his opinion of Pereira drop. He tested his feelings further and noticed a slight cooling in his love. Not a lot, not a whole degree's fall, but a drop. It was something to go on with. It gave him hope that someday he'd look at her photo and feel nothing but friendship. Someday.

The thoughts flashed though Richie's mind in seconds and when he looked up the Lexus was still in the Mitchell's driveway. Karen Mitchell was resting her head against the steering wheel and he could feel her vulnerability. He wanted to jump out of the car and ask her if she was OK. Take her in his arms and comfort her. Get comfort from her. An image of them kissing filled Richie's mind and he pushed it away, knowing exactly what it meant. He was attracted to her and it was growing.

Karen sat upright and pulled her cardigan straight as Richie watched, then she turned towards her daughter with a wet smile and said something that made the little girl laugh. She reversed out of the driveway and drove down the street with Richie close behind, grateful to be there for her, not to watch but to protect. He had no idea how necessary that would soon be.

***

"Your man has not been working. We gave him the new laboratory so that he could use it."

Javadi glared at Ilya and waved him to a seat. Ilya smiled, trying to placate the Iranian.

"Mitchell must meet research colleagues to keep up appearances, Behrouz. Until we are ready to extract him, everything must seem normal to anyone who looks."

"Who is this colleague? Are you sure that he exists?"

Ilya nodded firmly, hiding his own doubts. He wasn't certain that Mitchell had told him the truth about his Florida trip, but he was his son in all but blood. That bought him trust, and time.

"It will not be long now. He tells me his research has progressed."

"How far? What will its value be to us?"

"Billions of U.S. dollars." Ilya said the words firmly, brooking no retort.

Javadi scrutinised his face, suspecting the old man's relationship with Mitchell of making him soft. Ilya watched Javadi's expression change and he knew that a decision had just been made.

"In five days my scientists will come here from Iran. We need Mitchell's basic research by then. They will check every part of his work and tell me its true worth."

"Five days! It is too soon. Research takes time."

Javadi glared at Ilya for a moment then beckoned his bodyguard. The large man loomed over Ilya menacingly.

"It is decided." Javadi smiled malevolently. "Meanwhile we will be watching you all closely. If Mitchell's research is not what he says it is, then none of you will ever see your Mother Russia again."

***

Lloyd Harbor. 10 a.m.

The knife slipped easily between the wide glass doors leading from the Mitchell's deck, breaking the weak latch with one flick. The doors fell inwards; floating silently back against the family-room wall, and with one step the intruder was standing in the sunny room. They walked slowly, checking for life, already knowing that the house was empty. But there was always the unexpected. A sudden movement in the kitchen vindicated their caution and the intruder tensed, readying themselves for a fight, then a flash of ginger streaked across the floor and the tension eased. The threat was nothing but the family cat.

They wandered on, lifting ornaments and pictures, things that marked the house out as a home. They replaced them carefully, leaving no signs that they had been there, just noting each room's dimensions and where the locks were placed. A child's toy lay on the rug and they lifted it, scrutinising its bright colours and round shape and picturing the little girl who owned it before putting it back in place.

The visitor wandered upstairs, exploring, until only the master bedroom lay ahead; the heart of the home. The door swung open to reveal a cosy room, with throws and cushions scattered randomly across the bed. A large bed that said sex and love, its occupants entwined in each other's arms at night. The dressing table was covered in knick-knacks; feminine and perfumed. A bureau under the window was the man's. They ran their gloved fingers across the bed and then across the bureau, feeling the people who lived there and breathing in their scents.

A car back-fired outside and the visitor startled, moving downstairs swiftly and leaving by the open deck doors, replacing the latch behind them as if no-one had ever been there. No-one would ever know they had and the next breach would be easy. The house was open-plan, the only bolts at the front and back doors, allowing for easy access. The owners too confident in their decent neighbourhood to think that they needed an alarm. The visitor would return soon, once they had everything they needed for their plan.

***

St Augustine, Florida.

Mitchell turned into the short, dusty road and found the house he was seeking. He parked his car out of the sun and loosened his tie, wishing that he'd worn a summer-weight suit. Florida was only fifteen degrees south of New York, but the climate felt sub-Saharan by comparison. He felt in his pocket for his fake I.D. and walked to a gate that fronted a quaint wooden house onto the street. As it creaked open he saw something move behind the slatted blinds; a woman. His guess was confirmed a moment later when the porch door opened and she appeared.

She was a healthy looking woman of around seventy-years-old, dressed, not in the tracksuit and trainers that Mitchell had seen on every street since he'd arrived, but in a flowered summer dress that ended just below her knees. Her hair was set in soft waves of blonde with flecks of grey throughout and she wore no jewellery except a wedding ring. She looked nice, like someone's mother, which she was.

Nancy Chapman smiled warmly at Mitchell as if she was reading his thoughts and her smile sent a shockwave of recognition through him; so strong that he felt that he'd known her for years. He knew she was Greg Chapman's mother from the photograph, but the feeling was much more than that. Mitchell gazed at the woman's extended hand and then took it, holding it slightly longer than usual to see what more he could sense. The warmth he felt for her was unmistakable. He knew this woman, but he had no idea from where.

"Agent Mitchell, it's lovely to meet you. I'm Nancy Chapman. Please come in."

Mitchell was taken aback momentarily at her lack of recognition of him. He knew her but her eyes held nothing but politeness, as if they were meeting for the first time. The woman led the way to the back of the house where a man of her age was sitting at a table. He rose and shook hands with Mitchell, introducing himself as John. His grip and appearance had the same effect on Mitchell as his wife's and Mitchell stared at them both, bewildered. He couldn't possibly know them, except from the photograph in Chapman's flat, but he did. What's more his feelings said he loved them.

Mitchell dismissed the feelings as part of his illness, the tumour affecting his limbic brain, and took the proffered seat, accepting the offer of lemonade. The couple gazed at him in anticipation, as if they were looking forward to his questions. They probably were. It wasn't everyday someone wanted to hear you talk about your child. As Mitchell sipped the drink the woman brought out an album and Mitchell knew he would be seeing photos of Greg Chapman from birth. It was just what he wanted. He needed to find out who Chapman was, and why he knew so much about his life.

Two hours later he'd seen Greg Chapman age from birth to forty-two years. Chapman was an only child; they'd always wanted more but sadly it wasn't to be. Nancy Chapman looked wistfully at her husband as she said it and Mitchell wanted to comfort her. He curbed the urge quickly, forewarned of what he would feel by their earlier touch.

Chapman had been bright. Not PhD bright but bright enough to gain a degree in economics before entering the marines. His father's pride was obvious. He talked of his son's military exploits with excitement while his wife's face said that she was glad that they were done. John Chapman beamed as he talked of his son doing advanced training of some sort after his time in Delta Force, then entering government work. With whom? Mitchell voiced the question as a test, part of his security update to check if their son had been indiscreet and disclosed information at home. But they had no idea. Greg Chapman had only ever talked of 'the agency'.

Mitchell could only speculate again which agency had been on his tail. CIA or FBI? Was that who was watching him? No, he didn't think so. This bunch were specialists, some sort of sub-group. If they were CIA or FBI he would bet they had few more letters added on. Mitchell listened as the Chapman's talked lovingly about their son, then asked the question he was most reluctant to ask.

"That's really helpful, Mr and Mrs Chapman. I've just a few more checks to do before I sign off Greg's assessment. Just one more question. Could you tell me when you last spoke to your son, and roughly what the conversation was about?"

A worried look fluttered across Nancy Chapman's face and she reached for her husband's hand. Mitchell could see that he'd distressed her and again he wanted to comfort her. Instead he scribbled importantly in his notebook, writing nothing but his own name. It gave Chapman's mother time to regroup but when she finally spoke her voice was still tremulous.

"We haven't spoken to Greg since last Wednesday week. It's not like him at all, he usually calls us on Sunday nights but he's missed two weeks now."

Her husband intervened. "I've said he's probably on a job and isn't allowed to call. That would be it, wouldn't it?"

Mitchell saw the hope in his eyes and nodded kindly. "Yes, I'm sure it is. I'm often sent away at an hour's notice and can be out of contact for a month. It drives my wife mad."

It was a lie, but only a white one. The woman's relief was palpable. Mitchell scribbled his name again and waited for them to answer his question in more depth. Finally Nancy Chapman did.

"Greg called us about eight o'clock that Wednesday night and said he was following someone, but he couldn't tell us who. Just that it was somewhere in Manhattan. He probably shouldn't even have told us that, but he likes to keep his father up to date."

She smiled fondly at her husband. "John was in the army for twenty years and he misses all that running around. Don't you dear?" John Chapman nodded. "I think Greg's adventures make him feel young again."

Mitchell was only half-listening. Greg Chapman had been at Scrabo Tower on the Wednesday night that he'd visited the research suite in the lab. The night before he'd seen the blood in his shower. To think that Chapman was tailing someone somewhere else in Manhattan would be too far-fetched, especially when his phone had been found in Scrabo Tower. Was it him that Chapman had been tailing? Had they met that day? It might explain some of the things he knew about Chapman, but not all. No-one would know where Chapman's spare apartment key was kept except a lover or a good friend. The idea that he and Greg Chapman were lovers flashed through Mitchell's mind but he dismissed it quickly. His sexual experiences with Karen and Elza made it unlikely. Mitchell asked another question just to make sure.

"Does Greg have a girlfriend?"

Nancy Chapman smiled ruefully. "Oh, don't start me on that. He's brought more girls home than we've had dinners. The last one was somebody he worked with on a job in Washington, but since then there's been no-one. I always said he should have married Julie Richards, didn't I John?"

Her husband nodded, interjecting. "Julie was such a nice girl. She works as a teacher up at their old school. They were engaged at college but broke up. We never did find out why."

Mitchell smiled, imagining Greg Chapman's taciturn responses when they asked him. Julie Richards, it was another name that sounded familiar. Nancy Chapman was still talking.

"Still, I suppose it's still not too late for grandchildren. It would be lovely to have children around again and Greg would be a brilliant Dad. Do you have any children, Agent Mitchell?"

Mitchell smiled, thinking of Emmie. "Yes, a little girl. She's three."

"That's such a lovely age. They're so cute."

They chatted for a while about Emmie until finally Mitchell finished his drink and stood up, genuinely reluctant to leave. But he had other things to check out and the Chapman's had just added Julie Richards to his list. They showed Mitchell to the front door and stood there together, waving him goodbye. As Mitchell walked back to the car he felt like he was leaving home.

Chapter Twenty-Nine

11 a.m.

Richie followed the Lexus as it left the kindergarten, after safely depositing Emmie for the day. It meandered slowly through Long Island's suburbs, stopping at the Commack Wal-Mart and then at a delicatessen. Karen Mitchell placed her purchases in the trunk with a look that said she was just going through the motions of life. Richie wondered what she was thinking, already knowing what some of it was. How did you deal with the knowledge that someone you loved was dying? Richie allowed himself a moment's bitterness; could it hurt any more than knowing that they'd left you from choice? He felt instantly guilty. He wouldn't wish Karen Mitchell's sadness on anyone and he wouldn't wish Rosie Pereira dead even if he could.

The Lexus drove on for twenty minutes, meandering randomly through the suburban streets until it finally stopped outside a small row of shops five miles from the Mitchell's home. Richie parked three cars behind and watched as Karen Mitchell walked across the paved forecourt. On the spur of the moment he un-clamped his seatbelt and followed. It wasn't in his orders but he reckoned he could hedge it as 'using his initiative'. Richie didn't like letting Karen Mitchell out of his sight while her husband was away. He had a strange feeling that Mitchell would want him to protect her.

Richie spotted Karen's blue cardigan about ten feet ahead and kept his distance, leaning in doorways and perusing books, while she entered each small boutique in turn and gazed sadly at their wares. He knew that she wasn't seeing any of them. She was just using the time to think with other people around. It was less lonely somehow than thinking alone at home.

After twenty minutes browsing Karen stopped at a small café with its tables set outside to catch the morning sun. She sat down and ordered a coffee then lifted a journal to read. Richie watched from a doorway for a moment then broke with protocol completely and sat silently at the next free table until a waiter arrived.

"Espresso please."

Karen turned slightly towards Richie's warm voice then she turned away again, deep in her own thoughts. It was the closest Richie had ever been to her and he could see every angle of her face. He caught his breath, she was even prettier close-up. Her features were fine and delicately arranged, like a doll's. Her skin tanned the colour of honey and randomly sprinkled with fine freckles.

A moment later the waiter re-appeared. He placed Karen's cappuccino on the table and waited for her to pay. As she turned Richie saw her eyes. They were beautiful. Large pools of navy, fringed by long dark lashes that stroked her cheeks. He saw tears in them ready to fall and his heart broke again. Karen turned back towards her coffee then halted, gazing at Richie for a moment as if she really saw him. Then the moment was gone and they were just two strangers sharing a space for ten minutes, before they returned to their days. Ten minutes that would change both their lives.

***

Florida. 1 p.m.

Mitchell parked the car and removed his jacket, slinging it over his shoulder in a way he hoped was less intimidating than his suit and badge would suggest. The sun was perched directly overhead, casting a bright glow over some schoolchildren filtering back from lunch. They filed haphazardly into a small concrete building straight ahead, fronted by a plaque that said. 'Field High School. Founded in 1923.'

The name conjured images of lockers and desks arranged in rows, sports halls and music rooms. Filled with hundreds of bored teens; anxious about their grades and spots and lack of popularity. Mitchell watched as they wandered by in their cliques. The nerds and the cool kids, the jocks and the ones that no-one could place, walking by themselves from choice or cruelty. He shook his head and thanked God for being grown up. Adolescence definitely wasn't for wimps.

After a minute Mitchell noticed what looked like the admin block, its flip charts and office desks saying that no child should dare venture there. He crossed the yard, half-blind to the flirtatious stares of the older teen girls. Jailbait, even if he had been interested. Maybe twenty-five years ago.

Mitchell pushed at the block's heavy glass doors and wandered up three flights of stairs, following the signs to the principal's suite. The signs stopped outside a door with 'Principal' painted on the glass. Mitchell knocked and waited, watching as a plump woman wearing a suspicious look opened the door.

"Yes? Can I help you?"

She scanned him quickly. Mitchell wondered if she did it to everyone, or if his dark suit in the sunshine state made him seem extra strange.

"I'd like to see the Principal, please." He reached into his pocket and withdrew his badge, flashing it quickly in her face. "My Name is Agent Mitchell."

The woman was so startled that she stumbled back. Mitchell caught her quickly, surprised again by his reflexes. He shouldn't be; they'd been fast for as long as he could remember, although that wasn't saying much. He'd expected the tumour to slow him down but it hadn't yet. He was grateful for that at least.

The woman steadied herself and retreated into a corner office. After a murmured conversation the office door burst open and a man as tall as Mitchell strode out, extending his hand.

"Welcome, Agent Mitchell."

The Principal's words covered his anxiety well, but it was obvious from the shaking in his hand. Mitchell grasped it warmly to allay any fears that his title was causing and the teacher spoke again, with a tremor in his voice.

"Can I help you? Is there some trouble?

Mitchell shook his head and smiled. "No. No trouble at all, Mr…?"

"I'm sorry, that was remiss of me. Epstein, Todd Epstein. Please come in."

Epstein waved Mitchell into his office, nodding a coffee order to his P.A. Once they were alone Mitchell started, explaining that they were security checking an agent; Greg Chapman. Purely routine of course but, well, it had to be done every year and for some reason the school had been left out last time. He'd just come from the Chapman's parents and they'd directed him here. Please feel free to call them and check.

Epstein listened, his posture relaxing by the second. It wasn't every day that a man with a badge turned up at your door and Mitchell could only imagine what thoughts had run through his mind. When Mitchell had finished the Principal walked to a cabinet and searched through it for a minute, returning with a well-worn file. He flicked it open and sat back.

"What would you like to know?"

Mitchell turned to the list of questions he'd made, covering everything from Chapman's date of birth to his exam results, sporting achievements and merit badges. As Epstein answered Mitchell glanced around the room, knowing that he'd been there before, but also knowing that to say it would give him away.

"So all in all, Greg was a good student. Before my time of

course, but the records are clear."

Mitchell smiled vaguely at Epstein, noticing for the first time that he was the same age as himself. He couldn't have taught Greg Chapman; he was too young. Mitchell closed his notebook and smiled again, more broadly this time.

"There's just one last thing."

Epstein stared at him curiously, no sign of his earlier nerves. Mitchell could see him as the head teacher now and imagine him being fierce when school life required it.

"Greg's parents gave me the name of someone who knew him well in the past. Ms Julie Richards. I believe she's a teacher here now?"

Epstein smiled and Mitchell caught more than admiration for a colleague in his eyes. He glanced at Epstein's hands; no wedding ring, then back at his face. His expression had softened to an almost loving look. Epstein liked Julie Richards, a lot.

"Julie heads our drama department. Would you like to speak to her?"

"That would be helpful. Just as background."

Epstein left the room quickly, re-appearing five minutes later. Mitchell stood as he re-entered, with a slim thirty-something blonde. As soon as he saw her Mitchell gasped. He knew Julie Richards. It was more than that; he'd loved her, really loved her. It was impossible and Mitchell knew it but the feeling was very real. He staggered back against his chair and Epstein stared at him, concerned.

"Agent Mitchell, are you OK?"

Mitchell shook his head and looked at Richards again, hoping that his sanity had returned. It hadn't. He felt overwhelmed with affection for the woman in front of him and memories of the two of them together flooded his brain. Days at the beach and trips to the movies, holding hands and so much more. It had to be the brain tumour taking hold, making him feel things he couldn't possibly feel.

Mitchell sat down heavily and Julie Richards sat down beside him, watching him anxiously while Epstein fetched some water. Mitchell sipped at it gratefully and smiled at them, quickly covering his lapse.

"I'm sorry. It's the heat down here. New Yorkers aren't used to autumns like this."

Epstein nodded, relieved. "I'm sure wearing a dark suit doesn't help."

"No, it doesn't."

A minute later they were laughing and chatting and Mitchell felt like he'd known them for years; Julie Richards anyway. It must be because she looked like Karen. Of course, that was it. That was why he'd imagined feelings for her; she looked like the woman he loved. He and Greg Chapman shared their good taste in women. A bell rang in the corridor and Epstein glanced quickly at the clock. He stood up, apologising.

"I'm sorry but I have to teach a class. I'll leave you in Julie's capable hands. I know you have questions to ask."

Then Mitchell was alone with Julie Richards. He looked closely at her again, testing his feelings; they were still the same. She looked like Karen and the tumour was making him transfer his feelings for Karen to her. Mitchell pushed past the feelings and asked the teacher some basic questions then he moved onto how she knew Greg.

"We were students together." She blushed and looked down. "We…we were dating, even talked about marriage sometimes." Julie Richards glanced up and Mitchell could see brightness in her eyes and a tear perilously close to the edge. She'd loved Greg Chapman, so what had happened to break them up? She was still talking.

"But then Greg enlisted in the military and I knew it wasn't the life for me. I wanted to be near my parents and …" She glanced around the room. "I didn't want to leave St Augustine. Greg was always much braver than me, but I feel safe here."

She fell silent for a moment and Mitchell had an image of her and Greg Chapman saying goodbye to each other. He could see it clearly. They were sitting on a jetty dangling their feet in the water when Chapman had told her that he was joining-up. Mitchell knew that it had to be his imagination, but he needed to know for sure.

"Ms Richards, this will sound like a strange question, but could you tell me where you were when Greg told you he was joining the military?"

She glanced at him quickly and the tear that had been threatening rolled down her cheek. She said nothing for a moment and then whispered so quietly that Mitchell strained to hear. Her words shocked him to the core.

"Near Frances and Mary Usina Bridge. We'd been swimming and we were sitting on the jetty to cool off."

Mitchell couldn't breathe. He wanted to close his ears and un-hear the words, but he couldn't. He'd seen them on the jetty before she'd said the words. This wasn't the tumour, this was real. There had to be a logical explanation. He was a scientist, he believed in facts, not bloody telepathy. He could dismiss his affection for Julie Richards as the tumour messing with her resemblance to Karen, but how the hell had he known about the jetty where she and Chapman had said goodbye?

Mitchell stood up abruptly, knocking Greg Chapman's school file onto the floor. Julie Richards watched, surprised, as he raced from the room before she could say another word. Mitchell sprinted down the stairs and out of the school like something was chasing him, his only thought of getting home.

Tom Evans watched from the shadow of a white cedar as Jeff Mitchell ran into the street. Evans was shocked by the look on his face; Mitchell looked like he'd seen a ghost. Evans jumped into his blue Taurus rental just as Mitchell made a U-turn and accelerated past him down the suburban street. It soon became clear where he was heading; Jacksonville airport. Their Florida vacation was ending early.

Both men missed the van parked across the street, from which Anderson and Lemanski had been filming their every move. The two agents smiled at each other, well satisfied. They'd tailed Jeff Mitchell to the school to watch him and that's what they'd done, although they hadn't expected to see him leave it like a bat out of hell. But their surveillance had yielded a bonus; the man following Mitchell was someone the agency had been looking for a long time. Tom Evans was a completely unexpected gift.

Chapter Thirty

LaGuardia Airport, New York. Monday. 6.15 p.m.

Jeff Mitchell's plane had touched down almost forty minutes earlier and Amelia Howard stared at the arrivals board, willing it to hurry-up and disembark. She couldn't go home until Mitchell was safely back in Richie's sights, and she had a dinner to get to and a marriage to try and save. Howard pushed her hair back from her face and straightened her cream jacket, trying to look less like a government agent and more like someone waiting for a friend. Losing the suit had helped. In her floral skirt and t-shirt she could pass for someone's Mom, even though the fashion combination was making her teeth ache.

The crowd at the arrival gate surged forward, indicating that people were arriving. Howard stood waiting for the tall man she was expecting and a moment later Jeff Mitchell appeared. He looked drawn and pale, not what she'd expected after a day spent in the sun. Mitchell passed by Howard so close that she could almost feel his breath and the look on his face took her aback. He looked haunted, and years older than the man who'd left New York the day before. They all knew that Mitchell was ill, but even an aggressive cancer couldn't make that difference in a day. Something bad had happened in St Augustine.

Howard followed at a safe distance until Mitchell reached the long rank of cabs then she watched as he stepped into one, hailing the one behind. Cabbies loved playing 'follow that car' and the sight of her badge usually made them speed up even more. Her driver was true to form and fifty minutes later they pulled into Mitchell's road in Lloyd Harbor. Howard saw Richie sitting in the sedan and urged the cab around the corner; walking back to join Richie once she was certain that Mitchell had entered his house for the night.

Richie saw the cab drive past and watched as Jeff Mitchell turned his front door key in the lock, then he cleared the detritus from the passenger seat and waited for Howard to appear. A moment later the car door opened and she slumped in. Richie glanced at her skirt and was just about to make a wise-crack when Howard fixed his eyes with a warning look.

"I want no jokes from you, Cartagena. I was told to look like a tourist."

Richie couldn't resist it. "From Boulder?"

Howard laughed despite herself and reported quickly, then she turned to get out of the car. Richie stared at her, surprised.

"Where are you going?"

"I'm off duty. Dane is taking over."

"Not until midnight he isn't." Richie opened the driver's door and threw the car keys in Howard's lap.

"You're my relief until then; Magee's orders. Seems I've clocked up more hours than I'm allowed to and Human Resources are giving him grief. There are chips in the armrest if you're hungry. Enjoy."

A dark car pulled up behind them and Richie climbed in and disappeared quickly down the street, leaving Amelia Howard to explain yet another cancelled dinner party to the husband that she never got to see.

***

Ruth Lemanski knocked once on her boss' door and waited.

"Come."

She entered confidently, certain that he would be interested in what she had to say. The man behind the desk didn't look up, just kept on reading the file in his hand. He waved her to a seat and indicated the coffee percolator.

"Help yourself and get me one. I'll be with you in a moment."

Lemanski did as she was told and then took her seat again, waiting patiently. It didn't do to rush Brookman. He was a tricky bastard at the best of times, but interrupting his work was a bridge too far. Brookman set down his file five minutes later and took a long drink of coffee before looking her way. He seemed pleased, as if the file had contained good news. Lemanski hoped that he would view her report in the same light.

"Well?"

Lemanski didn't take offence at his brusqueness. They were used to it. It was fashionable to say that rudeness masked shyness or a heart of gold, but that wasn't always true. Leo Brookman was just plain rude. That was OK, she could deal with rude. At least it was honest. It was smarmy bastards that she couldn't take.

"Jake and I tailed Mitchell."

She tapped the paper in front of her and Brookman raised an eyebrow.

"And? You didn't come in to tell me that. You could have filed it on the net."

Lemanski indicated his computer. Brookman waved her on and she turned the screen around to face her, tapping a few times before turning it back to her boss. The video they'd taken outside the school appeared. Lemanski didn't need to explain any further.

Brookman leaned forward urgently and watched the film run then he tapped it back to the start and ran it again. There was no mistake.

"Tom Evans! What the hell is he doing here? He must know that he's a wanted man."

Lemanski shook her head and then hazarded a guess. "He thinks he's flameproof? Maybe he's earning his living tailing

Mitchell."

"And who's paying the traitorous bastard?"

Lemanski stared at her boss, shocked by his anger. His face was turning purple and his tone said that this was personal. She's never seen Brookman lose his cool but he was at boiling point now. She knew Tom Evans was on a wanted list, but that was all she knew. Brookman caught her questioning look and started to talk.

"Evans is a liar and a coward. He sold the President down the river in 2005 and the rest of us along with him."

Brookman thought back to the day that Tom Evans' leaked report on Iraq had reached the America's press, slandering the White House and the President's aides. He'd worked for years to become an aide and Evans' disclosures had turned him back into a grunt overnight. It had taken him years to get back on his feet. Brookman's voice grew louder.

"I'll ask you again, Lemanski. Who is Evans working for?"

Lemanski's eyes widened and she stammered a reply. "We're working on that now, sir. Should I share this with Agent Magee in New York?"

Leo Brookman thought for a moment and Lemanski watched as the vein in his forehead pulsed. Brookman wasn't an ugly man, just a brutal-looking one. His face could have graced Mount Rushmore; all hard angles and determination. His reputation made people fear him, but that wasn't always a bad thing. Bosses that you loved were great when you wanted a friend, but fear motivated people, and cocky junior agents sometimes needed motivation.

Ruth Lemanski had no idea what Brookman was thinking and if she had done she would have been shocked. He was thinking about a man who hated Tom Evans even more than him; Al Schofield, head of Special Ops in New York. They'd been Washington aides together and both of them had suffered the same fate after Evans' leak to the press.

Brookman turned to her, twisting his lips like a hungry

shark.

"Yes, give it to Magee. But tell him that we're interested in Evans as well and we need to be kept in the loop."

As Lemanski turned to leave the room Brookman lifted the phone to New York to give a gift to his old friend Schofield. Revenge; a dish that was best served cold.

***

Ilya paced the room rapidly, struggling to clear his head. Javadi's words had been unambiguous. If Mitchell's research wasn't worth having then they were all dead. He pushed away his doubts. Mitchell was brilliant. If he said that he'd discovered something new then he believed him. Mitchell wouldn't lie when he knew what was at stake.

Ilya's doubts returned faster than he expected. Mitchell had been behaving oddly lately; vague, almost disinterested. What if he'd decided not to hand over his work? What if it wasn't worth having? His mind raced with questions as Ilya searched for a safety net. He kept coming back to one, the very one he knew that he shouldn't use. Elza. She would make sure that Mitchell delivered, because she'd make him afraid not to, and Ilya knew exactly how she would make him afraid.

An image of Karen and Emmie Mitchell sprang into his mind. He'd met Karen at their wedding and many times since, always in the guise of an uncle. She was a nice girl, a gentle girl, and the malyshka Emmie was an angel. He couldn't let Elza near them; she would take pleasure in their harm. But… the threat might focus Mitchell's efforts.

The old man curled his lip in self-disgust, hardly believing what he was considering, but he had to. If Mitchell backed out now then his family would die anyway, all of them would. Far better that the threat should spur him on, and give everyone a chance.

Ilya stood frozen for a moment, as logic fought with love and logic won. Then he slumped heavily behind his desk and made the call that would give Elza Silin the green light to do her worst.

***

Lloyd Harbor. Tuesday 8 a.m.

It had been a silent evening followed by a silent morning and by the time Mitchell was ready for work Karen wanted to hit him, anything to make him talk. He'd returned from his trip taciturn and confused, not even telling her where he'd been or why he'd gone.

Karen had played the good wife game of smiling and kindness, then the other one of food and warmth. She'd moved towards her husband in bed, hoping that the dark would help them connect, but Mitchell had just smiled at her vaguely and stroked her hair gently back from her face. He'd gazed into her eyes as if they held the answer to something, then stared beyond them when he realised that they didn't. By eight a.m. the next morning Karen was ready to scream and as Mitchell turned to lift his briefcase she finally did.

"For God's sake, Jeff, will you talk to me? Say something, anything at all, just fucking well speak!"

Jeff Mitchell stared at his wife, shocked, not by her anger but by the language that he never heard her use. Karen was sweet, almost prim in some ways, and the swear word sounded incongruous coming out of her mouth, particularly with Emmie at their feet. Mitchell wasn't sure how to react, so he did what occurred to him first. He laughed.

Mitchell kept on laughing, uncertain what he was laughing at. The mess that he'd got them into, pursued by terrorists and the government? The fact that he would die soon and he didn't really care, as long as he solved the puzzle and kept them safe? Or the fact that he'd discovered he was psychic and had loved a woman called Julie Richards who he'd never met before, and remembered a shared history with her that could never have occurred? It was ridiculous! Every inch of him was a scientist steeped in logic, only ever believing in things that he could prove.

As Mitchell gazed down at his beautiful wife, getting more red-faced by the minute, he knew that he only wanted to do one thing, so he did. He dropped his briefcase on the floor and moved swiftly towards her and with one strong movement Mitchell scooped her into his arms and carried her upstairs, with Emmie scrambling to keep up. He kicked open the bedroom door like Rhett Butler and dropped Karen gently on the bed then put their daughter safely in her room to play. Undressing his wife gently Jeff Mitchell forgot everything for an hour, as they moved together in a way that said he had loved her forever, no matter what tricks his mind might try to play.

***

Richie watched the driveway's exit, expecting the Lexus to reverse out long before eight o'clock. When it still hadn't appeared an hour later he started to worry. Finally, at nine-thirty, the front door opened and Karen Mitchell emerged, looking pink-faced. Her husband followed, carrying Emmie and looking more pleased than anyone had a right to this early in the day. Richie knew immediately why they were late and his feelings surprised him. Normally he'd cheer for the guy and smile at the girl, but instead he felt a sharp pang of anger, and something else that he couldn't name. Why was he angry? So Jeff Mitchell and his wife had sex, big deal; it came with the ring. What business was it of his? Then Richie recognised the 'something else' he felt. He was jealous!

Jealous of what? The Mitchell's love for each other? Their little family? No. They'd had all of that two days before. So what had changed? Maybe he was bitter from losing Pereira, but

Richie didn't think that was it. Suddenly he knew exactly what it was; it was a teenage-boy jealousy, based on 'I want and can't have'.

The realisation hit Richie like a cold shower, taking his breath away. He liked her; Karen Mitchell. More than that, he wanted her. Enough to hate that she was having sex with her soon-to-be-dead husband! It told Richie something that he didn't know how to handle.

If he hated seeing Karen with her husband, hated thinking of them in bed, then he was too close to the investigation. He needed to take some leave. But if he told Magee how he felt he would take him off the case, end of subject, and then he wouldn't get to see her at all. Richie knew that there was nothing he could do but keep watching the Mitchells, and start getting hurt.

***

Magee stared at the e-mail in front of him, then lifted the phone and caught Ruth Lemanski at her desk. He started talking without introduction but she recognised his wheeze.

"You're certain it was Tom Evans?"

Lemanski paused, wondering whether to go for sarcasm or politeness. Cowardice made her opt for the latter.

"Good morning, Agent Magee. I take it you got my e-mail?"

"Of course I got your e-mail. Are you sure?"

"Absolutely. We have him on film. I'm sending you through the secure link now."

Magee said nothing, just refreshed his screen and clicked on the link that she'd sent. The man who appeared in front of him was well known to everyone at the agency. Tom Evans, ex-army Ranger, awarded the Medal of Honour and Bronze Star. One of the best agents that he'd ever trained. He'd lost track of Evans after he'd slipped custody for sedition in 2005. His last sighting had been on a plane heading for Cuba, where extradition to the

States wasn't enforced. Getting someone back up north from there required rendition.

How the hell had Evans got back into the States unseen? And why hadn't the Miami team picked him up? Magee vocalised his last thought and Lemanski jumped to her own defence.

"We didn't lift him because he was tailing your man, Mitchell, and we thought it might compromise your operation. Were we wrong?"

"Evans was following Jeff Mitchell? You're sure?"

"Absolutely. We think he tailed him from New York."

"Why?"

"Evans travelled back to LaGuardia from Jacksonville on the same plane as Mitchell last night, so we checked the inbound manifests for Sunday. He was on the same flight from New York to Miami, sitting two rows behind your man. More than a coincidence, I'd say."

Magee ran through the options. Evans was wanted States-wide, yet here he was, flying into LaGuardia cocky as hell. Like a man without a warrant on his ass. He knew Tom Evans; there was no way that he wanted twenty years in prison for sedition, or worse, to be executed for treason. There was only one way he was acting like he was untouchable; because he was. Evans had protection, and from someone so high up that he couldn't be stopped.

Magee ran through the possibilities; Senators, the President's inner circle and the rich list, plumping for the last. Evans was working for someone so rich that only God could touch them. It only took Magee a second to work out the name. Neil Scrabo; it had to be.

Scrabo wanted Jeff Mitchell watched and Evans was the tail. Poor bastard Mitchell had half the world following him because of his genius. That meant Scrabo must know that there were others after Mitchell's work by now, if not who they were.

Lemanski tapped her pen sharply against the phone,

reminding Magee that she was still there. Magee coughed deliberately loudly, hurting her ears in revenge and then he spoke.

"You did the right thing telling me about Evans. Now forget you ever saw him."

The call clicked off and Lemanski was left staring at the phone, shocked by Magee's economy of words. Who the hell did he think he was? Tom Evans was her case now and no self-obsessed New Yorker was going to tell her anything else.

Lemanski headed straight for her boss' office and rapped the door, looking for permission to follow Evans' trail. Leo Brookman's reply was as curt as Magee's.

"Leave Evans alone."

Brookman had his own plans for Tom Evans and they began and ended with the Special Ops team in New York.

Chapter Thirty-One

1 p.m.

Neil Scrabo stood in his spot by the Boardroom window and gazed out at 90 West Street's Gothic façade. When it was built its height must have been impressive, now every tenth building in Manhattan was the same. The intercom buzzed irritatingly and his P.A. Sylvie's voice echoed through.

"Mr Scrabo."

"Yes?"

"Mr Evans is here, sir. Shall I send him in?"

"Yes, and hold my calls until I say don't."

Scrabo turned towards the door just as the muscled shape of Tom Evans entered the impressive room. Scrabo glanced towards the whisky and Evans nodded, holding up three fingers. He needed a decent shot; it had been a long few days. They sat in silence, sipping at their drinks as Scrabo scrutinised the other man. Evans was the closest thing to a confidante he had, even though he paid his bills. He was fed up with sycophants and Evans was never that; he liked him for it. Scrabo surprised himself by admitting that he wanted their acquaintance to last longer than this contract.

When Evans had sipped for long enough Scrabo signalled him to speak. Evans ran through the trip to Florida, the visits to Greg Chapman's parents and High School, and the pallor on Mitchell's face as he'd left. Scrabo interrupted.

"Who is this Greg Chapman? Some old college pal of Mitchell's?"

Evans shook his head. "I don't think so. Mitchell was dressed like a Fed and I saw him flash a badge at the parents' front door."

Scrabo gave a wry smile. "Impersonating a federal agent? Can't he get done for that?"

They laughed together at his joke then Evans talked on.

"I'll find out whatever there is about Chapman. But whoever he is, whatever Mitchell heard in that school scared the crap out of him." He paused before continuing. "The local agents were tailing him too."

"Interesting. Do you think you were spotted?"

"Sure of it. They probably have a reel of film just of me." Both men smiled and Scrabo poured them another drink.

"Just as well I've got your back then, isn't it?"

Evans nodded and lit a cigarette, handing one to his boss.

"What now?"

"Keep following Mitchell. I want to see where else he goes in the next few days. It's time to suss out the North Korean's competition."

"And then?"

"Eliminate it of course."

***

3.30 p.m.

Richie watched as Karen leaned the groceries against the front door and rummaged for her key. She pushed the door open and ushered Emmie in, kicking it closed with her heel. She looked happier than she had in days and Richie smiled. He had his earlier jealousy under control. Karen Mitchell deserved whatever happiness she could get; God knows she had an ordeal ahead of her with her husband's health.

Richie turned the radio on and sat back, waiting for his relief to arrive. It was '90s day on the station and he laughed as the young disc jockey talked about the oldies he would play. Oldies! That was his youth they were talking about. Karen Mitchell's too. He imagined them both as teenagers and laughed, remembering the horrors of '90's fashion.

Karen walked quickly down the hall and put the groceries in the kitchen then she hurried upstairs to run Emmie's bath. It was their afternoon ritual, after kindergarten and before Jeff came home, and she loved the time alone with her little girl. Karen left out the towels and was just running downstairs to put the groceries away when she heard a faint bang at the back of the house. She glanced out of the family-room doors nervously, scanning the deck. There was nothing. She laughed at her own stupidity; she was afraid of her own shadow these days.

As she walked into the kitchen Karen heard another bang, this time from the family-room. Emmie was playing in there; she might have taken a fall! Karen ran into the room urgently to check and the sight that greeted her was worse than any fall she could have imagined. Her three-year-old daughter was lying unconscious on the floor with a woman that Karen had never seen before standing above her. The woman held an empty syringe and a patch of blood was forming on Emmie's neck. Another full syringe lay near-by.

Karen froze, afraid to move in case the woman emptied the second syringe into her daughter, and afraid not to in case she did the same. Elza Silin smiled coldly at her rival and watched as Karen's eyes flicked quickly towards a large paperweight beside the TV. Elza wagged an elegant finger at her, as if she was a naughty child.

"Naughty, naughty, Mrs Mitchell. I wouldn't if I were you. I'm a lot quicker than you think and by the time you reach me your daughter will be dead. She's just sleeping at the moment; I've given her a sedative. But if you attack me I will kill her."

Karen knew that the woman meant business. She restrained her urge to rush her and spoke, trying to sound calm.

"What do you want from us? We're not rich."

Elza laughed, showing perfect white teeth and making her green eyes shine. Karen knew the young woman in front of her should have been attractive, but her beauty was cold; empty somehow.

"Oh, but you *are* rich, Mrs Mitchell. You just don't value what you have."

Elza paused for a moment, scanning Karen from head to toe. She knew there was no rationale to men's taste, but how could Mitchell possibly prefer this anaemic weakling to her? She shrugged. It was academic. Soon Karen Mitchell and her brat would be out of the way and she would be flying off to Russia with Jeff.

Elza's next words were a lie to keep Karen Mitchell pliable, although Ilya would have thought they were the truth.

"Cooperate and you and your daughter will be safe."

Karen's temper flared and she took a step forward, then she stopped, knowing that she would never reach Emmie in time. Angry words would have to be enough.

"My husband will hunt you down and kill you."

Elza thought for a moment and then nodded. "Perhaps. Unless he blames someone else entirely, the one who ordered me here, and I will make certain of that. Now, enough chat, we're going on a trip. But not before you have a nice sleep."

Elza lifted the full syringe and beckoned Karen forward. Karen saw the gun strapped to her waist and knew that it was futile to fight. If she managed to grab the syringe the woman would shoot her, and the gun was too far round her waist to be seized from the front. Karen gave a last glance at Emmie's frail body and then walked forward, resigning herself to her fate. She felt the syringe push hard against her neck then she slumped to the floor with a thud.

Elza gave Karen a kick to check she was out then she carried the bodies to the waiting van one by one. As the van drove sedately down the back roads of Lloyd Harbor, Richie

Cartagena watched the front of the Mitchell's house, not suspecting a thing.

***

Karen opened her eyes to a kaleidoscope of colour, as blue, green and yellow melted to form abstract shapes above her head. Before she had time to focus a wave of nausea swept over her and she vomited hard, inhaling so much that she struggled for breath. A slim hand grabbed Karen and pushed her face into water. It held her down as she struggled, twisting and pulling to break free. Finally it yanked her up again and Karen gasped for air, shaking her shoulders free from the grip.

She fell back onto the floor and struggled to free her numb hands, but it was no good, they were tied tight. Karen could see the abstract clearly now. It was a rainbow painted on the ceiling above, a crudely crafted decoration. The room was bare and cold, with wooden floorboards and half-hung curtains patterned with cows and stars. They reminded her of an old nursery rhyme. Karen glanced at the ceiling again, understanding this time. She was in an old school. An abandoned one by the looks of it.

The thought was fleeting, replaced instantly by fear. Emmie. Where was she? Karen scanned the room frantically, but Emmie was nowhere to be seen. What had that bitch done with her? Karen's mind raced with possibilities, all of them bad. Her thoughts were interrupted by a voice that she'd heard before.

"The girl's fine and she'll stay that way as long as you behave."

It was a lie of course and they both knew it, but Karen grabbed at it like a life-line, holding on despite the voice in her head saying that it was crap. She sat very still and gazed at the voice's owner. The young woman was stunning. Karen scanned her face for some sign of compassion, but there was none. Just cool control and naked hatred filling her jade eyes. Who did she hate so much? Was it her? Really?

Karen's disbelief showed on her face and Elza laughed; the soccer Mom couldn't believe that someone wanted her dead. Believe it, Mrs Mitchell. They'd been conversing without words but now Karen broke the silence.

"Why?"

Elza smiled. It was an ugly smile. A dry sneer of contorted lips, twisted with emotion. Karen recognised the emotion at once and the weakness that it showed. The bitch was jealous. Of her, of Emmie, of their life. Clarity followed quickly. She wanted Jeff! She wanted him the way only a woman could want a man. That was why this woman hated them so much, they were in her way. Doubt froze Karen for a second. Had Jeff been this bitch's lover? She pushed the idea away. No. He loved her. That much she was sure of, and nothing else mattered today.

Karen's mind raced with plans. Jeff would be dead soon and she'd just as soon die as well, but Emmie had her whole life ahead. She had to protect her. Karen pulled herself to her knees and stared unblinking into Elza's eyes. The strength of her voice surprised her.

"Where is my daughter?"

Elza glanced carelessly towards the corner and Karen could just make out a small shape. She stumbled towards it and pressed her face fearfully against Emmie's thin frame. She was warm! She nudged her daughter's face towards her. She was asleep but unharmed and Karen whispered a silent prayer. Her thanks were interrupted by a sarcastic laugh.

"How touching. Mother and child reunited. I should take a picture."

Karen snarled and the ferocity on her face took Elza aback for a moment, then she smiled; the kitten had claws. Karen Mitchell might make a decent adversary after all. Elza stared at the tableau for a moment longer and then turned, leaving the room and locking the door. Karen didn't care that they were prisoners. Emmie was alive and that was all that mattered for now. She could think about escape another time.

***

5 p.m.

Mitchell collected a rental car and headed for the farmhouse. He'd spent the day wondering about Greg Chapman. It was self-indulgent and it wasn't moving him any further on. He needed to find out how far his research had progressed and exactly what Ilya had promised the Alliance.

As the car sped along the Interstate Mitchell thought of the papers from the café. He'd discovered a new carbon allotrope and applied it to plants, playing God by creating new strains. The cages at the café and farmhouse said that there were plans to do the same with animals. He shuddered, thinking of the grotesques that he might already have made. The potential for error was endless; he couldn't possibly have managed to eradicate it all.

In less than an hour Mitchell was sitting at the farms computer, reading a file and shaking his head. He'd done it! He'd applied the new carbon allotrope to animals, to change them into something else. But what? Clicking on a video file Mitchell watched as a monkey stood upright and walked with its arms by its side like a small child. It didn't scratch or shake its head; it looked almost human, except for its hair and face. Was this what he'd achieved? Some form of advanced eugenics?

But it was what the primate did next that surprised Mitchell most. The monkey rubbed its hands together and a shower of sparks appeared, then, with encouragement from an out-of-shot male voice, it grasped the bare wires of a lamp. Mitchell watched as the lamp's bulb glowed into life and the voice said 'well done'. The monkey was generating electricity!

Animals generating electricity was nothing new, several hundred species could, but they were mostly aquatic; one type of electric eel could generate five hundred volts. Some mammals also carried a charge; human beings did, but it was tiny, 10-100 millivolts, nothing like this. It would take more than one hundred volts to light a bulb!

As the video played on things grew even more bizarre. Over the next ten minutes Mitchell watched as the monkey powered a clock, then a computer and finally an electric car. It was a walking generator! If animals could be physically re-engineered to generate electricity then the possibilities were endless. It would be worth a fortune! And this was with only one change in carbon's form. What else could be achieved?

Mitchell couldn't believe that he'd managed it, but it was undeniable. It was his voice on the tape instructing the chimp. He rifled through the papers in front of him, shaking his head. He'd used carbon re-engineering to cause physical changes in a living thing! He couldn't remember any of it, but God, the logic was pure. Mitchell felt like patting himself on the back. He would have done if the potential applications hadn't been so perverse.

It was astounding work, so why did he still feel that there was more? Mitchell ran through each file on the desktop, opening and closing them one by one, but there was nothing else to see. He poured a cup of coffee and allowed himself a small smile; if Devon saw him drinking coffee near equipment again he would have a fit.

Clicking on the computer's document library Mitchell saw that it was filled with more files. A quick scan revealed that most were just the documents from Daria's coffee-shop and the equations from the 'Café' file that he'd seen before. Then he noticed a secure PDF labelled with one letter. 'A'.

Mitchell froze for a moment, considering what to do. A secure file was high level; it might have firewalls that would shut the whole system down. And what if it contained more advanced research? What could it be, and did he really want to know? The scientist in him overrode the man and he clicked to open the file, pushing through its series of passwords instinctively. Finally the PDF opened to reveal a document unlike any of the others that he'd seen. It was forty pages long and the word 'Archaeus' topped the first page. The word scribbled on the papers that he had at home.

Mitchell glanced quickly at the clock; ten p.m. Karen would be getting worried about him. He checked his cell-phone quickly. No missed calls. Maybe she was giving him some space to work. Mitchell turned back to the Archaeus file and made a decision, hurriedly pressing print, then he transferred all the computer files to a flash-drive and pressed delete, wiping them from the PC's memory. If the Alliance knew that the files existed they might still be able to retrieve them, but deletion would slow them down at least. Mitchell grabbed the hard copy and the flash-drive and headed for home, completely unprepared for what would greet him there.

***

Magee tapped his pen repeatedly against the desk, thinking through the options. If Scrabo was after Mitchell's research then he was going to sell it. That much was certain. The question was, to whom? Magee ran through the usual suspects. They knew the café was a front for the Russians, but they still weren't sure whether they were acting alone. If they weren't, then Syria and Iran had to be high on their partnership list, and neither of them was in love with the USA. They were dangerous, not just because of their fanaticism but because they believed in something; an ideal. Idealists were always lethal. They didn't have any price but death.

Neil Scrabo was a different proposition. A lone wolf, out for a fast buck. If he was prepared to screw his own company and its U.S. interests, then he could sell the research to anyone. Top of the list had to be the Arabs, or worse, the North Koreans. Zealots led by a dynasty convinced of its right to rule. There was no way of reasoning with them.

Magee shook his head in disgust. Not at the North Koreans but at the fact that Tom Evans was helping Scrabo make the deal. He'd trained Evans for God's sake, and before he'd gone rogue Evans had been one of the best men the agency had ever had. Evans had been a patriot, almost too much of one perhaps. He'd believed in the goodness of political leaders while the rest of them were saying 'I told you so'. Cynics, every last one of them, and him the worst of all. But not Tom Evans. He'd bought the whole shebang about flag and country. He'd taken the President's screw-up on Iraq really hard while the rest of them had just shaken their heads. God save America. From idealists.

Evans ideals had turned him into a whistle-blower and he'd gone rogue in 2005 and leaked classified information to the press, then he'd taken off to Havana with a warrant on his ass. The last they'd heard he was a mercenary somewhere in the middle-east. Now he was with Neil Scrabo, selling his country out. Magee shook his head again. No. He could call Tom Evans a lot of things, but all of them started with 'idealistic'. He refused to believe that Evans would help Scrabo sell dangerous research to the Koreans for money, no matter what the evidence said.

***

10.50 p.m.

Mitchell parked the rental car in the street and walked swiftly towards his house. He was dreading what he'd find when he read the Archaeus file, and he needed to hug his wife tight, to get the courage not to throw it in the fire. As he walked through the front gate Mitchell was surprised to see the house in darkness. He glanced at his watch, it was almost eleven o'clock. Karen might have gone to bed. No. That wouldn't explain the complete lack of light. She always left a lamp on in the hall.

Mitchell stopped in the driveway and stood completely still, scanning his home's pale wood façade. Something was wrong. A cold sweat covered his brow, matched by a trickle down his spine, but it wasn't fear, it was anticipation. He felt every muscle in his body tense, ready to fight and kill. Wherever his combat instincts were coming from they were welcome now.

Then he saw it. The front door was ajar. Mitchell slipped through the gap and crouched down in the hall, listening hard to the noises of the house, until they drowned out the pulsing in his ear. The wooden stairs creaked quietly, joining the refrigerator's hum to make it seem just like any normal night, but something was missing. He tuned out the background soundtrack, listening for movement of some kind, but there was none. Not even Emmie turning in her sleep.

Entering the kitchen first Mitchell moved swiftly from room to room, until he saw Buster in a corner of the utility room, asleep. As he got closer he saw that the dog wasn't sleeping; a single stab wound to his neck had ended his life. Bastards. But whoever had done it was no amateur. Mitchell thought of Emmie's tears when she found out that her pet was dead and his urge to kill whoever had done it grew. Slipping into his darkened study Mitchell pushed a book on the shelf to one side, revealing a lock-box. He prayed that his gun was still inside. It was. He loaded it and moved on, reaching the family-room across the hall.

The hairs on Jeff Mitchell's arms stood on end as he sensed that there was something there. He peered through the darkness searching for human shapes, but there was nothing. Then he stared again, his eyes falling on the glass deck-doors. Even in the darkness he couldn't miss it. A small white shoe was wedged between them, as if someone had dragged a child through and yanked so hard that their shoe had fallen off. Mitchell's heart dropped in his chest and he moved towards it, smelling the scent of Karen's perfume grow with every step.

As he bent to retrieve the small shoe he saw that a memory card was tucked inside. Mitchell seized it, already guessing what it contained, but dreading the moment that he was forced to find out. He checked the rest of the house for signs of a struggle. Signs of invasion filled their bedroom, bedcovers torn back and abandoned on the floor, ornaments and mirrors smashed, as if someone was angered by what happened in there. Karen was nowhere to seen. She and Emmie had been taken.

Mitchell re-entered the family-room and flicked on all the lights, gasping loudly at a patch of blood by the door. He stared at it for a moment, taking comfort from its size; it wasn't enough blood for a wound. What then? The answer came quickly and he pictured a needle piercing his wife's skin. Shaking off the image Mitchell re-entered the study, booted-up his laptop and inserted the memory chip. Then he braced himself for what he would see.

The screen opened to a video showing Karen and Emmie unconscious on a wooden floor. Mitchell squinted; it was the floor in the family-room. Whoever had done this had taken the time to film before they'd left the house. Mitchell's stomach turned over in disgust then something clarified. To know that they'd had the time to film meant that the intruder had known he wouldn't be home. This was someone who knew his movements.

Mitchell's mind raced with the possibilities then his thoughts jumped to the car outside. He'd seen the agent with dark hair watching as he'd pulled up. He could have done it! Even as the thought came it disappeared and Mitchell shook his head. No. The agent wouldn't still be there if he had. Besides, he would have come in through the front. Whoever had done this had crossed the deck at the back, both ways.

Mitchell kept on watching the video as the camera panned silently across Karen's face and then his child's. Their breathing was slow and laboured; they were alive, but only just. The camera moved to a syringe with a bottle of Morphine alongside. Showing that they were safe, or not? It all depended on the dose. It was exactly the message that Mitchell was meant to get and he knew it. 'See. We could have killed them with this if we'd wanted, we've just chosen not to. Yet.'

The camera moved around the room and then back to the sleeping shapes, focusing on a typed note by Karen's side. It was succinct. 'Act normally and work hard. We will be in touch.' Then the screen flickered and went dark, leaving Mitchell without 'We's' name.

Mitchell sat in darkness for almost half the night, his anger filling him with hate. By first light it was gone and logic had taken its place. Whoever had taken Karen and Emmie wanted him to 'work hard'. They wanted his research, that much was clear, but was it Neil Scrabo or the Alliance? He knew the Alliance was having him watched but was Scrabo still watching him as well, even though Devon had failed? They could both have known that he would be late home. Should he be adding the government to the list? No. They might be watching him but they would never harm a child. If they would then America was really screwed.

For some reason that Mitchell couldn't name, Neil Scrabo was fading from his list. Yes, the Board wanted his research, but surely they would just spy on him at work; Devon was proof of that. Mitchell shook his head, trying to clear his thoughts. Five more minutes of speculation narrowed his list to two names. Now he just had to decide what to do.

***

Thursday. 6.40 a.m.

Richie yawned and checked his watch then he rested back again, cranking up the car heater to keep warm. Six-forty. Handover was in twenty minutes then it was home for a shower and sleep and back again at seven o'clock tonight, to sit on his ass for another twelve hours. The glamour of being an agent was overwhelming.

He turned the radio dial and listened as Howard Stern told New York to wake up, using his rhetoric like an assault weapon. Easy listening would be kinder but then he would never stay awake. As Neal Peart beat the hell out of some drums Richie thought about Jeff Mitchell. He didn't like the man, but he had to admit that Mitchell seemed to love his wife, more so in the past few weeks. He was positively affectionate towards her nowadays. He felt sorry for Karen Mitchell that her husband would soon be dead, but if Mitchell was prepared to sell his research to corrupt powers then maybe his brain tumour was doing the world a favour.

An image of Karen sprang into Richie's mind and he admitted that he cared what happened to her. He shouldn't, after all she was just a subject, but he did. She and Emmie would be totally lost when Mitchell died and he would die very soon, either from cancer or a bullet. What would his little family do then?

Richie's reverie was broken by a sharp rap on the windshield. He startled, registering the time before he saw the outline of a man. It was too early for handover; Magee timed it to the minute. Richie reached for his gun, knowing that he'd be dead already if the man had wanted him that way. He turned slowly and was shocked to see Jeff Mitchell standing there. It was against every rule! Didn't Mitchell know that it was his job to be watched and Richie's to do the watching? It was just plain wrong to turn it around.

Richie pulled his gun from its holster, more from protocol than need, then pushed open the car door and stood facing his quarry in the street. It was an incongruous scene. One man exhausted, his hair standing up from a night spent holding his head in thought. The other pointing a gun. Not a sight you saw often in Lloyd Harbor at any time.

The men stared at each other warily. Similar age, similar height, nothing else in common except the hunt. Finally Mitchell broke the silence, smiling at Richie as if he'd known him all his life.

"Come in for coffee. We need to talk."

Mitchell turned on his heel, leaving the invitation hanging as Richie watched him re-enter the house, his mind computing the chances that it could be a trap. Every ounce of his training said to radio in, but his instinct and the week he'd had said to go ahead and take the risk. Richie Cartagena did both. He radioed Magee that he'd stay on until nine, without telling him why, then he left the safety of the sedan and headed to the neighbours for pot luck.

***

Tom Evans rubbed shaving foam into his stubble and lifted his razor to get clean. He stared at himself in the mirror, his features blanked out by the overhead fluorescent light. It was a pity that his conscience wouldn't blank out too. He stared for a minute longer, searching for some sign of the men he'd killed throughout the years marked on his face. No-one stared back except himself. His dark good looks gave no hint of the bad things that he'd done; he was a modern day Dorian Gray.

Evans pulled the blade roughly across his jaw, trying to hurt himself and feel alive, but even his razor wouldn't cooperate. It just slid across the foam to smooth his features even more. Evans threw it down in disgust; not at the metal; it had done its job. Coldly and sharply, just as he did his. His disgust was all for himself. Bile filled his mouth and he spewed it into the sud-filled sink, wanting to vomit up all his guilt.

Guilt for the life he led now, when it had all started out so well. Guilt at the money he'd taken as a mercenary; printed in dead men's blood. He'd been a patriot once, an honest-to-God George Washington; 'We the people' tattooed on his every pore.

And now what? A paid thug. A hired gun; without even the honour of a war to salve the wounds he caused.

Evans retched in self-disgust and then turned his eyes ahead, gazing at his face. He'd blamed the government for letting him down, and they had, but he'd blamed them for long enough. Handing himself in would mean prison and he wasn't doing time for any man, but he wasn't giving the North Koreans a weapon either. There had to be a middle way.

Tom Evans knew instantly what it was. He wiped his face clean and dressed very carefully, then sipped an espresso until it was dry, psyching himself up. When he was ready he scrolled through his phone for a number and dialled it quickly, before he had time to change his mind.

***

Richie entered the low-ceilinged hall slowly, not exactly wary, but cautious. The house was quiet, quieter than a family home should be at seven a.m. He stopped and gazed up the stairs, expecting the clatter of tiny feet to run down them any minute. Or more elegant adult ones. But there was nothing. Even the dog's bark was nowhere to be heard.

Mitchell turned, beckoning him into the family-room. It was warm and small with a wooden floor and an old settee, set opposite a large TV. It said winter movie evenings spent cuddled up, and popcorn in a big bowl. But it said something else today as well. He could see it in Mitchell's glance towards the door. Richie's eyes flew to where Mitchell's were already focused. There was blood on the floor. Not much, but enough to tell him why he was there. He looked at Mitchell quickly and Mitchell nodded then said the words that told Richie he'd completely blown last night's watch.

"They took both of them. Sometime yesterday evening."

Before Richie could speak Mitchell held out his hand, a computer card in his palm. Richie stared at it then followed

Mitchell to the study where they watched the video clip. When it ended Mitchell spoke again.

"I need your help."

Richie nodded, knowing that it might be his help alone that Mitchell got. He corrected his earlier thought. He hadn't blown his assignment. Their job was to know where Jeff Mitchell was at all times and they'd succeeded in that. Dane had watched Mitchell leave Scrabo and head in the direction of the farm. The satellites had followed him until he came home, where Richie was always waiting.

The agency would say that what happened to Karen and Emmie wasn't their concern, unless it affected Mitchell selling his work. They were collateral damage. Magee would echo that, accusing Richie of getting too involved. Magee would be right but it was too late. Richie already gave a shit about Karen and Emmie Mitchell and there was no way back from that. After a moment's thought Richie spoke.

"We need to plan this."

Mitchell smiled and Richie knew that he already had.

"First thing. What's your name? I can't call you 'agent'"

Richie thought about giving a false name and then shrugged. It rarely worked in the movies and it wouldn't work now.

"Agent Richie Cartagena."

Mitchell nodded, feeling like he'd met Richie before; another mystery to add to his list. "You already know my name and my birth weight too I guess, so let's get past the game-playing. I'm going to give your agency everything that it wants, but I need some things first."

"What?"

"I want Karen and Emmie back safe and in witness protection, then I'll talk to whoever you want me to."

"And take us to your accomplices."

Mitchell nodded; that had been his plan since he'd read the papers from the café, but he'd lied about one thing. He wouldn't be giving the agency everything. He hadn't read the

Archaeus PDF yet; he was deliberately putting it off. But if he'd guessed correctly about what was in it, no-one could be trusted with that information. Not even the good old U.S. of A.

Richie thought hard for a minute. There was no way the agency would sanction him helping find Mitchell's family. This had to be underground. But if he brought them Mitchell's research, witness protection should be easy to arrange and Magee would be kissing his ass for months. Richie shuddered mentally at the image but not at the promotion it would bring, then he made a half-hearted offer that he hoped Mitchell would refuse.

"It would be better to ask for the agency's help with finding them."

Mitchell shook his head vehemently. "Once they'd got my research they wouldn't care about the casualties." He looked at Richie and smiled, recognising his ploy. "But you already knew that. You just wanted to hear me say so."

Richie nodded. "I'm going off-radar on this and I need to be able to say that you insisted. OK, you've got me. Now tell me who has them."

Mitchell pulled out a piece of paper. It had two names at the top. Elza Silin and Ilya Tabakov.

"Who are they?"

Mitchell explained about his memory loss and Richie knew that he wasn't lying, or setting up a defence. It was a fact. After all, he had a brain tumour.

"The first thing I remember is being in the shower Thursday morning two weeks ago; the fourth of the month. Nothing before then."

Mitchell left out the detail about the blood, knowing that it would set Richie running in a direction he didn't want him to go. He hesitated, tossing up whether to tell Richie the thing he could barely bring himself to think about, and then he blurted it out. "I have a brain tumour. It must be that."

Richie feigned surprise, pretending that the information was new to him. He made a sympathetic noise, but his mind was racing. The Thursday before last; the day after Greg Chapman had disappeared.

"You remember nothing before that Thursday? Not about your childhood? College? Getting married?"

Mitchell shook his head. "It's made things tolerable in a way. If I can't remember doing things then I can't be blamed for siding with these pigs. I can't really be blamed anyway..."

Mitchell's voice tailed off and Richie was sure that he saw a tear forming in his eye. Why would Mitchell get tearful about things now, unless he felt guilty? No, that would be too big a shift for the bastard he'd been tailing for months. Mitchell stared at him for a moment and then spoke again.

"I was a sleeper."

A sleeper. The word conjured up the image of a normal life changed with one phone call. Average Joes activated into Manchurian Candidates by whatever language their employers spoke. Richie gasped, genuinely shocked; it hadn't been in their briefing on Mitchell. Why not? He asked and answered the question at the same time; because the agency couldn't possibly have known.

"How did you find out?"

Mitchell stared at the ground with a look that resembled shame. "They were discussing it. The day I went on the 295." He glanced up. "I'm sorry about your agent. There was nothing that I could do."

Richie scanned his face for sarcasm but there was none. Mitchell's regret about Brad Whitman was real. How could he change allegiance mid-life? Mitchell read his mind.

"The man they described as a sleeper doesn't feel like me. I have no memory of him at all." He tapped his head. "Maybe it's this tumour, or maybe if we don't remember who we are then we can become someone else. The person that we're supposed to be."

It made sense, and it could explain why Mitchell had become

'Family Man' in the past few weeks. So which one was the real Jeff Mitchell? The one he'd been bred to be, or the one he'd become when he was freed from the training of his past? It was too philosophical a question for Richie. He realised that Mitchell was still talking.

"I never knew my real parents. They chose me from an IQ test, took me from my family and brought me to the States when I was ten. I was bred to work for them."

Poor bastard. Richie almost felt sorry for him. Jeff Mitchell had been cursed by his intellect from the day he could think.

"Who are they? Russians?"

Mitchell nodded. "Some of them. You know about the café?"

"Yes. You killed one of our men there."

Richie knew Mitchell hadn't killed Brunet but it was a good test.

Mitchell gawped at him, horrified. "I didn't kill anyone. I knew nothing about it until they told me. I only ever went to see the old lady."

As Mitchell described Daria, Richie nodded. The old lady; Daria Kaverin. Old-school KGB and one hundred percent lethal. She'd been a Russian agent for years, one of their best, but the CIA had lost track of her after Perestroika. How the hell had she got to New York?

"Who else do you know about?"

Mitchell rubbed his face tiredly and Richie could see the stress starting to tell. Mitchell pointed to the piece of paper.

"The two names here. Ilya Tabakov." Mitchell paused and looked sad. "Apparently he brought me up. I don't remember it of course, but I felt something for him when he told me. Affection of some kind. And for Daria."

Richie tapped the paper.

"And this Elza Silin? Who is she?"

Mitchell filled Richie in on what he knew about Elza. He finished with an opinion. "She's poison and she wants me. I…I think she's in love with me. I can't believe Ilya would hurt

Karen and Emmie, but her…"

"Why now?"

Mitchell gazed at Richie, uncomprehending.

"Why would they kidnap your family now? You're working for them already so what's to be gained?"

Mitchell said nothing for a moment and Richie watched realisation dawn on him.

"They must have guessed what I was thinking! They must have realised that I was having second thoughts about giving them the research."

"When would they have known?"

"When I met the Iranians. They were at the farm facility the day your agent died in the crash, that's when I first remember meeting Ilya. I wasn't certain about the Russians, although I had a suspicion that they were involved after meeting Daria and Elza. But the Iranians were a complete surprise. They were there that day."

Richie struggled to hide his shock. Iranians. Fuck. His guess had been right. That made it a whole new ball-game.

"Who was leading? The Russians or the Arabs?"

"The Iranians, definitely. They were telling Ilya how it was going to be. Once they had my work they would get us out of the country."

"Us?"

"Karen, Emmie and me."

Something dawned on Richie. "Did this woman Elza hear?"

"What? What's that got to do with anything?"

God, Jeff Mitchell knew even less about women than he did. Richie asked again, more insistently. "Did she hear them say that you were taking your wife and child with you?"

Mitchell shook his head vehemently.

"No, she couldn't have. She was outside the room. The Iranian dismissed her like a servant. You know, the 'not for women's ears' crap."

Elza had overheard them somehow, Richie was sure of it.

And it had given her the motive to harm Karen.

"This Elza has taken your wife and daughter. I'd stake my life on it. She overheard them saying you were taking your family with you when you left and she wants rid of them."

Mitchell's eyes widened. "No! Elza could never take a decision like that alone. They would kill her. She was there to watch me, that's all."

Richie wanted to shake him. "She's a woman in love, for God's sake! She's taken them. I'd lay my life on it. The only question is, was it sanctioned higher up?"

"Ilya?"

Richie nodded. It was essential to find out. If Ilya Tabakov had OK-ed the kidnapping, then Karen and Emmie stood a chance of still being alive. He wouldn't want them dead, just Mitchell pulled into line until they were ready to leave. What better way to motivate him than to threaten the people he loved until he cooperated.

"Let's hope he ordered it."

Richie really meant it. Because if Elza Silin was acting alone then Jeff Mitchell's family was already dead.

Chapter Thirty-Two

Thursday. 10 a.m.

The old-fashioned café sat in a side-street in Greenwich Village, across from an antique bookshop and a new gallery showing Venezuelan art. People milled around the gallery's entrance, staring at signs that announced its opening date. Tom Evans stood amongst them, dressed down in the shabby-chic style that cost a fortune and made the rich feel 'real'. He fitted right in.

Evans cast a quick glance to both sides, scanning the crowd for an undercover goon. He would spot them immediately if they appeared. He should do, he'd been one often enough. There was no-one in sight so he leaned back against the gallery wall, his eyes roaming up and down the street. He was searching for one man in particular. A minute later Evans found him, seated in the café, just where they'd agreed. Dressed in a dark suit on a hot autumn day, Magee might as well have stamped 'agency' on his face.

Magee looked straight at Tom Evans, beckoning him across the street and ordering them both coffees before he arrived. He scrutinised Evans' outfit with a look of distaste; his fashion sense had degraded with his morals, and no faux-military jacket could hide the gun strapped under his arm.

Evans turned a wicker chair around so that his back was to the wall, and waited for the black filter coffee that he knew was on its way. When the waiter left he stared hard at Magee. Magee stared back for a minute then finally he spoke.

"You look like crap, Tom."

Evans gave a small smile. It was as close to affection as Magee ever got. He considered the older man carefully then grinned. "Well, you look just adorable."

Magee's face cracked into a smile, recognising an old 'in' joke. He closed the smile down quickly but not before Evans had read the nostalgia on his face.

"What do you want, Tom? I'm taking a risk meeting you and it will only happen once."

"Not as big a risk as I am. And you can park the attitude until you hear what I've got to say."

Evans paused and sipped his coffee again, knowing that as soon as he said his next words there was no turning back. He kissed goodbye to his expensive lifestyle and then spoke.

"I can give you the North Koreans."

Magee leaned forward urgently and Evans could hear the wheeze building up in his chest.

"You're a bastard, Tom! And a lying one at that. I stick my neck out for you and you come to me with this shit! The North Koreans aren't active in New York."

Magee sat back abruptly and grabbed at his inhaler. Evans gave him a moment and then shook his head.

"You don't know everything, Magee. The Koreans *are* here and they want whatever Jeff Mitchell's working on. Or are you going to tell me that you don't know about him as well?"

Magee pulled the inhaler from his mouth.

"We know that you've been watching Mitchell for Neil Scrabo. You were spotted in Florida."

"Good. I was being as obvious as I knew how. Even that dickhead Brookman couldn't have missed me."

Magee's eyebrows shot up and then he smiled wryly. He should have known. He'd trained Tom Evans far too well for him to be spotted unless he wanted to be.

"You know Neil Scrabo wants Mitchell's research, so you must know that he intends to sell it on."

It wasn't a question. Magee nodded.

"So? You're telling me that the North Koreans are buying and we just have to wait until Scrabo makes his move and lift him? We could have done that by ourselves." Magee's tone became sarcastic. "We do have some skills."

"Except that you didn't even know the Koreans were in New York." Evans paused and stared at his old boss. "What did I say?"

"What?"

Evans slowed his voice as if he was talking to a child. "What. Did. I. Say?"

Magee's face contorted in anger. Evans ignored him and carried on.

"I said that I would give you the North Koreans, not that I'd give you Neil Scrabo. Even I'd give you credit for being able to catch *him* by yourself."

Magee stared at his old protégé for a moment, his mind racing. Evans had been the best agent he'd ever trained. If anyone could trap the Koreans, he could. Magee took the bait.

"How?"

"You let me worry about that. Just have your men ready to move when I call."

Magee's sarcasm returned. "And you're doing this out of the goodness of your heart, I suppose?"

Evans laughed so loudly that a man at a nearby table turned to look. He smiled then turned away again. New York was no place to stare.

"That's right; the goodness of my heart. That and a presidential pardon. Oh, and some money to start again. I'm tired of running."

"Why would I do that when I could have you arrested right now and beat the information out of you?"

Evans smiled and patted his old friend's arm.

"A, because you like me and working together will be just like old times. B, because you know I can resist the agency's torture long enough to let the sale to the Koreans go down, and

C, because Neil Scrabo trusts me enough to let me close. Face it, Magee. You can't do this without me."

***

A stream of freezing cold water hit the ground, splashing Karen Mitchell's face and shocking her awake. She glanced around for its source and her search was halted by the sight of a stiletto heel an inch from her daughter's small hand. Karen pulled Emmie closer, marvelling how she'd managed to wriggle free of her embrace in her sleep. She listened to her child's slow breathing, worrying when she barely stirred, just turned her head slightly and then settled back to her feverish dream. She had to get Emmie to a doctor before she got really sick.

Elza tipped-up the jug she was holding and poured out more water, this time directly onto Karen's face, blinding her for seconds as it splashed into her eyes. Karen shook her head angrily, dispersing the cold droplets, and hissed at their captor, trying to clamber to her feet. She failed to notice the rope tied around her knees and fell backwards onto the floor, all movement limited by her tightly bound legs. At least her hands were free now, a concession earned by hours of begging. Karen drew in her breath and screamed with all her might, repeating the question that she'd been asking for almost a day.

"What do you want with us? We know nothing."

Then she added a phrase that she thought might appeal to the woman's vanity. "We're not important. No-one will pay to ransom us, if that's what you want."

Karen was wrong, it appealed to something much more base. Elza smiled down at her, watching as Karen flailed on her back like a beached fish. Karen Mitchell had just sealed her and her daughter's fates; no-one would pay to ransom them so they would have to die.

Elza gazed at her own reflection in the window, admiring her perfectly quaffed elegance and comparing it favourably to the woman's on the floor. She was far more beautiful. The knowledge made her angry instead of pleased. If it wasn't looks that had made Mitchell choose his wife that meant it was something she couldn't see. Something that made him love his wife but just fuck her. Elza stared at Karen Mitchell for a moment, searching for the something that made her unique then she flicked her eyes towards her child.

Emmie murmured in her sleep and Elza stared curiously at her small body. She couldn't understand Mitchell's love for this infant. She had no maternal feelings; in fact she had no feelings for anyone but herself. Karen saw her look and scrambled towards Emmie, throwing herself across her. Elza stared down at them like they were specimens in a zoo, her cold analysis replacing any human concern.

Finally she shrugged. If the woman cared for the child, what did it matter to her? It was only Mitchell's love that she was jealous of. Ilya would use Mitchell's feelings for his family to make him finish his work, promising their return, then they would be killed and Mitchell would turn to her. It was logical, but it wasn't human. Elza Silin had just made a huge mistake.

***

Neil Scrabo poured himself a whisky and leaned back in his chair, pressing his intercom impatiently. Where was Tom? He'd disappeared two hours earlier on some excuse about going home to change. Such a fuss about a small coffee stain. Well, OK then, perhaps not small. It *had* covered the front of his shirt.

He made a note to insist that Tom kept a change of clothes at the office and then turned back to his drink. Macallan1926; the most expensive whisky in the world. Scrabo sipped slowly at the golden liquid, savouring its fire as it slipped down his throat. He imported six bottles of it each year. When the deal with the North Koreans came off he would order it by the case.

Scrabo's thoughts flew to Jeff Mitchell. How far had Mitchell taken his research? And how much further could he progress it given time? It was a moot point. The North Koreans would see to all that, they had their methods of persuasion. All he had to do was deliver Mitchell into their hands. He'd been shocked when they'd first told him they wanted Mitchell, not just his work, but it made sense. Who knew what Mitchell might discover in the future? Why just take the water when you could have the well?

The North Koreans wanted Mitchell soon. He'd planned to give him more time to develop his work, but as soon as he'd mentioned it the Korean had shaken his head.

"Dr Mitchell will come now, with what he has. We will encourage him to take his work forward. His surveillance is becoming risky."

'Encourage him', now there was a euphemism if ever he'd heard one. They were right about one thing though, tailing Mitchell *was* getting dangerous. They couldn't be the only ones interested in his work; God only knew who else was out there making plans. They had to grab Mitchell soon before anyone else did.

Scrabo shrugged and took another sip of his drink. Jeff Mitchell wouldn't be his problem soon. He'd be out of his employ and out of the USA; they were only waiting for the word. Meanwhile Tom would watch him closely, he was sure of that. Dr Mitchell could make them both very rich.

Chapter Thirty-Three

1 p.m.

Jeff Mitchell walked quickly down the side-street, reaching Regan Plaza in five minutes flat. It was the only place he could think of to contact Ilya, except the farm, and it was too dangerous for Richie to tail him there.

Mitchell pushed open the café's door and listened as the bell announced his arrival. He peered through the gloom for some sign of life. It came a moment later when Daria appeared through the red beads. Instead of the warm greeting Mitchell was used to from her the old woman gazed at him surprised, a look of wariness in her pale eyes.

"What are you doing here? Ilya will not be pleased."

Mitchell smiled down at her, knowing that she would be friend or foe depending on what he said next.

"It's Ilya I've come to see. I need to contact him and I have no way except Elza."

"Then use her. You should not be here. This place has been watched since Elza disposed of the man."

Claude Brunet. Richie had told him the agent's name. Mitchell shook his head and gave Daria a fond look. It felt genuine and he knew that he'd known her since he was a child.

"Elza is nowhere to be found, Daria. I have looked around Scrabo Tower and she has gone."

A worried look crossed the old woman's face and Mitchell knew that he had her attention. Raising the possibility that Elza had been snatched would bring Ilya running, then Mitchell would find out what he knew about Karen and Emmie's disappearance. After a moment's hesitation Daria nodded Mitchell to a seat and hobbled towards the phone. She dialled a number, shielding it from his gaze and then murmured a few words of Russian that Mitchell understood. Ilya was coming, now all he had to do was wait. Richie would do the rest.

***

Richie stood on West Street, watching the turn-off to the square. He scanned each passing pedestrian; waiting for the man that he was certain would come. He wasn't disappointed. Ten minutes later a white-haired man walked purposefully past him and turned towards the café. He was Ilya Tabakov; there was no doubt of that. Even if he hadn't looked Slavic, Mitchell had described him perfectly.

Ilya walked briskly through the narrow streets, turning occasionally to ensure that he wasn't being tailed. Richie followed at a distance, pressing himself back against the side-streets' high walls and finding cover in the shadows cast by the afternoon sun.

As Ilya reached the square he gave a final backward glance then he pushed at the café's door, stepping warily into the darkness inside. He knew that Mitchell would kill him if he'd worked out that they had his wife and child. What he said next could save his life.

Richie watched as Ilya altered his expression from wariness to greeting as he entered the café, and imagined the thoughts running through the old man's mind. Survival would be top of his list, bargaining would be next. Richie wished that he could see what was happening inside but the Russians swept the café too frequently for any surveillance camera to survive. The wire that Mitchell was wearing would have to be enough.

Ilya's eyes adjusted to the gloom and he strode towards his surrogate son, his arms outstretched in hello. He halted abruptly at the look on Mitchell's face. Mitchell couldn't hide the venom in his eyes and in a split second Ilya saw that Mitchell knew his family had gone, and exactly who was to blame. Ilya was sad that they'd had to do it, but he'd known that Elza was right. Mitchell was wavering about giving them his work; the kidnap of his wife and child was the only leverage they had. He had to explain that before Mitchell killed him but the look on Mitchell's face said he only had seconds.

Jeff Mitchell moved towards Ilya with a speed that shocked them all. Daria gasped in surprise, glancing at each man's face in turn and knowing instantly that something was very wrong. She moved to step in between them but Mitchell stilled her with a look, then his hand shot to Ilya's throat without a word. He lifted the old man up and backwards, slamming him hard against the café wall, then he held him there, watching dispassionately as Ilya gasped for breath. Ilya's eyes rolled and he tore at his adopted son's fingers, trying to break his grasp. Daria tugged frantically at Mitchell's arm, but he pushed her away with his free hand. When he finally spoke, Mitchell's voice was wild, like an animal's.

"Stay away Daria or I'll hurt you too."

Richie heard the snarl that passed for Mitchell's voice and wondered if he should intervene. If he killed Ilya they would lose their contact and Mitchell's family. A second later Richie stopped wondering as Mitchell's voice became a cold hiss, saying that he'd got himself under control.

"Where are they?"

Ilya's eyes widened and Mitchell watched dispassionately as his colour changed to blue and he sucked frantically for air. Logic told Mitchell that he had to loosen his grip or kill Ilya, and a dead spy couldn't tell him where his family was. But hatred made him squeeze for a moment longer, savouring Ilya's gasps for breath. Hatred for what he'd done to Karen and Emmie, and to him when he was a child. Mitchell revelled in the feeling for a moment, sensing that one more squeeze would snap the old man's neck then he loosened his grip and watched as Ilya fell to the café floor like lead.

Daria rushed forward and Mitchell allowed her, staring coldly down at them both. The old woman glared at him, a stream of Russian invective spewing from her mouth. Her last few words were clear. "Where did you learn to do that?

Mitchell shook his head. He had no idea. They obviously hadn't taught him trade-craft or she wouldn't have been so shocked, yet it felt like something that he'd known all his life. Mitchell ripped Ilya's jacket open, reaching inside for his pistol. He'd seen the Makarov there the last time they'd met and Ilya wasn't getting a chance to use it. Mitchell motioned the old couple to two chairs then slipped-off the pistol's safety, pointing it straight at Ilya's head

Richie listened to the gun's slide pull back and smiled to himself. Mitchell had been in the military, he must have learned how to handle a gun then. Combat training too? As soon as Richie thought it he shook his head. No. He'd seen Mitchell's record. He'd been a doctor stationed in Balad, the main medical refuge in Iraq, so where the hell had he learned his fighting skills? There were three people in the café wondering that as well.

Ilya rubbed at his neck and tried to speak. He was shocked by the broken sound that emerged, but not as shocked as he was by what had just occurred. He'd reckoned on Mitchell being angry, but Ilya thought that he more than anyone would understand; they had to ensure the mission. The look in Jeff Mitchell's eyes said he understood nothing but hatred right now.

"They are safe."

The words wheezed out of Ilya Tabakov in a whisper that Richie could barely make out. If they were designed to reassure Mitchell then they failed.

"Where are they?"

Ilya's next words might sign his death warrant. When he

heard what they were Richie had to admire the old man's balls.

"They…they are safe. They will not be harmed if you do your work."

The sound that came next nearly burst Richie's eardrum. He yanked out his earpiece with a loud "Ow!" Mitchell had taken a shot! That hadn't been in the plan. Richie replaced his receiver and listened for the screams that said that someone was dead, but there were none. It had just been a warning that Mitchell meant business. When the gun's report died down Mitchell spoke again.

"I'll ask you again, Ilya. Where are they?"

Ilya looked into his adopted son's eyes and recognised what he saw. This was no calm scientist, this was a man who would kill him and not even blink. Ilya didn't know where he'd come from but he knew he was dealing with a very different man from the one he'd raised. The old spy re-calculated swiftly then exhaled, signalling defeat.

"Elza's holding them in an old warehouse at Brooklyn Waterfront."

"Address."

Mitchell slid the gun's mechanism back again menacingly. His voice was unwavering and Richie could hear an undertone that said he really wanted to kill. In that second he knew that Mitchell would shoot unless Ilya told him the truth, and perhaps even then. Fresh desperation tinged the old man's voice.

"Van Brunt Street, near the Gowanus Expressway. The dockers' family welfare centre."

The woman started babbling in Russian and Mitchell turned on her. "Be quiet!"

Daria fell silent, a soldier recognising a very real threat. Richie heard footsteps and he visualised Mitchell crossing the room to stand in front of Ilya. He was right. Mitchell's next words were a whisper that only Ilya and Richie could hear.

"If that bitch Elza has harmed a hair on their heads, I'll find you and kill you, old man. Very slowly. Right after I kill her."

Mitchell looked around for something to rope his prisoners together then he ripped the phone from the wall and used the cable to tie them both to their chairs. He grabbed Ilya's cell-phone and left the café without a backward look. Richie watched Mitchell emerge into the daylight and scan the square, then walk quickly towards West Street. Richie scanned the square for a moment longer to make sure that they weren't being followed, then he went to meet Jeff Mitchell at their agreed rendezvous.

***

Magee tapped his inhaler on the desk until he'd managed to annoy himself then he glanced at the clock, wondering what was holding-up his call. He walked to his office door and stood watching his staff at their work, counting the new faces drafted-in to replace the ones who had gone. Chapman, Brunet and Whitman; all lost or dead. And now Pereira, running away to a new life. Death and mobility were curses of the job, but that was four gone in two weeks. Somebody up there hated him.

Only Richie, Dane and Howard were left. Maybe he should ask that Lemanski woman to come up from Miami; at least she was sparky. Magee's thoughts were disturbed by the buzz of his intercom and he stabbed at it quickly.

"Yes?"

It was Lily, his P.A. She was bright and pretty and so was her voice. The girl deserved a medal for working with him. Even he knew he was a grumpy sod.

"You have a visitor, sir. An Agent Schofield."

Magee nodded to himself resignedly. He should have known that Al Schofield would come down in person. Special Ops were never going to sanction this over the phone. He pressed the buzzer again and spoke.

"Send him in please, Lily. And bring me the Evans file as well."

***

Richie pulled the sedan onto the wasteland, scanning the area for signs that they were being watched. He couldn't see anyone, but that didn't mean they weren't there. He peered through the windshield and then back at the GPS. They were in the right place but the only building around was a derelict concrete monolith with bricked-up windows and graffiti-ed walls. Even the agency had better welfare facilities than this.

Jeff Mitchell had been like a coiled spring the whole way there, now he was wrenching his seat-belt free and reaching for the handle of the door. Anger was making him careless and Richie said as much.

"Calm down. We need to look around first. I'm going to park over there."

He indicated the wall nearest the building's main door. Every window was blocked up so they couldn't be seen by someone looking out. It would give them cover for a while. Richie pulled the car parallel to the wall and they climbed out, pressing themselves flat against the concrete while he scanned the wasteland again. From what Mitchell said Elza Silin was lethal so he wasn't taking any chances. Mitchell went to move ahead and Richie hissed angrily at him, pulling him back into line.

"Me agent, you scientist. Remember that"

As Richie said it he remembered Mitchell's sang-froid in the café and wondered who was more lethal, Elza or him. They inched forward slowly until they'd reached the heavy main door, its paint peeling from years of weather and neglect. Richie pushed gently at the wood and winced as the door creaked, praying that their quarry was too high up to have heard. He was wrong.

Elza Silin startled at the sound and tore her gaze away from Karen Mitchell's face. She moved swiftly to the window and scanned the street. There was nothing to see, but whoever it was could be hiding. They could have parked on the building's blind side. Elza readied her Heckler-Koch and turned, just in time to see the look of hope in Karen's eyes. She'd heard the sound as well.

The Russian untied Karen's ankles and nudged her to her feet, signalling her to take Emmie into the corner. Re-checking the tape on their mouths and then reinforcing it with more; Elza positioned herself in front of them and waited. The noise might have been nothing. Ilya hadn't called to say that he was coming and no-one else knew that she was here. Then something occurred to her. Elza reached into her jacket for her phone, pressing dial without intending to talk. If it rang and Ilya answered it would tell her something. If he didn't it would say something as well. The call cut to answerphone, leaving her none the wiser.

Karen stared at Elza's back as she made the call, searching for her most vulnerable spot. Her eyes fell on the younger woman's legs, clad in tight jeans. One kick to the back of her knee could bring her down for long enough to grab the gun. All those self-defence classes Mitchell had made her take might not have been in vain.

Elza glanced back at Karen as if she'd read her thoughts and caught the determined look on her face. She reached down and grabbed Emmie, throwing her on the ground in front of her feet and then pointed the MP5's barrel down. The message was clear; try something and my first shot goes in the kid's head. Karen sat back, defeated, and prayed that the noise meant that help was near. Jeff must have noticed them gone by now. He would come looking, she was certain he would.

Richie climbed the stairs slowly, clearing each floor as they passed. Mitchell moved behind him like he'd been trained, turning each corner quickly, with his gun poised. Richie would worry later about how a scientist knew how to do that, probably watching too many cop shows on TV. But there was something about the way Mitchell moved that screamed combat vet.

Suddenly they heard a noise from the floor above. A soft thud, as if something small had been dropped. Richie felt Mitchell's tension heighten, saying that he'd heard it too. Richie raised a hand to still the man behind him and then indicated the next landing, where the floor split into left and right. Nothing about the sound had said which direction to take so Richie signalled Mitchell towards the right, positioning himself on the left. He turned briefly to stare at Mitchell, his gaze a silent reminder of what they'd discussed in the car. Elza was to be taken alive if possible, but she couldn't be allowed to escape. As it stood now, Ilya might still believe that Mitchell was acting alone; just a loving father, desperate to protect his family. With a bit of explaining Ilya would forgive him and Mitchell could go back to work, with the Alliance none the wiser. But if Elza escaped she would tell them Mitchell was working with a federal agent and a nine month operation would be blown.

The two men ascended the stairs in silence, pressing themselves back against the wall. At the landing they split off left and right. Richie turned left, moving down a corridor with rooms off it and a final door at its end. He cleared the rooms quickly as he went, knowing that any spy worth their salt would be waiting behind the end door. It was the best vantage point. Richie reached it just as Mitchell did the same on the right. They glanced at each other and then at the last two doors, kicking as hard as they could and entering the rooms with only seconds to make their choice.

As soon as Elza heard the kick she jerked her machine-pistol reflexly towards the door, pressing the trigger as she aimed for the intruder's head. Karen saw her aim shift away from Emmie and returned to her earlier plan, kicking Elza's knees as hard as she could and bringing her crashing to the floor. It was all the diversion that Richie needed. He scanned the room and saw Elza's gun, realising that he only had time for one shot. He made it count. If you only had one shot there was no ambiguity, head or chest; it was head every time. Richie's bullet whistled through the air and found its mark, but not before Elza Silin had managed to fire as well.

Mitchell scanned the empty room he'd entered just as shots rang out on the building's far side. He raced across the stairwell, down the corridor and into the small room. The sight that greeted Mitchell made his heart sink. His tiny daughter was lying on the floor with Elza slumped across her. There was blood everywhere; on Emmie's dress and face and soaking into her blonde hair. Mitchell heard nothing for a moment, only the shots ringing in his ear and then the sound of Karen's screams ripped through the air, forcing their way through the tape across her mouth.

"EMMIE, EMMIE..."

Karen Mitchell moved faster than she'd ever thought she could and pulled the woman's body off her child, pushing it roughly across the floor. She gathered Emmie in her arms and cradled her, pressing her ear against her child's chest and watching anxiously for its rise and fall. Finally she nodded to herself and smiled, tears streaming down her cheeks. Mitchell took them both in his arms, embracing them, his own tears mingling with his wife's. He glanced at the woman lying on the floor, her wide, unseeing eyes saying that Elza was dead. He was glad. Death was too good for her, but it would keep his cover safe.

A loud moan from the doorway reminded Mitchell that they weren't alone and he broke away from his family and headed for its source. Richie was lying in the corner, pressing hard on his bloodied shoulder. He gave Mitchell a rueful smile.

"Time for a refresher at the shooting range. I'm getting slow. She would never have got a shot off a year back."

Mitchell smiled gratefully and bent down to check Richie's wound. His left shoulder had a nasty graze but the bullet that had caused it was lodged in the wall behind. Part of a spray of Elza's bullets that formed a line six feet above the floor.

"You were lucky. She was aiming for your head."

"I know."

Richie nodded towards Karen and smiled.

"She missed. Thanks to your wife."

Mitchell glanced at Karen questioningly but her eyes were on her child. Explanations could wait. Right now, Emmie and Richie needed to be checked-out at a hospital and Elza Silin was heading for the morgue. The operation was still intact and Richie had kept his side of the bargain. Soon it would be time for him to keep his.

***

"You realise that this is impossible. Washington will never wear it."

Al Schofield tugged at his jacket, readjusting its perfect fit as Magee scrutinised his face. Schofield's features were a recipe for disaster; each one mis-sized or set a millimetre too far out of place. The overall effect was curious but not ugly; what the French called 'Jolie-laide'. Magee smiled inwardly, wondering what would happen if his visitor could read his thoughts. He shook his inhaler and puffed at it twice before speaking.

"The prize will be worth any crud Washington has to swallow."

"How so? Evans is a traitor, so anything he gives us is suspect. And then there's this so-called research, which frankly I find it hard to get excited about. Carbon atoms affecting human life! The nerds have been cloning sheep for years, so what's new? We'll lift Evans and I'll make him tell the truth. "

Magee shook his head tiredly and stared at his guest. The ignorance of some people in power was just depressing.

"Cloning is just copying, Al. Like if I made another one of you, God forbid. This is something else completely. Mitchell's work can alter the actual building blocks of life."

Magee could see that his cod science was passing over Schofield's head, so he shrugged, gave up on any attempt at educating him and went for shock value.

"This can build monsters that will do anything you want, Al. And a very dangerous country wants to buy the recipe."

The penny dropped and Schofield's face with it. He leaned urgently across the desk.

"Which country?"

Magee sighed, knowing that his point had flown straight over Schofield's head.

"The other countries are only one part of it; *we* want the research as well. And the man who is selling it.

But Magee still wasn't getting through. Schofield had returned to his favourite topic. Tom Evans.

"Get Evans in here. We'll make him tell us. Our interrogation methods have improved since he was an agent." Al Schofield waved his finger in Magee's face. "You were always too close to Evans. You've gone soft."

Magee swatted his hand away, refusing to rise to the bait. He sat forward, elbows on the desk and clasped his hands.

"Your desire for revenge against Evans is getting boring. So you were a Presidential Aide and he set your career back a few years. Boo-hoo. Get over it. Here's what's going to happen. We're going to give Tom Evans what he wants. *Everything* he wants."

An angry look crossed Schofield's face and he opened his mouth to object. Magee kept talking.

"And you're going to help arrange it. Because if you don't and the North Koreans get hold of this research, I'll make sure that *this* President knows your name and it definitely won't be in the way you want."

***

Karen wandered slowly around the family-room, picking up pictures and knickknacks and running her hand over the well-worn couch. She buried her fingers in the fake-fur throw across its back for comfort, as Mitchell and Richie watched her from the door. Karen stared at the glass doors that Elza had entered through and wanted to smash them. She knew that their fragility hadn't let her in, Elza had slipped the latch not broken the glass, but their very presence offended her now, symbolising everything vulnerable about their lives. Mitchell could read her mind and his decision took less than a second. They couldn't stay in this house.

He scanned the room, letting its familiarity sink in. It was his home, regardless of how briefly he remembered it, but it wasn't safe now. Mitchell wasn't worried for himself. He would be at work or the facility, and pretty soon he would be dead. But Karen and Emmie were still vulnerable.

Emmie was in hospital. She would be OK, but the drugs that Elza had given her were taking time to clear her system and it was better to be safe. She was well protected now; the armed guard Richie had posted outside her door would make damn sure of that. But Richie had been watching the house when Elza had broken in and it could happen again, no matter how many agents were around. It didn't matter to Mitchell if they killed him, but he couldn't allow his family to be used again, or worse, killed, for his work.

Richie watched them both and read their thoughts. "We'll move you to a safe house, Mrs Mitchell. We have plenty of them across New York." He turned to face Mitchell. "Until this is over you need your family safe."

Mitchell nodded then suddenly Karen gave a scream that shocked them both. It turned into a low-pitched moan that didn't stop. A keening sound, like at a Gaelic requiem where women mourn their loss. She was sitting on the small couch, doubled over, rocking herself back and forth as she cried. They couldn't see her face but the pain in her tears was impossible to ignore.

Both men moved instinctively towards her then Richie stopped himself, pulling back as Mitchell took his wife in his arms. Richie's urge to hold her shocked him and he turned away, but not before Jeff Mitchell had read the signs. Instead of being jealous he was strangely comforted by them. He wouldn't be around in the future to protect her, but Richie really cared. And he'd proved that he could be trusted with Karen and Emmie's lives.

Karen clung to her husband like a child, reliving the nightmare that Elza Silin had put them through and outlining her every fear. She needed a counsellor and when they got to the safe house they would get her one. Finally Karen's rocking slowed and her sobs became a sigh. When she spoke again her words were clear and what she said surprised both men.

"We're not leaving this house."

Richie went to protest but she stilled him with a glance.

"This is our family's home." Karen gazed at her husband. "I don't know exactly what's going on, but I trust you, Jeff." She shot Richie a watery smile. "I trust both of you. Do whatever you need to do to finish this and protect us from these people." A look of defiance filled her eyes. "Because no bastard from any country is making me leave my home."

***

Friday. 4 a.m.

Richie shifted uncomfortably in the armchair and finally gave up trying to sleep. He glanced at the clock. Four a.m. He was handing over at five so there was no point even trying any more. He unfolded himself from the leather chair and wandered, yawning, into the kitchen. One minute later he was staring into a coffee, deep in thought.

Karen would have to accept re-location eventually. If this went down the way that he thought it would then Russia would name Mitchell a traitor and make it open season on his wife and child. Richie's thoughts went to Jeff Mitchell. He was still hiding something, he was sure of it. Yes, Mitchell was going to give them his research, Richie believed him on that. So where was his 'but' coming from? Richie answered his own question. Mitchell wasn't giving them all of it, but he wasn't giving it to the Alliance either. Why? The answer hit Richie squarely between the eyes.

The dawning of realisation never got old and it was always unexpected. It couldn't be earned and it couldn't be planned for, it just appeared like a tree in heavy fog. Invisible the moment before, then suddenly there with all the substance that it would ever have. Richie suddenly knew that Mitchell thought something in his research was too dangerous to trust to anyone. Not even the U.S. Government. Mitchell was going to destroy it. He was sure of it.

Richie had a moment's thought that maybe it was for the best. Mitchell must know his own work's potential, if he thought it was too dangerous to exist then maybe it was. After all, who wouldn't un-invent the atomic bomb if they could? But the agent in him said no. If advanced research existed, then Mitchell had no right to hold it back if it could possibly be utilised for good.

A noise outside the kitchen made him jump and Richie grabbed instinctively for his gun, only to laugh a moment later when the cat wandered in. His imagination was playing tricks on him. Maybe he was imagining that Mitchell was hiding information too? He shook his head. No, Mitchell was definitely holding something back. Richie made up his mind to tell Magee his suspicions and trust in whatever he said.

***

Friday. 7.40 a.m.

Tom Evans stood for a moment gazing around the small office then he sat down and lit a cigarette, waiting for Magee to object. He was disappointed. Magee just kept staring at the screen in front of him, deep in thought. Evans could hear the whispers coming from outside and he smiled. He'd taken a certain amount of pleasure walking through the agency building's reception. The reception of a building that he'd been banished from eight years before. The wary looks hadn't bothered him. Nor had the knowledge that beneath their identikit jackets every agent wore a Glock and was itching for him to give them a reason to pull it. Evans smirked, remembering the hall of fame set high on one wall, with stars under each picture hailing patriotism and honour. Somewhere there was another wall for traitors and he knew his name was there.

The irony of his current situation didn't escape him. Define traitor. His crime had been too much belief in God and country, not too little, and being disillusioned by the truth. Instead of adopting the low-level cynicism that his colleagues seemed to have been born with, reciting their oaths from rote, he'd actually believed his. He'd believed it all, God, country and the American way. He'd even had faith in their political masters. Too much faith and look where it had got him.

Magee glanced up, watching the debate his old protégé was having in his head. It made him sad to know that Evans was still trying to make sense of what he'd done. He understood it perfectly, so why couldn't Tom? His fault hadn't been in believing too much, but in lashing out like a child when he'd found out that the fairy-tale wasn't true.

Magee stood up and gathered some papers, then gestured to a coffee area across the room, motioning Evans to sit across the low table from him, as if they were back in the café. Magee coughed once and glared at Evans' cigarette. Tom Evans smiled and stubbed it out. The look was all he'd wanted. Attention. Something to show that his old boss still gave a damn. Magee shrugged; more childish crap.

"I met with Schofield."

Magee's lack of preamble made Evans laugh. Magee was a man of few words and most of them barked. A quick shadow crossed the periphery of Evans' vision and he knew that a curious agent was lurking outside the room, not daring to pause too long for fear of Magee. It seemed that he was quite the celebrity. Evans decided to play Magee's word game and keep it brief.

"And?"

"Agreed."

Evans raised a sceptical eyebrow. Eight years in exile, treachery in the press and it was this simple. He didn't believe it and he said so.

"No way. Schofield's up to something."

Magee stared across the table and reached to pour them both coffees. Black, two sugars, just the way Evans liked it. He'd been touched that Magee had remembered in the coffee-house.

"I see that you've finally abandoned your naiveté, Tom."

"Not all of it, but I wouldn't trust that bastard as far as I could spit. Schofield has a life plan called 'Get Tom Evans'."

"It seems that you've replaced it with paranoia."

Magee half-smiled and Evans smiled back, shrugging an admission. "That's what eight years on the run does for you."

"Don't they call it 'on the lam'?"

"Only in James Cagney movies."

They descended into amiable silence and sipped at their drinks. Evans could hear the desks filling up outside and the eavesdropping agent being joined by several more. He glanced at his watch and tutted. Eight o'clock. He'd hoped to be out of there before the day-shift arrived. No chance of secrecy now. He glanced at Magee and saw that he wasn't worried; he was up to something. Evans tensed instinctively and Magee raised a hand in peace.

"I want us to talk."

Evans stared hard at Magee for a moment and then he slowly relaxed. The government could lift him now and throw away the key if they wanted to, except that they wouldn't. They needed him to get to the North Koreans and they were too big a catch for the agency to drop. He would walk out of here in an hour and go back to his life, and within weeks he'd be a free man, Magee would make sure of that.

But Evans' curiosity was piqued. Did Magee have an add-on? Something else that he needed him to do? It almost felt like the good old days. Tom Evans was surprised by how much he liked the thought.

***

Jeff Mitchell gazed through the bedroom window as the night turned into day. He glanced at his watch and then at his sleeping wife. The bruises on Karen's face would heal but he wasn't sure about the ones inside her head. She turned in her sleep and whimpered and Mitchell wanted to climb back in beside her and take her in his arms, but he had work to do and he needed to keep up his front.

Mitchell showered slowly in the bathroom where he'd first seen his wife, trying to remember her face through the steam. The feeling that went with the image was kindness; it was what Karen was. Loving and kind, always kind. A sob escaped from his chest, surprising him with its force. What was he crying about? His family's hurt? Or his own imminent death? There was no point crying about that, it was as inevitable as the dawn.

Mitchell shook off the mood and dressed quickly, then tiptoed softly down the stairs, lifting his briefcase and thinking of what was inside. He hadn't looked at the Archaeus file yet. That was today's shock; yesterday's had been bad enough. Mitchell nodded at the agent seated out on the deck, then at the one inside the hall; their position inside the house easier to hide than a sedan in the street. Then he lifted the keys to drive himself to work and find out the truth.

***

8.30 a.m.

Magee glanced at the office wall and Evans turned to see his target. It was a clock that he'd missed in his scan of the room. Magee was waiting for something. They'd covered the basics of his pardon in the first half-hour. He would get 20,000 dollars to start again and his slate would be wiped clean; no black marks. He could even take a job in law enforcement again, if that was what he wanted. Evans had shaken his head at the suggestion. He'd seen enough guns to last him a lifetime.

What else would he do? Magee was surprised by Evans' answer. He wanted to open a restaurant somewhere. He could cook well and host even better, and it was as far away from the violent world he'd spent his life in as it was possible to get. Somewhere in Italy, or maybe France; anywhere warm and relaxed.

Magee smiled as Evans' face lit up talking about it and he remembered the eager young agent that he'd met twenty years before. Tom Evans had been the best he'd ever trained, until he'd gone bad. Magee corrected himself quickly; Evans had never gone bad, he'd just had his ideals shattered and blown the whistle. Unfortunately he'd done it in the New York Times, and some people had never forgiven him for that. Wash your dirty linen by all means, just not in the Hudson.

Magee glanced at the clock again and Tom Evans stared at him, puzzled. His original thought that they were waiting for something was altered to someone. Magee had a meeting organised. But surely they couldn't be planning the operation yet? They'd barely had time to cover his benefits under the deal. Evans let his curiosity show.

"Are we meeting someone?"

"Yes."

Evans shifted irritably in his chair. "But we're less than halfway through. We haven't even discussed Scrabo."

Magee lifted a hand to still him. "The man that's coming will be helping you with the operation."

Evans sprang to his feet angrily. "I work alone. That was the deal!"

As soon as Evans said it he could hear how petulant it was. Magee gave him a jaded look. He didn't have the energy to placate anyone these days, much less a middle-aged man acting like a kid. He took a puff of his inhaler and waved Evans back to his seat.

"That's understood. He won't be working with you; he's on another strand of the operation."

Evans went to ask another question but Magee was saved by two sharp knocks at the door. A man's lean silhouette was visible through the glass. Magee shouted "enter" and as soon as the door swung back Evans saw that the man was shocked by his presence as well. Magee was up to his old tricks.

Richie stood in the doorway assessing the scene. When he'd phoned Magee asking him for a meeting he'd expected a one-on-one, not a group hug. There was no way that he would detail yesterday's events with some stranger in the room. Magee saw the questions on both men's faces and pre-empted them.

"Tom Evans, this is Agent Richie Cartagena."

Evans sprang to his feet and extended his hand. Richie took it without thinking, shocked by the name that he'd just heard. Tom Evans was the agency's bête noir. What the hell was he doing in the building, never mind here with Magee?

Richie scanned the man in front of him for threats, getting ready to move. There were none, so he took his hand back and sat beside Magee in the only free chair. A shocked silence filled the room. Magee let it fester, watching each man's face in turn and enjoying the show. After a minute he spoke.

"Alright. First things first. You're both working the Mitchell case and I'm not listening to any arguments."

Evans went to object then stopped, remembering Magee's

earlier reassurance that he would work alone. Richie hadn't heard it and he sprang to his feet again.

"No way."

His words were unambiguous. Magee was their boss and he could order them to do whatever he wanted, but the image of Emmie Mitchell on the ground was making Richie brave.

"These people trust me. I won't put them at risk."

Evans lurched forward. "What people?"

Confusion flicked across Richie's face and they both looked at Magee. He yawned theatrically and then spoke.

"If you both tried listening for a moment, this would go much quicker." He waved Richie back to his seat and started speaking in a bored tone.

"OK. To recap. Jeff Mitchell has been researching carbon for years, following the discovery of Graphene. If you don't know what Graphene is, then find out, and fast. The whole world is working on new applications for it; worth billions. We've had Mitchell under surveillance for some time because of his association with Russian agents. We know that there's a small cell in the city, working out of a café in Regan Plaza."

Magee sipped his coffee and continued. "We got wind that Mitchell's research had progressed way beyond the work being done elsewhere, but we couldn't get any details. If we'd tailed him too closely, he could have bolted. Unfortunately we believe that Greg Chapman, one of our most experienced agents, acted on his own initiative and tried to find out." Magee paused for a moment, looking sad. "Chapman's been un-contactable for nearly a fortnight. The last sighting of him was entering Scrabo Tower. Chapman radioed that he was following Mitchell and then nothing, so we have to assume that he's dead."

Richie interjected. "I still think we should go in and look for him."

Magee and Evans shook their heads simultaneously. Evans spoke first.

"It would blow the whole operation. Mitchell's lab is secured both ways by codes and retinal scanning. If Chapman did manage to get in, he never got out. He must still be there somewhere."

Magee re-started. "In the past few weeks things have started getting messy. Claude Brunet, another of our agents, tailed Mitchell to the café and was killed. The café has become redundant since then. We know they've moved operations to a farm of some sort; Mitchell has a secondary lab there where he's continuing his research. We have its exact location, but there's only one road in and it's heavily guarded, so any attempt to steal Mitchell's research would fail." Magee's eyes clouded. "We lost a third agent, Brad Whitman, tracking Mitchell there."

Evans interrupted. "So Mitchell's research at Scrabo might not be the full extent of it?"

"We're certain that it isn't, but we don't know how far his other work has gone."

"Neil Scrabo wants to get his hands on it."

Richie interjected. "But surely he owns Mitchell's research? He pays him to do it."

Evans shook his head.

"Only the work that Mitchell does on Scrabo Enterprise's behalf, and they think Mitchell needs more time to develop that further. I'm not so sure."

Richie nodded vaguely, giving nothing away. Magee carried on talking.

"Another recent development is that Dr Mitchell is very ill."

Evans looked shocked and Richie realised that he hadn't been fully briefed.

"He has an inoperable brain tumour. Even with radiotherapy and a lot of luck only a third make it beyond a year."

"He could become desperate."

"Desperate in more ways than one. Mitchell's intellect is his life. The race will be on for him to finish his work while he can still think clearly."

Evans shook his head. "There's no way Neil Scrabo knows

any of this. If he did he'd reckon Mitchell had got further than he said and he'd have already sold his research to the highest bidder."

What Magee said next shocked them both. "That's exactly what I'm banking on." He saw their shocked expressions and smiled. "The sooner that Scrabo thinks Mitchell has cracked his carbon research, the better; he'll think that Mitchell has something worth stealing." He turned to Evans. "That's where you come in."

Richie spluttered out his coffee and indicated at Evans. "You can't be serious. You're going to let this traitor and Neil Scrabo get their hands on Mitchell's research!"

Before Magee could stop them both men were on their feet and Tom Evans' hand was on his gun. "What did you just call me?"

Evans' voice was a growl and he slid his Glock from its holster and pressed it hard against Richie's chest, before Richie had time to move. Magee smiled at Evans' speed; he still had it.

Richie stared at Tom Evans without flinching and leaned forward into the barrel, repeating the word. "Traitor."

Magee watched them like a tired parent for a moment then he moved faster than either of them had ever seen. He knocked Evans' gun vertically with his left hand and shoved the men to the floor one by one with his right. He stood above them wearing a look of disgust, his voice cold.

"Grow up both of you, for God's sake! This is the biggest threat to national security for years and you're having a pissing contest."

Magee sat down abruptly and glared as they clambered back to their seats. Then he turned to Richie.

"Apologise, Richie, and don't even think about arguing with me."

Richie shot Evans a look of hatred and muttered a grudging apology under his breath.

Magee turned to look at Tom Evans. He was retrieving his

gun from the floor. "And you."

Evans shook his head hard. "Fuck you, Magee. He's responsible. And you, for arranging this blind date."

Magee's voice tightened. "Apologise, Tom, if you ever want to see your pardon."

The men locked eyes for a moment then Evans shrugged, saying the right words and meaning none of them. It would have to do. Magee turned back to the matter in hand.

"Now. Can we get back to work? The sooner Neil Scrabo thinks that Mitchell's progressed his research enough, the sooner he can steal it and arrange the drop with the North Koreans. That's where Tom comes in. He's going to set Scrabo and the Koreans up for us to grab."

Richie's jaw dropped. North Koreans; when in hell did they get involved? He decided not to ask just yet. He had his own secrets and he wasn't keen to discuss them in front of Evans.

Magee squinted at Richie, knowing that he was hiding something but letting it pass for now.

"Tom was never a traitor, Richie, he was foolish. He got burnt and shot his mouth off to the press. Remember that he's giving us Scrabo and the Koreans. We need his help to pull this off, so you're to give him all the support that he needs. Understand?"

They watched astonished as Richie shook his head. "No."

Magee stared at the younger man. "What do you mean no? Who the hell are you to question a direct order?"

Richie gazed at him coolly. "If you calm down I'll tell you. A lot's happened since yesterday, boss."

Magee glared and waited for him to start. Richie knew that he'd better make it good or he'd be pulling a twenty-four-hour shift.

"Karen and Emily Mitchell were kidnapped." Magee's gasp was gratifying and Richie struggled to keep the smug look off his face. "They were taken by a Russian woman called Elza Silin, on the orders of Ilya Tabakov."

Evans leaned forward, interrupting. "But aren't they part of the cell based at the café? Why would they kidnap Mitchell's family?"

Richie answered without looking at him. "They are, but I'll come back to that later. Mitchell's first loyalty is to his family, so when he found out that they'd gone he came out of the house to the sedan."

It was Magee's turn to interrupt. "How in hell did he know you were there?"

Richie laughed. "Give him some credit! The man has a PhD from Harvard and sedans aren't invisible."

Magee waved him on, making a mental note to improve surveillance training.

"Mitchell asked me for my help to find them and he said that he'd help us in return. To cut a long story short, Ilya Tabakov had commissioned the woman Silin to kidnap Mitchell's family, to pressure him to continue his work. It seems they've been starting to doubt Mitchell's loyalty in the past few weeks."

"Why?" It was Evans' question but Richie directed his answer to Magee.

"No idea, but they must have noticed something. Maybe it's because of Mitchell's tumour but he certainly seems a lot nicer than the man we were briefed on nine months ago. Anyway, we found Silin, but she had no intention of giving up easily. Shots were fired and she died."

Richie winced involuntarily and Magee noticed for the first time that he was holding his left shoulder lower than his right.

"You got shot." It was a statement not a question and Richie was surprised by the concern in Magee's voice.

"Just a flesh wound. I'll mend."

Evans watched the exchange thoughtfully. Magee's fondness for the younger man was obvious. It reminded him of how he'd used to treat him.

"And Mitchell's wife and child?"

Richie nodded. "Alive. The girl's in hospital with dehydration." His lip curled angrily. "The bitch drugged her. But Karen's fine; just cuts and bruises. I have them both under protection. I called in a few favours to keep it low-key."

Karen. Both men had noticed the soft way Richie said her name. Magee bookmarked the lecture on over-familiarity for later.

"Silin had no intention of letting them go alive. Seems she had dreams of a white picket fence with Mitchell in Mother Russia and they were in her way."

"So Mitchell's relationship with Tabakov is completely blown?"

Richie shook his head firmly.

"No. Tabakov doesn't know that I was involved. He thinks Mitchell acted alone to protect his family. If anything he's being conciliatory with Mitchell now, apologising for ever doubting him, etc."

He paused, considering his next words carefully and then he decided to say them straight.

"Mitchell's a sleeper agent. Russian."

The look of astonishment on Magee's face made Richie wish he could take a photo.

"What? How did we not know this?"

Richie shook his head. "No idea. Mitchell seemed as shocked about it as I was. Says he's only just found out. Apparently he was selected on the basis of his IQ when he was a kid and brought to the U.S. to assimilate when he was ten."

"What's his real name?"

"He doesn't know, but he says Tabakov calls him Durak. It's a term of endearment in Russia. Tabakov and Daria Kaverin became an uncle and aunt of some sort when Mitchell arrived here, but Mitchell swears that he can't remember any of it."

"Do you believe him?"

Evans knew that Magee's question meant he valued Richie's opinion. Maybe he'd better take the rude bastard seriously.

Richie nodded slowly.

"Yes, I do. Mitchell says that he can't remember anything at all before the past two weeks. Maybe it's because of the tumour, I don't know. But whatever it is I'll tell you this, his loyalty isn't with the Russians anymore." He paused then thought of something. "Maybe he's just lived here so long that he's shifted allegiance to the States?"

Magee nodded; Stockholm syndrome without the kidnap. "So now what?"

"Mitchell made me a promise. If I helped him get his family back safe and sound, he would work for us against Tabakov."

Evans snorted sceptically. "And you believe him?"

For the first time in ten minutes Richie looked at Tom Evans. His eyes were unreadable.

"Yes. I do." Richie turned back to Magee. "Mitchell's dying, sir and he wants his family safe. He's also questioning the safety of putting his research in the Alliance's hands."

Magee cut in. "The Alliance?"

Richie nodded. "The Russians aren't working alone. Iran is involved."

"Shit!"

No-one spoke for a moment as the implications sank in. Richie broke the silence first. "Mitchell is going to keep working, so that they won't catch on. But he'll be giving us his research, not them."

"If he doesn't give them something they'll kill him."

"He's not worried about that. His days are already numbered. But he's asked for his family to be re-located."

Magee nodded. It was small price to pay for life-changing research. Richie was still talking.

"Mitchell will give them some false research to play for time. He's mocking it up right now. It'll have to be close enough to fool their scientists, but it won't be the real deal. Tabakov and the old woman will leave the country once it's handed over. They think the Mitchell's are going as well."

Magee thought for a moment and then asked the only question that mattered.

"When?"

Chapter Thirty-Four

It was only a matter of time before the call came, and when it did Jeff Mitchell was prepared. Knowing that Karen and Emmie were safe had given him peace. Knowing that Ilya had ordered their kidnap had made him hate.

His cell-phone rang with the familiar number and Mitchell placed it on his desk, watching it vibrate just long enough to worry the man on the other end. It stopped ringing and then started again, sounding more desperate this time. Mitchell smiled, knowing that it was wishful thinking. Finally he pressed answer and sat in silence, waiting for the caller to speak.

"Durak."

Mitchell smiled coldly at the phone, savouring the fear in the old man's voice.

"Durak, it's me, Ilya. Forgive me."

Mitchell shook his head as if the man could see him. He would never forgive Ilya for what he'd done, but the best revenge would be the one that Ilya didn't see heading his way. Mitchell enjoyed a minute of pleading then he lifted the phone and spoke, moderating his anger with a neutral tone.

"What do you want?"

Ilya said a silent thanks to the God that he didn't believe in then he spoke again.

"I didn't know Elza would harm them. You must believe me."

Mitchell allowed righteous anger to tinge his words. If he seemed too ready to forgive it would be unbelievable, and Ilya's belief in him was essential to their plan.

"You didn't know. You didn't know! Do you think I'm stupid?"

"It's the truth, I swear."

"Why should I trust you when you didn't trust me?"

Ilya spoke again, conciliation in every word.

"I know, I know. I would feel the same if I were you. I must have been mad to doubt you. You are my son."

Mitchell couldn't resist the insult, knowing that it would hit the man right where it hurt.

"I am not your son. You kidnapped me from my parents, just as Elza kidnapped my family."

Mitchell was shocked by the old man's next words. "We did not kidnap you! Your father was proud that you would have a different life. You were the brightest and the best. He was ill and it was his dying wish that you should help your country."

His father was dead! An image flashed into Mitchell's mind. A wooden house at the edge of a lake. A woman standing holding a small girl's hand. They were waving at him. His mother! And he had a sister! The urge to know more overwhelmed Mitchell and he took a risk.

"I want their names, Ilya. My mother and my sister."

"I cannot, you know that. Please don't ask me."

He had to. Emmie had a grandmother and aunt somewhere that she didn't even know. He owed her that knowledge. Mitchell's voice cooled.

"Tell me or you can whistle for your research. And we both know what your Iranian buddies will do to you then."

Ilya swallowed hard and Mitchell could read his thoughts. He was weighing the odds. If he told Mitchell then the Russians might kill him. If he didn't then the Iranians definitely would. Mitchell heard the old spy's surrender before he heard his words.

"If I give you their names will you swear to go back to work?"

"When I have them in my hand."

Ilya sighed. The boy was hard, but then he'd taught him well.

"Tonight then. At the house, at eight."

The phone clicked off and Jeff Mitchell stared into space, reaching into the past. Vague fragments of sound and people's faces ran through his mind, until he stumbled again upon the wooden house. He felt its comfort warm him and he smiled, remembering his mother, and looking forward to eight o'clock.

***

"OK. You both know what you're doing. Tom, go back and act like nothing has changed. Do whatever Scrabo asks. When Mitchell gives us the false research, we'll get a copy to you to set up the exchange with the Koreans."

"When?

Magee nodded at Richie to take over.

"Mitchell's giving us the false version before he gives it to the Alliance. The handover to Tabakov is set for Sunday night at twenty-two hundred. Set up your meeting with the North Koreans for then. We need to exchange at the same time."

Magee interjected. "I'll act as liaison. It's imperative that the two exchanges go down simultaneously. If word leaks out on either side, lives will be put at risk." He looked at them both pointedly. "That includes you two."

"OK. So Scrabo gets lifted at the North Korean exchange. He gets stopped and we get the N.K. agents?"

"That's about the size of it. They'll have valuable intelligence that we can use."

"And Neil Scrabo?"

"Guantanamo probably, or federal prison."

Evans smirked at the thought of the silver fox wearing an orange jumpsuit.

Richie leaned forward. "What about my side?"

Magee rubbed his chin thoughtfully before speaking. "If Mitchell leads us to the Alliance, the intelligence haul will be massive. Not to mention strengthening the U.S. stance in the Middle East. But we won't lift Tabakov or Javadi immediately after the exchange. I want to see who else they lead us to."

"Russia will have egg on its face."

Magee shook his head. "It will embarrass the hell out of their government for sure, but all they'll get is a rap across the knuckles and a few diplomats expelled. They kick out a few of ours; we do the same to them. It's the game. The Iranians are much more valuable to us."

Evans interjected.

"And Mitchell's real research? It's ground-breaking stuff."

"Yes, it is. If he's willing to hand the real stuff over and brief our science teams, then he'll spend his last few months with his family in re-located peace. And his wife and child will be looked after when Mitchell dies."

Richie nodded. It was a fair deal. Karen and Emmie would be targets for retribution, so they had to start a new life far away from New York. The idea made him unexpectedly sad.

Evans stood and shook hands with Magee then he turned to Richie, watching as he slid his hand into his pocket. Magee saw it too.

"You know Richie, sometimes you can be a real prick. Tom gave years of service to this country."

Evans shook his head and gave a wry smile. "He'll shake my hand when he realises that he's wrong. I can wait."

Evans opened the office door then nodded goodbye and headed back to work. Magee turned towards his desk and lifted a file, ignoring Richie for a full minute. Finally he looked at the younger man grudgingly, annoyed at his childishness towards his old friend.

"Well?"

"There's something else I need to tell you, sir, but I'm not sure where to start."

***

7 p.m.

Mitchell drove quickly into the farm clearing, scanning the small house for signs of life. The windows were dark and there were no cars parked outside. Good, he'd got here first. He had time to look around.

He parked quickly behind the one-storey building and punched a key-code into the door before scanning his thumb print onto a pad. All that security for research that they'd never get. Mitchell allowed himself a wry smile; it changed to anger at the memory of Emmie in the hospital that afternoon. She was chatting now, but warily, and the bruises on her face were stark reminders of Elza's malice. He pictured Karen beside her bed, soothing her quietly, both of them permanently hurt. All sanctioned by Ilya, his ever loving Dad.

As Mitchell walked through the double-doors into the lab he halted suddenly, scanning the room. The cages still sat empty but now they were labelled with species, awaiting their new guests. He wouldn't be there for the house-warming party. Mitchell switched on his computer and ran instinctively through the firewalls, long past wondering how he knew things that he couldn't recall. He searched the directories for some sign of the Archaeus PDF but there was none. Good, he'd managed to wipe it completely. If he couldn't find it, knowing that it had been there, then anyone else would have one hell of a job.

A sudden thought occurred to Mitchell and he glanced at the doorway, searching for something. Then he saw it. It was unmistakable; a degaussing loop wound around the door. Ilya had installed the ultimate security tool. Anyone who tried to remove the computer would wipe its hard drive as they walked through the door and the last vestiges of his research would disappear for good. Ilya's security measures would lose him the very thing he wanted. Mitchell made up his mind to do it before the handover happened on Sunday. In the meantime he had work to do.

He searched every drawer and cupboard but they were all empty, waiting for him to list his needs. Excellent; the Alliance didn't know how far he'd got with his research. All they knew was that he was working on animals and whatever fragments of information they'd had the wit to retain from the café. They trusted him enough not to watch him. Big mistake. It would be child's play to create plausible fake research that they would believe.

Without warning an image of Greg Chapman flashed into Mitchell's mind. Their connection was still a puzzle and he made up his mind to ask Richie about Chapman soon. The agency'd had him under surveillance for a long time; perhaps Greg Chapman had spoken to him? It wouldn't explain everything that he knew about Chapman, but it would help stop him thinking he was going mad.

His brain tumour was a bastard and his memory was shot to hell, but Mitchell's fingers still flew across the keys. He slipped in the flash-drive and clicked-on a file marked 'trials'. Pages full of equations scrolled in front of his eyes. They might as well have been written by a stranger but Mitchell whistled in admiration at the work. It made perfect sense. Most scientists in his field had focussed on Graphene's conductive properties, their applications to new carbon allotropes timid, if at all, but his work was different. He stared at a row of equations, smiling. By changing carbon's form in living things he'd made it into a method of creation instead of just another element. It was brilliant, even though he did say so himself.

Mitchell ran through the pages quickly. Past the painstaking tests at atomic level to the first stab at making things work. Embedded videos flashed onto the screen, some of them so revolting that he wanted to throw up. He'd been working on two strands of physical research; enhancing the electrical power of existing species, like the monkey he'd seen three days before. And this; trying to create new species, bred specifically for the electricity they could generate. The results were revolting.

Bloody messes and distorted forms, dead before they could breathe. His creations certainly hadn't rivalled nature's, despite his brilliance.

As Mitchell scrolled on through the months the results improved. Some new species lived for minutes, before sucking in their last gasp of air. Others had features that could almost have passed for animal; in the right light. He clicked on a file dated two months earlier and as the video started to play Mitchell gasped aloud. The creature in front of him was from no species that he'd ever seen. Small, smooth-skinned and pink, like a new born. New born what? It turned its head slowly, gazing at the camera with sunken eyes. They were red like an albino's, but there was no photophobic blinking at the light, just the steady gaze of curiosity and a faint smile from the maw below.

Bile filled Mitchell's mouth and he averted his eyes from the image, scrolling frantically for information. He found it under a heading labelled 'Breakthrough: August 5th'. He read how specimen CH1 had lived for two weeks and generated one thousand volts! The trial had provided valuable information. The scientist in him was scarcely able to believe the words. But there was no doubt. He'd managed to create a completely new species! Not a plant this time but a living thing, and it could generate electricity, just as the monkey had. Carbon research had joined Frankenstein's. But he wasn't a geneticist so how had biophysics taken him this route?

Mitchell stared into space for a moment, unable to shake the feeling that there was even more than this. Scrolling to the end of the document didn't reveal it. Neither did a full search of the files. Whatever else there was it wasn't on the flash-drive. Mitchell knew instantly that whatever he'd discovered was in the Archaeus PDF that he'd taken home. He shuddered in disbelief at what he'd done. How could he have promised this work to anyone, never mind to foreign powers? The sleeper agent in him smiled ruefully. What was foreign to him anyway?

He came from somewhere very far away.

The sound of a car pulling into the clearing made Mitchell switch off the computer and pocket the flash-drive. He reached the wood-lined hall just as Ilya opened the front door. The old man was carrying an envelope in one hand; his other moved to his pocket. A gun. Mitchell smiled inwardly. It was what he would have brought if he'd been meeting a man who wanted him dead.

The men stood facing each other in silence. Mitchell watched as beads of sweat formed on Ilya's brow, staring idly as one trickled down his nose and fell onto his shirt. The aged Russian gazed fearfully at him and Mitchell smiled, malice filling his eyes. His voice was clear.

"Someday I may kill you, Ilya…"

Mitchell paused long enough for Ilya's hand to move towards his gun, then for his mind to register the word "someday" and hesitate. Was Mitchell playing with him? He was a man filled with hate and that made him a formidable opponent, but...

"But not today."

The relieved slump of the old spy's shoulders was almost comical to watch. Ilya stood hunched for a moment, looking like the elderly man that he was, then he held out the envelope to his adopted son. Mitchell walked forward slowly until he stood in Ilya's personal space, watching as he stepped back in response.

Mitchell snatched the envelope and gazed at it, turning it over in his hand, then he glared at the old communist with open contempt. He was reluctant to ask Ilya anything more, for the power that it would make him feel, but he needed to know.

"Are they alive?"

Ilya spoke quietly, his gruff voice tired with fear. "Yes. They are well."

"What do they know about me?"

"That you are a success in America and serving Mother Russia. They are proud."

Mitchell wanted to throw up. 'Mother Russia'; the words' patriotism made him sick. He didn't give a damn about countries, not Russia and not the USA. Neither of them could be trusted. All he cared about now was his family and not unleashing a lethal weapon on the world. He halted mid-thought, knowing that he had to give Richie his genuine research, to keep Karen and Emmie safe. If he had to, he had to, but even Richie would only get some of it and not without cast-iron guarantees on its use.

The thoughts ran through Mitchell's mind quickly and Ilya watched them flitting across his face, mistaking them for thoughts of his family in Russia. If he'd known what Jeff Mitchell's thoughts really were, he'd have shot him there and then. Mitchell stared at the envelope then ripped it open, quickly withdrawing the pages inside. He scrutinised the photographs, tears springing to his eyes.

The photos were arranged in order, year by year. A woman of forty with a young child; his grandmother and mother. Then two adult women, separately and together, the older slowly becoming the other's child, until finally the older woman was nc more. Mitchell turned the pages until he reached the last one then he stopped, staring at the picture beneath his hand. It was of a thirty-something woman with a young girl, standing outside a wooden house. The image in his mind! The last time that he'd seen his mother and sister.

Mitchell lifted the photograph, holding it close to his face as if he could smell their perfume. Each line and hair was studied as Ilya watched pain etch itself on the younger man's face and his heart sank as he saw the loss he'd caused. A murderous look filled Jeff Mitchell's eyes and Ilya knew that if Mitchell decided to kill him then and there he wouldn't object. He'd been the agent who'd taken the ten-year-old boy from his family. Perhaps he deserved to die.

Instead of Jeff Mitchell striking out, he dropped his head into his hands and wept. Harsh tears of bitterness and loss, and more loss to come. Finally he straightened up and strode silently past Ilya Tabakov, heading for home and the PDF that he'd hidden there.

***

"How much are the North Korean's paying me?"

Neil Scrabo topped-up his whisky and gave Tom Evans a sceptical look.

"You mean how much am I paying you, don't you?"

Evans bit back his next words, knowing that they would give too much away. Undercover was harder than he'd thought. Knowing that Scrabo's days were numbered made him want to tell the smug bastard a few home truths, but he couldn't and that was that. Instead he smiled at his boss' put-down, acknowledging that he'd crossed the line.

"Sure. That's what I meant."

Scrabo wandered across the Boardroom and took a seat at the conference table. He leaned so far back in his chair that Evans though he was going to put his feet up on the polished wood, but instead Scrabo just stared at him and smiled. He said nothing for a moment, just let the tension build. When he thought he'd put Evans in his place for long enough Scrabo set his glass down and fixed him with a look.

"Nine noughts."

Evans spat his drink across the room. "What? That's my cut?"

Scrabo's nod was barely perceptible but it was there. A thousand questions ran through Tom Evans' mind. The main one; was there any way to hand Neil Scrabo over to the agency and still get the money? He smiled to himself. His fresh start might be even fresher than he'd thought.

Scrabo was still talking. "Where are you with Mitchell? Our friends are keen to move."

Evans smiled again, ready to impress his boss.

"He has a secret lab."

Scrabo sat forward so quickly that he knocked his glass onto the carpet. As they watched the whisky spread across the cream wool Evans wondered how much it would cost to clean. Scrabo's voice was insistent.

"Where? How do you know?"

"I knew he wasn't going to do his research here. Too much chance of someone finding it."

Scrabo gazed at him in naked admiration and Evans smiled. So that was all he had to do to get respect; make a deal with the agency.

"And?"

"And I tailed him there."

"Good work."

"That's what you pay me for."

Scrabo shot Evans a warning look. There was hubris and there was taking the piss.

"Where is it?"

"Not far away. Long Island. I'll have the research soon."

Scrabo rose and walked over to the window. The sun had almost set and the lights of Manhattan were blinking on. It was a picture that graced a million postcards and he got to see it every night. Evans wondered how Scrabo could bear to live anywhere else, but it was surprising what money could make people do.

Neil Scrabo thought for a moment, then without turning he asked the same question Magee had asked.

"When?"

"Two days."

Scrabo nodded, more to himself than to his bodyguard. "Good, then I'll set-up the exchange. In two days we'll both be very rich men."

Chapter Thirty-Five

Lloyd Harbor. 9 p.m.

Mitchell opened his front door and entered the hallway, startled for a moment by the strange man standing there. He'd forgotten that there were agents living with them now. He smiled to himself at the surreal turn his life had taken, then grabbed a coffee from the kitchen and entered the study, taking a seat behind his desk.

Emmie was at the hospital for one more night, with Karen and Richie standing post. He liked Richie Cartagena. He was a little rough around the edges but his heart was where it should be. He could tell that Karen liked him too. A pang of jealousy rose in Mitchell's chest then died quickly. He had no right to mind. He would be dead soon, either from the tumour or his own hand, and he didn't want Karen to be alone. Better she was with a man that he knew would protect her, than some bum she'd meet in a wine-bar years from now.

Dragging his thoughts back to the present Mitchell re-opened the envelope that Ilya had given him, flicking through the pages until he reached the photograph at the back. He stared hard at his mother's face, tracing her smile with a finger, then he closed his eyes, trying to hear her voice. Vague sounds formed into words until finally he could hear her soft tones.

"Vadim."

His name was Vadim! Mitchell dashed away a tear and gazed at his little sister's pretty face. Her name was Galina, after their mother. She looked familiar somehow, but not from memory.

Then he realised why; she looked like him. They could have been twins. He remembered her crying as he'd left, hugging her doll tight to her chest. *"Vadim, ne ostavlyayte."* Vadim, don't leave.

Mitchell cursed Ilya Tabakov with a venom that he'd never felt before and wished he hadn't released his grip around his neck in the café. Ilya had stolen his childhood and his life, but now he was going to take them back. He would give Richie the photograph next time they met, so that the agency could find his family before he died. It would be a non-negotiable part of his deal.

Mitchell placed the envelope to one side and sipped at his cooling coffee then he reached for his briefcase and opened it, dreading the nightmare that he would find in the PDF inside.

***

The doctor held Emmie's arm for a moment taking her pulse, then he dropped it gently and smiled. Karen smiled back warily, waiting for the next shock. There wasn't one.

"She's fine, Mrs Mitchell. You can take her home tomorrow."

Karen exhaled, realising that she'd been holding her breath, and then glanced at Richie across the room. She liked him but she wanted Jeff to be there. She knew that he couldn't; he was busy upholding his side of the deal. As the doctor left Karen walked over to Richie and placed her hand on his.

"Thank-you, Agent Cartagena. Without you we would both be dead."

Richie gazed down at her hand, feeling the warmth of her small fingers and fighting the urge to entwine them in his. He could smell her perfume. It was warm and light and he wanted to breathe it in. Instead he stood up straight, composing himself into the professional that he knew he should be.

"It was my honour, Mrs Mitchell."

Karen clasped his hand insistently. "Karen. You can't call me

Mrs Mitchell when you've saved my life."

Richie stared into her dark blue eyes and blushed. "Karen then." He gently withdrew his hand in an attempt at officialdom. "I'll wait outside for my relief."

He crossed the room quickly, desperate for the safety of the door between them. If he stared at her any longer the closeness between them would grow and all sorts of trouble would lie ahead, most of which Magee had outlined for him a few hours before. Karen smiled at Richie's retreating back, surprising herself with a moment's curiosity about his life, then she turned back to her daughter and her last night spent sleeping in a chair.

***

"It's all set."

"When and where?"

Magee gripped the phone, waiting for Tom Evans to confirm the plan for Sunday night. He glared across the room at Al Schofield. He was standing by the bureau playing with Magee's ivory abacus. It was three hundred year's old and a birthday gift from his wife. Schofield liked to break things so Magee waved him irritably to a seat and turned back to his call.

Evans heard that someone else was in the room and he stopped talking, waiting for an explanation. Magee sighed, knowing from his silence that Evans wouldn't say any more unless he was told.

"Al Schofield is here."

"What the fuck? Why is that shit-head involved?"

Evans already knew the answer; because he had to be. Schofield headed-up Special Ops for New York State. Magee would never have had him there otherwise; he knew they'd crossed swords frequently when Tom had been an agent. Evans' press-leak costing Schofield his job as a Presidential aide had been the last quarrel in an already bad marriage.

Magee glanced at Al Schofield and pictured the look on Tom

Evans' face. He hated Schofield as well, so did most people, but his squad was a necessary evil in an operation that could get rough.

"We need Special Ops."

Evans bit his lip and kept talking, keen to get off the phone now that he knew who else was there. He liked Magee a lot and he could cope with Richie's moral superiority, but Al Schofield was a cold-blooded prick who'd rather shoot a man than take his name. Their enmity was the real deal; hallmark and all.

"The meet's on Sunday at twenty-two hundred, as agreed. Top of Scrabo Tower. I said I'd get Mitchell's research to Scrabo two hours before so he can take a look."

The roof of Scrabo Tower! What the hell? Magee stared at the phone incredulously and then realisation dawned. The helipad! The North Koreans were coming in and out of the city by helicopter. It was brilliant. New York ran hundreds of pleasure flights each week, who would notice one more?

"OK. You'll have it by then. Are you going with Scrabo and the Koreans?"

"I'll have to be arrested at the same as them or they'll catch on." Evans hesitated. "There's something else."

"What?"

"Scrabo wants to hand Mitchell over to them as well. For future work. The only way I can stop him is to tell him about Mitchell's cancer."

Magee thought for a moment and then said. "Go ahead." It was better if the Koreans thought that Jeff Mitchell had a sell-by date; that way they'd leave him behind.

Tom Evans paused for a moment, thinking. When he restarted his voice was cold. "Tell that prick Schofield not to go spraying any bullets around. I want to live long enough to be de-briefed."

Magee glanced across the desk, knowing how close Evans' words were to the truth. Schofield enjoyed killing, and he hated Tom. It would be the perfect opportunity to take his revenge.

Magee shook his head. No. It would be career suicide and Schofield was far too ambitious to destroy himself.

Magee ended the call with "OK. Check in at twelve hundred tomorrow" then he turned to his unwelcome visitor to finalise the plan.

***

The house was in darkness by the time Mitchell closed the Archaeus PDF, the noise of radios and phones in the hallway finally replaced by the occasional deep whisper between the agents protecting his back. Mitchell turned over the final page and sat starting into space, barely able to believe what he'd just read. His last shred of naiveté wanted to believe that it was just science fiction, but the scientist in him had read every equation with growing admiration for his own warped mind.

He remembered writing none of it and yet the work was unmistakably his. The PDF was covered with footnotes and comments, ranging from sharp mathematical amendments to ethical arguments so weak that Mitchell wondered why he'd even tried. The man who'd written this was on barely nodding acquaintance with morality.

Bile filled Mitchell's mouth and he grabbed at the waste basket, retching into it as quietly as he could. He was disgusted at his own genius, the warped intellect that had produced this file, and even more disgusted at what could follow unless he buried it.

The Archaeus research was eons ahead of his normal work for Scrabo, ahead even of the animal research work he'd seen earlier that evening at the farm. Mitchell had no idea how he'd made the discovery but he was certain of one thing. Absolutely no-one could be trusted with this work.

Mitchell lifted the file's first page and read the summary paragraph again, dialling down his horror just a notch. It was all just theory; the art of possibility. And theory without clinical trials was mere conjecture; generations of scientists could testify to that. From the page to the test-tube was a huge leap, from the laboratory to the street a much bigger one. There was nothing to say that anything he'd written here would work.

Mitchell exhaled, halting his self-chastisement for a moment. There was nothing in the file that even mentioned trials of this work. He sat in silence listening to the clock tick, his mind churning. It was unusual that there'd been no trials mentioned. Trial details were outlined for even the weakest research, regardless of whether they ever materialised. They were like a scientist's second date; a hopeful invitation to commitment for reluctant funders.

Mitchell's heart sank, knowing what it meant. He'd never seen research where trials weren't outlined at the earliest stage, and his work would be no different. There *had* been trials, they just weren't documented here. Why weren't they? And where were the results if trials had taken place? Mitchell knew the answer immediately. They were too secret to document. He must have hidden them in the same way that he'd hidden the PDF, under an obscure name. The same way he was skulking in the dark reading about it now.

The trial results must have been even worse than his work with the animals. If they weren't then he would have sold them to the highest bidder and be living in wealth by now, or be back in Russia getting a medal from the state.

Mitchell grasped for some shred of redemption. Perhaps he'd thought better of it and destroyed whatever he'd discovered? He shook his head immediately. Any man capable of creating the abominations outlined on the pages in front of him had no scruples. He was barely able to believe what he'd done. It felt like someone else's work; except that evil twins only existed in the movies. It was his name at the top of the page. Dr Jeff Mitchell. He had done this.

A deep laugh in the kitchen jerked Mitchell back to reality and he stared hard at the pages in front of him, gathering his thoughts. There were no signs of trials of this work at the farm facility, and there'd been none at the café. He'd wanted to keep the work secret even from the Russians, and for that he sent up silent thanks. What the Alliance didn't know about they couldn't hunt for. That only left one possibility. Scrabo Tower. He must have carried out the Archaeus research there. It would have been safe enough; the work was so advanced that even Devon wouldn't have known what to look for.

Mitchell's mind shot back to the missing time on the CCTV tape from Scrabo's basement lab. If this was what he'd been working on in the research suite that night, then he might have doctored the video to avoid anyone asking questions. It made sense.

Mitchell glanced quickly at this watch. Four a.m. He wanted to go to Scrabo Tower immediately to check the research out, but it would raise questions all round. Part of him was relieved that he could defer the time he had to face the monster he was. A man who'd used his gifts to pollute the world. The other part was desperate to see if his theory had actually worked.

Mitchell placed the Archaeus PDF in his lock-box and left the study, nodding at the tall agent in the dark. He had less than two days left as Joe-Public, to sleep and bring his family home, then he would face what he'd done and what he had to do.

Chapter Thirty-Six

Scrabo Tower. Saturday. 9.30 a.m.

Tom Evans sipped his breakfast coffee and smiled reassuringly at his boss. "There's nothing to worry about. Mitchell's just taken a day off. His kid was in the hospital so he's bringing her home."

Neil Scrabo sprang to his feet and started pacing. It was an annoying habit and Evans had to bite his tongue to stop himself yelling "Sit down." It would make Scrabo sit down for sure, his bass voice had a commanding effect, but it wouldn't score him any brownie points.

Evans smiled again, more tightly this time. "Relax, boss. We've plenty of time. Mitchell went to the farm lab again and met the Russian. They're gearing up to go. All I have to do is get hold of the stuff before they skip the country."

Scrabo swung around to face him. His normally well-groomed feathers looked ruffled today, like a hawk that'd been caught in a storm. Evans stifled a smile and gave Scrabo the attention that he knew he'd expect.

"So that's all you have to do, is it?"

Scrabo's sarcasm was palpable and Evans stopped drinking his coffee mid-sip. He was unperturbed, but he knew that to let Scrabo see that would tell him that something was up. Tom placed the cup down, composing his face into a mix of humility and panic. Unafraid but pretending to be was always a good way to go with sociopaths.

"Sorry, boss. I know I probably sound cocky, but that's

because I am. I'll break into the farm lab tonight and get the files. By tomorrow they'll be in North Korea's hands."

Scrabo glared at him. "And what about their security systems? Guards? File back-ups? We need to have the only copy or the Koreans won't pay us market price."

Evans smiled again, more broadly this time. He ignored Scrabo's raised eyebrow and slipped a hand into his jacket pocket, withdrawing the device that Magee had given him the day before. Scrabo stared curiously at the object.

"What is it?"

Evans turned the small box over then set it down between them.

"A little thing they were working on when I left the agency. An old pal of mine kindly stole it. It's an Electro-magnetic pulse generator. Creates an E.M.P. big enough to crash every computer within five miles. Once I have the files I'll set it to destroy Mitchell's research at the farm lab."

Evans smiled, admiring the device that he would never detonate, although Scrabo didn't know that. Neil Scrabo lifted the box and Evans shook his head nervously.

"Be careful with that thing. Unless you want every piece of research in this building to be wiped, along with every download in Manhattan."

Scrabo smiled maliciously. "We're near Wall Street. Just imagine. Merchant bankers without their screens."

They laughed together at the image of Uriah Heepish brokers being forced to write everything by hand. Quills would make the picture perfect. Scrabo set the box back on the table and then took out his phone. Evans feigned disinterest as he made the call, memorising every word.

"Yes... 8 p.m. tomorrow. Everything. Set-up the funds transfer as we agreed."

Tom Evans watched as his boss strolled to the window, surveying Manhattan as he talked; the King of New York. And somewhere else next week, unless he stopped him.

***

Karen watched as Mitchell lifted Emmie from the car and carried her gently into the house. There'd been moments when she'd been angry with him for risking their lives, but they were over and her anger had been replaced by pity now. The tears in her husband's eyes said that he knew what he'd done and would spend his last breaths making sure that they were safe. His last breaths. They would be few enough to be counted soon. She shook the thought from her head and turned to see Richie watching her.

Richie glanced away, embarrassed that she'd seen his stare, then he felt Karen's eyes resting on his face and he turned back to meet her gaze. For a moment they stood, their eyes speaking volumes, then the moment was over and Karen had gone, turning towards the front door and calling her husband's name. Richie watched her walk away, caring far more than he should.

He hid his feelings behind barked instructions at the agent on-call until he finally climbed into the sedan and drove away, giving Jeff Mitchell one last full day with his family before they played their final game.

***

2 p.m.

Richie stared at his cell-phone as if it was a snake. One that he'd like to kill. Good manners prevented him from cutting the call and respect for Magee kept him listening. Two more good reasons to hate the man at the other end. He swung his legs up on his desk and yawned loudly down the line at Tom Evans, knowing full well that he was being rude.

Richie had no illusions about himself; he was no angel. When character flaws were being handed out he'd been first in a lot of queues. But what he wasn't, was a traitor; not in any way.

Everyone had something in life that they could never get their head around; his was disloyalty in any form. From the school yard 'best friends' who suddenly weren't when someone else had a bigger toy, to infidelity. Right the way through the disloyalty list until you reached the top. Betraying your country.

Richie didn't fool himself that he and Rosie Pereira hadn't had an affair when they'd met. They had. A full-on, Kama Sutra fest of sneaked weekends in Cape Cod and snatched moments of groping in the lecture hall. This time round they'd graduated to expensive hotels and the sedan. But they'd sneaked around because of Rosie's husband, not his wife. He'd never been unfaithful to Dina after his and Pereira's first kiss. He'd gone straight home after it and packed a bag, ending his marriage to her that very day. He couldn't have lived with the lies, or the disloyalty. Dina had deserved better.

He'd only half-understood how Rosie had stayed married to Joey while she'd slept with him. He'd closed his mind to it then but he thought about it now and it hurt. It was disloyal for sure, but it paled into nothing compared to what Tom Evans had done. He was a full blown traitor. A sworn agent who'd got disappointed with the President who'd appointed him and had blown the whistle in the press. Evans wasn't the first; every country had their version. But he wasn't being asked to work with them.

Richie gripped the phone tighter as the traitor talked, outlining their handover of Jeff Mitchell's dummy file. He already knew the day and time that the North Koreans were collecting it from Scrabo Tower; the same time that Mitchell would put it into Ilya Tabakov's grubby hands. As Evans talked Richie only half-listened, gleaning the important parts. Times, places, agreed course of action if the meets went bad. He'd hear it again from Magee and he would listen properly then. Not to this man.

Suddenly Richie realised that Tom Evans had stopped talking, the silence alerting him that he had a part to play. He stumbled in with a few vague words as if he'd been paying attention all along.

"Sure. That all sounds fine."

The vacuum that greeted Richie's words said that he'd got it wrong. When Tom Evans spoke again his deep voice held an amused tone.

"So, it's OK if I steal your car then?"

"What?"

"That's what I've been outlining for the past three minutes and you've just said that it's fine."

Richie flushed with embarrassment and covered it with anger.

"Funny man. Lots of time to waste, have you? Well I haven't!"

Evans' voice cooled ten degrees as its volume ratcheted up.

"Who the hell do you think you're talking to, Cartagena? Do you think I've nothing better to do than be judged by a shithead like you? I'm putting my life on the line here, so get it together or the deal's off. And you can do the explaining to Magee!"

Richie thudded his legs off the desk and pulled himself up straight.

"Fuck you, Evans! I wouldn't even be talking to you if it wasn't an order. You make me want to heave, you yellow bastard. You didn't even stick around to see the shit-storm you created in 2005. First sign of trouble and you ran off to Ecuador!"

Evans' voice cooled further and sarcasm got added to the mix.

"Cuba actually, and I didn't run, I flew. Not that it's any of your business, but they wouldn't have listened to anything I'd said until all the facts on Iraq came out, and I didn't fancy sitting in jail until they did. Maybe you don't read the grown-up papers, but a lot of people agree with my view now. The man was a shit-head who caused an unnecessary war that we're still losing soldiers in."

"You're still a traitor."

"Only because those pompous pricks in Washington couldn't admit that they'd elected the wrong man. It was easier to blame me." Evans paused and they both drew breath, feeling better for the exchange. When Tom Evans spoke again it was quietly.

"Magee is getting me my pardon and if he wants to judge me then he can. He's earned the right. You haven't, buddy. Not by a long way."

Richie stared at the receiver and thought for a moment, then without apology or comment he said the six words that hinted he might someday concede that he'd been wrong.

"Tell me again. When and where?"

***

The farmhouse. Saturday. 7 p.m.

Mitchell switched on the computer and scanned the laboratory as it booted up. His gaze fell on the steel cages. He'd been surprised when he'd entered the lab five minutes earlier to find them half full. Unfortunate mammals of different sizes paced inside their small, meshed rooms, completely unaware of the fate awaiting them. With any luck, once he handed the dummy research over to Ilya they would be freed, although his knowledge of the Alliance's callousness led him to believe otherwise.

Mitchell looked at a small white rabbit. It gazed back at him with wide awake eyes, its pink nose twitching. He walked over to the cage and stroked its fur. A red tag around its neck bore a number and Mitchell punched it into the small pad beside the cage, pulling its history onto the screen. Three month's old, bred in captivity, fully vaccinated, no experimentation yet. It was clean. He made his mind up to take the rabbit home for Emmie; it wouldn't replace Buster but it might make her smile.

Turning back to the computer Mitchell pulled up the contents of the flash-drive. His carbon research was all there, except for the PDF that he'd hidden at home. Mitchell scanned for the pages that he'd earmarked and quickly got to work creating the fake research. After an hour of changing a variable here and there he went back to the start and re-read the file with a scientist's eye.

The changes were subtle. So subtle that the Alliance and North Korean scientists would believe it was plausible research, until they trialled it and found out that it wouldn't work. By then it would be too late; he'd be dead and his family would be safe. Javadi and Ilya could conduct as many experiments with this research as they liked, none of them would provide the key to changing carbon's form in living things.

Mitchell printed-off two copies then saved the fake file to a separate USB. He listened to ensure that he didn't have company then unplugged the computer and walked it back and forth through the door's degaussing loop, before plugging it back in. As the PC restarted Mitchell lifted the rabbit and ruffled its fur gently. Its clinging affection was the perfect antidote to the tension tightening his every sinew.

He watched as the PC's operating system flicked on and a new screen appeared; black and white and basic, with its decoders completely wiped. Mitchell clicked repeatedly on the keyboard, searching for some sign of the files that had been there ten minutes before, but there was nothing. Every file fragment and programme had been erased by the degaussing loop. Ilya's high security had destroyed the very thing it had been designed to save.

Mitchell lifted the false papers and drove his small companion home. His first task there was to send the most important e-mail of his life. As it showed-up 'delivered' more than two hundred times Jeff Mitchell allowed himself a satisfied smile.

***

Worth Street.10 p.m.

Richie swiped Mitchell through the agency's corridors and three floors up to see Magee. Tom Evans was already there when they arrived. Magee watched as Richie gave Evans a grudging nod and Jeff Mitchell extended his hand politely to shake. The spy who'd caused all the problems had better manners than his top man.

Magee nodded them to sit, then he poured the coffee and coughed to quieten the room.

"Dr Mitchell, this is Tom Evans. He works for Neil Scrabo but he's on our side. I'm Supervisory Agent Joseph Magee and Richie you already know."

Joseph, Joe. So that was Magee's first name. Richie was surprised; he hadn't imagined Magee with a first name, especially not such a friendly one. Without further preamble Magee waved Jeff Mitchell on. Mitchell removed the fake research print-outs from his briefcase and set the USB on Magee's desk before he spoke.

"I altered the research sufficiently to make it redundant and saved the false version onto the USB." He held out the papers. "These are hard copies of what's on the stick."

Mitchell paused for a moment, wondering how to explain things simply to three non-scientists. He gave up, deciding that they were intelligent enough to ask about anything they didn't understand.

"The changes I've made to the research are subtle. So subtle that it will take their scientists months to figure out why no amount of trials will make it work."

Evans leaned forward urgently. "Will they notice anything when they open the fake file?"

Mitchell shook his head. "No. No-one else in the world is doing this level of research, so they're working completely blind.

Your men will be perfectly safe at the handover."

"And your real research?"

Mitchell turned slowly towards the question's source. Richie was staring at him coolly. He'd seen first-hand the change in Mitchell over recent weeks. The man in front of him wasn't the bastard that he'd started tailing nine months before; Mitchell had developed a conscience. For what reason Richie didn't know, but he had, and he knew men well enough to know that a change of heart could make them unpredictable. Jeff Mitchell's gaze said that Richie was right. His eyes held a struggle, but it wasn't the one that Richie thought.

Mitchell held the younger man's stare for a moment then he slid his hand into his jacket, withdrawing a computer disc. He turned it over in his hands as he talked. "This is the genuine research." Mitchell paused before continuing. "And I don't want to give it to you."

Magee tensed and Tom Evans smiled to himself. Mitchell's mistrust of the U.S. Government just about matched his own. Mitchell stared directly at Magee.

"What's on this disc will give the holder the key to altering the carbon atoms in living things. That means both physically changing existing beings and creating new life-forms. It's dangerous research, so dangerous that I need some assurances before I hand it over to you."

Mitchell turned to face Richie again, defiance etched on his face. "Don't even think about taking it from me by force, Richie. The disc's encrypted and any attempt to decrypt it will wipe it clean."

Richie glared at him. "We had a deal! You give us the genuine research and we look after your family. Are you welshing on it?" He paused menacingly. "That would be very dangerous."

Richie hated himself for the implied threat against Karen, a threat that he knew he could never carry out; but they needed the research. Mitchell scrutinised him for a moment and then smiled knowingly. Richie Cartagena wouldn't harm a hair on Karen's or Emmie's heads, regardless of whether he gave the agency his research or not. Richie was in love with Karen, even if he didn't know it yet.

"OK. Let's make another deal, Richie. You don't make idle threats and I won't call your bluff. We both know that you'd never harm my family. And I'm not welshing, as you put it, I just want some assurances."

Magee leaned forward, interrupting. "Alright. Like what?"

Mitchell pulled a sheet of paper from his pocket and started reading. It was a list of every Nobel scientist in the States, almost two hundred and fifty of them. Mitchell had sent them an e-mail saying that his research existed, although not its details. Evans smiled again, openly this time. Clever bastard. If Nobel scientists knew about the research then they would make damn sure that the government used it for everyone's good. There would be no back-room weapons being made in Jeff Mitchell's name.

Magee held up a hand, halting the monologue and Mitchell placed the list on the table with the computer disc on top.

"What do you want?"

"First, I want Richie to be the one that guards my family. They know him and I have faith in him. Agreed?"

Magee baulked at the thought of his best agent being used as a baby-sitter but Richie nodded firmly in agreement and both men stared at Magee determinedly. After a grudging pause Magee agreed, with a caveat. Richie could do it for three months, long enough to settle the family wherever they moved. Mitchell nodded. Three months should be plenty of time for Richie and Karen to fall in love. He moved on to his second condition.

"There are some people that I want you to find for me. My birth family. I want Emmie to know her grandmother and aunt."

Magee nodded. He'd expected it. "And?"

Mitchell smiled. "Nearly finished, I promise. I want to know about an agent called Greg Chapman. Who is he and was he tailing me?"

Mitchell missed the glance that passed between Richie and Magee. He kept talking, bracing himself to deliver his final bombshell. None of them were going to like what he said next, even though he knew it had been the right thing to do. Mitchell tapped the computer disc pointedly.

"I've e-mailed the decryption key for this disc to all of the scientists on the list and told them that it's for the advanced research I've given to the U.S. Government. The key is in over two hundred parts, one part to each name. I figured that you might gag one of them, but not every Nobel scientist in the States."

Richie's mouth flew open and Magee joined Tom Evans in his smile. He gave Mitchell a mock-salute, even as his mind was running through possible ways to crack the code. Magee already knew that there wouldn't be one.

"Very clever, Dr Mitchell. You trust scientists more than you trust the government. OK, we have a deal. Now, let's run through the handovers to the Alliance and the North Koreans."

Chapter Thirty-Seven

Sunday. 6.30 a.m.

Dawn's first light shone through the bedroom curtains and Jeff Mitchell watched as it played across his wife's pretty face, dappling her cheeks with gold. Karen turned fitfully in her sleep, huddled-up in an untrusting ball. It contrasted sadly with her relaxed posture of a week ago. Mitchell sat on the edge of the bed watching her as the distant glow of New York's night blended with the sunrise, then faded slowly, handing over to the new day.

They were finally here. There were no more plans and no days to wait. Today was the day that he gave Ilya and Javadi what they thought they wanted and Evans did the same with Neil Scrabo. Mitchell smiled, remembering Richie's look of shock at his Nobel list. It had been a stroke of genius on his part; a failsafe to keep America honest. And a one hundred percent pure act of mistrust in his adopted country.

At least he'd trusted them enough to hand his real animal research over. They should be flattered. It was more than the Alliance or North Koreans would get and a second fake version would have been child's play for him to create; one that would have fooled the American Government's scientists for years. Long enough to see Emmie through school and Karen safely re-married.

Mitchell's heart stung at the thought of another man sleeping with his wife and raising his child but he brushed it aside. He wanted them safe and loved when he was dead. He glanced at Karen and sent up a silent prayer that Richie would make his move soon; three months wasn't very long. He wished that he could guarantee it happening; people missed each other too often in this world. Mitchell shrugged. There were some things that even he couldn't control.

As he stared at the brightening street outside Mitchell thought about Greg Chapman. He was a piece of the puzzle that still hadn't found its place. Why did everything about Chapman's life feel so familiar to him? Magee had looked strangely at him when he'd asked who Chapman was. Someone that worked for him was all that he would say. Greg Chapman had been Magee's agent; that much he'd already guessed. But what did he have to do with him? If Chapman had been tailing him then perhaps they'd talked; it might explain how he knew so much about the agent's life. But where was Greg Chapman now?

Mitchell rubbed his eyes tiredly and crossed to the window, gazing out at the garden that he'd cut two weeks before. It felt like he was saying good-bye. He left the bedroom quietly and wandered downstairs, nodding at the suited agent in the hall, pristine even without a wink of sleep. He walked into the study and took the papers that only he knew existed from the lock-box then read the Archaeus file again, still unable to believe what it said. That was tomorrow's task, today he would finally deal with Ilya Tabakov and make his family safe.

***

The day passed like any other day but Mitchell was surprised by the number of staff who graced the corridors of Scrabo Tower. It was a Sunday for God's sake; didn't they have anything better to do? Most of the workers were juniors, eager to impress their bosses by starting the week on top. The people at his level were home in bed or on the golf course, already secure in their lives. But he had to be seen working normally. It wouldn't do to alert Neil Scrabo or Ilya that something was amiss.

At five p.m. Mitchell checked his watch, switched off his computer and left, waving cheerfully at the guards in reception like he always did. The Lexus was waiting by the kerb and he made small talk with Karen as she drove him home. But instead of climbing out when they reached the house Mitchell shifted to the driver's seat, just as Richie slipped under the car's rear seat for the journey's next leg.

The drive was quick and silent and in thirty minutes they were parked in the clearing outside the small farmhouse. Richie could tell from Mitchell's rise in tension that they weren't alone. They'd expected as much; it was all going to plan. Richie lay totally still as Mitchell turned off the engine then said a few words to a man outside the car; Ilya Tabakov. Mitchell didn't get out of the car to join him, just waited in hostile silence for another hour.

At 19:40 a second car arrived and Mitchell climbed out of the Lexus. As the driver's door opened Richie heard Russian words. He kicked himself for not paying more attention in language class but he wasn't kept in the dark for long. Mitchell changed the conversation smoothly to English and left the door open so that Richie could hear. A third man's voice joined in. It sounded Middle Eastern. Iranian. Behrouz Javadi.

Richie slipped the safety catch off his weapon and listened hard. The plan was for Mitchell to hand over the false file and leave, but Richie had been an agent for too long to think that the exchange would be that clean. Ilya's next words were clear.

"You have the file?"

"Yes." Mitchell's voice was cold, just what Ilya would expect after their last encounter.

"Good, good. Let us go inside."

"No."

Richie heard a sharp intake of breath from Ilya then Javadi interjected.

"We cannot exchange out here. You must need your computer."

"I have a laptop in the trunk."

Richie knew that Mitchell's next move would be to take the USB from his pocket. The click of a gun's safety sliding off said that Mitchell had reached for it; the sarcasm in his next words confirmed it.

"Are you going to shoot me, Javadi? Is that how you treat your friends? I'm reaching for the USB that holds the data, if that's OK with you?"

Richie listened to the exchange, knowing that Jeff Mitchell had a gun pointed at his face and admiring his balls. He wondered if Evans was having this much fun with the Koreans.

***

Evans watched as Neil Scrabo booted up his laptop and inserted the computer-chip that Magee had downloaded the fake research to. Evans smiled as he watched the suave owner of Scrabo Tower staring intently at the computer screen, pretending that he understood what the equations meant. Good luck with that. He had a Master's degree in Physics and he'd got lost on the first page.

Scrabo kept up the pretence for a moment and then ejected the chip, smiling confidently. He had no idea what the research was about but it looked official enough to keep the North Koreans happy and get the first half of his funds. Their nerds would check the file and the second half would hit his account in ten days' time. Tom Evans smiled, knowing that Scrabo planned to be in an inaccessible country lying on a beach very soon. He was completely unaware that the shit was about to hit the Korean fan.

Scrabo nodded. "Good work. This should keep them happy. Any fatalities in the retrieval?"

The question was asked in a bored tone and Evans knew that

whether he'd answered none or ninety Scrabo wouldn't have cared. It was just asked to be asked. Evans shook his head and glanced at his watch; 19:45. In five minutes time Scrabo would make the call, then it was ten more minutes to show-time and the helicopter would land on the roof.

Evans sent up a prayer that Magee and Schofield had everything arranged. The last thing he wanted was to have to climb inside a chopper. He hated the bloody things at the best of times; he'd seen too many of them crash in combat. Add North Korean heavies to the mix and it would be the flight from hell. Scrabo cut across his thoughts by handing him a whisky then he raised his own in a toast.

"Salut. This time tomorrow we'll be in Venezuela with half the money in the bank, and in a week's time we'll both be richer than God."

Evans stared at his drink distractedly then downed it in one. He poured another, praying to Neil Scrabo's God that it wouldn't be his last.

***

Richie could feel the tension building outside the Lexus, less in the words being said than in the silences in between. Suddenly the car's trunk swung open and he tensed, listening as Mitchell's laptop was removed. Mitchell was using the laptop to show them the research; anything to avoid entering a building that he knew he might never leave. Once he told Ilya he wasn't going to Russia with him anything might happen.

Ilya said something in Russian and Behrouz Javadi reacted with chagrin.

"Speak English. It's the only language we all know."

Ilya's voice was tired and impatient, as if he was speaking to a spoilt child.

"I said. Just show us the research and we can be on our way. That was all."

Richie heard the laptop being placed on the Lexus' hood and its start-up music play, then Mitchell clicked at some keys and called the others over to see.

"That's the summary and conclusions. The other pages are the detail."

The clearing was quiet for a few minutes and Richie visualised Javadi and Tabakov peering at the screen. He had no idea if they understood Mitchell's research or not, but even if they didn't they would pretend. Richie imagined an identical scenario being played out at Scrabo Tower.

Javadi asked a few questions that showed he actually knew what he was talking about and Mitchell answered him in strained tones. Finally Richie heard the USB being ejected then the Iranian spoke again.

"We must go inside."

Richie's hand slid to his gun, ready to move. Then he heard Mitchell's reply.

"If you think I'm going anywhere with you, Javadi, you've got another think coming. I barely trust Ilya and I've known him since I was ten, there's no way I'm getting in a room with you alone."

There was silence for a moment before the Iranian admitted defeat.

"Very well, Dr Mitchell. But if this research is not genuine, or if it fails to deliver what we need, we will find both of you, and your families."

A second later Richie heard some words being barked-out in Farsi then a car revved-up and screeched out of the clearing. Richie prayed that only the Iranian was inside when it did. His prayers were soon rewarded.

"You did well, Durak."

It was Ilya Tabakov's voice. His words held more than a hint of relief. Mitchell's were just plain angry.

"You evil bastard. You stole me from my family and set me to making weapons for scum like that."

"It was for Russia, for the motherland."

The venom in Mitchell's voice shocked even Richie.

"Russia means nothing to me, nothing! This is where I live, this is who I am. Not your Durak. We're done, Ilya. I did as you asked; now if I ever see you again you're dead."

Tabakov's next words were almost pleading.

"But we are leaving together, Durak, to go home. That has always been the plan."

Mitchell jerked the driver's door wide to leave, then he stopped and spun around. Richie could hear Mitchell hadn't entered the car and he froze, uncertain of what to do. If Mitchell killed the Russian there would be hell to pay, and if he showed himself to stop him, the whole operation would be blown. They'd have to lift Tabakov or kill him and Richie knew that someone in Moscow and Tehran would be primed to check how the exchange had gone. It would only take minutes for Javadi to find out that Ilya had gone.

Richie heard Mitchell's feet crunch across the dry earth of the clearing and he knew that he was heading straight for Ilya Tabakov, to take his life. What the hell could he do? The answer came to Richie in a flash. He pulled out his cell-phone and pressed dial, holding his breath as Mitchell's phone started to ring. Mitchell grabbed for his cell and stared at the screen, recognising Richie's caller I.D. It was a bold move and enough to break his fugue.

Ilya yelled at Mitchell angrily.

"Don't answer that! This is important."

Mitchell stared at the old man for a moment as if he couldn't see him, then he knocked the phone off and turned swiftly on his heel. Mitchell climbed into the Lexus and spat out the last words that his 'uncle' would ever hear him say.

"We're done, Ilya."

He underlined them with the dust from his wheels as he screeched away.

***

Neil Scrabo made the call at 19:50 on the dot. The North Koreans were nothing if not precise. Night-time was better for the meeting. The helicopter would blend in with the myriad of tourist flights that covered Manhattan's evening skies, and any attempt to shoot it down would be hampered by the fading light.

Evans watched as his boss made his plans, knowing that in less than an hour Neil Scrabo would be in jail. He smiled, making certain that Scrabo didn't see. If he knew what his bodyguard had planned he would shoot him on the spot. Evans had spotted the tell-tale bulge in Scrabo's jacket as soon as he'd entered the room.

Scrabo's suits were always immaculate; slim-cut testaments to Parisian style. He never even carried a wallet in case it ruined the line, so a bloody great gun was always going to be seen. Evans wondered vaguely if Scrabo even knew how to shoot it, or whether it was just an accessory to suit the day. He imagined him dressing that morning. 'This is the day I commit treason, so what would be a good look?' Matching his suit and gun in some attempt at gangster cool.

His reverie was interrupted by a loud whirring overhead then Scrabo's phone rang once, giving their signal to move. Evans downed his whisky in a single gulp and rose, tugging his jacket straight, then he un-holstered his Glock and walked swiftly ahead. He scanned the hallway expertly then beckoned Scrabo out and pressed the elevator's button for their single storey ride. The whirring noise grew louder as they ascended and when they opened the door to the roof it deafened them both.

Evans stood in the doorway scrutinising the scene. A Kai Surion helicopter was hovering twenty feet above the helipad, throwing dust and debris across the Tower's roof. He shielded his eyes and squinted hard, trying to see the pilot's face. He was black and fit; ex-military without a doubt. Evans squinted again and made out the shape of two East Asian men seated inside the craft. One was small and clever looking, the other pure muscle, carrying an RPK and obviously hired for his blunt force approach to life. Both men's guns were aimed at them.

Evans raised his weapon and pointed back and for several seconds no-one moved. The small man broke the stale-mate, tapping the pilot on the shoulder to land. Evans waited until the rotor stopped then approached the chopper cautiously, pushing Neil Scrabo behind him. He didn't give a shit if they shot his boss, but he had to keep up appearances till the end; his own life depended on it. Somewhere on another rooftop Al Schofield was watching everything, ready to give Special Ops the sign to move in. Evans just had to keep everyone fooled until then.

The small North Korean stepped onto the roof as they approached. His bodyguard joined him, his weapon primed. Scrabo moved forward and reached out his hand.

"Kim-Jong Bae. Right on time."

The man shook Scrabo's hand limply and gave what passed for a smile.

"Do you have it?"

Evans wasn't surprised at his lack of small talk. The Korean's must have known that they were being watched, without being certain who by. Scrabo reached inside his jacket for the computer-chip. He held it in his palm for a moment as if reluctant to let it go, then handed it over. The bodyguard passed his boss a laptop and Kim-Jong Bae clicked the chip in, scrolling quickly through the screens until he was satisfied. Mitchell's fake had passed inspection.

The leader bowed politely, waving them onto the chopper. Evans hung back, searching for some sign that Al Schofield's men were about to appear, but there was nothing. No sound of feet on the landing and no back-suited troops bursting through the roof's door. Only a faint glint of sunlight off a lens to Evans' left said that they were even there. What the hell was Schofield waiting for? He must have seen the exchange. Once the helicopter was airborne the North Koreans would be impossible to catch.

Then it dawned on him. Schofield wasn't interested in catching the Koreans; he wanted to shoot them all down! Evans couldn't see the rocket-launchers but he knew that they were there. Schofield was going to send a message to the North Korean Government and any traitors on American soil. This is what happens if you fuck with us. There was no way that Joe Magee had sanctioned this!

As Scrabo climbed onto the chopper Evans did the only thing he could to stop Schofield executing his plan. He'd spotted a water tank as they'd entered the roof, now he sprinted behind it for cover. The bodyguard saw Evans run and pumped a stream of rounds into the tank's side, spurting water all over the ground. Evans rolled onto his back and pulled his Glock's trigger twice, hitting the man square in the chest. He watched him fall, thinking fast as the small Korean screamed at the pilot to take off. He had to stop them. Once they were airborne Schofield would shoot them down. They would all die and Magee would lose the N.K.'s intelligence.

There was no point trying to alert Magee. By the time he got his men there they would all be dead. He couldn't involve the cops either; pitting the NYPD against Special Forces would be a massacre. Tom Evans dialled the only number that he could think of then he turned his attention back to the scene.

The Surion was rising slowly off the helipad with the small Korean still screaming. A look of panic covered Neil Scrabo's face. Evans put two shots expertly into the chopper's fuel tank, then another in the pilot's back, watching as he slumped forward across the controls. The pilot wasn't dead, he was too good a shot for that, but there was no way that he'd be flying anything for a while.

As the helicopter began to fall, Neil Scrabo glared at his erstwhile friend, his panic and anger escalating. Scrabo didn't know it but Tom Evans had just saved his life, not that he'd ever say thanks. Evans reloaded and watched as the chopper started turning in a slow spin, getting perilously close to the roof's edge. Kim-Jong Bae was pushing a gun against Scrabo's head and shouting. His words got lost in the wind and he shouted them again.

"Your boss is going to die."

Evans yelled back. "Unless you listen you're all dead. Look to your right."

The North Korean turned slowly to his right, moving Scrabo in front of him as he did. Evans watched his expression change as he caught the glint of the Special Ops' sights. This time Scrabo did the yelling.

"You bastard. You set us up."

"They want you dead. I don't. Do what I tell you, it's your only chance."

Kim-Jong Bae thought for a moment then nodded, watching as Evans pointed towards the building's electrical hut.

"When I say 'go', run behind it. I'll get the pilot. Wait until I give the word."

Evans knew that Schofield's next move would be to launch a rocket at the Surion; they had about ten seconds before everyone inside was dead. He shouted "GO!" and the two men jumped from the chopper, running for cover behind the hut. Evans raced forward and pulled the pilot out, dragging his body behind the water tank just as the chopper spun out of control.

It spiralled over the building's ramparts and careered into the street below. The sound of crushing metal was deafening as the rotor's steel blades shredded and screeched against Scrabo Tower's walls on its progress to the ground. Thirty seconds later the Kai Surion hit West Street with a sickening crash, followed by an explosion that Evans knew would have killed anyone nearby. He prayed that the business street was empty on a Sunday night.

Evans lay back against the tank's cool steel, making plans to put a bullet in Al Schofield's brain. It would have to wait; they weren't safe from the Special Ops team yet. Suddenly a loud whirring sound cut through Evans thoughts and came to a crescendo overhead. He glanced up to see another helicopter appear and hover above them, generating a cloud of dust. It was just the cover they needed to prevent Schofield sending in ground forces to finish them off.

Evans grinned up at the Channel W news-copter and then laughed out loud, hoping that Al Schofield could see his face. Some journalist had acted on his last ditch phone-call and had just got the scoop of their life. Schofield wouldn't try anything now, not unless he wanted to wave goodbye to his career on live TV.

Evans phoned Magee to say they needed evacuated stat, unless he wanted his covert operation all over the evening news.

Chapter Thirty-Eight

10 p.m.

Richie and Mitchell reached Magee's office at the same time as Tom Evans, and Magee nodded them all to sit while he gave an update. Neil Scrabo and Kim-Jong Bae were safely in custody, looking at long days of questioning in padlocked rooms. The pilot and bodyguard were at a nearby hospital, the latter in its morgue. The Alliance thought they'd got the genuine research and it would be months before they realised that they'd been had, if they ever did. The North Koreans still thought that they'd bought their copy then been robbed of it by the Feds. All in all it was a good day's work, except for one thing.

"Where's Schofield? I want him, Magee. He tried to kill us."

Magee swung his chair round and stared at Tom Evans, scanning his ex-protégé's face; it wore a murderous look. Evans was furious and he'd every right to be, Schofield had tried to kill him. But if Evans retaliated, no matter how much Al Schofield deserved it, he'd end up in federal prison. Then the pardon they'd both worked so hard for would go down the tubes.

They faced-off for a moment while Richie and Mitchell looked on, then Magee nodded. If Evans was expecting an argument from him he wasn't going to get one.

"You've every right to be angry, Tom. Schofield acted against orders and threatened your life. His men were supposed to intercept you on the rooftop and capture the targets before the chopper took off again. Instead he hung you out to dry." Magee paused, knowing that his next sentence would elicit an angry retort. "We can only speculate what Schofield intended to do once you were in the air."

Evans cut across him, outraged. "You know damn well what he was going to do! Shoot us down like dogs. The man's an assassin and he's wanted me dead for years!"

Evans saw Richie's shock in his peripheral vision. Richie hated him too, for the traitor that he thought he was, but he was a better man than Al Schofield would ever be. Mitchell caught the exchange. It was another tick in Richie's box as far as he was concerned; he'd stopped him killing Ilya as well. Mitchell felt safer by the minute leaving Karen and Emmie in his care.

Magee waved Evans into silence and nodded heavily. He was right. Schofield *was* going to shoot him down once the helicopter was airborne. Schofield wanted him dead and he was prepared to lose valuable intelligence to achieve it. Magee decided to tell them what he'd resolved to keep quiet.

"Schofield's being interrogated."

"About what? It was pretty clear what he was going to do!"

Magee shook his head. "Not all of it. Yes, he wanted you dead, Tom, and we can all guess at his motive for that. But he was ready to kill Kim-Jong Bae as well, so either Schofield didn't care if we lost North Korea's intelligence or he actually wanted us to. We're beginning to think that it was the latter."

Richie interrupted. "But why would he want that? The leverage that Intel can give us is huge!"

Magee turned to look at him. "We think Schofield was working for the North Koreans and didn't want it coming out. It seems Internal Affairs have had him under surveillance for some time."

Evans' face contorted in fury.

"You let him back me up on that roof-top knowing that he might try to kill us all!"

Magee wheezed angrily. "I didn't know anything! I've just found out what Internal Affairs were up to. They wanted to draw Schofield out and they saw their chance. You weren't in any danger. They had one of their men in his team. One sign that Schofield was going to shoot you down and he'd have been stopped in his tracks."

Evans froze at Magee's words and the others watched, disbelieving, as Evans' anger morphed into a loud laugh. He moved towards Magee and Richie tensed, ready to protect his boss. He needn't have worried. Evans just slapped Magee hard on the back in congratulations, making him cough.

"You clever old bastard! You used me as bait to draw Schofield out."

Magee shook his head then spoke in a wheeze.

"Not me. Internal Affairs. I knew the North Koreans had moles inside the agency but we were getting nowhere on finding them. Schofield can lead us to everyone now."

Evans laughed again. "I wouldn't want to be him once I.A. gets going. A win-win for the agency. Nicely done, boss."

Magee gave a rare smile, then Richie gawped as he started to laugh with Evans about I.A. setting him up. Finally Richie couldn't keep silent any longer.

"Am I the only one who thinks that this was risky?" He motioned towards Evans. "He could have died!"

Both men turned to look at Richie then they laughed again. Evans spoke first. "Walk in the park, son. Back in the day we did a lot worse than that."

Mitchell and Richie shook their heads incredulously as the two men laughed on. After a few minutes the room quietened and Magee nodded Richie to report on the handover to the Alliance.

"OK. I'll keep it short and sweet. Tabakov and his partner Javadi have the dummy file. It all went smoothly."

Mitchell smiled, grateful that Richie hadn't mentioned his momentary loss of control at the farm. Magee read their body language and instantly knew that something else had happened. He shrugged. It hadn't interfered with the operation and that was all he cared about. Richie continued.

"Javadi sounded like an aristocrat. Someone high up in the Iranian regime."

"You're certain he was from Iran?"

"Positive. He was speaking Farsi and five years working in Tehran gave me a good ear for their class structure. He said something in Farsi to Tabakov. 'This will accelerate our bio-tech programme. Our weapons will benefit.'"

Mitchell gave him a shocked look; Richie hadn't told him Javadi had said that. Then he nodded. It made sense. If the Iranians had a biological and technical weapons programme, his research would be have been manna from heaven. His real research, that was.

"We got it all on tape."

Mitchell startled again. What tape? Richie reached across and withdrew a pin from behind Mitchell's lapel. It was the smallest microphone that he'd ever seen. Richie smiled at him reassuringly and Mitchell knew that when he transcribed the tape his angry exchange with Ilya would be cut-out.

Magee shook his head ruefully. So the Iranians had a bio-tech weapons programme. Another set of fanatics with lethal toys. Just what the world needed.

"Get the transcript straight to the White House, Richie. If the Iranians have biological weapons then that changes the game completely."

"Aren't we going to lift Javadi and Tabakov?"

Mitchell had been thinking the same thing.

Magee shook his head, surprising them both. "Ilya Tabakov and Daria Kaverin are just tired old reds who'll be put out to pasture now. And Javadi will be more use to us free, now that we know what he's up to. Our people and the British will keep a good eye on him here and in the middle-east, and follow wherever he leads."

After a minute's more silence Magee stood up, signalling them all to do the same.

"OK. I'd like to thank all of you gentlemen. We've managed to stop valuable research getting into enemy hands. We've captured one valuable asset and we have a good trail on another one. Plus, we've uncovered a mole in the agency. I'd call that a good day's work, wouldn't you?"

He turned to Mitchell. "Dr Mitchell. Thank-you for your part in this. Once you've tidied your affairs you and your family will be taken to an interim safe place under Agent Cartagena's guard. After a short debrief you'll be re-located to your new life." Magee reached forward and shook Mitchell's hand. "We may have started this operation with you as an enemy but I hope that we've ended it as friends."

Mitchell nodded, shocked at the depth of feelings the words provoked. He'd never been what anyone might have called a patriot, but he felt proud that his research might help someone after he was dead. Magee read his thoughts and smiled.

"Richie will help you with the search for your birth family and to get your affairs in order."

Mitchell interrupted. "I'll need another day or two in Scrabo's labs, to tie up loose ends and make sure that I've wiped all the files."

"One day?"

Mitchell smiled. "I'll do my best to be finished tomorrow, but I can't guarantee it."

"Fine. Richie, give Dr Mitchell and his family whatever help they need." He patted Richie on the arm. "You did well. There'll be a promotion waiting when you get back."

Magee turned briskly towards the door, pulling it open. "Now, get out of here. Tom and I have some catching up to do." He threw a smile at Evans. "Over quite a few beers, I think."

***

The ride back to the Mitchell's house was quiet, so quiet that

Richie clicked-on the radio, grateful even for Country and Western to fill the void. What could they possibly say to each other? The normal come-down after an operation was multiplied by the fact that they both knew Mitchell was going to die. Maybe not tomorrow, but soon. He would only be part of his family's life for a few more months. Richie couldn't read Mitchell's thoughts but if he could have done, he would have known Jeff Mitchell planned to make it much sooner than that.

Mitchell wasn't sure how he was going to commit suicide yet, or when, but he knew one thing; he wasn't rotting away in some hospital bed with sad faces all around. He couldn't remember much about his life, but he knew himself well enough to know that he didn't want that.

He would kill himself soon. After he'd tidied up things at the lab. There were some small research trials that he had to hand over, and a letter he needed to write Devon. He smiled. Devon would be safe to return now that Neil Scrabo was safely locked away. The organisation would need a new Director of Research and Devon deserved the chance. It couldn't have been easy playing second fiddle for five years.

Mitchell needed to find his mother and sister as well, but Richie already had people in Moscow working on that. They would have to get them out of Russia. Once it came out that Mitchell had betrayed the Alliance it wouldn't matter that his family hadn't seen him for thirty years, they would be killed just for being related. He would get to speak to them on the phone before he died at least, and ensure that Emmie had the chance to know them someday. That only left two things to sort out. Greg Chapman and the Archaeus PDF secured in his lock-box at home. Mitchell switched off the radio and turned to Richie, wondering how to start. He decided on the direct approach.

"Richie. I need to ask you some things."

"OK. Shoot."

"I need to know more about Greg Chapman. Will you tell me about him?"

Richie swallowed hard. Magee had warned him that this might come, but he was still unprepared. Chapman had been his friend, not just a colleague. They'd sunk beers and chased women together after his divorce. Greg had been tailing Jeff Mitchell on the night that he'd disappeared. Richie liked Mitchell now, so he prayed to God that he wasn't about to say something about Greg that would make him want to kill him.

Richie screeched the car to a halt and turned towards the passenger seat.

"What about Greg?"

Mitchell shook his head. He looked genuinely confused.

"I don't know for sure. It's just...I can't shake the feeling that I know him."

'Know him'. Mitchell was using the present tense. That meant he thought Greg Chapman was still alive. Or else he was playing games. The look of confusion on Jeff Mitchell's face made Richie dismiss the second idea. The man looked tortured, like he was trying to remember things that kept slipping away. He recalled Magee's briefing about Mitchell's brain tumour. It made sense.

Maybe Greg *was* still alive somewhere? Even as the thought came Richie rejected it. It was over two weeks since his last report. Wherever Greg was, if he wasn't dead he probably wished that he was by now. Richie nodded slowly, reluctant to give anything away.

"I know Greg Chapman. When did you meet him? Was it at Scrabo?"

Mitchell shook his head, not in the negative but as if he was trying to shake something loose. The effort frustrated him and he banged his fist against the dash.

"I don't know. I really don't know." Mitchell was almost shouting. "I know things about Chapman that I couldn't possibly know, and his phone appeared in my desk-drawer at work one day. I found out that the building's cleaners had put it there. They'd found it near my lab at Scrabo Tower. I checked

Real Estate records and found Chapman's address and when I went to his apartment to check it out, I already knew where to find his key."

He turned towards Richie with an anguished look. "How the hell did I know where to find his key?"

Richie knew all about Mitchell's trips to Greg Chapman's apartment. He spoke slowly, trying to calm Mitchell down. "Where was it?"

"Above the front door, on the ledge."

"Lots of people leave their spare keys there. It could just have been a good guess."

"NO!"

The sheer volume of Mitchell's words took Richie aback and years of experience made his hand twitch for his gun. The reflex died as soon as it rose and Richie watched Mitchell's anguish deepen as he talked on.

"When I got inside, it was like I knew the place. Even his pictures seemed familiar." He looked at Richie and half-smiled. "I checked Chapman out. He came from St Augustine in Florida. It's a small town near Jacksonville. Picturesque. Flowers, churches, the works."

Mitchell's expression changed to sadness. "I went down there to see what I could discover. I met his parents, they were nice people. I felt like I knew them. The girl he used to date too. She teaches at his old school." Mitchell hesitated, knowing that his next words would make Richie think he was insane. "I ...I knew things about her, Richie. Things that I couldn't possibly have known. It scared the crap out of me."

Richie nodded. He knew all about Mitchell's Florida trip. Brookman's team had watched him carefully, but Richie hadn't understood why Mitchell had gone until now. Mitchell was still rambling. He looked desperate.

"I feel things all the time, strange things. I have memories of times that I don't remember living through, even physical reactions that feel like they don't belong to me, like I've been combat trained, except I never was. I…I'd think I was going insane…hallucinating from the tumour, if Chapman didn't really exist. But he does. He's real. Greg Chapman has a life and I know too much about it. I need to talk to him. I need to find out how I know so much."

He shot Richie a pleading look. "Can you help me? Can you help me find out?"

Richie's heart sank, knowing that he had no answers to give. Chapman was missing in action and they had no leads. Nothing except the fact that he'd been in Scrabo Tower the day he'd disappeared.

Something occurred to him - they could go in and search the Tower now that Neil Scrabo was secure. Richie made a mental note to clear it with Magee then he looked at Jeff Mitchell again. The look of sadness on his face was almost pitiful. He couldn't tell Mitchell about his plan to search Scrabo Tower for Chapman; it might push him over the edge. Instead he took the line that he and Magee had agreed.

"Yes, I'll help you. We have men out looking for Chapman already, in all his usual haunts." It was the truth. "We'll add St Augustine to the list. Now that the operation's over we'll have more resources to put on the search."

Jeff Mitchell's look of relief was worth the half-lie. Richie watched as he relaxed back against his seat, then he turned the key gently in the ignition and drove them both home.

Chapter Thirty-Nine

Souths Bar, Tribeca. 1 a.m.

"How would you like to come back to work, Tom?"

"No thanks, I just want my pardon and my share of the money that's frozen in Scrabo's account."

Magee stared at his old student across the table and saw the beginning of a smile in the bar's dim light. He could feel a punch-line coming.

"Besides, you could never cope with me becoming your boss."

Magee laughed until he wheezed and Evans reached over and slapped him on the back, still talking.

"I'm still the same whistle-blowing malcontent that I was eight years ago, Joe. Do you really think any White House administration would let that pass?"

When Magee stopped coughing his reply took Tom Evans by surprise.

"Actually yes, this one would. You were right about the government back then; it was just your public exposé of it that was wrong. This is a very different administration."

Evans snorted. Magee stared hard at him and Evans knew that he was being serious.

"I've been authorised at the highest level, Tom, not only to give you a full pardon but to offer you your old job back, with a promotion. I'll even throw in five minutes alone with Al Schofield."

Evans fell into stunned silence as Magee continued.

"Look, Tom. We need men like you. I've never doubted it but your quick thinking on that roof-top confirmed it again. At most I have five years left and then you'd end up running the show." He smiled. "Besides, we need to keep you off the streets."

"What about Cartagena? He's a good agent, despite the attitude. Surely the job is his?"

Magee smiled. "Let me handle Richie. He's good and he'll get better, but you were the best I'd ever trained. Look, you've heard the offer, so just think about it. That's all I have to say, except..." He held up his glass. "It's your round."

***

Mitchell couldn't sleep no matter what he tried. His head was buzzing with questions, so at five a.m. he entered his study and opened the lock-box, removing the flash-drive and papers inside and slipping them into his briefcase. He shrugged on his jacket and headed for the front door, only to see Richie leaning, arms folded, against the leaded glass. He looked as rough as Mitchell felt.

"Going somewhere?"

"Work. I need to tidy things up if we're leaving."

"At dawn?" Richie's look was as sceptical as his voice.

"Let me go, Richie. You know where I'll be and I'll be back as soon as I can."

Richie glanced towards the stairs. His message was clear, but Mitchell couldn't worry about Karen's feelings right now. He was thinking of her long-term happiness, not just today's. Mitchell shook his head and moved towards the front door, then something occurred to him and he stopped, giving Richie a small smile.

"I'm trusting you to take care of them."

Mitchell was out the door and in the Lexus before Richie realised exactly what he'd meant.

***

When Mitchell reached Scrabo Tower dawn was breaking. He watched it through his office window, wondering how many more of them he would see. He breathed in its beauty as if it was his last and then turned towards his work, making fast progress in the early morning peace. By seven a.m. there were three neat piles on his desk. One for the research team, one for Devon with a note, and the last one for shredding. In two hours' time the outer office would be full of people and his day would be filled with queries to answer and papers to sign. If he was ever going to act it had to be now.

Mitchell lifted his briefcase and pulled out the flash-drive, slipping it into his computer. Thirty minutes later he'd read the Archaeus PDF twice, feeling again the shock he'd felt in his study that first night. It confirmed all his fears. He'd taken carbon engineering far beyond the animal research on the disc he'd given the agency. That had only outlined the physical changes that the new form of carbon could create, it was nothing compared to this. What was in the Archaeus file was far too dangerous to fall into anyone's hands.

Mitchell knew now why he'd named the file 'Archaeus'. It was apt. Archaeus; alchemy's creation of the vital spark. This research wasn't about mere flesh and blood; the physical changes that he'd made to t animals. This work was about the very essence of living things; the thing that made him Jeff Mitchell, and Richie Cartagena himself.

Scientists and philosophers had spent centuries trying to describe it, as far back as the ancient Greeks. Even the churches had weighed in, calling it the 'soul'. What was it really? Identity? Personality? Conscious and unconscious thought? Maybe even some sort of Quantum energy, if recent publications were correct. Whatever you called it, it was what turned a human body into a human being, and made each one of them unique.

Mitchell stared at the equations in front of him, stunned by their impeccable logic. Had he really discovered this? A way to capture people's very essence? He read it again, still disbelieving, but there was no doubt. Just as carbon was the building block of physical life, his research had shown, through work on the neurotransmitters in the brain, that carbon held the basis of human consciousness itself. It was brilliant work but Mitchell knew that he couldn't trust it to anyone. It had to die with him.

He sat for a moment considering what the work might mean to the future of the human race. Telepathy? Maybe, but the world had been looking at that for generations; it was nothing new. Collective consciousness? Remote viewing? Spying on enemies from your office chair using only the power of thought? Perhaps. There'd been work on that before; the Stargate project in the seventies, twenty million dollars spent before it was called a dud. Perhaps this was the leap forward that it would take to make it work. Mitchell ran through the possibilities, not knowing that the truth he was about to discover would make all his speculations seem like children's games.

Mitchell left the office, locking the door behind him, and took the elevator down to the basement lab. The last time that he'd been there was with Devon, the previous time the night before his blood-filled shower; the night that Greg Chapman had disappeared and the CCTV had lost time. The cleaners had found Chapman's cell-phone there and Mitchell was sure that he'd carried out the Archaeus trials there as well. It was the logical place. But wherever he'd done the trials he needed to make sense of it all before he died.

As he pulled open the basement door the lights flickered on and Mitchell gazed around the laboratory where he'd spent the last five years of his life. A place that he would have to say goodbye to soon. Jeff Mitchell had no idea that what he was about to find there would give him his future back.

***

Karen walked into the kitchen and pressed the kettle on to boil. She took her tea out to the deck to drink, admiring the peace of the autumn morning. Richie watched her from the doorway, smiling at how tiny she was in her bare feet. With her soft blond hair and make-up free face she could pass for a student instead of a thirty-something Mom. He felt protective of her, and of Emmie. They hadn't asked for any of this.

Karen knew that Richie was watching her and she didn't mind. He was a kind man, gentle and strong, and he made her laugh. She couldn't remember the last time that she'd laughed. In a different life they might have had something together.

A sob caught her unexpectedly and Karen covered her face with her hands. She cried softly until it was wet, and she could barely breathe. She thought sadly of her handsome husband. She loved Jeff so much and he would be dead soon, no matter what anyone did. Suddenly all her worry about being safe paled against the reality of a future spent alone. Her shoulders dropped and her sobs grew so harsh that they racked her slim frame.

Richie let her cry alone for a minute, knowing that she needed the release, then he walked over and took her in his arms. Karen gazed up at him, surprised for a moment, then she slowly relaxed, feeling safe in his arms for that instant, no matter what the future would bring.

***

The outer lab was empty apart from a haze of dust that drifted past Mitchell in the flickering lights. It was an icy, grey-white space; almost colourless, but not in a drab way; it was just the colour of science. Mitchell thought of the bright kindergarten corridor that he'd stood in two weeks before, smiling at his daughter's pretty world and its contrast to his own. There were no bright collages hanging on his walls, just square blocks of concrete and upper-case words screaming

'CAUTION. HIGH VOLTAGE' above every door

Mitchell walked through the huge lab slowly, his footsteps dulled by the polymer underfoot. He scanned the long room as he went. Right and left were exactly the same. Row upon row of work-benches and computers, with no personal touches to break the sombre mood.

In a moment he reached the back wall; cool, pale stone, broken only by the smooth steel door to the research suite that said private without a single word. Mitchell ran his hand slowly down its patina and stood for a moment, considering flight. Whatever had caused the gap on the CCTV tape, the reason lay behind here. Did he really need to know? Did he want to? Mitchell shook his head and turned, striding towards the lab's exit as if he was being chased. Then he stopped.

Jeff Mitchell stood still, listening to the silence around him and then to the voice inside his aching head. He couldn't run any more. If there were answers to his questions then he had to find them before he died. He reached the steel door again in two steps, punching in the entry-code before he changed his mind. The door swung open and Mitchell stepped inside, pulling it behind him to avoid prying eyes. They weren't likely while Devon was away, but you never knew.

The internal light flickered on, revealing that he stood in a short hallway with a room on either side. 'The Research Suite', accessible only to him. The left hand door led to a refrigeration facility, the one on the right to the small office that he and Devon had seen on the CCTV. The office door lay open. Mitchell frowned. The tape said that the last person in there had been him; he must have left it unlocked. But he was normally fastidious about security.

Mitchell recalled his blood-stained shower two weeks before. He'd been here the night before it, the video-tape proved that. Had he been attacked by someone, was that where the blood had come from? Mitchell shook his head, knowing that the answer was no. The blood hadn't come from injuries on his body.

What then? Had he been the attacker? It was unlikely, but if he had been then the question was why? The answer came quickly. There was only one reason that he would have attacked someone in his research suite. If they were an intruder.

Mitchell walked forward cautiously and pushed at the open door with one hand; the other one curled, ready to fight. One half of the office held a desk and work-bench, the other was made of glass with a self-hinged door. The glass room that he'd seen on the CCTV. Two empty cages sat on the floor beside the desk.

Mitchell scanned the room for signs of an injured intruder but there were none. He exhaled noisily, relieved; they must have got away. He thanked his lucky stars and turned to leave, then stopped as a dark-red patch in one corner caught his eye. Blood.

Small drops of dried blood covered the room's black polymer floor. There'd been a fight here, but not a fatal one; it didn't explain the amount of blood on him in the shower. Whose blood was it? Mitchell searched the room frantically for clues, knowing that whoever it was might still be there. The key-codes showed that no-one had entered or left the suite since that night.

As Mitchell rifled through the desk drawers for information something nagged at him. If no-one had been on the CCTV that night but him then how had his attacker entered? And why hadn't the guards in reception noticed a stranger? More importantly, when had they fought? It must all have been during the gap on the video-tape; had they knocked it off during the fight or had he wiped it? Mitchell's head hurt with questions that he couldn't answer and he slumped heavily onto the desk chair.

The Archaeus work had been trialled here, he was certain of it. It would have been easy to hide. Only he and Devon ever visited this floor and Devon wasn't allowed in the research suite.

Mitchell glanced at the cages and then through the open door at the refrigeration room, built in perfect proximity for scientific trials. He walked into the hallway and examined the floor. There was a trail of blood leading towards the fridge. More blood, but still not enough to explain his shower.

Snatches of memory filled Mitchell's mind. A man fighting with him in the hallway. Fists flying, him evenly matched with his foe. The man had followed Mitchell into the office and they'd fought again. And then what? A searing pain ripped through Mitchell's head and he staggered back against the wall. A series of images flashed through the pain. The small, glass room, flooded with light. Animals changing, but not physically this time.

Mitchell huddled on the floor, banging his head against the wall for relief. But there was none. Not from the pain and not from the images in his head. They filled his mind, showing him the horrors that his Archaeus work had achieved. This was no sci-fi movie, it was real life.

He didn't know the date or time of the experiment but he could picture the result. A rabbit; timid, docile, nibbling on some leaves. An angry dog, a pit-bull; snarling and snapping at the air, searching for something to bite. Mitchell watched, filled with dread, as they sat in cages inside the glass room and were flooded with light. No, not light, radiation of some sort. He kept on watching until it cleared.

The dog was lying quietly now, cleaning its paws, the rabbit snarling and biting its own fur, blood smearing its whiskers. Mitchell retched at the memory. The changes in the animals hadn't been physical this time; they'd swopped consciousness. The dog's mind and personality were in the rabbit's body and vice versa!

These were the Archaeus trials he'd held; playing God with animals' minds. He'd altered the carbon atoms in the creatures' brains and in the process he'd managed to transfer their consciousness and personality from one to another. As the memory faded Mitchell's headache waned and he stared reluctantly at the refrigeration room door, dreading what he would find behind it. There was no choice but to look; he couldn't run away now.

He clambered to his feet and turned off the CCTV, then he drew the heavy door back slowly, breaking the vacuum seal. Mitchell shivered as a blast of cold air hit him and he braced himself for what he would find inside. As the fluorescent light flickered on, his eyes accustomed slowly to its glare, making out first the large shapes and then the small.

The sight that greeted Jeff Mitchell made him gasp. A man's body lay propped in one corner of the room, surrounded by cardboard boxes, as if he was just another item being stored. His black suit was paled by frost, and congealed blood formed a dark patch on his shirt. More blood covered the sealed floor. Not droplets this time but a flood.

The man's grey eyes were wide open but there was no doubt that he was dead. Mitchell knew immediately that he had been since the night before his bloodied shower. This was why the CCTV had been off that night. Judging by the blood trail he'd dragged the man's body from the office to place it in here.

Mitchell stared at the dead man's face, recognising him. It was Greg Chapman; Magee's lost agent. Mitchell stood for minutes, staring down at Chapman sadly, as more images filled his mind. This time there was no pain, just an overwhelming relief that he finally understood.

This movie was of two men in the suite's office, fighting to the death. A gun drawn by Greg Chapman and then a struggle. They'd staggered backwards into the small, glass room and the door had slammed closed; trapping them together, both of them fighting desperately for their lives. The gun had discharged, firing a shot into Chapman's chest. It was an accident, a struggle. An agent killed in the line of duty. It explained the blood on Mitchell in the shower the morning after; Greg Chapman's blood. But why hadn't he remembered any of this earlier? In that instant Mitchell knew that there was more. Something else had happened as they'd fought. The glass room had flooded with light!

Mitchell hunkered down beside Greg Chapman and stared into his sad, dead eyes, suddenly realising that he and Chapman were sharing more than just this space. They'd been trapped together in the glass room and irradiated, just as the rabbit and dog had been. Radiation had mutated the carbon atoms in their brains, just as it had done with the two animals.

As Greg Chapman had breathed his last, Mitchell's body had absorbed the agent's dying mind. It explained so much. But the transfer had been incomplete. Chapman was dead so Mitchell's consciousness had nowhere to go and the radiation level had been set for animals; too low for adult men. The result was that now both their minds existed inside Jeff Mitchell. He was a hybrid of them both.

Mitchell gazed at Greg Chapman and smiled. He understood at last. *This* was why he'd known so much about Chapman's life. They'd been sharing space inside his head for weeks. It had fogged his own memories before the night it'd happened and the fog was taking time to clear. His brain tumour had confused things even more.

Mitchell nodded to himself. It explained everything. From his newly heightened physical responses to his changing personality and the things that he couldn't possibly have known; even him forgetting Ilya. Thank God he'd eventually remembered enough scientific information to keep his family safe.

Mitchell scanned the floor urgently, searching for Greg Chapman's gun. It had to be nearby. He saw the barrel protruding from behind a cardboard box and lifted it, turning it over carefully in his hand and startled by how familiar it felt. It was bigger than the ones he'd seen on Richie and Tom Evans. Then he remembered, it was the same as the gun he'd seen in Chapman's apartment. Mitchell stared at the weapon, knowing what his next step should be.

He had to tell Magee. Chapman's parents deserved to know what had happened to their son and bury him in peace. No jury would find him guilty of murder; it had been self-defence. Besides, he'd be dead from cancer before the trial.

Mitchell smiled at the man at his feet. He knew Greg Chapman now and he really liked the guy; he was kind. Chapman wasn't really dead; they'd co-existed in his mind for weeks. Jeff Mitchell may have been a genius but he'd been a hard bastard too. A sleeper agent, prepared to give dangerous research to countries that would use it for God only knew what. Mitchell shook his head; that was only half-true. Jeff Mitchell may have been a bastard but maybe Vadim had been a good kid, before Ilya had got his hands on him. Thirty years of indoctrination and living a double life was bound to have taken its toll.

Either way, Greg Chapman's decency had given him back some of the compassion and honour that he'd lost, and in return Chapman had got the child that he'd never had, and fallen in love with Karen. Mitchell's smile widened. Chapman was brave and strong; stronger than Jeff Mitchell. Ultimately Chapman had won the fight inside his head, taken over and made him a better man. It was a pity that they would both be dead soon.

Mitchell stood for a moment longer, thinking, then he walked back into the office to make the call. He was just about to dial Magee when something stilled his hand. Mitchell lowered the phone and thought for more than an hour, until the noise in the car-park above said that people were arriving for work and his presence upstairs would soon be missed.

Mitchell moved swiftly, hiding the gun in the small office and turning the CCTV back on, then he locked up the research suite and lab and returned calmly to the fifteenth floor. He'd made a decision about his future that some people would consider selfish. That was, if they ever knew.

***

"Do you have the Mitchell's re-location sorted yet?"

Magee nodded and slid the papers across the desk. Richie read the file and smiled. The Mitchell's new house was large and white. Set in an acre of garden that held a slide and swing for Emmie. Richie could imagine them being happy there.

"Where is it?"

"Boston. We thought a change of coast wouldn't be fair. Mitchell's wife went to Yale, less than two hundred miles away, so she should feel right at home. Her new name is Kerri Morrison. We left Emily's name alone."

Richie nodded. Kerri. It suited her. He read the legend and smiled approvingly. They'd got Karen's law licence changed to her new name. She would get to practice again.

"Mitchell's name is Jerry Morrison, for as long as he's alive. We've got him into a trial of a new cancer drug at Massachusetts General."

"You've thought of everything. Thanks, boss."

Magee gazed thoughtfully at the younger man. Letting Richie go with the Mitchells went against his better judgement. Richie was already too attached to Mitchell's wife.

He should really send someone else to guard them until Mitchell died. Once he was dead the threat to his family would plummet and they could get on with their new, re-located lives in peace.

He *should* re-assign Richie, but he wasn't going to. Magee knew all about his relationship with Rosie Pereira; both times. Richie needed Karen Mitchell's friendship right now as much as she needed his.

Magee took two puffs of his inhaler and then straightened up, looking stern.

"OK. Here's the way it's going to be."

Richie raised an eyebrow and wondered what was coming next.

"I know all about you and Agent Pereira."

Richie went to object but Magee stilled him with a glance.

"I also know that you like Karen Mitchell more than is healthy."

He watched Richie blush and sniffed.

"I could re-assign you, but I'm not going to, and before you say thank-you, I'm going to tell you why. Karen Mitchell has suffered enough. Now she's going to be uprooted and have to leave her whole family behind. Her husband's going to die soon and she's not going to know anyone in Boston, so you're going to provide continuity for a while, until she can cope alone."

Magee stared hard at the younger man, his voice becoming firm. "Then I want you back, Richie. No arguments. Understand?"

Richie Cartagena smiled, understanding. Magee was giving him a chance to find love again, in the full knowledge that it meant he might never return. He stood and extended his hand. Magee shook it then concluded the meeting briskly.

"I want them out of New York by tomorrow evening. Let me know when you're on your way.

Chapter Forty

Jeff Mitchell ran over his plan repeatedly, until he was finally certain of every step. Then he packed-up his office and drove himself home, smiling as Emmie wrapped herself around his legs at the front door.

"Daddy, daddy, come and see what Richie has. We have a new house. It's white with a garden and everything, and he says we can build a hutch for Fluff."

Mitchell threw his briefcase in the corner and scooped his small daughter into his arms, carrying her though the family-room onto the deck. Karen was pouring some lemonade into a glass and Mitchell caught his breath at the sight of her. She looked really happy. Happier than he'd seen her in weeks.

Mitchell set Emmie down and walked across to his wife, taking her in his arms and kissing her deeply. Karen moved towards him so that their bodies melted into one, and she kissed him back long and hard. Finally she broke away laughing, embarrassed by Richie's averted gaze. Richie smiled and waved them on.

"Don't mind me. It's great to see you happy."

Mitchell knew that the words were aimed at Karen not him, but he didn't mind. After tomorrow it wouldn't matter anymore. They sat out in the evening sun and Mitchell nodded at the file on Richie's knee.

"Is that what my daughter's getting so excited about?"

Richie nodded and handed him the folder. Mitchell flicked through the pages quickly then he looked at Karen, sensing her excitement. She would get to practice law again. She'd wanted it for a long time. Magee had thought of everything, even a new cancer treatment for him that he would never use. Mitchell placed the file face-down on the table.

"When do we leave?"

Richie hesitated, as if waiting for an objection.

"Magee wants you out of New York tomorrow evening. Can you do it?"

Mitchell thought for a moment. That only gave him the next day to carry out his plan. He swallowed hard before he spoke.

"Yes, I just need another day at the lab. I'm almost done. I have to leave things ready for Devon when he gets back."

Karen sat down on Mitchell's knee and turned his face firmly towards her.

"Only one more day, Jeff. You promise?"

Mitchell smiled and kissed her gently on the nose.

"One more day, honey, then everything will be different."

Karen Mitchell had no idea just how much.

***

Richie finished his phone-call and beckoned Mitchell inside the house. They stood in the family-room watching as Karen and Emmie reclined outside, catching the last rays of the sun. Mitchell looked curiously at the other man, knowing that he had something important to say. He was unprepared for just how quickly the agency achieved its goals.

"We've found your mother and sister."

Mitchell gasped as if he'd been punched in the gut. His childhood memories were about to come to life. He stood silently as the photographs Ilya had given him ran through his head. Richie waited for a moment then handed Mitchell something; the agency had managed to find a school picture of him at ten, just before he was brought to the States. His name was Vadim Alenin.

Mitchell sat down heavily on the room's well-worn couch

and stared at the white-blonde boy as if he was a stranger. Slowly his memories started to return. Walking to school in the winter snow and summers spent fishing and swimming in the lake. He'd had a happy childhood; stolen by Ilya Tabakov.

Finally Mitchell spoke, in a hoarse voice.

"Where did you find them?"

"In a small suburb of St Petersburg. They're both well. Both widowed unfortunately, but your sister has a little girl, just a year older than Emmie."

Richie paused and stared at Mitchell, giving him a second to recover before he went on.

"We've explained everything and they've agreed to come to Boston. They're waiting to talk to you now, if you're ready?"

Mitchell felt the tears on his cheek and he let them fall, unashamed in front of the other man; Richie knew almost everything about him now. Richie watched as Mitchell wept and he felt like weeping too; so much had happened to them both in the past few weeks. He shook himself for being so selfish; there was no comparison. He had a future to look forward to, even without Rosie Pereira, but Jeff Mitchell's time was very short. He could only imagine how that felt.

Finally Mitchell nodded that he was ready and Richie made the call, handing him the phone. He watched as Mitchell said "Mother", the word that made him someone's child no matter what his age, then Richie turned and walked back to the garden, leaving Vadim Alenin to talk to his family in peace.

***

8 a.m.

The next day dawned bright and cool and Mitchell was in his Manhattan office by eight, leaving Karen and Richie to sort out the domestic debris in preparation for the move. His last view of them had been on their knees, buried in boxes and tape, with

Emmie running between them tangled in string. Karen had looked up and smiled as he'd said goodbye and Mitchell knew that it was the last time she would ever look at him that way. He just prayed that it wouldn't be the last time he'd get to see her.

Mitchell sorted out his office at Scrabo in the same way the others were sorting out the house, putting his pictures and keep-sakes in boxes, marked for shipping to their Lloyd Harbor address. The agency would forward them to Boston. Mitchell stared at Greg Chapman's cell-phone for a moment, turning it over in his hand. He knew who all the numbers belonged to now. He scrolled through them one by one, putting faces to each of the names. All Greg Chapman's memories were clear now, and strangely so were his own. Once he'd understood what had happened, he'd concentrated hard, sifting through the years and allocating this memory to Chapman and that one to himself. Mitchell knew that Greg Chapman was living inside him and that he'd made him a better man. He wasn't afraid of the next step.

***

1 p.m.

Mitchell made the call to Richie at one o'clock, shaping his voice to mimic panic and shock. "You have to come to Scrabo. I've found something important."

Richie's agent's curiosity didn't disappoint him. He was coming now. Mitchell left instructions with reception to send Richie down to the basement lab, then he took the elevator to the lower-fifth floor to wait. Fifty minutes later security rang through that a Richie Cartagena was on his way. Mitchell stood by the main lab door, composing his face in a mask of distress and as soon as the elevator opened he spoke.

"Richie. I've found him."

Richie stared at him, uncomprehending.

"Who?"

"Greg Chapman. I recognised him from the photo at his apartment. He's...he's dead."

Mitchell watched as Richie's hand flew to his gun, freeing it from its holster; he'd expected the move. He led the way through the outer lab and they reached the research suite quickly. Mitchell pointed Richie towards the refrigeration room and ran quickly into the office across the hall. He retrieved Greg Chapman's gun from its hiding place and entered the glass room, wedging the door open with an easily broken phial.

Mitchell grasped the revolver in his right hand and gazed at the picture of Karen and Emmie in his left. He loved them and Richie loved them too; whatever happened next they would be in safe hands. As he listened for the sound of Richie exiting the refrigerator, Mitchell thought of his little family and said au revoir, praying that he would see them again, even if it was through different eyes. If his plan was successful then both his and Greg Chapman's consciousness would live on in Richie Cartagena's body. He would get to stay with Karen and Emmie and meet his mother and sister when they came from Russia, and he'd keep in touch with John and Nancy Chapman. If it failed then the note that he'd slipped into Richie's pocket that morning would explain everything, including Greg Chapman's death.

Mitchell pressed the gun barrel hard against his abdomen and waited, bracing himself for the pain. At the sound of the refrigerator door opening he pulled the trigger hard, hearing the shot and feeling its impact at the same time. It skewered through him, severing the major artery in its path. Mitchell gasped in shock and slumped back, watching as a pool of bright blood oozed through his shirt, signalling that in under a minute he would be dead.

Richie heard the shot and came running, to see Jeff Mitchell lying on the dark office floor. He rushed forward to help, crushing the phial in his way and letting the heavy glass door swing closed. A blinding light filled the room instantly and radiation flooded through the two men, then it faded and there was nothing but peace.

***

4.10 p.m.

Richie Cartagena came-to slowly and gazed around him, confused. He ached as if someone had kicked every inch of him and his vision was so blurred that he could hardly see. The last thing he remembered was a shot being fired, and then pain, pain in his stomach like he'd never felt before. Richie felt his body frantically for injuries, searching for a bullet hole to match his agony, but there was nothing. He hadn't been shot!

He glimpsed a red stain on his sleeve and remembered. Chapman. Greg Chapman was dead. No, it wasn't Chapman's blood. Too fresh. Greg was long gone. Richie felt for the wall and pressed his back against it, trying to focus on where he was. He was in a small, glass room in Scrabo's lab and it was eerily quiet; the only thing audible was New York's soundtrack in the street above. He remembered the gunshot again and reached urgently for his Glock, but the safety was still on. If he hadn't made the shot then who had? Richie clicked off the catch, ready to shoot whatever moved and then a memory of Jeff Mitchell bleeding hit him like a train. He turned swiftly towards the corner, squinting until a man's body came into view. Richie stared at it for a moment and then holstered his gun. He wouldn't need it; Mitchell was dead.

Jeff Mitchell lay in the corner, his head hanging awkwardly to one side. Fresh blood leaked from a hole in his abdomen, much too large to have been made by any Glock. Richie scoured the floor for the weapon and finally found it. A Smith and Wesson 500. The only person he knew with one of those had been Greg. They'd often kidded him about its size. But Greg Chapman couldn't have shot Mitchell; he'd been refrigerated for weeks.

Richie shrugged, too confused to work it out. Forensics would tell the story, but his money was on Mitchell shooting himself. He already knew why; cancer. Jeff Mitchell couldn't bear a fight that he was bound to lose. But why was *he* feeling pain in his abdomen when it was Jeff Mitchell that had been shot?

Just then a searing pain ripped through Richie's head, knocking him back against the wall. He slid to the floor, gripping his head in agony as an image of him shooting himself in the stomach filled his mind. He could feel the weight of the Smith and Wesson in his hand as he pushed it down hard over his aorta. Knowing exactly where to shoot and fully aware that once he did he'd have less than a minute left to do what needed to be done.

Richie felt his body cool and his blood seep away as he fought hard not to die. He was waiting for something. He was waiting for a black-haired man to enter the room. The man's face was blurred but it grew clearer as Richie watched, until he could finally see who it was. It was him! But that didn't make any sense.

A sudden light blinded him and Richie Cartagena felt himself die. Except that he couldn't be dead, he was still here! Richie threw up from the shock and then his vision started to fade away. He just had time to dial 911 before blacking out.

***

The sound of breaking glass woke Richie again and he opened his eyes to the sight of a uniformed woman checking his pulse. His head throbbed mercilessly as memories that didn't belong to him rushed unbidden through his mind. His wedding to Karen; his Russian childhood; his mother Nancy sunning herself on the porch in St Augustine. They were Greg Chapman's and Jeff Mitchell's memories! Richie scrambled frantically to find a memory of his own and settled on his childhood in Queens.

A moment later the medic sedated him and Richie Cartagena was stretchered from the room. As they carried him past Jeff Mitchell's cold body he saw Mitchell's face close-up. He was smiling, as if he was pleased with what he'd done. In a moment of awful clarity, Richie knew exactly why.

THE END

Fantastic Books
Great Authors

Meet our authors and discover our exciting range:

- Gripping Thrillers
- Cosy Mysteries
- Romantic Chick-Lit
- Fascinating Historicals
- Exciting Fantasy
- Young Adult and Children's Adventures

Visit us at:
www.crookedcatbooks.com

Join us on facebook:
www.facebook.com/crookedcatpublishing

Lightning Source UK Ltd.
Milton Keynes UK
UKOW02f2357280814

237719UK00001B/2/P